PRAISE FOR CAROLYN BROWN

The Daydream Cabin

"I absolutely loved this novel. With moments of laughter and tears, I could not stop reading and imagining the beautiful changes that were taking place within each character's heart! Author Carolyn Brown's novels always give me a feeling of hope!"

—Goodreads reader review

Miss Janie's Girls

"[A] heartfelt tale of familial love and self-acceptance."

—*Publishers Weekly*

"Heartfelt moments and family drama collide in this saga about sisters."

—*Woman's World*

The Banty House

"Brown throws together a colorful cast of characters to excellent effect and maximum charm in this small-town contemporary romance . . . This first-rate romance will delight readers young and old."

—*Publishers Weekly*

The Family Journal

HOLT MEDALLION FINALIST

"Reading a Carolyn Brown book is like coming home again."
—*Harlequin Junkie* (top pick)

The Empty Nesters

"A delightful journey of hope and healing."
—*Woman's World*

"The story is full of emotion . . . and the joy of friendship and family. Carolyn Brown is known for her strong, loving characters, and this book is full of them."
—*Harlequin Junkie*

"Carolyn Brown takes us back to small-town Texas with a story about women, friendships, love, loss, and hope for the future."
—*Storeybook Reviews*

"Ms. Brown has fast become one of my favorite authors!"
—*Romance Junkies*

The Perfect Dress

"Fans of Brown will swoon for this sweet contemporary, which skillfully pairs a shy small-town bridal shop owner and a softhearted car dealership owner . . . The expected but welcomed happily ever after for all involved will make readers of all ages sigh with satisfaction."

—*Publishers Weekly*

"Carolyn Brown writes the best comfort-for-the-soul, heartwarming stories, and she never disappoints . . . You won't go wrong with *The Perfect Dress!*"

—*Harlequin Junkie*

The Magnolia Inn

"The author does a first-rate job of depicting the devastating stages of grief, provides a simple but appealing plot with a sympathetic hero and heroine and a cast of lovable supporting characters, and wraps it all up with a happily ever after to cheer for."

—*Publishers Weekly*

"*The Magnolia Inn* by Carolyn Brown is a feel-good story about friendship, fighting your demons, and finding love, and maybe, just a little bit of magic."

—*Harlequin Junkie*

"Chock-full of Carolyn Brown's signature country charm, *The Magnolia Inn* is a sweet and heartwarming story of two people trying to make the most of their lives, even when they have no idea what exactly is at stake."

—*Fresh Fiction*

The Barefoot Summer

"Prolific romance author Brown shows she can also write women's fiction in this charming story, which uses humor and vivid characters to show the value of building an unconventional chosen family."

—*Publishers Weekly*

"This story takes you and carries you along for a wonderful ride full of laughter, tears, and three amazing HEAs. I feel like these characters are not just people in a book, but they are truly family and I feel so invested in their journey. Another amazing HIT for Carolyn Brown."

—*Harlequin Junkie* (top pick)

The Lullaby Sky

"I really loved and enjoyed this story. Definitely a good comfort read, when you're in a reading funk or just don't know what to read. The secondary characters bring much love and laughter into this book; your cheeks will definitely hurt from smiling so hard while reading. Carolyn is one of my most favorite authors. I know without a doubt that no matter what book of hers I read, I can just get lost in it and know it will be a good story. Better than the last. Can't wait to read more from her."

—*The Bookworm's Obsession*

The Lilac Bouquet

"Brown pulls readers along for an enjoyable ride. It's impossible not to be touched by Brown's protagonists, particularly Seth, and a cast of strong supporting characters underpins the charming tale."

—*Publishers Weekly*

"If a reader is looking for a book more geared toward family and long-held secrets, this would be a good fit."

—RT Book Reviews

"Carolyn Brown absolutely blew me away with this epically beautiful story. I cried, I giggled, I sobbed, and I guffawed; this book had it all. I've come to expect great things from this author and she more than lived up to anything I could have hoped for. Emmy Jo Massey and her great-granny Tandy are absolute masterpieces not because they are perfect but because they are perfectly painted. They are so alive, so full of flaws and spunk and determination. I cannot recommend this book highly enough."

—Night Owl Romance (5 stars and top pick)

The Wedding Pearls

"*The Wedding Pearls* by Carolyn Brown is an amazing story about family, life, love, and finding out who you are and where you came from. This book is a lot like *The Golden Girls* meets *Thelma and Louise*."

—*Harlequin Junkie*

The Yellow Rose Beauty Shop

"*The Yellow Rose Beauty Shop* was hilarious, and so much fun to read. But sweet romances, strong female friendships, and family bonds make this more than just a humorous read."

—*The Reader's Den*

Long, Hot Texas Summer

"This is one of those lighthearted, feel-good, make-me-happy kind of stories. But, at the same time, the essence of this story is family and love with a big ole dose of laughter and country living thrown in the mix. This is the first installment in what promises to be another fascinating series from Brown. Find a comfortable chair, sit back, and relax because once you start reading *Long, Hot Texas Summer* you won't be able to put it down. This is a super fun and sassy romance."

—*Thoughts in Progress*

Daisies in the Canyon

"I just loved the symbolism in *Daisies in the Canyon*. As I mentioned before, Carolyn Brown has a way with character development with few if any contemporaries. I am sure there are more stories to tell in this series. Brown just touched the surface first with *Long, Hot Texas Summer* and now continuing on with *Daisies in the Canyon*."

—Fresh Fiction

Riverbend Reunion

ALSO BY CAROLYN BROWN

Riverbend Reunion

CAROLYN BROWN

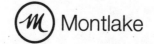 Montlake

Text copyright © 2022 by Carolyn Brown
All rights reserved.

Published by Montlake, Seattle

www.apub.com

Amazon, the Amazon logo, and Montlake are trademarks of Amazon.com, Inc., or its affiliates.

ISBN-13: 9781542038249
ISBN-10: 1542038243

Cover design by Leah Jacobs-Gordon

Printed in the United States of America

To Mr. B
With all my love forever and a day

Chapter One

"Uncle Elijah, why did you build a church out here in this Godforsaken place, and why didn't you get rid of the empty eyesore before you died?" Jessica asked as she stood in the middle of the sanctuary and looked around at the mess she'd inherited.

Dust was as gray and thick as fog on the floor, the pews, and the blades of the ceiling fans.

A huge bunch of hair hung on the back of two pews. A closer look revealed millions of daddy longlegs huddled together.

Jessica sneezed and sent dust and spiders going seven ways to Sunday.

The only light in the huge room came from the setting sun shining through dirty windows and gave the whole place an eerie look. Jessica could imagine spooky music playing in the background as she turned around to be sure ghosts weren't floating toward her.

Paint had peeled from the walls, and the place smelled like an old attic full of sweaty clothing with a little mold thrown in.

This was her life in a nutshell—her future looked as grim as the dust that coated the pews and the pulpit. Just like the dim light coming through the windows, nothing seemed clear to her. Ideas had filtered through her mind like all those baby spiders wiggling together, and yet nothing—not one blessed thing—seemed to take hold.

She looked up and noticed a wallpaper border around the room depicting angels with white wings and halos, but even that hung in long strips.

"Where's *my* guardian angel when I need one?" she groaned. "What in the hell"—she glanced up at the ceiling fan with cobwebs hanging from every blade—"am I supposed to do with a decrepit old church building?"

Dust boiled up all the way to the knees of her camouflage pants as she headed down the aisle, leaving footprints behind her.

"Do those impressions in the dust mean something? If so, I'd sure like someone to explain it to me," she muttered when she reached the foyer and glanced over her shoulder.

She locked the door, brushed the dust from her pants, and made sure she didn't have any spiders hanging on her anywhere. Gravel crunched under her feet as she walked from the porch to the motor home that had been her home for the past two weeks. She slung the door open, grabbed a washcloth, wet it with cold water from the sink, and cleaned her face. Then she took a beer from the tiny refrigerator, twisted the top off, and took a long drink.

Sweat still ran down her neck and into her bra, but the cold beer helped some. "My church," she mumbled, and then a smile covered her angular face.

Thank goodness no one was near enough to hear Jessica Callaway belt out Maren Morris's song "My Church." Jessica had shot the eyes out of a horned viper during her tours in the Middle East, but she couldn't carry a tune in a galvanized milk bucket.

She carried her beer outside, where a soft breeze ruffled the leaves of the pecan trees surrounding the old church's parking lot. The song seemed appropriate as she stared at the white church in front of her and wondered again what she was going to do with it. That decision had to be made before she could move on to the next step—whatever that was—in her life.

"Why didn't you just donate it, and the land it's sitting on, to the city of Riverbend, Uncle Elijah?" Jessica wondered out loud. She had been talking to herself a lot since she finished her last enlistment in the army a couple of weeks ago, but then she hadn't had anyone to visit with on her travels from Maine to Texas.

If this had been two decades before, when Jessica graduated from high school, the parking lot would have been filled with cars and trucks. Loud music would have filled the air, and some of the teenagers would have been dancing. A handful would have been popping the tabs off cans of beer that they were too young to be drinking, and still others would have been making out in the back seats of vehicles. But that was usually on Friday and Saturday nights, and this was just the middle of the week.

Now the place looked as abandoned as the church itself. Most of the letters on the sign that once read "Community Church" had faded and chipped away. Only the one *m* and the *y* were still legible on the first line, though the word *Church* was still intact below that. It seemed like an omen that she'd been singing a song with that title and now the sign declared it to be true.

"Yep, it's definitely *my* church," Jessica muttered with a sigh, "but what the hell do I do with it?"

According to her friend Mary Nell, there were already half a dozen struggling churches in Riverbend, so who would want to buy another one? Especially one three miles out of the small town. Jessica took a deep breath and inhaled the musky scent of the Lampasas River, which was only a quarter of a mile down a path grown up with weeds.

Yes, she was home—at least until she figured out what to do with that ugly building full of dust and spiders. She went back inside the RV, reached into the refrigerator, and brought out a six-pack of long-necks with one hand and a lawn chair from beside the door with the other and carried them outside. She set the beer on the ground, popped open the lawn chair, and then stretched to work the kinks out of her tall frame. Every bone in her nearly six-foot body whined from sitting in the driver's seat for eighteen hours that day. She twisted the top off her second bottle of Coors, took a long drink, and then eased down in the lawn chair.

"Nothing like a couple of cold beers and a Texas sunset." She raised her bottle in a toast to the orange, yellow, and purple streaks that filled the sky to the west.

Then she took another long look at the old community church her Uncle Elijah had built back in the day, when he got sober for the seventh time—or was it the eighth or ninth?—and got religion.

The windows in the white building were dirty, but it was a miracle they were all intact. Scaling paint testified that no one had kept up the building since the day Elijah gave up trying to build a congregation and headed to the nearest liquor store down in Burnet, Texas. Seven posts held up the roof to a wide front porch. Jessica wondered whether that number was significant.

She heard a noise to her left and glanced that way to see a squirrel fussing at her. The critter's tail twitched as he barked out a warning.

"This is my church, and it looks like you're sitting on my steeple, even if it is laying on the ground," she argued with the animal.

She and her cheerleader friends—Risa, Haley, and Mary Nell—had thought they were being so rebellious when they were in high school. Now she wondered whether drinking beer, dancing, and making out with guys in a church parking lot had brought all of them bad luck. Risa was headed for a divorce. Mary Nell had given almost twenty years of her life to a boyfriend who'd kicked her out a while back. Haley had lost her mother recently. And Jessica had inherited a church from her last living relative. There was also a lot of money involved in Uncle Elijah's estate, but she had to deal with this church sitting here like a white elephant with a bad case of peeling skin before she could think about what to do with the rest of her life.

Risa had said that her mother, Stella, had had some roof damage to her house when a tornado or straight-line winds had hit Riverbend the year before. Evidently, that same storm had whipped the steeple from the roof and tossed it out onto the ground beside the building. Jessica glanced over at the squirrel, and the sassy critter started barking at her again.

"You want to buy this?" she asked. "I'll sell it to you for a reasonable price, and finance it for you, but I want payment in dollars, not pecans."

The squirrel flicked its tail a couple more times and then ran away.

"See there, Uncle Elijah? I can't even sell the place to a squirrel." She groaned.

Since the pandemic, folks had gotten spoiled to watching Sunday morning services online rather than going to an actual church. Jessica was surprised that the existing churches didn't have "For Sale" signs out on the lawns. With a population of less than nine hundred people and six different denominations trying to stay afloat, a person or persons would be crazy to try to start up a new place to worship in Riverbend. Add to that the fact that it was so far out of town—the only reason the squirrels stuck around was for the pecans they could eat on the trees around the old church. Then it was down a dirt road—that got a car dirty every Sunday morning, and the nearest car wash was at least thirty minutes away, down near Burnet. No one wanted to drive that far every week to remove all the dust from their vehicles, and everyone knew it was a sin to drive a messy car. Just a minor sin in the scheme of things—at least according to Jessica's mother before she was killed in a plane crash. Nowadays, according to what she heard from Risa, Stella carried that list of sins high in the air so everyone could read it.

Maybe Jessica should just donate the church to the town and keep driving until she found a place that felt like home. Other than the church, there was nothing for her in Riverbend except her besties—Mary Nell, Haley, and Risa, who were all waiting for her call that evening—and who knew how long they'd stick around when the summer ended?

Haley might go back to her old job in Alabama. Risa could easily give her husband in Kentucky another chance. And Mary Nell could get homesick for Tennessee at the end of summer. Jessica just needed to find a place to put down roots as soon as the monstrosity in front of her was taken care of, and she didn't have a clue where they would be.

Memories of a church a lot like the one she was staring at flashed through her mind. It had been a white building, but the stained-glass windows were shiny clean, and the paint wasn't peeling. She'd had her folks' memorial services there on Orcas Island when they'd been killed in a small plane crash. She'd read the report dozens of times, but all the technical legalese didn't make much sense to her. Something with the fuel tank had gone wrong, and the plane had crashed, killing the pilot, her folks, and two other passengers as they traveled from Orcas Island, where they lived, to the mainland.

The crematorium had asked her about an urn, but she couldn't decide on one, so they'd given her the ashes in simple cardboard boxes. Afraid that the boxes would get wet and disintegrate, she had mingled her parents' ashes together in a red plastic coffee can, taped the lid shut, and carried them with her for the past five years.

Even after all this time, her chest still tightened at the memory of how she'd felt when she got the news that they were gone, and tears hung on her eyelashes. The feeling of being so alone—except for an alcoholic uncle—that had hit her as she realized the finality of a memorial service five years before wrapped itself around her again as she stared at the white clapboard church that was now hers. The building seemed to be trying to tell her something, but she couldn't grab hold of whatever it was.

Her plan had been that someday she would retire from the military and live on Orcas Island, close to her folks. She would be there for them as they got older and needed her help. Then, like a puff of smoke, they and a place to put down roots were gone. The money they'd left for her brought little comfort, and she'd never touched a dime of it. Then her

Uncle Elijah passed away and left her his estate, which included more money and that church she had to deal with.

Her father had told her that money was just dirty paper with dead presidents' pictures on it, and that pennies didn't buy happiness. A song she'd heard that day got stuck in her mind as she continued to stare at the building in front of her. The lyrics said that money couldn't buy happiness, but it could buy the singer a boat. She smiled as she hummed the snappy little tune. Was the church trying to tell her that it could bring her happiness?

The damn thing didn't make me happy. Elijah's voice popped into her head. *I don't care what you do with it, but be happy no matter what you choose to do.*

With a sigh, she fished her phone from the hip pocket of her pants and sent a message to her three friends: I'm here. Beer is cold, but in this heat, it won't be very long.

In just seconds she had three dings on her phone. They were all on the way and would be there in a few minutes. She'd barely sent a smiley face to the group when she heard the rumble of a truck coming down Preacher Road. Which one would it be? Risa, Mary Nell, or Haley? Jessica would put her money on Risa, since she'd do about anything to get away from her mother, Stella, who held the crown for being the biggest gossip in all of Burnet County, and who had been about to drive Risa crazy since she'd come back home from Kentucky with her sixteen-year-old twin daughters.

Jessica's eyes widened when the truck came to a stop not far from her RV and a tall guy wearing faded camouflage pants and a black T-shirt crawled out of the vehicle. His boots matched hers. A dead giveaway that he'd spent some time deployed overseas. His squared-off shoulders and posture were further proof that he was a product of the military. The sun behind him put him in silhouette so she couldn't see his features, but he looked familiar.

"You lost?" she called out.

"No, are you?" His slow Texas drawl sounded like someone she'd known in the past.

"Nope." She squinted, trying to make out his facial features. "I'm the proud owner of this place, and I came home to do something with it. Who are you, and what are you doing on my property?"

The man took a few steps toward her and frowned as she paused while trying to put a name with his face. His dark hair was a little longer than it would have been in the military and curled below the back of a camouflage cap bearing an army insignia. His square jaw and high cheekbones reminded her of someone she'd gone to school with.

"I come here to think," he finally answered. "And to remember the good ol' days, Jessica. I don't expect you to—"

"Wade Granger!" she butted in and finished his introduction. "I remember you now. Your brother, Danny, graduated with me at good old Riverbend High School." She stopped herself from saying that she'd had a major crush on Wade back in high school. But as a lanky, brainy guy, he'd always hung back in the shadows, and there was no way she'd ever admitted liking him to her friends.

Danny had been very proud of his older brother when he had joined the army right after he graduated, but Jessica hadn't heard anything about him for the past twenty years. Danny had been more outgoing, had played football for the Riverbend Gators, and had gone to college somewhere in Arkansas . . . or was it in Alabama?

"Yes, he did." Wade nodded. "Welcome back to Riverbend, Jessica. You home to stay?"

"Who knows?" She shrugged. "I don't know where I belong after being shifted around from one place to the other for twenty years. How about you?"

"I'm here to stay," he answered.

"Where's Danny these days?" she asked.

"My brother was killed a year ago in a freak accident, just a few months before he was to finish his last enlistment." Wade's voice cracked.

"I'm so sorry. He enlisted, too?" Jessica could sympathize and could tell him that he'd still have that catch in his voice five years down the road. Folks told her that it took time to get over the loss of a close relative, but time sure hadn't done much in the way of helping her find closure for her parents.

"Thank you and yes. I was his only living relative, so I buried him here in Riverbend by our parents," Wade said.

"Your folks passed?" She understood his pain. She'd been an only child, but losing her parents had been tough enough. She couldn't imagine adding the loss of a sibling to that.

"Mama went five years ago. Daddy only lasted six months after that. Cancer got them both," Wade said. "I'm sorry for your loss, too. Do you remember Oscar Wilson, Mary Nell's dad?"

"Haven't seen Oscar in years, but thanks, Wade," Jessica answered. "I appreciate the thought."

"He told me that your folks were both killed in a plane crash the same year that my folks died."

"It's tough being alone in the world, isn't it?" Jessica said.

Wade nodded. "Are you really going to sell the old church?"

"I'd like to sell it tomorrow, but I doubt that I'll have that kind of luck," she answered. "It's been on the market for more than ten years, and no one has even asked about it. Maybe I should turn it into something else, but then it's too far out of town to be used for much of anything."

She didn't tell him that the building itself seemed to be trying to tell her something.

Instead, she changed the subject. "Hey, you want a beer?"

Before he could answer, the noise of approaching vehicles filled the air. Dust boiled up behind them and settled slowly when they came to a stop beside his truck.

"I didn't know you were having a party," Wade said. "I should be going."

"There's five beers left in this six-pack. That means there's extra. You might as well stick around and have one. That's Risa, Haley, and Mary Nell. It's not a party, just a gathering of friends for a cold one and some catching up."

"How long has it been since you've seen them?" Wade asked.

"Years and years, but we kept in touch—kind of," she replied, not knowing why she didn't want him to go. Maybe it was the ache in his voice when he talked about his brother, or perhaps it was her nosiness in wanting to hear more about Danford—Danny—Granger. Or, if she was honest, maybe it was because she remembered the crush she'd had on Wade himself when she was in high school. Or perhaps she recognized a kindred spirit, not only in his service to the country, but in his grief. "Grab that extra chair from inside the door and join us."

"Thanks." His brief smile didn't reach his green eyes. "You sure I'm not intruding?"

"I'm sure," Jessica said.

Car doors slammed. One. Two. Three. Four. Five.

"Risa must have brought the twins with her," Wade said.

"You've met them?" Jessica asked.

Wade nodded as he headed for the RV. "Did some work for her mother last week. Saw them there. Cute kids, but not a thing alike, even if they are twins."

Jessica stood up and finger combed a few stray hairs back into her blonde ponytail. When the four women met in a group hug, she towered above the other three, but then she'd always been the tallest kid in her class. Risa had always been the pretty one, with her dishwater-blonde hair and big brown eyes. Haley had been the short, curvy one of the group when the four of them had been senior cheerleaders twenty years before—the smart one who always seemed to make the right decisions. Her eyes were the color of a chocolate Yoo-hoo, and her hair was so black that it looked blue when the sunrays hit it. Then there was Mary Nell, the smallest of the four cheerleaders from that year, who had always taken the place at the top of the pyramid. Jessica had envied her friend's thick, curly red hair and light blue eyes—but even more, her Dolly Parton boobs. Jessica had wondered at the time whether Mary Nell wasn't jumping into a relationship that would end up breaking her heart—and she'd been right.

None of them had changed much. Mary Nell might have put on a few pounds and Risa had lost a few, but Haley was about the same. Jessica still felt like a giant among them, even though Mary Nell was the only one who'd be considered short.

Another song about always being seventeen in your hometown came to Jessica's mind as the four of them took a step back from one another. She had put twenty years into serving her country and was now thirty-eight years old, and yet for a few moments, she felt like she was a teenager again.

But they'd graduated, gone their separate ways, and reality had hit them all like a category-five tornado. Risa's daughters were proof that none of them were still seventeen, and that they could never go back to those days, even though they were meeting in the same place—a gravel parking lot—to have a beer and catch up.

"Hey, y'all, this is Wade Granger, home from a stint in the military just like me. His brother, Danny, graduated with us," Jessica said.

"Hey, Wade." Risa waved.

"I was sorry to hear about Danny," Haley said.

"Me too," Mary Nell said with a sad frown.

"Thanks." Wade popped open the lawn chair a few feet from Jessica and sat down.

"Would you girls please get out the lawn chairs from the back of the truck, and set them up for us?" Risa nodded toward the older-model pickup that she had shown up in that evening.

"Yes, ma'am. Do we get a beer for doing that?" Lily, the taller twin with blonde hair and big brown eyes, asked.

"Sure thing," Risa said, "when you are twenty-one and can buy them with your own money."

"I figured you'd say that." Daisy giggled. "We won't talk about the times Daddy let us have one."

If Jessica hadn't seen pictures of them from the day they were born, and then watched them grow up through the benefit of the internet, she would have never believed they were sisters, much less twins. Daisy, the shorter one, was the spitting image of her mother, with her hair color and curvy figure. The only things the girls had in common were Risa's milk chocolate–colored eyes.

"Or about the times he showed us how to roll a joint," Lily said as she reached over the bed of the truck and picked up all five chairs at once.

"I don't believe either one of you, because if your Granny Martha found out he was doing that, she would disown him," Risa said. "And his mama's word was the law."

"Amen!" Lily handed off two of the chairs to her sister.

"Mama has talked a lot about all y'all. The picture of y'all when you were cheerleaders is still on her dresser these days," Daisy said. "We've already met Haley and Mary Nell, so it's good to see you in person rather than just on FaceTime. I'm jealous of your height. God could have been better to me and shared what he gave Lily."

Lily set up all the chairs in a semicircle. "Stop whining, Daisy. God gave you big boobs. You don't get to have both height *and* a figure to die for."

"Glad to finally meet you girls in person," Jessica said to hide her grin. "This being tall is a curse and a blessing all rolled up into one enchilada, isn't it, Lily?"

"Yep, it is. On one hand, I can reach everything on the top cabinet shelf for Granny Stella and Mama. On the other one"—she sighed and shot a look over toward Risa—"if Mama ever lets me date, I can probably never wear high heels."

"Wear them, darlin'," Jessica said, and began to pass bottles of cold beer around to everyone. "Be who you are, and to hell with any boy who don't want to date you because you're taller than he is."

"Amen!" Mary Nell raised her bottle in a toast.

"Y'all sure you don't mind if I stay awhile?" Wade asked. "I feel like I'm butting in on a private party since you haven't seen each other in so long."

"We've FaceTimed every month or two, and always got in touch on Christmas. Sometimes Jessica was in a place where she could join us on a conference call," Mary Nell told him. "We understood her situation when she couldn't, though. You two were off saving the world. Since you are one of the heroes, Wade, you should stay. Besides, we never told anyone to go home when we came out here as teenagers and thought we were ready to set the world on fire."

"Saving the world and inheriting a church. Story of my life." Jessica passed a beer over to Wade, then motioned toward the church. "Y'all want to tell me what I'm going to do with that thing?"

"You could always start preaching." Haley sighed and wiped a tear from her cheeks. "Maybe you could even do your first sermon on that commandment about not lying to your kid."

"No thanks, but why would I preach on that?" Jessica asked. "I don't have kids, and other than a few little white lies about the tooth fairy and Santa Claus, I don't think my parents ever lied to me."

"You mean there's no Santa?" Lily gasped and then giggled.

"Or tooth fairy?" Daisy slapped a hand over her mouth. "Mama, you lied to us."

"Yes, I did." Risa sat down in a chair beside Lily.

"I found a letter in Mama's things today." Haley's voice quivered as she sat down in one of the chairs. She put her head in her hands, and sobs shook her body. "I don't . . . ," she stammered, "want to . . ."—more sobs—"throw cold water on our reunion."

Jessica handed her beer to Wade and went over to drop down on her knees in front of Haley and wrap her friend up in her arms. "We're here for you. I wish my mama would have left a letter for me," she said as she patted Haley on the back.

"No, you don't." Haley hugged her back and whimpered, "Not this kind of letter."

Haley had always been the most level of all the cheerleaders. She'd listened to their problems with parents, boyfriends, even issues that arose with each other, and given them great advice when they were teenagers. Jessica hadn't been a bit surprised when she had gone into the teaching field and from that on to counseling. Something about that letter had to be pretty bad to affect her this way.

Haley broke down again and, between sobs, said, "Mama left a letter, along with my original birth certificate and adoption papers. I'm ruining our evening that we've all looked forward to, and I'm so sorry."

Wade stood up, whipped a red bandanna from the hip pocket of his jeans, and handed it to Jessica. *What a sweet gesture,* she thought as she wiped Haley's tears away with it. "Talk to us. We're all here for you. I didn't know you were adopted."

"I am, but then I'm still family, and I never knew." Haley took the bandanna from Jessica and blew her nose on it. She seemed to steel herself as she straightened up and wrung her hands. "Remember me talking about my sister who went to California when I was just a little girl and seldom ever came back home to see my folks?" Her voice quivered, and tears continued to flow down her cheeks.

"I remember her." Wade sat back down. "I was five or six when y'all moved here, and I got to admit, I kind of had a crush on her. She was fifteen or sixteen that year, and I thought she was the most beautiful girl in the world with all that blonde hair and those big blue eyes."

"Blonde hair and blue eyed is right, and I have black hair and brown eyes. You'd think I'd look in the mirror and ask questions, wouldn't you?" Haley finally got control.

"What happened?" Jessica asked.

"I found the letter in Mama's Bible telling me that Frannie isn't my sister. She's my mother, and that my father was half-Latino, and they were both just fifteen, so they were too young to even think about marriage, and . . ." Haley stopped and took a breath. "I always wondered why I was an oddball in the family. Now I know, and both my biological mother and my grandmother, who I thought was my mother, are gone, and I don't have anyone to be mad at. This hit me like a ton of bricks."

"Good Lord!" Mary Nell gasped. "Why didn't you call us for a FaceTime conference?"

"I found the letter about five minutes before I got the text that Jessica was home," Haley answered. "I wasn't going to tell y'all until later, but I had to talk about it. I've barely got past the denial stage in the grief process for the woman I thought was my mama and now this."

"I can sympathize with you." Mary Nell scooted her chair over closer to Haley's and draped an arm around her shoulders. "I'm going through some of the same things, only mine is about a failed relationship. And, honey, your mama was your mama. She didn't birth you, but she raised you from the time you were born, so she was your mother."

"Mary Nell is right," Jessica said, "but that's a big chunk of news to get handed to you before you can even find closure for your mama's passing."

"I'm a high school counselor, and I've had a little training in therapy. But right now, I realize what it feels like to be on the other side. Why don't we talk about something other than our problems tonight?" Haley raised her beer bottle high and said, "To being back home together again and riding on the float as representatives of our class this fall."

They all raised their bottles. "To homecoming!"

When they'd all taken a sip, Daisy raised her disposable cup of root beer from the local convenience store. "To me and Lily being cheerleaders in the new school this fall. We couldn't do that in Kentucky."

"Why?" Jessica asked.

"Granny Martha said no, and nobody ever crosses Granny Martha, especially not Daddy. The whole family does what she says," Lily answered.

"That would be talking about problems, so let's put that story on the back burner," Risa said.

Mary Nell glanced over at Wade. "So, what's your story? Why did you come back to Riverbend when you got out of the service?"

He shrugged. "It's home. How about you, Jessica?"

She raised one shoulder. "Same as you. It was home for eighteen years, and the only place I remember having roots. When I enlisted, my folks moved west. They wanted me to join them on Orcas Island when I finished my twenty years in the service. I'd planned to do that, to be near them, but I don't know where I want to land since they're both gone now. Where are you living, Wade?"

"I bought a small travel trailer that hitches up to my truck. Right now, it's parked out behind Sparky's old convenience store that closed up when COVID hit. He lets me keep my tools in the store building." Wade nodded toward her RV. "It's not as fancy as that, but it's bigger than the tiny area I could call my own in the military."

"Yep, that one is really small compared to some that I looked at, but it seemed pretty big after living out of a duffel bag for twenty years. And the owners were being sent to Germany for two years, so they had it up for sale."

"I know Risa is living with her mama right now, since I hung a new screen door for Stella last week. What about you other two?" he asked.

"I'm at Mama's place," Haley answered, "trying to go through all the stuff. I never realized what a hoarder she was. It'll take all summer, but that's all right. It will give me something to do to keep my mind off this adoption thing. I don't have to be back at school in Alabama until August."

"I'm at home until I find a job," Mary Nell said. "Daddy has said 'I told you so' a dozen times since I got here last week, but it's the truth, and I deserve it. He told me that if Kevin ever got a contract in Nashville, he would toss me to the curb, and that's exactly what Kevin did. But that's another of those stories that we'll talk about later."

Jessica patted Mary Nell's shoulder on the way back to her chair. "Kevin is a jackass for not appreciating the fact that you've supported him for twenty years so he could follow his dream."

"Amen!" Risa and Haley both chimed in at the same time.

"Now, changing the subject." Jessica pointed toward the church building. "What can I do with that thing? Y'all got any ideas?"

"You could always turn it into a bar," Wade suggested. "Riverbend hasn't got one of those, and the church is sitting right in the northeast corner of Burnet County, which is a wet county in the middle of a whole bunch of dry ones. Fort Hood is just over the county line, and you'd get all kinds of business from the soldiers stationed there. They have to go quite a way to find a place to dance some leather off their boots and get a drink."

"Sounds like you've given this some thought." Mary Nell cocked her head to one side. "Have you mentioned the idea to my daddy? He would love the idea of a bar close by so he could sell his moonshine and wine to the owners."

"Nope, I haven't talked to Oscar about it, but the thought has crossed my mind," Wade said. "Danny and I used to joke about starting a bar, but he wanted to build a tiki bar on a beach somewhere, and I was thinking about an old western honky-tonk, maybe in Wyoming or Montana."

"In a town with a population of eight hundred ninety-three people, a bar would never support itself. And all the churchgoing people would fight you tooth and nail at even suggesting such sacrilege as turning a church into a beer joint," Risa said.

"And Granny Stella would lead the protest march," Daisy said.

"You got that right," Lily agreed with a nod.

"If all four of us plus the twins decide to stay here, that would make it eight hundred ninety-nine," Risa said.

"They haven't counted me yet"—Wade turned up his bottle and took a long drink—"so that would make it an even nine hundred. I was in a bar over in Mingus, Texas, a few years ago, and that town only has a little over two hundred people in it. It's got two bars and all the counties around it are dry, so they flat out do a business on the weekends. You're sitting on a virtual gold mine, Jessica. All the surrounding counties except San Saba, and that barely even touches Burnet County, are dry. Folks would come from all around us to have a little fun. Throw in a grill and you could even serve up burgers and fries."

"I can already hear Granny Stella's screams." Daisy giggled.

"Right along with everyone else's here in the county," Haley said.

Jessica was glad to see that Haley's tears had finally dried up, and she was sipping on her beer. If nothing else, the old church gave them something to talk about that evening.

"Not my daddy," Mary Nell disagreed. "He makes moonshine in the barn out back of the house. He's even got a license to make and sell it. He would love to see a bar go in this close to town."

Lily looked up at the sky. "Granny Martha is probably talking to God right now, and the two of them are planning to send lightning streaks down to strike all y'all dead for even thinking about turning a house of God into a bar."

Jessica took a long look at the building. Wade was probably teasing, but it *was* a pretty good idea. She could visualize Uncle Elijah giving her two thumbs up from his grave. The old guy had tried to reform and become a preacher back when she was in middle school, but his church—the very one she was staring at—had failed to bring in enough of a congregation to even pay the electric bills. He had shut the doors a year after he'd opened them, and then he fell off the wagon again. His liver finally had enough of his drinking and had failed him just last year.

"A bar sounds like a crazy idea," Jessica said and wondered if her Uncle Elijah had bought his moonshine from Oscar. "What about a bed-and-breakfast place?"

"Who'd come to Riverbend?" Haley asked. "In case you've forgotten, this isn't a resort area. And did you learn to cook while you were in the service? A bed-and-breakfast would require serving up something fancy every morning at the very least."

"I can make toast and pour cold cereal in a fancy bowl," Jessica answered.

"I can cook," Risa said. "Hire me to run the kitchen and my girls to do the cleaning."

"Hey, we're going to be cheerleaders, remember?" Daisy reminded her. "We won't have time to work and do all our school stuff, too. This is our senior year."

"Maybe y'all could buy a boat and become fishing guides," Mary Nell suggested.

Wade chuckled and started a few lines of "Buy Me a Boat."

Lily joined right in with him on the Chris Janson song, and then Daisy harmonized with her when she reached the chorus.

"Y'all are pretty good," Jessica said. "You should try out for the choir at the Riverbend school this fall."

"Never thought of that," Daisy said.

"I'd rather sing in your new bar," Lily said with a grin.

Jessica eyed the building with a new perspective. Chase away the spiders, sweep up all that dust, and take out the pews. That would create a nice big room for a bar. The Sunday school rooms could be used for an office, and if Risa's mama threw her out, she and the twins could live right there.

"You could turn the sanctuary into a beer, bait, and bologna store for fishermen and use the Sunday school rooms for the bed-and-breakfast," Haley suggested.

"My mother would go into a rigor if I worked in a place that sold beer." Risa shook a finger at her girls. "And don't either of you tell her that I drank one here tonight, either."

"How did we get two grannies that are so religious?" Daisy groaned. "I thought when we left Granny Martha's place in Kentucky that this one might be better, but Granny Stella is just as bad—or maybe the word is *holy* . . ."

"*Self-righteous* is what you are looking for," Lily told her sister.

"Whatever. She and Granny Martha could be sisters," Daisy said.

"And they're both so bossy," Lily added.

"Fate," Risa answered. "That's what brought us to Riverbend at this time in our lives. For some reason we all need to be here, and it's got something to do with that church. I can feel it."

"For real?" Jessica raised an eyebrow. "The building seemed to be trying to send me a message, too. Maybe it's saying that whatever I do with it, we should all be involved together."

"Then I don't like fate." Daisy swatted a mosquito from her arm. "But I do like the idea of having a job."

"I'll get some candles to burn next time y'all come out here. I'd forgotten that the skeeters in this part of the world were as big as buzzards." Jessica killed one that had alighted on her neck. "Or better yet, I'll get the electricity turned on in the church tomorrow, and we can all visit in there. I went into the sanctuary when I first got here, and everything is covered with dust and daddy longleg spiders. I've got some bug spray in the RV, so I'll take care of those little critters first thing tomorrow morning."

"Are y'all really goin' to drink beer in the sanctuary?" Lily asked.

Daisy covered her head with her hands. "Granny Stella and Granny Martha are calling down the lightning for sure."

Jessica laughed at the girls. From what Risa had told her, the twins had taken the whole bit about getting kicked out of the Jackson family better than most teenagers would have. They'd had to leave cousins by the dozens, a close-knit family, and the school they had attended their whole lives, but they were adapting—maybe even doing better than their mother.

Jessica tipped up her beer and took a sip. "I'll give all these excellent ideas some thought."

"We could just make it into a house," Risa suggested. "How many Sunday school rooms are there?"

"Have no idea," Jessica answered. "I was only in it a few times when it was a church, and I was only in the sanctuary a few minutes this evening. Daddy didn't like Uncle Elijah's preaching. He was one of those hellfire-and-damnation preachers, and Daddy liked a more conservative church. I'll try to get lights and water hooked up before y'all come out tomorrow evening, so we can take a tour."

"Think it's haunted?" Lily whispered. "Does your Uncle Elijah's ghost live in it?"

"Guess we'll find out when we go in there. His spirit might have been what knocked the steeple off," Jessica said with a giggle.

Wade stood. "Thanks for the visit, but I'm going home now. If you need some carpentry work done on the place, holler at me. I'm between jobs right now."

"Thanks," Jessica said. "You might as well come on back tomorrow. We can see if there are rats in there as big as the ones in Kandahar."

"How'd you know?" Wade asked.

"The boots." Jessica held up a foot, showing she was wearing the same boots the military issued for deployment in the sandbox. "When were you there?"

"Four years ago," he answered. "You?"

"Just finished my last tour a couple of months ago, after we pulled out," she answered. "Boots are from a previous tour, though."

"So are mine. Just now getting them broken in good," Wade said as he started toward his truck. "See y'all tomorrow evening, then. Who knows, we might even find a snake or two hiding in the pews."

Daisy shivered. "I'm not going in there until y'all clear it. I hate rats."

"I hate snakes, so I'll hang back with Daisy," Lily told them. "And y'all just changed my mind about enlisting in the army when I graduate high school."

"Both our grandmothers would disown you," Daisy said. "Granny Martha almost kicked Daddy out of the family when he joined the army."

Lily shot a look toward her twin sister. "But he got back in her good graces when he let her name us after her mother and grandmother."

Jessica whipped around toward Risa. "You didn't even get to name your kids?"

"That's only a minor detail of my ill-fated marriage," Risa answered. "Right now, we'd better get on back to Mama's. She starts calling if we're not home by nine o'clock. That's her bedtime, and she locks the doors promptly at nine. Out of the frying pan, into the fire—the story of my life. But I'm hunting a job so the girls and I can get our own place."

"Want to live in an old church?" Jessica asked.

"Don't tempt me." Risa stood up, bent to give Jessica a hug, and motioned for her girls to follow her. "Is it all right if we leave the chairs right here? We might need them tomorrow."

"Perfectly fine," Jessica answered.

"I'm turning in, too," Haley said. "I should go through some more of Mama's stuff before bedtime. Maybe there'll be something in another note about why they hid things."

"Me too," Mary Nell said. "See y'all tomorrow. Same time?"

Jessica walked with them out to their vehicles. "If you need to talk, Haley—or any of you, for that matter—give me a call, or just come on out here. You don't have to wait for an invitation or a specific time."

When the dust from the vehicles had settled, she turned her beer up for a long drink. The burp it produced wasn't very ladylike, but then, if there was no one to hear a beer burp, did it really happen? ·

"How could we all split seven ways to Sunday, and yet when we get back together, it's like we were just here having a good time last weekend?" she muttered as she headed back into her RV.

That's close friends of the heart for you. Appreciate what you've got here, girl. It could be the beginnings of putting roots down for all of you. Uncle Elijah's deep voice popped into her head.

She wondered why she would hear from him after all these years. "Well, Wade Granger was barely an acquaintance in high school. I wouldn't consider him a close friend, and yet, he kind of fit right in with us," she argued as she pulled a box of junk cereal from the cabinet and filled a bowl with it.

He might be if you give him a chance, Uncle Elijah said.

"Since you're passing out advice, you could tell me what to do with that church." She poured milk on the cereal and carried the bowl over to the tiny table to eat.

There was no answer, so evidently, Uncle Elijah was finished with his advice. So, she ate her cereal and thought about Wade. What would bring a guy back to Riverbend to work odd jobs? He'd always been considered a nerdy type of person who never participated in sports—or in much of anything else, for that matter. He'd been one of those supersmart kids who made good grades and kept his head down between classes.

He had seemed lonely that night, and glad to be invited to join the circle of friends. Jessica decided that she'd hire him to put the steeple back on the roof. Maybe that would increase the chances of unloading the place as a church.

"I wonder if this area is zoned commercial and if I could get a liquor license," she mused as she stared out the window at the building, barely visible now. The moon was dark that night, and the stars didn't do much to light it up for her.

Chapter Two

Wade knelt in front of the three tombstones at the Riverbend Cemetery. One for his mother, one for his father, one for Danny, and an empty plot where he'd be buried someday. Losing his parents within a year of each other had been tough, but he'd still had his brother. Even though they were often on different continents, they had used modern technology to talk to each other every week—and then Danny, his only sibling and his best friend, was taken from him, leaving him totally alone.

He swiped a single tear from his cheek and whispered, "We should be starting a business together like we always talked about. Jessica Callaway has come back to town, and Elijah left her that old church out there on the river. You remember the one that Mama took us to when we were kids? Do you think the building would make a good bar? Do you want me to use your insurance money to do that? I always thought we'd come to some kind of agreement and build a bar in between a beach and the mountains—kind of like a compromise. I never thought of building one right here in Riverbend, until last night. What do you think?"

A south wind rustled the leaves in the old live oak above his head. Wade had never been superstitious, but it seemed like Danny was saying that he agreed with the idea. A bright red cardinal settled on a low branch and began to put on a show for him. Wade's mother used to say that cardinals sang "pretty boy, pretty boy." She had always called Wade and Danny her "pretty boys" and even had a set of gold dog tags made for each of them engraved with *Mama's Pretty Boy*. They couldn't wear them every day, but when they were off duty, they used them like a necklace, leaving their regular ones behind.

"I hear you, Brother," Wade said as he walked back to the truck that had belonged to Danny. He slid in behind the wheel; touched both sets of his brother's dog tags, which were hanging from the rearview mirror; started the engine; and drove toward the old church. Now, he just had to figure out how to either buy the place outright or else talk Jessica into taking him on as a partner in the business. He weighed the pros and cons on the way across town. On the pro side, if he bought the place outright, he would be his own boss, and all the profits would be his. The biggest thing on the con side would be finding help. Folks who owned the local convenience store said they couldn't get anyone to work, and he knew from experience that he was the only handyman in the area.

Jessica has friends who might help you out if you go in with her as partners. Danny's voice popped into his head. *Use my insurance money to go in business with her. Then you'll have some working capital left over in the bank account until the place begins to earn its keep.*

That was the first time since he'd lost his brother that Danny had spoken to him. He pulled over on the side of the road and said around a lump in his throat, "Tell me more of your thoughts."

Evidently, Danny had said all he was going to say that day, because the only thing that Wade heard was the whine of the AC in the truck. "Okay, then, partners, if possible," he said as he pulled back onto the road and turned on the radio. It was still tuned to the same station that his brother had left it on the last time that he had driven it. A quarter, two dimes, and three pennies were in the cup holder, where his brother had tossed the coins when he had parked it on post the day he left for his last mission.

Wade wasn't superstitious—at least not until that very day—but he wished that Danny would send him another sign. He felt guilty that Danny had taken his advice and joined the army right after he graduated from high school. He missed him. If only he had encouraged Danny to go to college, he might be alive today. The next song on the radio was "Broken Halos" by Chris Stapleton. Tears hung on Wade's thick, dark lashes as he listened to the words that told him not to ask Jesus why.

"But I want to know why," he whispered. "You were a techie who sat behind a desk, so why were you even in that vehicle that day?"

He turned onto Preacher Road, which led back to the church, and nodded in agreement with every word Stapleton sang. Apparently, Danny did have something more to say, and he used the song to relay his message. Wade finally had a smile on his face as he pulled in beside the other vehicles in the parking lot.

Even with all the mosquitoes buzzing around, he had enjoyed sitting out there with friends from his past the night before—especially Jessica. Maybe it was their matching boots or the fact that he had always thought she was the prettiest girl to ever come out of Riverbend that made him feel more of a connection to her than the other women. Whatever it was, she had invited him to come back, and he wasn't going empty handed. He had driven down to Burnet that afternoon and picked up a couple of six-packs of beer and one of root beer for the twins if they came with Risa. He turned the engine off and sat there for a moment before he opened the truck door. The next song on the radio was an old George Jones tune, "Choices."

He listened to about half of the song and said, "I get the messages, Danny." He opened the door and picked up the cooler from the back of the truck.

"Did y'all even go home?" he yelled at the women sitting in the same chairs they'd been in when he left the night before.

"We're waiting on you, so we can go see inside the haunted church," Lily called out. "We need two heroes to chase away rats and snakes. One's not enough."

"It's not haunted," Daisy declared. "Did you bring a gun to kill the varmints? Jessica says that she killed all the spiders and even swept their carcasses up so they won't scare us."

"We don't waste ammo on those things," Jessica said in mock seriousness. "We use our Ka-Bar knives to take care of critters like rats the size of possums."

"Avoids the noise of gunfire." Wade was amazed that he could joke after the morning he'd had.

"I want to grow up to be like y'all," Lily said. "I may go into the army or the air force when I get out of high school."

"The army is better," Jessica said.

"And," Wade said, "the army has even begun to let women go to sniper school."

"Oh, no!" Lily shook her head. "I went hunting with Daddy one time, and I hated the idea of killing an animal. I sure couldn't ever draw a bead on a person, but I could be a dang good nurse to help the ones who get wounded."

"How about you, Daisy?" Jessica asked. "Army or air force?"

"Neither one," Daisy declared. "I'm going to go to college and get a job in an air-conditioned office. I'm going to wear high heels and pretty dresses to work every day."

"There you have it." Wade set the cooler down beside the last empty chair. "One goes to the military, or maybe to nursing school and then the military. The other one to college. They're already planning their careers. Shall I leave the beer and root beer out here or take it inside? It's been on ice for a couple of hours, so it should be cold."

"Big as these mosquitoes are, I think we should take it inside." Jessica got to her feet and headed that way. "The power and water have both been turned on, so we have electricity and bathrooms. I didn't go back inside until everyone was here, so you might have to fight a few cobwebs. I can grab some toilet paper from my RV."

"That's better than squatting behind a tree," Lily said.

"And that's why I wouldn't go hunting with Daddy," Daisy declared. "Granny Martha said that ladies stayed home and cooked the food. They didn't go out in the woods and hunt."

"She also said that we weren't part of her family anymore, so whatever she said don't matter anymore." Lily fell into the line behind Jessica and Wade.

"Go on in, Wade." Jessica opened the door and stood to one side.

"My mama would rise up out of her grave and cut a peach-tree switch to whip me with if I went into a place before a lady," he said.

"Well, we wouldn't want that." Jessica smiled as she stepped inside the cool building.

"Ladies?" Wade set the cooler on the porch and stood to one side.

"Thank you," Mary Nell said and followed Jessica into the church.

When everyone had gone inside, he picked up the cooler, walked through the foyer, and went from the sanctuary through an open side door into the fellowship hall. The whole place seemed quiet as a tomb, and like Jessica had said, every pew, the floor, and even the light fixtures were covered with dust. Cobwebs hung beneath the pews and were thick in all the corners, but he didn't see any spiders. He plugged the refrigerator in, and it immediately began to hum. Half dreading to open the door, he was surprised to find it cleaned out and smelling only slightly musty.

"This place smells like Granny Stella's attic." Lily's voice carried through from the sanctuary.

"Or like the well house at Granny Martha's place," Daisy suggested. "But I haven't seen a mouse or a snake."

"I killed one spider so far," Haley said. "And I haven't seen a mouse or rat, but then I'm not surprised. There's nothing in here but dust and cobwebs for them to feed on. I've never been in this church before, but it doesn't look a lot different from the one Mama took me to when she was alive."

"A church is a church is a church," Risa said, "and by any other name, it would still be a church."

"So, if we put a bar in this building, would it still be a church?" Wade leaned on the doorjamb.

"It would." Mary Nell nodded. "Remember what happened when they started up a little nondenominational one in that old service station on Main Street a few months ago."

"Yep." Wade left the cooler and went into the sanctuary. "Folks still ask me if I'm parked out behind Sparky's church, and he just rented the building out. He never even went to the services there."

"What happened to it?" Jessica asked.

"They built up a congregation that got too big for the service station. They pooled their money then, and built a cowboy church in an old barn between Burnet and Riverbend. I heard that they baptize in a galvanized tank that folks use to water cattle," Wade answered. "Guess it don't matter, long as it holds water, what a person gets baptized in."

"Granny Martha says if you ain't baptized in natural water, like a creek or a river, it don't count," Daisy said. "Seems like you know your way around this place. You took the cooler into that other room?"

"My mama liked Elijah's preaching and was disappointed when he closed down the church and started drinking again," Wade answered. "That room is the fellowship hall. We had some after-services potlucks in there, back when I was a teenager. I would have sat through preachin' every Sunday without even wiggling if they'd had a dinner afterwards every week."

Risa breezed past him and squealed when she saw the kitchen. "A person could really live in this building with a full-sized kitchen like this."

"Yep, and there's a pretty nice bedroom suite back there by the Sunday school rooms," Wade said. "Elijah had visions of evangelists coming to preach revivals, and since there's no hotels or places to stay in Riverbend, he fixed a little place for them to stay right here at the church."

"Are you serious?" Mary Nell asked. "Is there a private bathroom?"

"I wouldn't know about that. Danny and I . . ." He swallowed the lump in his throat at even the mention of his brother's name. "We just peeked in there one time. It was all fixed up nice in those days with a bed and everything like a hotel would have. Don't know what it looks like now."

"Maybe you should be our tour guide," Jessica suggested.

"No, ma'am." Wade shook his head. "I've done told you everything I remember, so you're on your own."

While everyone else went snooping around the church, Jessica took a moment to stand in the center aisle between two rows of oak pews. She turned around slowly, taking in the whole room once again. With good lighting, it didn't look quite as bad as it had the night before. The windows were still dirty, and she was surprised that her uncle hadn't paid someone to put in elaborate stained-glass windows. She looked up at a vaulted ceiling with four big fans that had started turning slowly when she flipped on the lights. From there, her eyes went to the hardwood floor with footprints now in the layer of dust, and she imagined the noise of folks doing a line dance to jukebox music. The place would make a great bar, but of all the ideas that had gone through Jessica's mind concerning her life after retirement from the military, owning a bar wasn't even on the list.

The lyrics to "My Church" popped into her head again, and she visualized a jukebox where the choir had been set up behind the pulpit. She could almost feel the vibrations of boots on the hardwood floor as folks did a fancy line dance to the song. The sanctuary would make a nice-size room for dancing and throwing back a few drinks. The bar itself could be over on the side where the door was into the fellowship hall. And the raised stage where the choir and the preacher had stood really would make a good place to set a jukebox and, maybe later, even have a karaoke night.

Stop it! You can't make a bar out of a church. The folks in town would crucify you. Her father's voice was plain in her head. *Elijah built that place to be a church, and that's what you need to sell it as.*

Even hearing her dad fuss at her didn't stop her from imagining a food-prep table in the fellowship hall, and maybe one of the round tables for her and her friends to sit around for meals or to visit before and after hours.

"Come look at all these rooms," Lily squealed. "There's five of them, and they've each one got a big closet. And one of them still has a king-sized bed in it. It's not made up for company, but I didn't see a single mouse living in the mattress. I could so live in this church, and I wouldn't even have to share a room with Daisy. We've had to share with each other since we were born, Mama. Talk Jessica into renting this place to us for a house."

"Honey, we couldn't afford the electric bill on this big old building," Risa told her. "I bet Jessica is going to have an enormous bill just for cooling it down for us to have a tour this evening. But we will hunt a place of our own when I find a job, and maybe it will have enough bedrooms that you girls can have your own space."

Jessica felt a strange sense—almost eerily—that the building was talking to her as she listened to Risa and the girls. The walls seemed to be saying that she should look around and think of her friends, and what it would mean to them to have jobs.

What would it mean to you to work with your best friends every day? Uncle Elijah's voice popped into her head. *I should've made this place into a bar in the beginning rather than a church, so don't just dismiss Wade's idea.*

"What if . . ."—Jessica hesitated, almost afraid to even say the words out loud—"we did make a bar here? Risa, what if you did the cooking for us? You'd have to leave your mama's house if we did this, so what if we made a small living room in one corner of the fellowship hall so the twins could have a place to hang out? We could turn one of the Sunday school rooms into an office for Mary Nell to run the business out of. What if I did waitress work and tended bar? Maybe Haley could help out in the summers. I'm already pretty good at mixing drinks, and I can learn how to make the fancy ones." She paused to catch a breath, and wondered if she'd really just said all that.

"What if . . ."—Wade took up where she left off—"I put half of the money up for renovations and did the work for free? I would have half ownership in it, and I can already see tearing all these pews up to use to build the bar and the shelves behind it, and make some barstools. That would save a lot of money on lumber."

"That's a helluva lot of *what-ifs*," Haley whispered. "You'd have to get a lawyer to take care of all the legal stuff, like making sure this land is zoned right for a bar, and to check into people living in the back, and liquor licenses, and . . ."

Jessica held up a hand. "I've retained Uncle Elijah's lawyer out of Killeen to help me with the legalities of selling the place. What if I just told him I want to keep it and for him to look into the possibility of a bar? I've got the money that my folks left me, plus what I inherited from Uncle Elijah's estate sitting in the bank, so we could get whatever we need to do for remodeling, but I like the idea of using the wood we've got before we go buying more."

"There was money involved, and not just this old church?" Haley asked.

"Yep," Jessica answered. "He left his entire estate to me. There's enough to pay a lawyer to take care of all the legal stuff and redo this place, and probably float us for a year until we can start making a profit."

"I wouldn't be surprised if the lawyer found out that you'd need to close up the doors from the sanctuary into the former Sunday school rooms." There was excitement in Wade's voice. "You could probably leave the one from the fellowship hall to the bedrooms if it worked out. But I'm sure the lawyer will find out all the particulars for that kind of thing."

"Are we serious?" Haley asked. "I've got money saved, and I've got a place to live, so I wouldn't need to take up any of the rooms. I could just keep Mama's house and live there, or I could sell the house, and we could use all the furniture in her house to furnish this place like a home, and I could have one of the bedrooms."

"We've got bathrooms in the foyer for guys and gals," Risa said, "but what about a shower or tub?"

"The room that the evangelist was supposed to use has both. A garden tub and a walk-in shower," Lily said. "Daisy and I found it when we were looking around. Can I have that room?"

Risa shook her head. "Nope, Jessica should move into that room, but maybe she would let us use the tub and shower. What am I saying? This is just a pipe dream, isn't it? Kind of like playing house when we were little girls and drawing up the rooms in the dirt with a stick."

Jessica remembered those days fondly, but this was a lot more serious than their imaginary playhouses and pint jars filled with wild daisies and whatever flowers they could pilfer from their mothers' flower beds.

"The people in town might set fire to the place, but fate is sure telling us that this is a possibility," Wade said with half a chuckle.

"Naw." Risa shook her head slowly. "They'll cuss and rant and rave, but they wouldn't burn down a building. God would be madder at them for doing that than He would be at us for making a bar in a church."

"Granny Stella will lead the ranting party," Daisy said.

"Yep, she will," Lily agreed. "Are y'all *really* thinkin' about this?"

"Right now, we're *just* thinking about it," Jessica said, but her mind was going ninety miles an hour. "I'll have to talk to my lawyer and see if it's even possible." She turned to look up into Wade's green eyes. "Are you serious about buying half interest in this thing?"

"Yep, especially if you'll let me park my trailer out behind the bar for free and move my equipment into that storage barn out back," he answered.

"I didn't even know there was a storage barn." Jessica went to the end of the hallway and threw open one of the back doors. Sure enough, there was a metal barn out back. "I wonder what's in it?"

"A couple of old lawn mowers and some extra pews." Wade headed back toward the fellowship hall. "I peeked in the window a few weeks ago, when I came past here on my way down to the fishing dock. The road has gotten pretty rough and not many people use it anymore, but I like the peace and quiet at that particular place on the river."

"We'd all have jobs." Mary Nell's tone was full of hope and excitement. "Haley, you could come work here in the summers, and we could all be together for a few months every year."

"I might not even go back to Alabama if we decide to do this," Haley said. "I might be ready for a change in my life."

"Oh, yeah?" Jessica asked.

"Yep," Haley answered. "Besides, I'd be jealous that y'all would be here together, and I'd be off in Alabama."

"Having you here would be great," Jessica said. For Haley to even consider staying in Riverbend seemed to put the icing on the cupcake for her.

"Y'all want a beer?" Wade asked. "We just made a pretty big decision. We should celebrate with a beer at least. If I'd known we would get serious about a bar, I would have brought champagne."

"Yes," the women chorused.

"How about you girls?" Wade turned around. "I've got cold root beer in bottles."

"Yes, and thank you," the twins said in unison as they rushed past him.

"We'll get them, and bring y'all each a beer," Lily said.

Wade turned to face Jessica. "I have a confession. I wanted to buy this place from you and put in a bar myself, but I didn't have enough money to do what I envisioned doing with it. I can go half with no problem, though."

So that's why he made that suggestion last night, Jessica thought.

"Did you already look into the legal stuff?" she asked.

He shook his head. "No, but I did find out that Elijah had it zoned commercial before he built the church. Y'all can think about it if you need to, but I am very serious about my offer."

"What if you used your money to buy into the place, and then you hated working with us?" Jessica asked.

Wade flashed half a smile. "I've worked with easy people, and I've worked with total butts. You do your job, and I do mine. Why wouldn't we get along? We'll be together quite a bit during the remodel, but after we open, our hours will probably be from six in the evening until two in the morning, like most bars. I'll live in my trailer, and you probably won't even see me during the day."

Lily and Daisy returned with soda pop and beers in their hands, brushed away a few cobwebs from the corner of the back pew, and sat down side by side.

"We'll be in school, so we won't be around during the day, either," Lily said.

"And if we get to be cheerleaders, we'll be gone some at night, too," Daisy added.

"If we don't get chosen, we can help Mama in the kitchen. I'm pretty good at dishwashing, and I do a mean job of cutting up tomatoes for hamburgers," Lily said.

Jessica sat down on the end of the pew, and peace fell around her shoulders like a nice warm blanket on a winter night. This was where she was supposed to be, and what she was supposed to do. The bar would provide a job for Risa and her girls, as well as a place for Mary Nell—and Haley, if she decided to stay in Riverbend.

"If we're serious"—Jessica let out a long breath of air that she hadn't even realized she was holding in—"I'll talk to my lawyer as soon as I can get a hold of him."

"I better be looking for three beds because Mama is going to throw us out, but I'm dead serious," Risa said. "I need a job. I have no skills or experience, but I can cook, and I can clean. At least I won't have to dust mounted deer heads, stuffed squirrels, and antlers that are hanging in every spare corner of Paul's trailer house."

"I'll supply beds," Haley said, "and the living room stuff, too. Wade, can you help move them in your truck?"

"No problem," Wade answered, "but, Risa, you might want to wait until we know for sure this is a reality before you break the news to Stella. If she says that you've got to leave, I'll bring the flatbed trailer that I use to haul all my tools around in over to Stella's place and move whatever needs to come this way."

"And I won't tell Daddy until we know for sure," Mary Nell added. "It would disappoint him to think he might have a local outlet for his moonshine and wine and then find out that the whole thing fell through because of some legal problem. I vote that if that happens, we go back to the drawing board and figure out something that will let us all work together."

"We've got a secret." Lily giggled.

"And wild hogs couldn't drag it out of us." Daisy draped her arm around her sister's shoulders. "But it would be tempting when Granny Stella starts preachin' at us about our souls."

"Not a word," Risa warned with a shake of her finger.

"Let's toast to a partnership and, if this doesn't work out, to whatever does." Jessica held up her bottle of beer, as did Wade.

"To friendship." Mary Nell raised her bottle.

"To friendship," Haley and Risa chimed in at the same time.

"To moving away from Granny Stella." Lily held up her root beer.

"Amen!" Daisy agreed.

Chapter Three

Isaac Yandell, Jessica's lawyer, pushed his wire-rimmed glasses up on his nose and ran a hand over his bald head. "You do realize that Riverbend is a small, conservative town, don't you? Are you absolutely sure you want to turn a church building into a bar? You're going to get a lot of arguments from the local folks."

"Yes, sir, I do know that Riverbend is a small town, and I also realize that the church is a prime spot for a bar because it's sitting right at the corner of three dry counties and is only a few miles from another one to the south and a fifth one to the north," Jessica told him.

"Plus, Fort Hood is right over the county line," Wade said from the corner where he'd chosen to stand rather than sit in one of the chairs in front of the lawyer's desk.

"Well, there's no reason the building couldn't be used for anything commercial. Elijah said you could use it for anything, or you could burn it down if you wanted to. I also can't see a valid reason why you couldn't get a beer and liquor license, but that will take about three months. If everything goes smoothly, you might be able to have a grand opening the middle of September. To do that we need a name for your bar, and we'll need to submit forms for everyone who will be serving liquor. That means a valid birth certificate and social security card for each person," Mr. Yandell said. "Should I start proceedings today, or do you need to think about this a little longer? It's a really big decision. You are saying that you are going to live in Riverbend under the shadow of contention for a long time."

"What do you think Uncle Elijah would say?" Jessica asked.

"He'd think it was a royal hoot," the lawyer chuckled. "He was a salty old dog. He and I played golf together, and we both enjoyed a double shot of Jameson too often to talk about."

"Then I'm ready to get on with it." Jessica figured that she hadn't had the church or the inheritance before her uncle died, so if her bar didn't work out, she really wasn't losing anything. And all her friends would have jobs, which was a big selling point to her.

"All right then." Mr. Yandell looked up at Wade. "Since you're going to be a partner, you'll need to bring everything that I've already mentioned, plus you'll both need bank statements showing that you are each putting up half the money to start up the business."

"I'll get it all together for you, sir," Wade said with a nod.

"Okay then," Mr. Yandell said. "I'll get the paperwork started. Make an appointment with my office manager on your way out to come in on Wednesday and sign everything. Go ahead and bring all the folks you told me about at that time, too, so we can get their signatures on the permits to sell liquor."

"Do you know offhand if there will be a conflict about my friends living in the back of the place?" she asked as she got to her feet.

"I don't think there would be, but I'll check into it. Just to be on the safe side, when you remodel, you might want to consider closing any doors leading from the sanctuary into the hallway where the Sunday school rooms are. That would be for privacy's sake. You wouldn't want folks who had too much to drink wandering into your living quarters looking for a bathroom. But I will see what the law says about that," he answered.

She stuck out her hand to shake with him. "Thank you, Mr. Yandell."

"Isaac," he said as he shook her hand. "If we're going to be working together, just call me Isaac."

Wade took a couple of steps forward and shook his hand also. "I'm just Wade, then."

"Thank you, and I'm Jessica." She smiled.

"Then Jessica and Wade it is," he said. "I'll see you on Wednesday."

"We'll be here." Jessica slung her purse over her shoulder, and she and Wade stopped by the desk out in the lobby to make an appointment for three o'clock on Wednesday.

A blast of hot wind hit her in the face when she stepped out of the air-conditioned office. She figured the heat was what made her a little dizzy, but then it could have been the fact that she'd made such a huge life-changing decision after such a short time. She certainly had not considered living in Riverbend permanently before the idea of a bar came about.

"Are you okay?" Wade asked. "You look like you just saw a ghost. You aren't already regretting this, I hope."

"Little shocked at how hot it is," Jessica answered, but she held on to the porch post a few more seconds. "The deal is all in motion now, so I guess we're going to brave the elements—meaning Stella and the people in Riverbend—to put a bar in what used to be a church."

He tucked his arm into hers. "Let's get you out to the truck where it's cool. And, Jessica, I've never been surer of anything," Wade said. "How about you?"

"It's all been pretty fast, and when Isaac reminded me that the folks in Riverbend are not going to be happy about this, I thought of Risa and what she'll have to endure." She let him guide her out to his vehicle. "Thank you so much for driving me up here today. It would have been tough to find a parking spot in that RV."

"No problem," he said as he opened the passenger door for her.

This is the kind of guy you want for a partner and a friend, the voice in her head whispered.

Wade slid in behind the wheel. "We should go by the Dairy Queen and get an ice cream to celebrate. Maybe a little something cold will bring some color back in your face. I thought you were going to faint when you came out of the building."

"That sounds great," she said, "but, Wade, what if we spend all this money, and then the bar doesn't do well? We'll have payroll to meet and overhead to pay, and if it all bombs, my best friends will have lost their reputation in town, plus their jobs. What if—"

He butted in before she could say another word. "Don't think like that. Just remember that it could take a year before we start making a profit, but that's all right. As long as we pay Haley, Risa, and Mary Nell, you and I can live on our retirement from the military. At least I can. How are you set?"

"I've got a pretty good savings on top of my pension and inheritance," she answered. "How do we even go about figuring out how much it will take for our renovations? You've done odd carpentry jobs, so maybe you can figure a rough estimate?"

He nodded the whole time she talked. "With all the wood in the pews, there will be very little money involved with that. The main outlay will be to buy the liquor license and do all the legal stuff for inspections to run a kitchen." He started the engine and backed out of the parking lot.

Jessica giggled. "Stella will *sure* have a fit when she finds out we tore up the pews to build the actual bar. To her that would be as much a sacrilege as having beer and liquor in what used to be a church house."

"Yep, but that's okay." Wade grinned.

"How do you figure that it's okay?" Jessica asked.

"You ever taken a vehicle out on a back road and ran it as fast as it would go to blow the cobwebs out of it?" he asked.

"We've all done that, but what's that got to do with Stella?" she asked.

"A hissy fit will clear out her mind." Wade chuckled.

What started out as a giggle quickly turned into a guffaw. Jessica never did laugh like a lady, but more like a burly truck driver. The laughter was so infectious that soon the whole truck cab was filled with their mirth.

Finally, Wade got control and said, "That felt good. I can't remember the last time I laughed so hard that I got tears in my eyes."

Jessica pulled down the visor to check her reflection in the mirror. "We better order ice cream from the drive-through window. My mascara is making black streaks down my cheeks." She wiped at her cheek with her palm, but it just smeared. "Rumors will have it that you've made me cry if anyone sees me like this."

Wade opened the lid to the console and handed her a couple of individually wrapped wet wipes. "This ought to take care of the problem, but it would be a good idea to stay in the truck anyway. It's only just now cooling down."

"Thank you." Jessica opened a package and cleaned her face with it.

With a man that sweet, why was she feeling doubts about taking him on as a partner? Or even becoming the half owner of a Texas honky-tonk?

Because it was an impulse decision, something you never make, the voice in her head said. *That does not mean it wasn't the right one.*

"I hope so," she whispered.

"Are we still talking about Stella's hissy fit?" Wade asked.

"No, I was woolgathering, and hoping that the bar is a big success for all of us, and that we're making the right decision. Just a few days ago, I didn't know what I was doing with that building, my life, or even where I was going to settle down, and things are happening so fast that I'm second-guessing myself," Jessica answered.

"Do you ever watch *NCIS*?" Wade asked.

"Every chance I get," she said. "What's that got to do with anything?"

"Remember Gibbs's rules?"

"There's no such thing as coincidence," she recited.

"Rule number ninety-one: don't look back." He drove straight to the Dairy Queen and pulled up to the window. "Whether we made this decision on the spur of the moment or we took five years to think about it, we should commit to it and not look back."

Jessica took a deep breath and let it out slowly. "Since Gibbs is never wrong, I'll accept that rule, and remind you of it if I catch *you* having regrets."

"Sounds good to me." He smiled across the console at her.

Risa carried a basket of cucumbers and tomatoes from the vegetable garden in her mother's backyard to the back porch. She left her shoes beside the door and got a whiff of fresh bread baking in the oven when she went inside. She set the vegetables beside the sink, poured herself a tall glass of sweet tea, and carried it to the table. Her mother had the remote phone lying on her shoulder and was talking as she arranged lunch meat and cheese on a plate for lunch.

Maybe *talking* wasn't the right word. She mostly just listened and shot dirty looks toward Risa every five seconds. Stella finally put the phone back on the base, tapped her foot—a clue that always meant trouble was on the way—and glared at Risa.

"I'll slice up some of those tomatoes and cucumbers to go with our sandwiches." Risa hoped she was wrong, but her gut feeling said that the only thing she wasn't right about was the fierceness of her mother's anger. "Nothing smells as good as bread baking in the oven."

"I hope you enjoy it and the sandwiches we'll have for lunch"— Stella's tone was even colder than her stony stares—"because if what I just heard is the truth, and you're involved in it, this will be your last meal here in my house."

Risa's heart missed a beat. Surely the news of even the possibility of making the old church into a bar hadn't spread that quickly. Jessica had just called Risa while she was harvesting the vegetables to tell her that it was a go and what all she needed to have ready on Wednesday for the lawyer. Jessica said that she and Wade were having ice cream to celebrate, and they had lots of ideas on how to save money on the renovations that Jessica wanted to discuss with everyone that evening.

"What are you so angry about, Mama?" Risa knew the answer, but hoped she was wrong. She and the girls might very well be sleeping on the floor at the old church until Wade could get some beds moved in from Haley's place.

"Hey, what's going on in here?" Lily popped into the kitchen.

Risa hoped that the girls being in the kitchen would break the tension, but Stella's expression didn't change at all.

"Smells like lunch. Looks like lunch. My stomach says it's time for lunch," Daisy teased. "What can I do to help? Set the table? Pour the sweet tea?"

"You"—Stella whipped around and pointed a finger at Daisy—"can be honest with me. Did you know that your mother has been going to the old Community Church the past three nights, and that she and her friends are talking about turning it into a bar?"

Daisy bore up under the heated glare pretty well—for about five seconds. Then she turned to her mother and raised a shoulder in a shrug.

"Yes, it's the truth." Risa pushed back her chair and stood up. Stella Sullivan—mother or not—was not going to intimidate her or run her life, either. Sleeping on a floor wouldn't be so bad if it meant getting away from her mother's self-righteous, overbearing, controlling issues when it came to Risa and her girls.

"Then get out of my house." Stella pointed toward the door.

Risa held her head high and kept her back ramrod straight. "Wade Granger and Jessica Callaway are going to partner up on the deal. Mary

Nell and I are going to work for them, and possibly Haley if she doesn't go back to Alabama in the fall. I'll be cooking since it will be a bar and grill."

Stella's finger shot around to point at Risa. "It's bad enough that I have to explain to my friends that your husband and his family kicked you out, and now this. I've tried to convince folks that it wasn't your fault, but it was, wasn't it? Were you working on the sly in a bar there, or doing something even worse?" Her face got redder, and her voice got higher and squeakier with every word. "Your father would rise up out of his grave if he knew this. He was so proud of being a deacon in our church. I'm glad he's gone and can't see what our only child has become."

"What happened in Kentucky wasn't Mama's fault." Lily came to her mother's rescue.

Stella's finger found its way to her in a split second. "Don't you speak to me in that tone. I've given you a home when you didn't have one, young lady. What's going to happen is this, Risa Sue. You are going to call—"

Before she said another word, Risa's phone and the landline rang at the same time.

"Saved by the bell." Daisy's giggled words were thick with nerves.

Poor kid had heard a tirade like the one Stella was giving them as they left Kentucky a few weeks ago. Their paternal grandmother, Martha, had yelled and screamed at them, but she had given them twenty-four hours to get off her property and out of her son's life, not half an hour at the most. Stella grabbed the phone and went into what Risa called her mother's martyrdom voice as she talked to one of her friends.

"Hello, Haley, bad time," Risa answered her call in a whisper. "Can I call you back?"

"Give me just a minute first," Haley said. "I've got a wonderful idea. Why don't I keep this house, and you and the girls can live here?

There's lots of room, and that way they wouldn't be teased at school about living in a bar."

"Are you serious?" Risa didn't even realize she was holding her breath until she let it all out in a long whoosh. "Mama just found out the news, and she's throwing us out. If we could even stay there for a few days, it would be wonderful."

"Yes, I'm serious. I don't know why I didn't think about doing this before. I guess it was because I was so upset over that damned letter," Haley said. "Can I expect you in a little while? I'll make some sweet tea and open a pack of cookies."

"Yes, you can." Risa had lost her belief in miracles years ago, but right then she began to believe again.

Stella put the phone back on the stand once again and turned to face Risa. "I'm giving you an ultimatum. Either call Jessica Callaway and not only tell her you will not be working in her bar, but that you won't be talking to her anymore, either."

"Or?" Risa continued to stand even though her knees felt weak. Living with her mother wasn't any better than being under Paul's and his mother's thumbs.

"Or you and these girls can find another place to live," Stella said.

"I heard that," Haley said. "Pack your things and come on over. You and the girls can have the three bedrooms and bathroom on the second floor. I've been using the master bedroom right off the foyer, anyway, because I'm too lazy to climb the stairs several times a day."

"Are you sure? What about rent when you go back to Alabama?" Risa's clammy hands trembled so badly she almost dropped the phone.

"We'll discuss all that kind of stuff tomorrow," Haley said. "This is today. You and the girls need a place where you don't feel so much tension. I'm sorry I didn't offer sooner, but with all that's been going on, my mind has been off in la-la land. I'll be waiting on the porch and heaving a sigh of relief that we don't have to move anything to the old church."

"Thank you. Be there as soon as we can get things packed and in my truck." Risa ended the call and closed her eyes for a second to give a silent prayer of thanksgiving for her good friends.

"Mama?" Daisy looked like she was about to cry.

"This is bull crap," Lily said through clenched teeth.

"No, it's your grandmother's house, not ours," Risa said in a calm voice. "She has the right to decide who lives here and who doesn't, just as much as your Granny Martha in Kentucky had the right to be mad at me and kick us out. Go pack your bags, girls. Don't forget anything, not even a hair clip."

"Are we going to live in the bar?" Lily asked.

"No, Haley has offered to let us live in her house," Risa answered.

"So, you're choosing your low-life friends over me?" Stella crossed her arms over her chest and gritted her teeth. "After all I've done for you—giving you a home and putting food in your mouths all these weeks—you are going to leave me alone?"

"Mother, you are the one who is making me choose. I'm going to take the girls over to Haley's house and stay there, and I *will* be work-ing for Jessica and Wade. I don't have many skills outside of cleaning a trailer house and cooking, so it's a good job for me. It's your decision as to whether you want me and the girls to be part of your life. When you get over your fit, call me if you want to see us." Risa started out of the kitchen.

"Don't hold your breath until you get that call, girl," Stella yelled at Risa.

"Are you serious, Mama? Do we really get to go live with Haley?" Daisy whispered.

"Yes, I am," Risa said around the lump in her throat. When she had been thrown out of Kentucky, she had called her mother to ask if she could bring the girls to Riverbend for a few weeks. Stella hadn't sounded happy about the idea, but she hadn't refused. At that point Risa should have listened to Haley and driven down to Alabama to stay with her until she could get on her feet. But Risa couldn't impose on Haley like that when she was living in a tiny one-bedroom apartment.

Lily took her sister by the hand and tugged to get her moving. "Let's go before she changes her mind. I'll have my things in the truck before you know it, Mama. Is Granny Stella going to inspect our bags to be sure we didn't take anything that doesn't belong to us?"

"Of course not!" Stella gasped.

"Good," Daisy said, "but I wouldn't take anything that wasn't mine, anyway. She's going to have to apologize to you before I want to see her again."

"I don't owe anyone an apology"—Stella's voice got even louder—"and if you leave, don't expect to ever be welcome in my house again. Not ever."

The girls disappeared down the hallway to the room they shared, and Risa turned around at the door to face her mother. "Are you sure you don't want see the girls every once in a while? They won't be working in a bar, and they're your only grandchildren."

"Not if *you're* working at a bar. Good grief, Risa Sue, the whole town is already talking about the sacrilege of turning a church into a bar. Whatever gave y'all the idea to do such a horrible thing?" Stella fumed.

"Location, building, and there's already too many churches in Riverbend as it is," Risa answered. "The place has been on the market for years, and from what I understand, there hasn't been one bit of interest from anyone in buying it. It sits in a prime location with Fort Hood just over the border and lots of dry counties around Burnet County. I don't know why someone hasn't latched on to the idea before now. And, Mama, you go into places to eat that serve liquor. What's the difference?"

"I go into restaurants, not bars," Stella shot back at her. "I cannot and will not have someone living in my house that works in a place like that. I have held up a Christian example in this town for years, and I will not tarnish it this late in life." Stella took two loaves of bread from the oven. "And being the Christian woman that I've always been, I can't have someone in my house who is working there. I'm going to take a loaf of this bread over to Lulu, my neighbor and my sister in Christ. I will *let* you have lunch if you want to eat before you go, but I expect you'll be gone when I get back?"

"It's just a building, Mama," Risa said. "Like Sparky's Service Station. It was once a place to get gas, candy bars, and soda pop, and then it was a church, and now it's an empty building again."

"You can't say anything that will make me change my mind," Stella said.

"Thank you for giving me and the girls a place to come to when we had to leave Kentucky," Risa said with a sigh, "and know that I love you even if you are kicking me out."

"If you did, you'd choose me." Stella dumped a beautiful loaf onto a plate and removed her bibbed apron. "And I love you because Jesus says I have to love you, but right now, I don't like you, and I'll be glad you and the girls are out of my house."

Risa took the first step out of the kitchen. "I'm sorry I've upset your life."

"Then why do this?" Stella asked.

"Because when I left Kentucky, I made myself a promise that no one, no matter how much I loved them, was ever going to tell me how to live my life again. That includes you, Mama. It's been a bad example for my girls, and I don't want them to grow up thinking that anyone has that kind of power over them," Risa answered. "Paul had his antlers and deer heads all over our trailer, even in our bedroom. I was supposed to keep them spotlessly clean, but he was the king of our double-wide. He and his mother made the decisions, and I was supposed to be the submissive wife."

"Why did he kick you out? Were you having an affair?" Stella eyed her carefully.

"I wasn't, but after the twins were born, I decided I didn't want more children. My body belongs to me, not Paul, so I took birth control pills. That's a no-no in the Jackson family. Kids are blessings from God. Mother Martha had half a dozen sons, and each of those, other than Paul, are still producing kids every year or two. According to her, I cheated Paul out of a son, and was an abomination to God for using birth control. When Paul found my pills, he took them to his mother. They made a family decision to excommunicate me," Risa said.

Stella crossed her arms over her chest. "Kids *are* blessings from God, and you should have obeyed your husband's wishes."

"Bye, Mama. We'll be gone by the time you get back from Lulu's place." In one respect, Risa's heart felt heavy with even more grief. Twice now, her daughters had been uprooted. In another way, she was relieved to leave her mother's house, where she and the girls had as many strict rules as they'd had in Kentucky. "You've got my phone number if you change your mind about seeing the girls or if you need anything."

"I don't need or want anything from you," Stella said.

"You aren't proud of me for standing up for my rights?" Risa asked around still another lump in her throat.

Stella shook her head. "A woman's responsibility is to her husband. I took care of this house and your father for forty years and never wanted more."

"Good for you." Angry tears flowed down Risa's cheeks. She heard the back door slam when her mother left, and then another one at the front of the house echoed that noise.

"Hey, need some help?" Lily asked as she came into the foyer from outside. "My stuff is already in the back of the truck."

"Yes, I do." Risa smiled through the tears.

Lily hurried across the room and wrapped her arms around her mother. "It's okay, Mama. We got through Granny Martha's hissy fit, and this one isn't nearly as bad as some of hers have been. I love the idea of living with Haley. She's cool, and Daisy and I can help her out with whatever she needs to pay our way for letting us live there."

Daisy came into the room and made it a three-way hug. "I heard what Lily said. I'm really, really happy about not living next door to Granny Martha or right in the house with Granny Stella. My things are in the truck. Let's get you all packed and ready to go. We didn't realize it at the time, but not being able to bring so much with us from Kentucky was a blessing."

Out of the mouths of babes, Risa thought.

Chapter Four

*W*hat a way to start off a new month," Jessica said and wished that Wade would drive faster. No one ever saw a police officer on the back county roads, and Risa needed her support right then. Time and distance had nothing to do with the kind of friendship she and Risa, Haley, and Mary Nell had. It didn't matter that she hadn't seen them in years; they were just as close as they'd been when they were high school cheerleaders. And Stella had kicked Risa out of her house that day. What kind of mother did that? That her mother-in-law had gotten her underwear in a twist and told her to leave Kentucky was one thing. That her mama's-boy husband hadn't backed her up was another thing, but for a mother to tell her own daughter to leave and never come back—that was totally inexcusable, and Jessica had to go comfort her friend.

"The good always comes with a little taste of the tough going. If it didn't, we wouldn't appreciate the easy times nearly as much," Wade replied. "That's what my mama always said."

"So did mine," Jessica said with a nod. "We knew this would happen when Stella found out about the bar, but I didn't expect it to be today."

"Word has it that she really didn't want Risa to come back to Riverbend when the Jackson family kicked her out, but she couldn't say no. This is actually a blessing for Stella. She's got an excuse to be the martyr, and she gets rid of two teenage girls and a daughter that she'd rather have living a thousand miles away," Wade said.

"How do you know all this?" Jessica asked.

"Oscar." Wade shrugged. "He's a fountain of information about anyone in Riverbend. Lived here his whole life, and he hosts a domino game at his house on Sunday afternoons. I attend almost every week, and sometimes I even win. Back to the gossip. Old women don't have a monopoly on knowing everything that goes on in a small town. Old men talk as much as old women."

A line of vehicles was already parked outside Haley's house when Wade made the turn down the short, tree-lined lane. The sight of the old two-story house with its wide front porch brought a flood of memories back to Jessica's mind—chasing fireflies in the yard when they were little girls, crying over boyfriends lost and sighing over boyfriends wished for as they got older, making plans that last year they were in high school, and shedding tears right there on the porch when Jessica was the first to leave town.

"I spent a lot of time here," Jessica muttered past the lump in her throat. Where had the time gone? Almost four decades of friendship, and a lot of it was spent right there in that house. They could never go to Risa's house because Stella didn't want kids running in and out of her place. Mary Nell's mama didn't care if they came over to her house to play, and Jessica's folks were warm and welcoming.

"I remember that y'all were all friends even when we were just kids." Wade parked beside Risa's old truck, which had once been shiny and red but now had faded to somewhere between a dull pink and an ugly shade of orange.

Jessica would bet dollars to doughnuts that Paul didn't drive a vehicle that old. He would probably have a new one every two years, plus an old one to use for a hunting wagon. She slung open the door and took the porch steps two at a time, expecting to find Risa in tears. But everyone was sitting around a table with a gallon jug of sweet tea and a bowl full of ice in the middle. No one was crying, but they all stopped talking at once when she reached the top step.

"I'm so sorry, Risa," Jessica said.

"We're not," Lily and Daisy chorused together.

Risa motioned toward an empty rocking chair right beside her. "It's not your fault, and probably for the best all the way around."

Jessica sank down into the chair and set it in motion with her foot. Risa didn't look or sound upset, but being tossed out of two homes like a bag of garbage couldn't be good for her. She must be putting on a brave front for her girls. If Jessica had daughters, she would certainly do the same thing.

"Welcome to the party," Haley said as she poured two glasses of sweet tea and handed one to Jessica and the other to Wade. "This solves a lot of problems for all of us. The twins have a home that's not in the back of a bar. I don't have to rush to make a decision about the house, and even if I go back to Alabama in the fall, someone will be living here to take care of things for me. And I'll have time to help with the renovations at the bar."

"Mary Nell tells me things went well at the lawyer's. When do we start to work?" Oscar asked as he came out of the house and sat down in a lawn chair beside Wade.

Oscar hadn't changed much. He still wore what Jessica called his signature look—bibbed overalls and a faded T-shirt. She could have hugged him for starting a new conversation about the renovations on the church. Risa needed to think about something other than her mother right then.

"Tomorrow morning too soon?" Wade took a long drink of his tea.

"Not one bit. Mary Nell tells me you're moving your trailer and equipment out there. I'm free this afternoon if you want help doing all that," Oscar said and then looked over at Jessica. "Girl, you ain't changed a bit since high school, and you ain't gained a pound, neither."

"Neither have you." Jessica smiled. "I was sorry to hear about Miz Nellie passing."

"She was a good woman, more wife than I deserved, and a good mama to Mary Nell." Oscar sighed.

"I miss Mama so much and more here lately than ever," Mary Nell said.

"I miss her every day, but I'm glad to have all you girls back in town and going into business together." Oscar took a drink of his tea. "My Nellie would like that. Most of all, I'm happy that Wade is going to be working for you so that I can be in the middle of all the fun. Elijah would have been happy to see you use that old church for something rather than letting it just sit there and rot. He probably should have made it into a bar rather than a church in the first place. He would have had a helluva lot more success. Folks have enough religious places in Riverbend, but they ain't got a good bar and grill."

"Thank you. When I heard that Stella had . . . ," Jessica stammered and took a long drink of her tea. "Well, you know."

"Hey, if Haley didn't have a place for Risa and these girls, I would have insisted they come live with me and Mary Nell. We've got lots of room. Nellie wanted a house full of kids, so we built a big house," Oscar said.

Oscar's red, curly hair poked out around a cap with a US Marine logo on the bill, and a matching, faded tattoo peeking out from under his shirtsleeve testified that he had spent time in the marines. His blue eyes were a little darker than Mary Nell's, and they twinkled with happiness.

"That's awfully kind of you," Risa said.

"We all should have thought to offer you a place so you wouldn't have to move in with Stella. A band of angels couldn't live with that woman," Oscar said and then tipped his hat toward the twins. "Begging your pardon, ladies. That is your grandmother, and I shouldn't be saying ugly things about her."

"No problem," Lily assured him. "Forget the angels, though. Daisy and I don't think the devil himself could live with her."

"Lily!" Risa scolded.

"Truth is truth, no matter if you cover it in pig poop or chocolate." Daisy took up for her sister. "I'm just glad neither me or Lily look like either of our grandmothers, and if we ever act like them, then, Mama, you should take a peach-tree switch to us."

"I never believed in whipping," Risa said, "and I don't intend to start now."

"Me neither," Oscar said, "but I was sure tempted to lock Mary Nell away when she decided to quit college and move to Tennessee with that worthless piece of crap. I've always been glad that my daughter got my hair and eyes, but I was even happier that she got her mother's sweet disposition." He finished off his tea and refilled his glass from the gallon jug. "That's a good thing most of the time, but she's always been a little too trusting, as we all know from what happened with that low-down skunk she left in Nashville. But at least he's there and she's here, and he would do well not to cross over the Texas line if he values his life."

"Daddy," Mary Nell scolded.

"It's the truth. She should've married Danny Granger. That boy thought she hung the moon and stars," Oscar declared. "But that's water under the bridge, and we can't call it back."

When Jessica glanced over at Wade, she found him smiling, but it didn't reach his eyes.

"But we can burn that bridge and move on, can't we, Mary Nell?" Risa suggested.

Mary Nell nodded.

"I'll drink to that and provide the matches and kindling." Oscar raised his glass. "I'm going to view today's event as a positive thing. Let's talk about our new bar. I'd be glad to buy in as a silent partner."

"Thank you," Wade said, "but what we're really interested in is buying your local moonshine and wine."

"And maybe letting this old Vietnam vet man the bar some of the time?" Oscar asked. "I could swap stories with all these young whipper-snappers from over at Fort Hood."

"We'd be honored to have you behind the bar anytime you want to help out," Jessica said.

"Thank you, darlin'." Oscar's face lit up. "I sure do like the idea of helping make this old building into a bar and then spending time with all you kids."

Wade finished off his tea, refilled his glass, and turned to focus on Jessica. "Oscar and your Uncle Elijah were best friends. They served together on the worst day in that Vietnam War. They hardly ever talked about it, except with each other."

"January 1968, but right now I want to know if these two young'uns here"—Oscar nodded toward Daisy and Lily—"think they'll be happy living with Haley? If not, then they can bring their mama and come to our house. It's pretty far out of town, but the school bus runs right past it. And speaking of that, any of you girls are welcome if you need a place, either for a few days or permanently." He turned to nod at Jessica. "That goes for you, too, if you get tired of living all cramped up in that little bitty trailer."

"Thank you, Oscar. I appreciate that offer a lot," Jessica said.

"Oh. My. Gosh!" Lily fanned herself with the back of her hand. "We won't ever get tired of living here. This is like living in a fairy tale. Daisy and I each have our own room for the first time in our lives. I don't have to listen to Daisy whine about me taking more than half of the top of the dresser."

"And I don't have to put up with Lily missing the dirty-clothes basket with her socks, and never making her bed. We even have each got a queen-sized bed in our rooms. I'm sure I'm going to feel like I'm sleeping on clouds after having a little narrow, twin-sized one my whole life," Daisy added. "And the best part is that"—she took a deep breath and shot a look toward her mother—"we left all the tension behind in

Granny Stella's house. We never knew when she was going to get mad at us, or start telling us how lucky we were that she took us in so that we didn't have to live on the street."

"That's good," Oscar said. "Now, you, Risa. Are you really all right with this move? It had to have stung for Stella to tell you to get out of her house. She is your mother, after all, and a mother should love her child unconditionally and support her."

"I was feeling like I didn't belong anywhere, but I'm grateful that Haley has taken us in, that Jessica is giving me a job, and that I've got good friends," Risa answered, "and that y'all are all here to support me and the girls. It seems like maybe things might work out after all."

"Anytime," Haley said. "Going back to the bar conversation. What time should we be there in the morning?"

"Oscar and I usually start at eight, knock off an hour for lunch, and quit about four," Wade answered, "but that's not set in stone."

"How about the girls and I get there a little earlier than that, have breakfast ready for y'all at eight, a light lunch at noon, and then we all have supper together at five?" Risa asked.

"Home cooking?" Oscar's blue eyes lit right up. "I'd work for free for that kind of schedule."

"We all have to eat, and that's what I'll be doing when the bar opens, so I can get acquainted with the kitchen this way," Risa said.

Jessica pulled a credit card from her purse and handed it to Risa. "This is going to be our account card. Buy whatever you need at the grocery store with it and bring the receipts to Mary Nell. She's going to be in charge of the office, payroll accounts, and all that stuff. Seems strange to call the place a bar after it being a church for so long."

"Might as well get used to it." Wade grinned, and this time it did reach his eyes. "That's what it's about to become."

"What are y'all naming it?" Haley asked.

"That should be a joint effort," Jessica answered.

"How about the Preacher's Bar and Grill since it's located on Preacher Road?" Lily asked.

"Or My Church since that's what's left on the sign right now? Seems like an omen to me," Risa suggested.

"Can't you just see a young trainee from the base saying that he's going 'to church'?" Wade air quoted the last two words. "His training officer would probably think the kid had gotten religion."

"Name it whatever you want. Folks are going to call it the Old Church," Oscar said. "Remember when those folks rented Sparky's little store and had services there until they could build something better? The little paper sign taped to the window with the times for services called it the Cowboy Church, but everyone called it Sparky's church. You probably would have a legal name for the business when you apply for your liquor license, though."

"Speaking of that," Jessica said, "you all need to go with me to the lawyer's office on Wednesday. Each of you have to apply for a license to sell liquor and beer."

"I'll be in the kitchen, not behind the bar," Risa argued.

"And I'll just be doing waitress work, but only in the summer," Haley added.

"Better just get it done for all of you at once, just in case one of you have to do fill-in work," Oscar told them. "But don't get me one. My license to make and sell liquor and wine will hold up. I guess this means that tomorrow we'll only work until noon, right?"

"Probably so," Wade answered. "We can measure and figure out the dimensions for the actual bar, and get it sort of designed."

Jessica glanced over at Wade. "Hey, this is a joint project. Everyone here gets a vote about each step along the way."

All the talk about names, licenses, and legalese wasn't what was in her thoughts at all. Now that she'd seen that Risa wasn't too upset, her thoughts went back to worrying about whether she and Wade would make good partners in this impulsive decision. Neither of them had had a permanent home in twenty years. What if one or even both got the itch to travel or to do something else?

Live for the here and now, not tomorrow or yesterday, the voice in her head whispered ever so softly.

Wade looked up and flashed a smile at her. "Then the next step in this is to make a decision about the name of our new bar."

"We've all been gone for years," Jessica said, "and fate has brought us back home at pretty much the same time. What about Back Home?"

"I tell you," Oscar chuckled, "it wouldn't matter what you put on the sign, folks are going to call it the Old Church."

"Probably so, but naming it that is a little too much for me since I'm still mad at God right now," Wade said.

"Back Home Bar and Grill," Daisy said. "It has a nice ring."

"It sounds generic." Lily frowned.

"What if we leave the *Bar and Grill* off and just call it Back Home? Everyone in the southern part of the state is going to hear about it, and know that we serve food as well as liquor and provide a dance floor," Risa suggested.

"I like it, but I agree with Lily. It's a little generic," Haley said.

"Anyone got another suggestion?" Mary Nell asked.

"Well, the boys from the base could say they're going back home for the night," Oscar said with a wide grin that deepened the wrinkles around his blue eyes. "But I've got another name to throw in the pot. How about Danny's Place?"

Jessica's eyes shifted back toward Wade. He jerked his head around and locked eyes with hers, then shifted his gaze over to Oscar.

"Why would you suggest that?" Jessica asked.

"I know that Danny and Wade wanted to put in a bar together, and that Wade is using Danny's life-insurance money to go into business with you, so it seems like a good idea," Oscar said.

Jessica stole another look over toward Wade. The glassiness in his eyes told her that he was thinking of his brother.

"Thank you, Oscar, but let's think on it for a couple of days before we make a decision this important," Wade said. "The name sounds good to me, and it sounds like more than just a bar. Folks might come from miles around just to get good food."

"Not anything against Risa's food, but I wouldn't bet on that," Mary Nell said. "Folks can eat in dozens of places, but finding a bar around here is another story altogether."

"Just what are you going to cook?" Haley turned to focus on Risa.

"She's real good with roadkill like possum and raccoon," Lily said, but she couldn't keep a straight face as she fell out laughing. "I'm just teasing."

"She watched those cooking channels all the time when we were in Kentucky," Daisy piped up from her corner of the porch. "Daddy hated anything fancy, but she can do anything from Cajun to Tex-Mex and all in between."

"Paul was—is—a meat-and-potatoes man. Give him a venison roast or steak, fried potatoes, and gravy, and he was happy." Risa shrugged. "We can go over menus and all that later. Like Jessica said, everything we do needs to be joint decisions."

Warmth that had nothing to do with the hot breeze blowing through the pecan trees surrounding the porch wrapped itself around Jessica's shoulders. She had found where home was after two decades of traveling from one post to another, and she loved the feeling.

How could so much change so fast? Haley wondered as she laced her hands behind her head and stared at the ceiling. The security light her mother had installed years ago at the edge of the backyard filtered through the lace curtains and created an ever-changing pattern of shapes above her head.

She hadn't planned to come home until the end of summer and then only for a week or two, and then her mother—at least, the person she'd thought was her mother all her life—dropped dead with a heart attack. She'd talked with the lawyer about the will, had her mother cremated as was her wish, and someday when she was comfortable with the idea, Haley would take her ashes to the beach in Florida and scatter them. She had good memories of going there for vacations when she was a little girl.

When she'd tossed and turned for an hour, she finally got out of bed, poured herself a tall glass of milk, and padded barefoot to the screened-in porch just off the kitchen. She eased down in an old rocking chair that had been her mother's favorite, set her milk on the table beside her, and gazed out at the stars. Knowing that Risa and the twins were in the house with her made her feel less lonely and upset with the idea of her birth.

Thinking of the beach brought back memories of the times when she was a little girl, and her parents would take her out to Laguna Beach for a week. She remembered one time that her sister, Frannie, had joined them for a couple of days. Frannie had hugged her extra tight when she had left and had even wiped away a few tears.

"Were you trying to tell me that you were my biological mother? Was it difficult for you to keep the secret?" she whispered.

"Is someone with you, or are you talking to me?" Risa asked from the other end of the porch.

Haley jerked around, startled to hear someone else in the room. "I'm alone. I was thinking about my parents. Remembering a time when Frannie hugged me and cried when she had to leave. We were vacationing on the beach, and she had come down for a couple of days. Why didn't Mama tell me when I was grown, or at least before Frannie died so we could have the option of a relationship?"

"Most likely she didn't know how to after all the years had passed," Risa said from the other end of the porch. "I hope I didn't wake you when I came downstairs. That bottom step on the staircase squeaks."

"Always has," Haley said. "You couldn't sleep, either?"

Risa moved over closer to Haley and sat down on a settee. "I'm trying to process everything. The girls have been through so much lately. Do you think I should take them to a therapist?"

"They seem to be adjusting very well to me, but I think *you* could use some help," Haley said. "I'm a counselor, not a therapist, but I've got broad shoulders and listening ears if you want to talk. What happened between you and Paul? I thought y'all were the model couple, and I used to wish that I'd find a husband like him."

"I can bluff with the best of them." Risa's chuckle was brittle. "Mama always told me that I had to sleep in the bed I made, and if I married *that boy* and went to Kentucky with him, then I was on my own. The Paul I married was not the one I left, or maybe I should say *who left me*. I married a romantic, fun-loving man who picked a bouquet of wildflowers and tied them with a piece of twine so I would have a bouquet when we eloped. He turned into a man I hardly knew after the first three months of marriage. His mother had a double-wide trailer set up on the property for each of her six sons, and they all worked for the family business. She was the queen, and everyone bowed to her wishes."

Haley stood up and went to a small cabinet on the back wall, took out a bottle of Gentleman Jack, and poured two fingers in a red plastic cup. She handed it to Risa and then sat back down and held up her glass of milk. "To accepting change, no matter what."

Risa sipped the whiskey and nodded. "Thanks for this. I didn't know your mama ever drank. Aren't you going to have one with me?"

"Nope, my stomach is a little touchy. Nerves and stress, I'm sure, but I don't think I'd better have whiskey," Haley answered.

"Okay then, to accepting change, but we don't have a choice in the matter, for the most part," Risa said. "It can blow in like a tornado, or kind of slow—strolling along humming, in the case with Paul. But it will come, and it will affect a life no matter what."

"When we look back, we can see that we didn't have to do the things we did, but maybe at the time, it seemed to be the right choice, but we did have one. I didn't have to take that job in Alabama. I could have stayed in Texas, but at the time I wanted to be totally on my own, and as long as I was in Texas, I would depend too much on my parents. Now I wish I would have stayed here so I could have spent time with Mama."

"How are you really holding up after finding that letter?" Risa asked. "Evidently you're having as much trouble sleeping as I am."

"I've got questions that will probably never get answered." Haley took a sip of her milk. "Was I born because my mama and her boyfriend were careless, or was I the product of date rape or something like that? If that was the case, why didn't she just put me up for adoption?"

"Or terminate the pregnancy?" Risa said.

"Mama would have never let my sister do that." The icy-cold milk settled her nervous stomach—a condition that she'd been battling since her mother passed away so suddenly—but it did nothing to answer all the questions in her mind. "She wasn't super religious, but she couldn't have handled a termination. Maybe I'll find something in this house that helps me get through all this. Right now, I want you to know that having you and the girls here is a big plus. I feel like I've got family around me."

"Thank you. I sure don't want to be a burden, and if—" Risa started.

Haley held up a palm and shook her head. "Don't even think like that. We are more than friends, and you are helping me as much as I'm helping you. We're talking through problems, so basically, we're in a group therapy session. Speaking of that, why did the queen bee in Kentucky kick you out, anyway? If I'm prying, you don't have to answer that."

"Birth control pills." Risa shrugged. "It all boils down to birth control pills."

"What?" Haley's brow furrowed.

"Just what I said. According to Martha, any kind of birth control was taboo, and using it was right next to worshipping Satan. She believed wholeheartedly in the Quiverfull movement and quoted those verses in Psalms almost on a daily basis: *Children are a heritage from the Lord. Offspring are a reward from Him. Like arrows in the hands of a warrior are children born in one's youth.*"

"And you used birth control pills, right?"

Risa nodded again. "I got them right after the twins were born and managed to keep them secret for sixteen years. Martha was of the opinion that babies are blessings straight from God, and sons are put on pedestals. She told me that I must be sinning because God had closed up my womb like he did when women sinned in the Bible."

"Sweet Lord!" Haley gasped. "How did you survive as long as you did? Do any of the other daughters-in-law sneak around and use birth control?"

"I think some of them have figured out how to get around producing a baby a year by using the rhythm method, but it wasn't something anyone talked about, not even in the kitchen when we all gathered around to wash dishes after Sunday dinner. Several of them had ten or more children, so the weekly family dinner was a big affair."

"Paul didn't take up for you?" Haley could hardly believe that her friend had lived in that kind of situation. "That's like living in a commune."

"You got it!" Risa raised her glass in a toast. "There was the underlying fact that Paul's old girlfriend became a widow last year. She's the woman that Martha had picked out for him, so I wouldn't be surprised to see them get back together real soon."

"Why didn't he marry her back then?" Haley asked.

"They dated from the time they were in junior high school. After graduation, she broke up with him for one of his buddies. Paul joined the army without asking or telling anyone in his family. They almost disowned him over the whole thing, and then he married me—that was two strikes, since his mama didn't approve of him marrying a woman outside of their faith. Somewhere in Corinthians it talks about not being unequally yoked with unbelievers. I thought I'd been raised in a strict religion, but Martha's was even worse, and it wasn't until I had the twins that Martha accepted me into her church."

"Her church?" Haley asked.

"We all lived in a sort of community of our own, and Matthew, the oldest son, was the preacher. They had fixed up an old barn to serve as a church, and we were required to be there for services every Sunday morning and Wednesday night. I was just grateful that she hadn't built a school or made us all homeschool our kids," Risa answered.

"And Paul went along with all that?" Haley was stunned that a grown man wouldn't stand up for his wife and kids no matter what.

"He didn't want to get a third strike, so he buckled down and became the son that his mama wanted him to be." Risa finished off her whiskey. "It wasn't so bad, really. Matthew usually preached on the value of family and loving one another. He didn't talk about hellfire and damnation, and for the most part I tuned him out, just like I did when Mama made me go to her church all those years."

"Why did you take the pills when you knew they were taboo?" Haley said.

"I was pregnant by the time I figured out that my life wasn't mine, and Paul's wasn't his, either. We both belonged to the queen bee, a witch by the name of Martha Jackson. Before I even left the hospital after having the twins, they were already talking about me maybe having twin boys the next year. I didn't want to be pregnant again that quick, so I asked the doctor for a prescription." Risa's tone sounded flat and lifeless. "Martha and the six sisters-in-law had told me that God must love me because He double blessed me with twins. The only thing better would have been if they had been boys. The Jackson family puts a lot of stock in male heirs, just like the folks in the Old Testament did. She often talked about how that she had asked God for a quiver full of sons, and He had answered her by giving her seven."

"How did they find out about the pills?" Haley asked.

"I got careless and left my newest package in my purse," Risa answered. "At least I was lucky for sixteen years, or maybe, looking back, those were an unlucky sixteen years, because I lived with constant ridicule from Martha. According to her I needed to spend some time on my knees in repentance."

"Holy smoke!" Haley gasped. "How did Paul find the pills if they were in your purse?"

"He was digging around for my truck keys and found them. After he threw a fit, and a few dishes, he took the pills to his mother, and the rest is history. To be honest, since I had girls, and apparently was never going to be able to give him a son, he was more interested in how many deer heads and antlers he could hang on the walls than he was in being a husband or a father. He took the girls fishing a few times when he figured out that we weren't going to have more children, but even that didn't satisfy him. He wanted sons and lots of them, like his brothers all had."

Haley finished off her milk. "I'm sorry you had to live like that. You should have told me years ago about all this. I would have gotten a bigger apartment, and you could have come to stay with me."

Risa set her empty whiskey cup on a side table. "There were good times, but . . ."

"Most of those involved the girls, not the family, right?" Haley asked.

Risa nodded. "You'd think seventeen years would amount to something. I did what he wanted, catered to his mother and the family, but you can't imagine how mad he was when he found those pills. He accused me of cheating on him, of robbing him of sons, and of being a horrible wife. I was afraid he might finagle a way to take the girls away from me."

"Has he called to check on them or sent you child support?" Haley was genuinely worried about Risa and the girls now that she knew the whole story. With that kind of mother behind him, Paul might try to take the twins from her.

"All I got from him was a note saying that divorce papers were on the way. He said in the text that I can have whatever I brought into the marriage, and full custody of the girls. Since he doesn't actually own property, then there's nothing to fight about," Risa said.

"How do you feel? Empty? Relieved? Liberated?" Haley asked.

"All of the above," Risa answered, "plus angry, and now kind of sad since my own mother kicked me out. Then I'm worried that all this will have a snowball effect on the girls' self-esteem. They've always had to take a back seat to the boys in the Jackson family."

"We're kind of in the same boat," Haley said, "only my mother did that years ago in a sense. Maybe the reason I wanted to be a counselor and help kids is because I knew down deep in my heart that something wasn't right in my own family. But concerning your girls, I don't see signs of them being anything but happy, so you can wipe that worry off your list. It's okay to be angry and even sad. Embrace it. Own it. Let the girls feel whatever emotions they're going to as well. And then toss it all out with the trash."

"Good advice." Risa sighed. "Got any special tricks on how to do that?"

"Hard work," Haley answered. "You'll be cooking for the crew and then, when the bar opens, for the public. You'll be earning wages, making your own decisions, and living the way you want to."

"You were right." Risa covered a yawn with her hand. "Talking about all this has helped. I think I can sleep now."

Haley pushed up out of the rocking chair and hugged Risa. "Good friends make good listeners, and you've helped me as much as I've helped you."

"Anytime I can repay you for tonight, just let me know." Risa gave Haley an extra hug.

"You already did. I don't have to worry about selling this house or trying to move furniture." Haley paused by the door.

"Funny how twenty years changes things, isn't it? Hey, on a different note, do you think Jessica and Wade . . ." Risa wiggled her eyebrows.

"Nope." Haley yawned. "Remember when we thought she might have a crush on him in high school? She would never admit it. I believe that was their moment and it has passed, but it *is* strange how he showed up at the church parking lot at the same time we did that night."

"And how he's offered to put up half the money for renovations and paychecks." Risa started up the stairs. "Thanks again for taking us in."

"Hey, I feel better with y'all in the house, so this is a win-win situation," Haley said.

Risa stepped on the squeaky step and stopped. "We've got to fix this step."

"No, we do not." Haley giggled. "That step is going to tell you when Daisy and Lily come home past curfew. You don't want to fix that thing until they are grown and gone."

"Good advice." Risa's smile even reached her eyes that time.

Chapter Five

*J*essica awoke to the sound of a vehicle's engine right outside her new RV. Figuring it was a fisherman using the church parking lot to get to what was now just a pathway leading down to the fishing dock on the Lampasas River, she turned over and shut her eyes. The sun was just coming up and sending a thread of light through the window blinds right into her eyes. Since she couldn't get back to sleep, she crawled out of the narrow space in the overhang above the cab of the RV, bumping her head on the way.

"Dammit!" she swore as she rubbed her forehead and slung the door open to see the tail end of a trailer carrying heavy equipment parked between the church and the barn. "Well, *you* got up at the crack of dawn," she said and then heard the crunch of gravel signaling the approach of at least one more vehicle. Oscar waved as he passed in an old blue truck that looked pitiful, and yet the engine still purred like a baby kitten, and after that Risa's truck came to a stop in front of Jessica's RV.

Risa rolled down the window and said, "Good morning. The girls and I got up early and made a run up to Walmart for today's food supply. I need keys to the church so we can get inside and put on a pot of coffee."

"Bless your heart." Jessica grabbed the keys from the hook beside the door and made a mental note to have extra keys made for all her . . .

What were they? Friends? Family? Partners? She slipped her feet into a pair of flip-flops and headed out to the truck. "Turn on the AC when you get inside. No sense in us working in heat when we don't have to, and thanks. I'll be out there in a few. Risa, grab a piece of paper and write down your hours. You're on payroll when you go to the store, just like you are when you are at work."

"Thanks, but are you sure you can afford that even before the bar opens?" Risa asked.

"I told you that Uncle Elijah left his entire estate to me," Jessica said and Risa nodded. "There was a lot of money in addition to the church building. Mary Nell says she can take care of the business end of this, so she'll be doing payroll every Friday at the close of business. So yes, ma'am, I can afford to pay you. How about double what minimum wage is?"

"Holy cow!" Risa gasped.

"Hey, the bunch of us couldn't go out to eat three times a day for what we'll be paying you to cook for us. Just keep track of your hours and give them to Mary Nell on Friday evening," Jessica said. "I'll see y'all soon as I get into some work clothes."

"And run a brush through your hair?" Daisy giggled.

"That too." Jessica smiled and waved as Risa rolled up the window and drove across the lot to park in front of the church.

Jessica started back toward the RV, but heard another vehicle, so she waited. Mary Nell came to a stop, sending dust rolling up behind her. She rolled down the window and said, "You look like crap. We could sure use a rain to cool things down around here. I see that Risa beat me, so I guess she's going to open up the church."

Jessica leaned down to talk to Mary Nell through the open window. "You didn't have to get up so early."

"I'm used to getting up before the sun," Mary Nell said. "I had to make a living for Kevin. That meant working an early shift at the doughnut place, getting to my office job from nine to five, then hitting the bar on the strip for a four-hour shift after that. I've got my laptop in the back seat. Does it matter which Sunday school room I take over for my office?"

"Not one bit, and put yourself on payroll at whatever you made as an accountant in Nashville." Jessica didn't care if they used every bit of the money Elijah had left her getting things set up and ready for the bar to open.

"Thanks," Mary Nell said. "A job, a free place to live, three meals a day that I don't have to worry about cooking or getting yelled at if I don't make Kevin's favorite food. It don't get no better than this."

"I hope we're all as happy a year from now as we are right now today. You do know we're going to face a lot of . . ." Jessica searched for the right word.

"Bitchin'?" Mary Nell finished the sentence for her.

Jessica nodded. "What do you bet they ask us to keep our degenerate asses off the homecoming float for the cheerleaders?"

"Maybe we'll just make a float of our own." Mary Nell did a head wiggle. "We'll be a true local business."

The morning breeze blew Jessica's blonde hair across her face as she went back into the RV and gave the bed a dirty look. She'd thought the RV would be ideal when she bought it from her friends in Maine, but she hadn't figured in getting into and out of the loft bed. She got dressed in a pair of old jeans and a faded olive drab T-shirt, brushed her hair up into a ponytail, and took time to brush her teeth.

She was almost to the church when Wade fell in beside her. There were vibes again, sending sweet little sparks dancing all around them. Evidently, Wade didn't see or feel them, which was probably a good thing, since if he flirted, she might not be able to resist the temptation to flirt right back.

"This remind you of going to the mess hall?" he asked.

See there, the voice in her head said. *He's not feeling anything. Talking about the mess hall is about as romantic as talking about weaponry or bombs.*

"Little bit." She opened the door and the scent of coffee wafted out. "That does smell good, doesn't it? Did you get up for breakfast every morning when you were in the service?"

"Oh, yeah." Wade flashed a brilliant grin. "I believe what they say about breakfast being the most important meal of the day."

Jessica led the way through the foyer and across the sanctuary. "Do you make a hot breakfast every morning?"

"Nope, I just grab a bowl of cereal and add a banana to it if there's one layin' around," Wade admitted. "But that doesn't mean I won't be first in line every day that Risa cooks for us."

"Even after we don't get home until three o'clock in the morning when we open the bar?" Jessica asked.

Wade drew his eyebrows down into a frown. "Maybe when that happens, it'll be like working the midnight shift, and we'll have breakfast at noon every day."

"That's an idea." Jessica followed her nose straight to the coffeepot.

"What's an idea?" Risa cracked eggs into a bowl.

"That we have breakfast at noon when the bar opens," Wade answered. "We'll all be going home at three in the morning."

"Except us," Lily reminded them as she finished setting the table for eight.

"I'll pick you girls up for school," Mary Nell said, "and after I drop you off, I'll come to work in the office. Haley's place is right on the way from my house to here. You can have leftover biscuits for an after-school snack when your mama comes and gets you once school is done for the day."

"Y'all have got it all planned out, don't you?" Daisy set a bottle of orange juice and a gallon of milk on the round table she and Lily had set up close to the kitchen.

"Not yet, but we're working on it," Haley answered. "I vote that we close the bar on Sunday and Monday nights. That will be our weekend and time for all of us to play catch-up with our lives."

"That works for me." Risa nodded.

"And we can fill in for each other if one of us needs to do something else during the week, like Risa going somewhere with the girls on a school event." Jessica poured two mugs of coffee and handed one to Wade. "Risa might want to be at a ball game on Friday night if the girls make the cheerleader squad."

"That can be the night we just serve burgers," Mary Nell suggested. "I can manage that, but don't expect me to do fancy cooking."

"This remind you of anything?" Wade asked Jessica.

"Oh, yeah." She took a sip of her coffee.

"What?" Mary Nell asked.

"Teamwork," Jessica said. "I worked with a team, and I'm sure Wade did, too. We depended on each other, had each other's backs, and after a little while, we could almost finish each other's sentences."

"Do we get uniforms?" Lily's eyes twinkled.

"I hope to hell not!" Oscar came into the room and headed straight for the coffeepot. "I like working in overalls and oversized T-shirts."

Before he reached the section of counter where the coffeepot sat, Jessica poured another mug full and asked, "Cream and sugar?"

"Black as sin and strong as Hercules. That's the way I like my coffee," Oscar said. "Now, what's this about uniforms?"

Wade quickly explained what they'd been discussing. "I liked being able to depend on others, but I wouldn't want to have to wear a uniform every day again, either."

"Except for the boots?" Jessica asked.

"Hey, these are broken in and comfortable." Wade held up a foot.

"Can we all have boots like that?" Daisy asked.

"If you join the military after you finish high school," Jessica answered.

Risa whipped around and popped her hands on her hips. "I'm not so sure I want them to do that."

Oscar shot a look over toward Mary Nell. "Sometimes we don't get what we want."

"Amen to that," Jessica agreed.

"Don't look at me." Mary Nell threw up both her palms in a defensive gesture. "You know I didn't get what I wanted, and neither did Risa or Haley. How about you, Jessica? Have you gotten what you wanted out of life?"

Jessica thought about the question before she answered. "Depends on what time of my life we're talking about, but for right now, I'm very content with this team."

"I was thinking about the business supplying T-shirts with our logo on the back with a catchy phrase for all of us to wear this fall when we are working at the bar," Jessica said.

"I love it," Lily said. "Daisy and I'll put our heads together and come up with a slogan idea."

"Remember it's got to go on a shirt, so keep it short," Jessica said.

"Beer, Burgers, and . . . ," Risa started, then stopped.

"Back Home Moonshine," Oscar finished for her.

"That sounds more like the hills of Kentucky." Risa laughed.

"Write your ideas down, and we'll talk about them before we have the shirts made," Jessica suggested.

By evening, Jessica had filled two pages with quips and ideas for the bar's name, but she was too dog-tired to even look at them as she crawled up into her loft bed. She had helped move and stack pews against the far wall of the sanctuary all day so that Wade and Oscar could measure for the bar. They had a plumber in mind who could come and do whatever was needed to bring water up through the floor and a local electrician who could wire the area for what they'd need to put in the machinery for draft beer and a small hot-water tank to run the dishwasher.

"Making the decision to turn the building into a bar was easy," she muttered. "Making it all work—not so much."

She closed her eyes and dozed to the humming noise of the air conditioner on top of her RV. Then suddenly everything in the RV went so quiet that her eyes popped wide open. She tried to figure out why she could hear tree frogs and crickets, then groaned when she realized that she was sweating and sticking to the sheets. The couple she'd bought the RV from had said the air conditioner had been repaired and would probably last another year or two. They had seldom used it in Maine because they almost never needed it.

"But this is Texas," she groaned, "and this thing is just a glorified tin can."

She sat up and bumped her head for the second time that day, cussed loud enough that all her superior officers would have been proud of her, and finally got out of the bed to open the windows. The first one she tried was stuck, which brought on another round of cussing, and then when she had it open and turned around, the damn thing fell back down. She found a wooden spoon in a drawer, propped the window up, and as luck would have it, the only breeze that flowed through it felt like it had come from an oven. That's when she remembered the evangelist room in the church. The bed was still there. Granted, it didn't have sheets on the mattress, but the church was cool.

"I've got sheets." She opened a drawer and pulled out what she needed to remake the bed, tugged the comforter from the loft bed, slipped on her flip-flops, and headed back out across the parking lot. She was still muttering about the heat when she realized that someone was sitting at the end of the porch in the shadows. The shadow of a full-grown man startled her, but she wasn't running away from her own building. Whoever was over there in the dark could gather himself up and get off her property.

"Who are you, and what do you want?" she asked in a testy tone.

"It's me, Wade, and I was thinking about going inside for a midnight snack, but the door is locked." Wade got to his feet. "Are you having trouble sleeping, too?"

"I wasn't until the AC went out in my RV, and it got hot as hell in there pretty fast. I opened a window, but evidently tonight you can't beg, borrow, or buy a breeze. I'm taking over the evangelist room in the church. It's bigger than my RV, and it's cool."

"Sounds like a smart plan to me," Wade said. "Is it okay if I have another bowlful of Risa's peach cobbler for a night snack?"

"Of course—you can have whatever you want. We're in this together, and I might have one with you when I get my bed made." Jessica held up a key with her free hand. "That and a glass of milk might help me sleep. I'll get keys made for all of you soon as we go to the lawyer's office. That way you can get in and out anytime you want."

Wade crossed the porch, opened the door for her, and followed her inside. "It's been a good day, but my mind won't stop running in circles. I keep going over and over my notes on the bar, trying to be sure that I've got it all laid out to be the most efficient. This will be the biggest undertaking of the whole remodeling job. I want to get it right."

She flipped on the lights in the fellowship hall and tossed the sheets on one of the long tables that Risa and the girls used for a prep table. The bed making could wait until later. Since Wade mentioned peach cobbler, her stomach had begun to growl. She opened the refrigerator and looked over at him. "Milk or beer?"

"Milk with cobbler," he answered. "I'll get the bowls and glasses from the cabinet."

"If you ever get tired of your trailer, you are welcome to claim a Sunday school room," she said as she poured two glasses of milk.

"Thanks for the offer, but I like my little home on wheels." He opened three drawers before he found the one with cutlery. "I'm kind of having second thoughts about where to put the bar."

"Why? Seems like the original place we talked about is a good place." Jessica dipped cobbler into two bowls.

Wade stuck a spoon in each one and carried them to the table. "What if we put it where the pulpit is instead of on the wall? It's already built up about six inches, so that would give us a little better vantage point to keep an eye on everything. It runs across the whole front of the church except for that little section where the piano used to sit, so it would be about the same length."

Jessica didn't really want to talk about where Wade and Oscar built the bar. That part didn't matter a bit to her. She wanted to talk about more personal things, and yet she wasn't really sure how to change the subject. She wanted to know how Danny had died, and why Wade was mad at God for his brother's death, and if he was ever going to get over the anger. She wanted to tell him that she had found a measure of peace at the idea of putting down roots in Riverbend in spite of the conflict they were facing over the bar.

"I'm going to leave that part of the business to you and Oscar," she said, "but remember where the kitchen is. I suppose we could keep the door where it is for a waitress to pop in and out if folks just wanted to come in and eat."

"Thanks, Jessica, for having that kind of trust in me," Wade said with a grin and then dug into the cobbler.

"Hey, you and Oscar are the carpenters"—she shrugged—"and after tomorrow we'll all have keys. We should be able to get them at any hardware store while we are in Killeen to talk to the lawyer about all this."

"That will be great," Wade said.

A long, pregnant silence settled over the kitchen. Jessica had never been without words in her whole life, but then she'd never been so attracted to a guy in her life, either—whether she wanted to admit it or not. Her mind stalled out when she tried to latch on to something to say, and the silence got even heavier.

"You said you buried your folks here in Riverbend, right?" she asked, then wanted to take the words back. That might be entirely too personal. "I'm sorry. I shouldn't have pried."

"Nothing is personal between partners, and besides, have you forgotten where you are? Riverbend might be small, but it should probably be in the *Guinness Book of World Records* for citizens that know everything about everyone—including when they did it and what the results were. But to answer your question, yes, my parents are buried here in Riverbend. Danny is right beside them," Wade answered. "I know Elijah didn't want a service of any kind, which thoroughly aggravated Stella Sullivan. What about your folks?"

"Uncle Elijah was cremated, and his ashes were dumped in the Lampasas River at the spot where he liked to fish. My folks were also cremated, and I mingled their ashes together. I've got them out in the RV in a coffee can, but I can't make up my mind where to spread them, or if I want to bury them so I have a place to go to visit them." She took another bite of her cobbler.

"That's something you'll have to decide, but for myself, I like having a place to visit. There's something peaceful about being able to just . . ." His voice cracked, and he took a couple of sips of milk.

"Just to be able to talk to them, even if they can't really hear you?" she asked.

"That's right," he said with half a smile. "Sometimes they answer, but it's not in the way you think." He went on to tell her about his visit with Danny. "When those trees rustled above my head, I felt like he agreed with me."

"Uncle Elijah popped into my head and gave me a thumbs-up when I got serious about making this building into a bar, like he used to do when I was a kid and he agreed with me," she admitted.

"Seems like a pretty good omen when we have both of their blessings." Wade reached across the table and laid a hand on Jessica's. "I believe with all my heart that this is going to work for us, Jessica. I've got Danny's insurance money to keep us afloat until we're showing a profit, and that shouldn't be long, since the only overhead we'll have is utility bills and the stocking of liquor and food."

"I've got Uncle Elijah's money as well as what my folks left me, so I'm really not worried about that, either. We can each put an equal amount into the working account that Mary Nell will set up for us," she said and hoped her voice wasn't as high and squeaky as it sounded in her ears. Evidently Wade didn't feel the sparks dancing around them when he touched her hand, or he wouldn't be talking about money.

Never work. Her father was in her head now. *You can't date a partner. If you break up, there's bad feelings that will bleed over into your business.*

I know that, she thought with a little sigh, *and besides, I've got to help my friends get through all their problems. I don't have time to fall in love with Wade Granger.*

Chapter Six

The room that Mary Nell chose for an office had originally been the pastor's office. A desk sat at an angle so she could see out the window into the parking lot. Empty bookcases that might have once held extra Bibles or maybe volumes of sermons lined the back wall, and two burgundy wingback chairs had been placed in front of the desk. She had dusted, swept, and even cleaned the window. Now sunlight flowed into the room and warmed her face. She'd set up spreadsheets for payroll, for expenses, and for debits that morning, and liked the room better than the tiny cubicle she had at her job in Nashville. Later, she would put some pictures on the bookcases, and maybe add a couple of green plants over by the window.

She couldn't imagine Jessica's uncle, Elijah Callaway, sitting in the office chair any more than she could imagine him standing behind the lectern. Elijah had spent a lot of time out around the barn where her dad made his moonshine and beer, so she'd seen him almost every year when she came home for a visit. Visualizing the old guy on a barstool with a beer in his hand was a whole lot easier than picturing him with a Bible.

Oscar rapped on the door and poked his head inside. "Does this mean you're staying in Texas and not going back to Tennessee?"

Mary Nell motioned him inside. "I didn't leave anything in Nashville that I need to go back for."

"Not even your job and the friends you made?" Oscar asked.

"I've got friends here, an office of my own," she said with a smile. She pointed toward the window. "And a view. It might just be of the parking lot, but it beats a cubicle with a fluorescent bulb on the ceiling."

"And you've got me," Oscar said.

"That's right." Mary Nell's smile got even bigger. "I've got you, Daddy, to always tell me that you told me so. I wonder where I'd be today if I had listened to you all those years ago."

"We can't go back and undo what we've done, sugar," Oscar said, "but we can learn from it and go forward with determination not to make the same mistake twice."

"Amen!" Mary Nell got up and walked around the desk to give her father a hug. "I love you."

"Love you, too, sweetheart. Always have. Always will. It's good to have you home, and to hear you say that you're here to stay. I want you to find a good man like Wade. One that will worship the ground you walk on," Oscar told her. "And then I want you to have a whole yard full of grandbabies for me to spoil."

"Wade is a friend." Mary Nell caught a movement out of her peripheral vision and turned to look at a bright red cardinal on the other side of the window. "And I need to find myself before I get into another relationship."

"You'll be letting a good man slip right through your fingers, and let me tell you . . . ," Oscar started.

Mary Nell didn't like the "let me tell you" speech any more than she did the "I told you so" statements, but her father was usually right, so she turned back to focus on him rather than the pretty cardinal. Hopefully, the cold glare she shot toward him would shut him up.

It didn't.

He went right on. "Your mother and I were good friends before we fell in love. That makes the best kind of relationships, the kind that stands up through the tough times," Oscar finished. "And on that note, I'm going to leave you to your work. If you get finished, we can use all hands on deck to help stack wood after Wade and I take the pews apart."

"I'm almost done here. I just have to back up my work," Mary Nell said with a smile. "And, Daddy, thanks for loving me."

"Always." Oscar smiled back at her and then disappeared out into the hallway.

She recognized the tune he whistled as being the one that she and her mother had heard every evening when he came home from work.

"That's the kind of man I want, not one who comes in whining about how he's the best country singer in Nashville and no one will give him a break," she muttered as she went back to work.

Jessica sat on the raised platform at the front of the church and waited for the two guys to finish taking apart a few more pews. She'd only been there a minute when the twins came out of the kitchen and plopped down on either side of her. The morning had been a whirlwind of signing papers, both at the lawyer's office and the bank. Wade had been right there beside her the whole time, sometimes close enough that she could catch a whiff of his shaving lotion—something woodsy with a hint of vanilla—that sent her senses reeling. Now, she was watching the muscles in his upper arms stretch the fabric of his T-shirt as he and Oscar tore apart the oak pews. When they finished with two, she and Haley carried the lumber from the backs and seats over to an empty Sunday school room where they were storing the wood until Oscar and Wade were ready to start building the bar.

"Jessica!" Lily touched her on the shoulder.

With a jerk, Jessica focused back on anything but those upper arms. "I'm sorry. Did you say something?"

"No, but there's a spider on your other shoulder, and I'm afraid of them," Lily said.

Wade came by, brushed the spider away, and stomped on it with his boot. "It was just a little one, nothing like we had in the sandbox."

"He's your knight in shining T-shirt," Daisy said with a giggle.

"I'm not afraid of spiders," Jessica said. "Maybe he's not my knight, but yours?"

Daisy shook her head. "He's way too old for me. He's as old as my daddy. You'll have to take him, since he saved you from getting a spider bite."

"Ouch!" Wade threw a hand over his heart. "That hurt."

"What?" Jessica asked. "That you're old or that someone *has* to take you?"

"A little of both," Wade said as he headed toward the kitchen. "I'm going for a bottle of cold water. Anyone else want one? You better speak up now while I'm still strong enough to carry more than one. I can feel the feebleness sneaking up on me."

"Yeah, right!" Daisy giggled. "And yes, on the water."

"Don't worry," Lily piped up. "You can still outrun it for a little while yet. I'll take a water, too."

Wade raised an eyebrow at Jessica. "Water, tea, beer?"

"Whoa!" Lily put up a palm. "I didn't know beer was a choice here."

"Water." Jessica smiled and turned to Lily. "And you two don't have a choice."

"I was just joking with you," Lily said. "I don't even like beer."

"I'm the beer girl," Daisy chimed in. "She likes whiskey."

"Water for both of them," Jessica said with a slight giggle. "They're just trying to get a rise out of us."

"Truth." Daisy crossed her heart. "One of our cousins, a daughter of Uncle Matthew's, who was our preacher, invited us for a sleepover a few months ago. She had stolen a can of beer from one of our other uncles and one of those little bottles of whiskey. We all tasted them."

"It was for spiritual reasons," Lily declared with an impish grin, "so that we would know what it tasted like so we would know the enemy of our souls."

"Teenagers!" Wade headed on into the fellowship hall to get the water.

"Does your mama know that you tasted liquor?" Jessica asked.

"We tell Mama everything, but Granny Martha didn't know. She would have kicked us out of Kentucky before she did if she found out. Boys could drink beer and have a shot now and then, but girls couldn't," Lily said. "Granny Martha ran the town where we lived, and nobody, not even God, crossed her."

"Granny Stella didn't know, either, or she wouldn't have let us move in with her," Daisy added.

How on earth did these girls get to be so well adjusted? Jessica wondered.

Wade returned with bottles of water and passed them around, then went on over to the other side of the sanctuary, where Oscar stopped working long enough to take a bottle from him.

Lily took a long drink and then twisted the lid back on the bottle. "I'm going to help Mama finish up with supper."

"I'll go set the table." Daisy stood up and dusted the seat of her cutoff denim shorts. "We love our mama, Jessica. Granny Martha tried to turn us against her when she found out about the pills, but we're glad we don't have a bunch of brothers and sisters."

"Yeah," Lily agreed, nodding several times. "Our cousins are always bitchin' about the boys and girls having different standards. Boys do one thing and get away with more in the Jackson family. They say, 'Boys will be boys.'"

"But girls are supposed to be angels who want to be married and have babies. They aren't supposed to have dreams of careers unless Granny Martha wants them to help her out with bookkeeping or in the lumberyard itself, and then it wasn't for pay," Daisy said.

"That sounds kind of old-fashioned and sexist," Jessica said.

"Exactly!" Daisy crossed the room and disappeared into the kitchen with Lily right behind her. "But Granny Martha didn't see it that way."

Jessica hadn't realized until that moment what a gift her parents had given her when she had come home from school in the spring of her senior year and announced that she wanted to go into the military. They had both told her that they would support her if that was what she really wanted, but if she changed her mind, there was money for her to go to college.

"That was probably part of what my inheritance was." She picked up the ends of one of the pews and carried them back to the room they were using for storage.

"Hey," Mary Nell called out when she passed by the office door. "Got a minute?"

"Be there soon as I put this where it belongs." Jessica kept walking, left the end of the pew in the room with half a dozen others, and went back to talk to Mary Nell.

"Close the door," Mary Nell said.

"Oh. My. Goodness. This must be serious," Jessica said. "Something wrong with the accounts? Should we have put more money in to cover payroll and the overhead for the next six months?"

"Have a seat, and this has nothing to do with the business. We're starting out on a fine foundation where that is concerned," Mary Nell answered. "I'm done with that for now and was about to come out into the bar and help y'all, but we need to talk first."

The hair on Jessica's arms prickled, and that meant something was wrong. "Then what's going on that I needed to shut the door?"

"Daddy is trying to fix me up with Wade, and I'm not ready for any kind of a relationship. It's too soon after everything went south with Kevin. I need a year or maybe two to find myself. I feel like it's been . . ."

Haley rapped once on the door and then stuck her head inside. "Am I interrupting anything?"

"No, come on in and shut the door." Mary Nell motioned her into the room. "You're a counselor, so maybe you can help me, but we shouldn't leave Risa out." She picked up her cell phone from the desk and made a call.

"Did someone die?" Risa asked as she came into the room and closed the door behind her. "What are we having a meeting for?"

Jessica pointed at Mary Nell. "She's the one that's got a problem, not me."

Liar, the voice in her head scolded. *You don't want her to be interested in Wade, so you've got a problem, too.*

She opened her mouth to argue, but then clamped it shut.

Risa pulled up a folding chair from across the room, popped it open, and eased down into it. "Spit it out. Are you fixin' to tell us that Kevin called and you're going to give him another chance?"

"God no!" Mary Nell's voice went as high and squeaky as a mouse caught in a trap. "In some ways it's even worse than that. Daddy wants to fix me up with Wade, and like I just told Jessica, I need some time to figure out who I am. I've got a feeling Daddy won't give up on the idea. What do I do?"

"You're a grown woman," Haley told her. "Stand up for yourself and tell Oscar that you are just out of a disastrous relationship, and you sure don't want to jump into another one."

"I did, but once Daddy gets something in his head . . ." Mary Nell sighed.

"Tell him that I've got a crush on Wade, and you would never want to do something to ruin our friendship." Jessica could almost feel the wind from all three of her friends when they whipped around to focus on her.

"Do you?" Risa asked.

"I did in high school, so it's not a total lie," Jessica admitted.

Haley narrowed her eyes into slits. "We kind of knew even though you didn't say anything."

"That's right," Mary Nell said. "We would have probably told you that was crazy. Wade was a nerd, and you were a cheerleader. Y'all were way too different to have ever been a couple."

"Guess we all had a few secrets," Risa said with a slight shrug. "I had a crush on Danny for two years, but I knew Mama would throw a hissy if I even mentioned his name. I was supposed to date boys from her church, preferably one who was going to be a preacher, and Danny was one of those bad boys who drove too fast and drank beer on Saturday nights."

"And went to the church parking lot," Mary Nell added.

"At least until Sparky, who was the town night cop in those days, shooed us away," Haley said with a giggle. "Little did he know that we just came back as soon as he went to the diner for pie and doughnuts."

"Then he retired and put in a gas station about the time we graduated," Jessica said. "I wonder who took his place."

"We'll have to ask Daddy about that," Mary Nell answered.

"Thank God Mama didn't know that's where we all went, too," Risa said with a giggle and then turned to face Jessica. "We can't tell Oscar that you like Wade. He'd see through that in the blink of an eye."

Haley cocked her head to one side and squinted her eyes. "You do like him, don't you? I can see it in the way you're all flushed. It's understandable. You've both lost your folks and been in the service. Even beyond that, this bar is already throwing you together every day, and will be doing even more so when we open the doors. But be careful. You might ruin a perfectly good partnership if things didn't work out."

"I like him as a friend and a partner." That was as much as Jessica intended to admit—even to her best friends. "But I'm willing to let Oscar think there's more if it will help Mary Nell out."

"We'd probably be better off, to be honest." Mary Nell sighed. "But thanks for the offer to pretend to like him, or like him for real, whichever the case might be."

"You are welcome," Jessica said with a slight nod.

"Let's talk about all those secrets we've been keeping through the past twenty years. I was silly enough to think that we knew everything about each other," Haley said with a wide grin that lit up her brown eyes.

Risa stood up and headed for the door. "I'm going to the kitchen. I'm not discussing any more secrets today."

Mary Nell pushed her chair back and stood up. "And I'm all done with bookwork for right now, so I'm going out to the sanctuary—or should I call it the bar?—to help Daddy and Wade tear down pews."

"You know that I'll drag every single one of your secrets out of you before the end of summer, don't you?" Haley asked.

"Maybe so," Jessica said as she stood and raised her arms to stretch the kinks out of her back. "But not right now. And beware! While you're unpacking our baggage, we'll be doing the same for you. Do you have a crush on Wade?"

"Never did. Never will. He's not my type," Haley answered. "I like . . ." She stopped and shook a finger at Jessica. "Are you sure you weren't a chaplain or a counselor in the military?"

"Positive," Jessica threw over her shoulder as she left the room. "I'd tell you my exact job description, but then I'd have to . . ." She stopped at the door. "You know the rest. What I did was so classified that it went from my building over to headquarters in a locked briefcase."

"Was it handcuffed to the courier's wrist? That sounds so James Bond–ish." Haley followed her out of the room.

"Sometimes, but not always," Jessica said.

"So, you were an analyst?" Haley asked.

"Something like that"—Jessica lowered her voice to a whisper—"but just between me and you, I like the idea of being a bartender a lot better than what I was doing."

What Jessica did wasn't necessarily classified anymore, but she didn't like talking about her job in the military, and she sure didn't talk about the nightmares that she still had concerning some of the decisions she and her team had to make.

Back in the bar, Haley popped her hands on her hips and said, "Carrying these one at a time is ridiculous. I'm going to go out to the barn and bring in that thing that guys lay on to roll up under a vehicle. I saw it out there when we were snooping around. I bet we can stack at least four on it, maybe more."

Jessica popped a palm on her forehead and groaned. "Why didn't one of us think of that before now?"

"Hey, everyone, I'm going to make a trip to the grocery store in town for some sugar," Risa called out. "Anyone want me to pick up anything while I'm out?"

"I need to go to the lumberyard for drill bits and a box of screws, and I noticed we're getting low on bottled water. I can pick up the sugar for you," Oscar said.

"I'll go with you," Jessica said. "I've got to pick up a prescription at the drugstore."

"Okay, then." Risa waved. "Supper is in the oven, so the girls and I can help out here until y'all get back with the sugar for the sweet tea."

Jessica grabbed her purse from the bedroom, made sure she was at least semi-presentable to go out in public, and walked out into the summer heat with Oscar right beside her. "I guess we're going in your truck unless you want to wait for me to unhook everything on the RV."

"Nope, I surely do not." Oscar opened the door to his vehicle for her. "I'm glad we'll have a few minutes alone, though. I've got a couple of things I need to talk to you about."

"Oh, yeah, what's that?" Jessica felt a twinge of concern about his comment. What if he wanted to enlist her help in getting Mary Nell and Wade together?

He slammed the door shut, and took his own good time walking around the truck and sliding in under the wheel. "I'm worried about Mary Nell," he said as he started the engine and drove out of the parking lot. "She was in college and planning to be a CPA when she met Kevin. He sweet-talked her into believing that he was the next big thing in country music, and she quit school. You know all this already, but I'm worried that some other smooth-talking man will come along, and it'll be the same thing all over again."

"She told me that she needs some time to find herself," Jessica said. "She won't make the same mistake twice."

"I hope not." Oscar sighed. "I'm getting old, but I'd hate for my grandkids to ever have to visit me in prison, and if another man treats her ugly, that could be where I spend my last days."

Jessica laid a hand on his shoulder. "We'll help her stay on the right track. Matter of fact, with all the problems we've all come back to Riverbend with, we'll be helping each other through this tough time."

"Thanks." Oscar turned off the dirt road onto the paved highway and pointed the truck toward town. "That makes me feel better. Maybe if you four girls would have stayed together right out of high school, you wouldn't have had all these troubles." He looked puzzled. "I can see that Risa and Mary Nell have men problems, and Haley has got grief from her mama's passing to get past, but what have you brought home, anyway?"

She removed her hand and pasted on a fake smile. "Mine are job related, maybe with a little PTSD tossed into the mix."

"If you ever need to talk, I'm a good listener." Oscar turned into the parking lot at the lumberyard, sending up a cloud of gray dust behind his truck. "If you need to cry, I don't do well with weeping women, but Wade has big shoulders."

"Oscar Wilson, are you trying to find a girlfriend for Wade?" Jessica asked.

Oscar shrugged. "He's lonely and needs someone in his life. You girls have each other now, and you kind of took him in. But he ain't getting no younger, and if he ever wants to have a family, he needs to get started."

Jessica could hardly wait to get back home and tell the girls that Oscar was trying to fix Wade up with *any* woman, not just his daughter. Mary Nell didn't have so much to worry about. But then she realized that she'd called the bar *home*, and a smile tickled the corners of her mouth. She had mulled over where she would land when she left the base in Maine, and now she had found a home right there in the same little town she'd left two decades ago.

"He'll find someone when the time is right," Jessica assured Oscar.

"It can't be you," Oscar said. "That could ruin a partnership in a split second. Maybe we should steer him toward Haley?"

Jessica wasn't shoving Wade toward anyone, not until she figured out what all those sparks were that his touch generated. Besides, Wade was probably not finished grieving for his brother. He was driving Danny's truck, and she'd noticed that Danny's dog tags—two sets of them—were hanging from the rearview mirror.

"Let's just get through the summer, and maybe by then, everything will work out the way it's supposed to," Jessica suggested as she got out of the truck.

"I'm not a patient man." Oscar removed his cap and then repositioned it on his head. "But you're probably right." He held the door to the lumberyard open for her.

A cool blast of air hit her when she walked out of the Texas heat into the building. Her eyes took a moment to adjust, but when they did, she was staring right into Stella Sullivan's angry eyes. The woman's hand shot up, and for just a split second, Jessica thought she had a pistol. Jessica blinked a couple of times and figured out that it was her forefinger pointing straight at her. Stella's expression looked like she was shooting fire at her and left no doubt that she was upset beyond words.

"Mrs. Sullivan!" Jessica pasted on her best fake smile and tried to be cheerful. "How are you today? A bit hot out there, isn't it?"

"You are an abomination unto our Lord and Savior." Stella was practically humming with anger. "I wish you would have never come back to Riverbend. I wouldn't have even cared if you'd gotten killed like Danny Granger did." The finger began to shake so fast that it became a blur. "If you think you're going to be asked to ride on the cheerleader float, you are dead wrong. I'm on that committee, and I'll see to it that neither you or any one of your friends, including my daughter, ever ride on a homecoming float again."

A smart remark about how Risa would rather have a job in a bar than ride in a parade was right on the end of Jessica's tongue. Yet before she could open her mouth to say a word, Oscar was right there beside her. His eyes narrowed until they were little more than slits, and he set his jaw tightly for a moment before he spoke.

"Who gives a rat's rump about riding on any stupid float?" Oscar said through clenched teeth. "It's a good thing these girls are doing. They're supporting each other and trying to make a business out of a building that in a few years would go to rot, which is more than you can say you did for Risa and your granddaughters. You should be ashamed for treating your own kin like you have, Stella Sullivan."

"You *would* agree with them"—Stella raised her voice until she was almost yelling—"since you spend time out there in your barn making moonshine and wine. I'm telling you the town is going to shun all of you."

Jessica had known drill sergeants who scared her less than Stella did. The woman looked like she was ready, willing, and able to slice Oscar's throat with nothing but words. Then she whipped around to say something more to Jessica, but before she could, Oscar slipped right in between them.

Oscar's nose was just inches from Stella's. "Jesus made wine from water at that wedding in the Bible, didn't he?"

Stella popped her hands on her hips. "Don't you throw that up to me. Of course he *drank* wine, but he didn't sit out and brew it in his backyard."

Oscar's face relaxed and he chuckled. "Just think of it this way. We're doing all the church folks a great service. Folks will need a place to go on Sunday morning to repent for the sins they commit at the bar on Saturday night."

Stella's face turned scarlet. "I'm going to get a petition going to shut down that bar before you even get it ready to open. I'll take it to the city council and—"

"You can scream and yell, but my lawyer says nothing is standing in the way of turning the old church into a grill and bar, plus what can the city council do?" Jessica had been taught to respect her elders, but standing up to Stella after the way she'd treated Risa felt right—and good. "My church isn't even in the city limits, and it is zoned commercial. Maybe Uncle Elijah did that so that he could turn it into something else, like a bar, later. But I do know that all the screaming and yelling you do will not change a blessed thing, Stella, so save your breath."

"We will stand in the middle of the parking lot and sing hymns in a peaceful protest on Tuesday night," Stella threatened. "I'm going to tell everyone to come, and we'll have a petition for them to sign. We'll just see who has power in Riverbend."

"If you get hungry, send someone into the bar for a burger. Maybe we will run a special on a hamburger, chips, and a cold drink that night." Oscar chuckled. "Risa is a mighty fine cook, and I'm sure all that singing might make people hungry."

Stella finally dropped her finger and glared at Oscar and Jessica. "I wouldn't put a foot in that place."

"It's nothing but a white frame building." Jessica was surprised that her voice sounded so calm.

"It's a church, a place to worship God," Stella shot back at her.

Jessica tried one more time to reason with her. "It has not been a church in ten years."

"And God don't want it to be a church anymore. He sent straight-line winds to knock the steeple off the roof." Oscar chuckled.

"God didn't do that," Stella argued.

"I believe He did. He makes the wind blow, according to the scripture, and He sends all kinds of signs. Evidently, He doesn't want that old place to be a church, and never did, or else it would have taken off when Elijah built it," Oscar argued. "You can believe what you want, but me and Jessica have some shopping to do." He tipped his hat toward her. "You have a nice day now." He turned to walk away, and Jessica followed him.

"God will rain fire and brimstone down upon that church if you continue with this horrid idea," Stella shouted at them.

"Let her have the last word," Jessica whispered.

"That's a hard thing to do when she's bad-mouthing you girls," Oscar growled.

"I know, but you can't fix stupid," Jessica told him.

He chuckled. "Guess that's one way to look at it, but some duct tape over her mouth would surely stop it for a little while, and I would so enjoy slapping a strip across her lips."

"Nope." Jessica found boxes of screws and nails and turned to Oscar. "It would just make her explode, and then someone would have to clean up the mess on aisle one."

"I'd offer to do the job for free"—Oscar was back to growling—"but you're right. Let's get what we need and go home."

There was that word, *home*, again. It didn't matter how many hymns Stella and her cohorts sang in the church parking lot, there was no way they could take that away from Jessica.

Chapter Seven

*J*essica turned her back to the shower spray and let the pulsating water massage the aching muscles in her back. In the past two days, the team had torn down half the pews, stacked the backs and seats over to one side of the bar, and taken the ends to the storage room. Wade had drawn up plans for the bar, but they hadn't voted on whether to put it against the wall shared with the kitchen or on the end that had been the pulpit.

Another thing that they had to think about was the baptism tub behind the pulpit. Curtains covered the oversize bathtub, but something would have to be done about that. An idea to fill it with whiskey or vodka popped into her head, but that might really cause lightning to come down through the rafters and strike her graveyard dead.

She turned off the faucet, stepped out of the shower, and wrapped a towel around her wet hair and another one around her body. Then she padded into her bedroom and continued to think about the baptismal. The thing was simply a nice deep bathtub with stairs leading down into it. When it was filled, it would come up to a grown person's waist, and maybe to a teenager's chest. Once she'd finished drying her body, she dressed in a pair of sleep shorts and an oversize T-shirt. She picked up a mystery book she'd been reading about a small town where young, newly married women were being killed. She propped two pillows against the headboard and settled in to finish the story.

"Another reason not to get married if you live in a small town," she whispered as she turned to the page where her bookmark had been placed. She read through five pages and then laid the book aside when she realized she was looking at the words but not remembering a single detail.

The leftover lemon pound cake in the kitchen seemed to be calling her name, so she slung her legs over the side of the bed, stood up, and headed down the dark hallway to the sanctuary/bar. Someday the doorway would be closed, and one made from right outside her bedroom into the kitchen. That would be a lot handier for Risa since they had decided to use one of the Sunday school rooms for a pantry. She'd already asked Wade and Oscar to build lots of shelves in the room to hold big quantities of staple food.

"Hey," Wade said from the pulpit, where he was sitting in the dark.

Jessica flipped on the lights and sat down beside him. "You having trouble sleeping, too?"

"Yep," he answered. "I sure am."

"What's on your mind?" Jessica thought he was trying to figure out something about the placement of the bar.

"I've got this favor to ask, and it's so personal that I don't know how to begin," he said.

"Just spit it out," she said.

"Sparky had lived in the back of his store at one time, but when I rented the building from him, the room was filled with old tires and batteries. It did have a tiny bathroom with a shower." Wade stared off into space as he talked.

"You are welcome to use my shower anytime you want," Jessica said. "Is that what you're trying to ask me?"

"Yep," Wade said with a nod. "I've been washing up in the men's bathroom off the foyer, but after two days of sweating, I would love a shower."

"Then go on back there and take one. There should be plenty of hot water left even though I stood under the water for an extra ten minutes," Jessica told him. "Towels are on the ladder-back chair beside the shower."

"Thank you, but I can go get my own towel," he said as he stood up.

"That's not necessary," Jessica said. "We've got the washer and dryer in the kitchen, so just toss the towels in the basket out there. We'll be doing laundry nearly every day, so it's no problem. Feel free to do your washing here at the bar rather than going into town."

"Thanks," Wade said with another nod. "I hated to ask, but . . ."

"Hey," Jessica butted in, "we're partners in this business and friends, I hope, so don't ever feel like that." She couldn't control her thoughts, though, and they went to the fact that Wade would be using her shower and brushing his teeth at her vanity. But what was even more disturbing was the visual she got of the two of them *sharing* that shower.

"Thanks for that, too," he said. "I'll go out to the trailer and get clean clothes and my shaving kit."

"I'll be in the kitchen when you get done," she told him. "That leftover lemon cake is what brought me out of the bedroom. I'll save you a slice."

"I would love one, and maybe a cup of coffee to go with it." He waved over his shoulder as he left the bar.

Jessica closed her eyes and pictured the bedroom. The bed was rumpled because she'd been stretched out trying to read. Her towels were hung over the shower rod and there was underwear in the clothes basket. She hurried back to the hallway, slung the towels into her basket and carried it to the kitchen, put a week's white clothing into the washer, and started it. She and Wade were partners and friends, but from now on she would keep her dirty-clothes basket in the closet. There was something way too personal about him seeing her underpants—even in a plastic basket.

The coffeepot was still half-full from what had been made at supper, so she figured they could heat up a mugful each in the microwave. She took the pound cake from the refrigerator and sliced off four pieces; put them on a couple of plates, which she set on the table; and then sat down to wait.

The picture of him in the shower popped into her head again, but she blinked it away and replaced it with that huge baptismal in the sanctuary. She wandered out there to stare at it for a few minutes. Then she opened the side door leading up the stairs to the edge of the thing and would have stepped down into it if it hadn't been coated with dust and spiderwebs. She remembered when she was baptized back when she was thirteen years old. The preacher had said something about leaving her old self behind when she went under the water and being a new soul when she came up out of it.

"Is that what I'm doing these days? I'm leaving my old life behind and beginning a new one with this bar and my friends?" she wondered out loud.

Yes, you are, Elijah whispered so softly that she expected to see him in the baptismal. *You've got my blessing, so to hell with Stella and everyone that stands with her.*

Wade could tell that Jessica had been in the military by her room. He couldn't have bounced a quarter on her bed, but then the pillows against the headboard and the book on the nightstand said that she'd been reading. Everything else was inspection-ready—pretty much like he kept things.

He adjusted the water in the shower and left his dirty jeans, socks, and shirt on the floor when he peeled out of them. The scent of vanilla mixed with coconut filled the bathroom and reminded Wade of a beach. He could almost hear the ocean waves slapping against the sandy shore.

The last time he'd seen his brother in person had been in Wells, Maine. They'd had a lobster dinner right across from the Atlantic Ocean and had listened to the sounds as they talked about the future and the bar they wanted to build someday. They hadn't really planned on going into business in Riverbend. Danny had thought more about a tiki bar somewhere on a beach. Wade had envisioned one in somewhere like Wyoming or Montana—an Old West type of saloon.

"Well, Brother, we're getting the bar, but it's not on a beach or in the mountains. I guess we've kind of met in the middle," he muttered as he stepped into the shower and pulled the curtain.

He enjoyed every moment of standing under the spray and was grateful for Jessica's offer. Her bathroom was so much nicer and cleaner than the old makeshift shower in the back of Sparky's store. By the time he had gotten out and dried off, he was humming the tune to "Knee Deep" by Zac Brown. Part of the lyrics talked about him finding his own kind of paradise, and he nodded as he heard the words in his head. The peppy tune made him think of a tiki bar out on a beach somewhere. "I swear everything makes me think of you, Brother. Is your spirit still with us?" Wade asked his reflection in the mirror. "Like the song says, it doesn't matter where we are; we can always climb out of being lost and find paradise. The words make it sound easy, but it's not always."

He dressed in a pair of baggy pajama bottoms and a loose-fitting tank top and headed to the kitchen. On the way he stopped to look at both areas for the bar and finally decided that building it near the kitchen would be the better choice.

"Wondering what in the world we're going to do with that baptismal font?" Jessica asked from the kitchen door.

"Yes, I was. You got any ideas?" he asked.

"Nope," Jessica answered, "but I bet we come up with something. What if we took it out and used the space as a small wine and extra liquor cabinet? We could lock our extra stock behind the closed doors on either end."

"That's actually a pretty good idea," Wade agreed, "but for tonight let's just have some cake and coffee and forget about the bar for a little while."

"Cake is sliced and ready. We just have to heat up the coffee." She turned and went back into the kitchen.

Wade flipped off the lights in the bar area and made his way across the wide room. "Thanks again for the use of the bathroom. Been a long time since I've been in one that clean."

"Military sticks with us, doesn't it?" She set the cake on the table and put two mugs of coffee in the microwave.

"Oh, yeah, it does," he said with a nod. "I cleaned Sparky's little bathroom half a day, but it still didn't look too good. That's not the only thing that sticks with us, though, is it?"

The microwaved dinged and she removed the coffee and set both cups on the table before she took a seat across from Wade. "Nope. Did whatever your job was cause you to have nightmares?"

He took a sip and remembered the recurring dreams that plagued his sleep. "I was a sniper, and yes, I still have nightmares. I probably should be in therapy, but . . ." He shrugged. "I'd have to go to Killeen or to the post at Fort Hood, and I've convinced myself that I can deal with it on my own. Are you asking because you have the dreams, too?"

Wade couldn't only recognize the pain in her face—he could feel it. He wasn't sure whether to ask another question or change the subject.

"I . . ." She took a deep breath and let it out slowly. "My job was in special reconnaissance." Her voice sounded hollow. "I expect it affected me as much as if I'd been a sniper. I was the only woman on the team, but after the first year, the guys accepted me fairly well."

Wade reached across the table and laid a hand over hers. "I understand. Sometimes I didn't even see the face of the person, but I still wake up in a cold sweat hoping that I didn't rob a child of a father. I'll never get over knowing that no matter how bad that person was in my sights, I did rob a mother of her child."

"National security," Jessica said, "takes its toll on us folks who have to do the work, doesn't it?"

He gave her hand a little squeeze and wasn't a bit surprised that his was still tingling when he picked up his fork. Every time he'd brushed against her when they were working on the church pews, sparks had flown. It was a wonder she didn't feel the heat like he did, but then she probably hadn't had a crush on him, like he had on her, when they were just teenagers.

"You got that right about those of us who are ordered to do things that bother us." He cut off a piece of the pound cake and put it in his mouth. "We do what we're trained for, and try to compartmentalize it, don't we?"

"We do it for the greater good," she said just above a whisper. "That's the words we're told, but do you think the greater good helps those mothers who lose their sons and daughters, or the children who lose their parents?"

"Nope," Wade answered. "That would be like talking to a preacher about putting a bar in a church. He's never done it, never even thought about it, so how could he give advice on whether to take out the baptismal and use part of the area to make shelves for liquor or not?"

"Or to a committee who never taught a day in school and expects to give advice on how to teach kids anything," she said.

"What brought on that idea?" Wade asked.

Jessica raised one shoulder in half a shrug. "Thinking about Haley going back to school in the fall. I want her to be happy, but I also don't want her to leave. We've got a good team here."

"Do you often shy away from talking about what you did by thinking of something else?" Wade asked.

"Do you really think that's what I'm doing?" she asked.

"Yes, because I do the same thing," he answered. "I'll talk about building the bar over out there in what used to be the sanctuary to avoid a discussion about Danny."

"Do you want to talk about him?" Jessica asked.

"I haven't, not even to Oscar." Wade shrugged. "I just say that he was killed in the line of duty, but the truth is that it was a tragic accident. He worked in technology, and there was a problem with their equipment during a field training exercise. He loaded up what he needed and started driving. They told me it was only a mile away from base, and the road had been cleared. Evidently, they either missed an IED or one had been planted since they left."

"And Danny ran over it?" Jessica stood up, moved around the table, and sat down next to him. Then she draped an arm around his shoulders. "I'm so sorry, Wade."

He reached up and covered her hand with his. "Thanks for listening. He only had one more year, and then we were going to get serious about putting in our bar."

"Well, I think when the lawyer has to have a definite name for this bar, we should call it Danny's Place." She removed her arm, but she didn't go back to her original seat.

"He'd like that." Wade knew a moment of peace because he had finally told someone what happened to Danny, yet felt empty because he had liked having Jessica so close that her arm was around him.

"Danny did die in the line of duty," Jessica assured him. "You know that down deep in your heart, Wade. In the field we depend on technology. Without it, we'd fail in our missions."

"Thanks, but I already know that." Wade managed a smile, but it was only on his face, not from the heart.

"No thanks necessary." She nudged his shoulder with hers. "That's a fact. Whether our technology is during a full-fledged battle or in a training exercise, it's important, and Danny was doing a good thing. He died a hero, Wade. Don't ever forget that."

He laid a hand on her shoulder and tried to stop his chin from quivering. "I won't, but I also can't forgive myself for talking him into enlisting. I'm glad you came home and that we are partners, Jessica. You'll never know how much talking to you means to me."

"I think I do, because talking to you means that much to me. No one understands unless they've been there." She laid her hand on his and gave it a gentle squeeze.

"You got that right."

Jessica had teased about having to kill someone if she discussed her job with them. In reality, what she did really was classified, but by joking about it, she didn't have to answer any more questions.

"I never realized it until now, but I guess I do change the subject to avoid difficult conversations," she said after a moment.

"So do I," Wade said with a nod. "I don't want to remember how many people's lives I was responsible for ending when I pulled the trigger, so I switch to talking about something else to avoid the questions. How did it affect you the first time you shot a person?"

"I went out that night and cried until there were no more tears," she answered. "The next morning, I told myself I deserved the pain. I'd passed all my psych evals, so I thought I was prepared for the aftershock, but nothing gets us ready for that first time, does it? Or, for that matter, any time after that. I still have nightmares."

Wade nodded and then changed direction and shook his head. "I did the same thing and felt the same way. The only person I ever talked about this with before tonight was Danny. I think that's why I have missed him so much. We could share things that I couldn't talk about with anyone else, even though we had such different jobs." He chuckled. "Kind of a role reversal from the way we were in high school, isn't it? I was the brainy kid, and he was the football player."

Jessica was stunned at the different paths the two Granger brothers had taken. If she'd guessed which one would be a techie and which one would be a sniper, she wouldn't have put Danny in the former role.

Wade finished off the last bite of his cake and washed it down with coffee. "He was going to run the business end of our bar for us. We were both going to share the bartending work so we could spend time together."

"Danny's Place sounds better every time I think about it," Jessica said.

"Like Oscar said, it's going to be referred to as the old church no matter what's on the sign out front. Which reminds me, do you think we should have a neon sign or just a wooden one?" Wade asked.

Jessica was glad to get away from the memories of what she had done when she was following orders. "Maybe we should set the steeple up where the old church sign is and put the sign on top of it." She made a sweeping motion up in the air. "Danny's Place."

"Or Cheers, for cheerleaders." Wade chuckled.

"We might get into copyright problems with that," Jessica said with a smile, "and besides, you weren't a cheerleader, and you are a partner in this business."

"I'd forgotten about that old television sitcom." He flashed a brilliant smile toward her. "We should think about advertising in the nearby newspapers about our grand opening and say that it's a place where the beer is always cold and the food is always hot."

"And a place where everybody might not know your name, but you can get hymns sung to you in the parking lot, and maybe even a preacher to absolve you of your sins before you even leave the premises." Jessica's heart felt lighter than it had in years.

"What?" Wade asked.

"Didn't Oscar tell you that we had a little altercation with Stella in the lumberyard?" she asked.

"No, but I'm all ears now. Why on earth was Stella in the lumber-yard?" Wade leaned forward in his chair and propped both elbows on the table.

"She had a petition she was trying to get everyone in the place to sign," Jessica answered and went on to tell him what Stella had said. "So, when we open, we may have a choir and a preacher out in the parking lot either singing hymns or passing out church literature."

"Seems only fitting since this started out as a church, doesn't it? Maybe we should consider naming it the Preacher's Place in honor of Elijah. Then the protesters could fuss at us for that, too. We are located at the end of Preacher's Road, so it would make sense." Wade's grin got even wider.

"I wonder why they named it that."

"I asked Oscar about it, and the original name for the church was Preacher's Church, so when they had to name all the roads for the emergency crews, they just named this one Preacher's Road. Then Elijah decided to call it the Community Church, in hopes that he could lure folks into it from the other religious organizations, but the road was already named, and it was too much trouble to change it."

"But it was always called the Old Dock Road before Uncle Elijah built the church," Jessica said.

"Yep, and folks still call it that. Just like Oscar said they'll do about calling the bar the old church." Wade covered a yawn with his hand. "Not bad company, darlin', just a long day. I'm glad we're all taking Sunday off even during the building of this place. After tomorrow we'll need a day of rest."

"I guess we should take Sunday off since this started out as a church."

"Yep, but we've really adapted very well to the idea of this being a bar. We've already stopped referring to that room as the sanctuary"— he motioned toward the door with his hand—"and this one as the fellowship hall. It's now the kitchen, and your quarters and Mary Nell's office aren't Sunday school rooms anymore."

"Progress," she agreed.

"By the time we open for business, we will have forgotten that this was ever anything but a bar and grill." He finished off his coffee. "Thanks for listening to me, and for confiding in me, too."

She smiled at him and said, "BTT."

"What does that mean?" he asked.

"It means Been There Therapy," she answered and picked up her dirty dishes.

"Amen!" he said as he got up and carried his plate and glass to the sink. "That's the only kind of therapy that works for people like us."

His shoulder brushed against hers when he put his plate and cup in the sink, and there was that little burst of electricity. She glanced over and saw the dreamy look in his green eyes and knew in that moment that he could feel the chemistry between them, too.

Not that it would do a bit of good—they were partners, and mixing pleasure with business was too risky.

"And you got that right," she told him as she headed for the door. "See you in the morning."

"Good night, Jessica," Wade said.

"Sweet dreams." She managed a smile, but what she really wanted to do was take a step forward and wrap her arms around him. Wade had suffered—was still suffering—just like she was from the jobs they'd had. Would a simple hug be so bad?

Yes, it would, because it would start something that has no future, the voice in her head warned her.

"See you tomorrow morning at breakfast," he said and disappeared into the darkness of the bar area.

The moment was gone, and there was a good possibility it would never happen again. With a sigh, Jessica turned out the lights in the kitchen and made her way across the dark bar to the hallway leading back to her quarters.

She went right to the bathroom, flipped the switch to turn on the light, and was met with the lingering scent of Wade's soap, which smelled a lot like leather. She took a long breath and held it for a moment. If he took a shower every night, which she expected he would, how was she ever supposed to go to bed and not think about him?

Chapter Eight

Dust hung over the weathered wooden bleachers like smoke in an old-time honky-tonk, blocking out the stars and what there was of the moon over Jessica's head that evening. Wade and Oscar had come up with the idea for them all to go to the ranch rodeo. According to them, everyone had worked so hard that they deserved a little fun that Saturday night, but Jessica figured the evening was mostly for the twins' sake.

Jessica had been to a couple of local rodeos, but seeing the events through the eyes of a couple of teenagers was a whole new experience. They were both wide-eyed though the bull-riding event, and when the second contestant stayed on for the full eight seconds, their whoops and hollers put the enthusiasm of everyone around them to shame.

"I want to do that," Lily said. "Can I take lessons? Maybe on one of those fake bulls?"

"Not me." Daisy shook her head. "I'm like Mama. I'm as graceful as an elephant on ice."

"Hey, now!" Risa argued. "I can do better than that."

"Want me to start giving examples?" Daisy teased.

Risa nudged her daughter with a shoulder. "Only if you want me to tell secrets, too."

"I will shut up right now." Daisy giggled.

"That kid that just managed to stick to the bull's back for the whole time has been riding since he was mutton busting, and he's your age, Lily," Oscar said. "I'll introduce you to him if you want, and you can talk to him about learning to ride."

"Are you serious?" Lily asked. "Would you really introduce me to him?"

"What's mutton busting?" Daisy blurted out over her sister's question.

"It's when kids from four to seven climb on a wild, woolly sheep and try to hold on for six seconds. Cole and his cousin, Peyton, have been competing since right after they turned four. It's also known as wool riding," Oscar explained. "But yes, I will introduce you. Can you girls two-step?"

"Yep, we can," Daisy answered, "but don't tell Granny Stella or Granny Martha. They don't believe in dancing."

"Mama taught us how to dance," Lily said.

"My lips are sealed," Oscar chuckled, "and good for Risa. A girl needs to know how to dance, but I'm not so sure about bull riding."

Wade nudged Jessica. "Want to put a mechanical bull in the space between the pulpit and the north wall? That would give Lily some practice."

"Are you serious? Aren't those things expensive?" Jessica leaned close enough to him so that she could be heard, and the electricity between them seemed to crackle.

She took a deep breath, cleared her mind, and tried to think about a beach to still her racing pulse. She hadn't dated in two years, not since she got sent to her last duty station and her boyfriend was reassigned to a base in California. Two months later they'd figured out that long-distance relationships didn't work for them. The split was amicable, and now he was married with a child on the way.

"Somewhere around eight thousand, but just think of the customers it would pull in," Wade said.

Jessica glanced over at Lily and made another impulse decision. "We'd probably be the only ones for miles and miles with a bull. Let's talk about it with the rest of the team. We're the two supporting partners, but they should have a say-so, too."

"Have you ever ridden one?" Wade asked.

"One time. I hit the sawdust in two seconds. He was named Fu Man Chu, just like in that old country song. I'm a little like Daisy and not very coordinated," she admitted.

"Me either, but I really think a bull would generate a lot of money," Wade said.

"How's that?" she screamed over the noise of everyone screaming and yelling for the first bareback bronc rider.

"The night I rode one"—Wade leaned over close to her ear—"my friend bet me two beers I wouldn't do it. Another one bet a shot of whiskey that I couldn't stay on eight seconds at high speed."

The warmth of his breath on her neck sent tingles dancing down her spine, and she had to keep reminding herself that they were business partners. Oh, yes, sir, she really did need to get back into the dating game so that she could get over this teenage infatuation with Wade.

"I had to buy a round of drinks when I didn't stay on the full eight," she said, "so I see your point. Let's discuss it over breakfast tomorrow morning."

"Everyone is free on Sunday, so there won't be a breakfast," Wade reminded her.

"Then we'll talk about it Monday morning," she said in a loud voice just as things got quiet.

"Talk about what?" Daisy asked.

"Putting a mechanical bull in the bar. We can all discuss it Monday morning," Jessica answered.

"I'll ride one of those," Daisy said with a nod. "I bet I can stay on longer than Lily. She's even clumsier than I am."

"Am not! And you cannot!" Lily declared.

"Wait and see," Daisy told her with a smug little grin.

"I bet you a root beer that I can beat you," Lily said.

"You're on!" Daisy nudged her sister with a shoulder.

"Point proven." Wade chuckled and turned toward Jessica again. "Hey, are you going to church tomorrow?"

"I'm sleeping in until noon," Jessica answered. "What's your plans?"

"Since you offered to let me use the washer and dryer, I thought I'd do that and maybe organize the bar a little better," Wade said.

"Look!" Oscar pointed. "Peyton, Cole's cousin, is next up in bronc riding."

"How do you know those guys?" Jessica asked.

"Their granddad and I were in the military together. We still play dominoes at the senior citizens' center or cards at my house on Sunday afternoons after church," Oscar answered. "After he rides, I'm going to the concession stand for a beer. Anyone want to go with me?"

"I'll go," Risa said.

"Me too," Jessica added. "I've been getting a whiff of those nachos every few minutes, and I want some."

"Yes!" Haley pulled a bill from her purse and handed it to Oscar. "I want nachos and a root beer."

"We'll go help bring it all back." Lily stood up.

Daisy and Jessica both got to their feet at the same time.

"Burger with mustard and no onions for me"—Mary Nell handed her dad a bill—"and a beer."

"I'm getting a hot dog." Risa fell in behind the group. "What do you want, Wade?"

"A candy bar and a root beer." He pulled a bill from his shirt pocket and handed it to Risa. "I'm not picky about the candy, just so long as it's chocolate."

Jessica repeated all the orders in her head a couple of times as the five of them made their way from the bleachers over to the concession stand. She had them memorized until she reached the wagon that traveled from rodeo to rodeo and saw Stella making nachos. She heard Risa suck in air behind her, and said, "I'll take care of this. You and the girls go on back up to our seats."

Risa shook her head. "Thanks for the offer, but I'm not running away from my mother. No one is ever going to have that kind of power over me again."

Lily marched up to the window and looked her grandmother right in the eye. "Hey, Granny Stella, what are you doing here?"

"Are you going to the dance after the rodeo?" Daisy smirked. "Want me to ask Oscar to dance with you so you won't feel like a wallflower?"

"I'm here because the church is selling the nachos tonight for the missionary fund, and no, I will not be attending the dance," Stella said through clenched teeth.

"Oh, come on, Stella." Oscar chuckled. "I really will dance with you. I remember when we were all teenagers and you used to be real good at doing the twist and the jerk down at the fishing docks where we gathered up on the weekends to drink beer."

"That was before I started going to church," Stella hissed, "and I would not dance with you, Oscar—not for any amount of money. You are helping these people turn a church into a bar. That is pure sacrilege."

"And we might get a mechanical bull so I can learn to ride," Lily said with a cheeky grin.

Stella laid a hand over her heart and rolled her eyes upward. "Father, forgive them for they know not what they do."

Jessica bit back a giggle. No way on God's great green earth could she imagine Stella dancing one of those old dances or drinking a beer. Haley would probably say that Stella had gotten such a case of religion because she felt guilty for her teenage sins.

"You're not Jesus, Mama"—Risa frowned—"but we need to order so that these folks behind us can get their nachos. We need . . ." She rattled off the order.

Jessica was amazed that Risa could remember everything after the dirty looks Stella shot her way. When Jessica saw Stella in the concession stand, her mind had gone blank, and yet Risa didn't forget a single thing they had all asked for.

"You'll have to get the beers on the other end. I don't sell those vile things," Stella huffed.

Jessica imagined flames shooting out of Stella's ears and eyes, but the women simply whipped around and began making baskets of nachos. When she shoved them out the window, Jessica thought they looked a little scant, but she didn't say a word.

Not so with Lily, though. "Granny Stella, it's not very Christian of you to short us on nachos just because you're mad at us."

Stella glared at her granddaughter. "Don't you tell me what's Christian and what's not, young lady, and you don't deserve what you've got in those baskets. You don't respect your elders, and—"

"Love you, Granny Stella," Daisy said, cutting her off. She picked up a couple of the baskets. "Come on, Mama. We've got drinks to get, and she's not going to tell us that she loves us anyway."

"Jesus says I have to love you, but He didn't say I have to like any of you," Stella snapped. "Now, go on, so I can wait on these other people."

"I'm sorry," Jessica told Risa.

"Thanks, but I'm not sorry." Risa got in line to get drinks. "I've never been happier in my life, and I mean that. I'm totally at peace living with Haley and working at the bar. I keep finding myself humming while I'm cooking or helping with whatever needs to be done. It's like a heavy weight has been lifted off me."

"And we love our new world," Daisy chimed in.

"I just wish I could tell our cousins about Texas and this rodeo." Lily sighed. "I know that Rachel, Sarah, and Myra would love to be here with us."

"Ain't never goin' to happen," Daisy assured her as they all headed back to the bleachers.

Wade hung back with Jessica, bringing up the rear. Another burst of dust flew up in the arena, and the crowd jumped to their feet and roared. The announcer in the press box sounded as excited as the rest of the folks when he announced the name of the young man who'd stayed on the bronc's back for the full eight seconds.

"We should both count our blessings that we had good parents. You might have to hold me back if Stella makes good on her threat to show up in our parking lot trying to convert our customers," Jessica said for Wade's ears only.

"Honey, I'll be out there with you, not holding you back," Wade told her. "If I'd known Stella was going to be here, I would have suggested a movie and ice cream afterwards, rather than this rodeo."

"Like Risa said, she can't run from her mama," Jessica told him. "She's actually taking all of this a lot better than I am."

Wade glanced over at her for the hundredth time that evening. She wore a pair of tight-fitting jeans and an off-white shirt that hugged her body like a glove. Her blonde hair floated on her shoulders, and she smelled like the beach—coconut suntan lotion, vanilla, and maybe a little piña colada thrown in. At that moment, he wished that he and Jessica weren't business partners.

When they reached the bleachers, places had shifted, and now Jessica was sitting between Wade and Oscar.

"I was proud of the way the twins and Risa handled things," Oscar whispered.

Haley leaned around Oscar so she could hear better. "What happened when y'all went to get something to drink?"

"Stella is working the concession stand, selling nachos for the church," Oscar answered.

"Sweet Jesus!" Haley groaned. "You think she poisoned the ones we ordered?"

"Only if words dripping with ugliness can poison them," Oscar said. "Risa held her own, so you don't have to worry about her."

"That's more than I would have done, and it could always be a bluff, but I'm here for her if she needs to talk about it. As far as that goes, I'm always here for any of the team," Haley assured him.

"We're lucky to have you," Wade told her.

"Thanks, but the feeling is mutual." Haley smiled.

"And that's the last event of the evening," the rodeo announcer said. "While we're waiting for the band to get set up for the dance, let's give our rodeo clowns a big hand. Their job might look easy, but believe me, it's a tough one, so let's hear it for them."

The clowns all came out, lined up, and took a bow. The crowd gave them a standing ovation complete with whistles and ringing cowbells. The dust settled somewhat but was still hanging in the air a few minutes later when the band struck up the first notes of an old country song, "Heaven's Just a Sin Away."

Wade stood up and extended a hand to Jessica. "May I have this dance, partner?"

She put her hand in his and said, "I might be a little rusty, but I'll give it a shot."

His inner voice warned her against dancing right out in public with Jessica, but he ignored it. He didn't give a tiny rat's rump what people thought of the church being a bar or of him and Jessica being partners—or if they banned her from riding on a float at homecoming, either, for that matter.

That song had ended by the time they reached the middle of the area. The lead singer started singing "My Church." Wade wrapped his arms around Jessica and drew her close for a fast-moving two-step.

"Seems fitting for our first dance, doesn't it?" Wade said.

"I imagine that Stella would say that heaven being a sin away would be more like it, only she would substitute *hell* for *heaven*," Jessica told him.

When the singer asked if she could get a hallelujah, the folks still up in the stands all jumped up and yelled, "Hallelujah." Wade glanced over Jessica's shoulder and smiled when he saw Oscar giving him the thumbs-up sign.

When the next song started, Wade swung Jessica out and then brought her back to his chest. The singer sounded a helluva lot like Mary Chapin Carpenter as she sang "I Feel Lucky."

Wade could agree with the lyrics because he sure did feel lucky with Jessica in his arms. The whole arena filled up with other couples, but Wade didn't even see them. In his mind, he and Jessica were the only couple out there in the dusty arena.

Haley grabbed a quick shower, got dressed in a pair of loose-fitting pajama pants, and glared at the pregnancy test lying in the drawer beside her toothpaste. Still in the box and just lying there tormenting her every time she brushed her teeth. She couldn't be pregnant—she'd been on the pill for years and years. She kept telling herself that all the recent stress, not pregnancy, had caused her to miss a couple of periods. Losing her mother, finding out about her biological mother, not knowing whether she should even try to find her father. Then add on the fact that she was having trouble deciding whether to quit her job in Alabama and stay in Riverbend—all that would cause any woman to be irregular.

She slammed the drawer shut with force so she wouldn't even have to see it. Sure, she wanted a family, but not now. Lots of women were starting a family in their early forties these days, and she was only thirty-eight, so that meant she had a few years left. She'd always plowed right into a problem, so why was she procrastinating and worrying about that test? If she was pregnant, the decision would be made for her about going back to Georgia in the fall. Here in Riverbend, she would have support and help. There she would be completely alone.

"I can't think about this right now," she muttered.

She went to the kitchen without turning on the light in the foyer, poured herself a glass of milk, and carried it to the back porch with intentions of watching the stars dance around the moon. She and her mother used to do that, and it always calmed her nerves.

Like the stars did the night you probably got pregnant? the pesky voice in her head asked.

"Hush!" she said as she stepped out onto the screened porch and remembered that last bittersweet night.

"I didn't say a word," Risa said from one end of the settee.

"Sorry," Haley said with a sigh. "I was arguing with myself."

"I've done that a lot lately," Risa said.

"Oh, yeah." Haley caught a whiff of whiskey, and her stomach did a roll. "Please don't tell me you are drinking because Paul called and you're all going back to Kentucky."

"Where did that idea come from?" Risa asked.

"It's just the scariest thing I could think of." Haley crossed her fingers when she thought of that pregnancy test, because that scared her even worse.

She had invited Risa and the girls to live with her to be a help to them, but now they were there, she had figured out it was a two-way street. If that pregnancy test turned out to be positive, she sure would need support from them.

"Oh, no! That ship sailed. I can't even see it out there on the horizon," Risa assured her. "After seeing my mother again and hearing her say such ugly words to my girls, I needed a good stiff drink, and I'm going to have another one. If that's a sin, then I'll ask forgiveness tomorrow morning in church." Risa stood up and headed toward the little cabinet where Haley kept the liquor. "Want one?"

Yes, I want one, but I can't—not until I figure this out about a baby, Haley thought, but she said, "No thanks. Milk helps calm me down so I can sleep. Talk to me. Is this about Stella?"

"We've had a wonderful evening," Risa said, "so let's not ruin it by hashing out all this crap."

"It'll lay inside you and eat away until you talk about it." Haley wasn't sure if she was talking to herself or to Risa. "You'll feel better if you get it off your chest, and I can't sleep anyway. So, you're going to church tomorrow?"

"Yep, I vowed that I wouldn't run from Mama, and the girls need to be in church. I might not believe like she does but . . ." Risa took a sip of her whiskey.

"You could go to a different church," Haley suggested. "There's more than one in town, and maybe thirty in the county."

Risa set her mouth in a firm line, shook her head, and took another sip. "Nope, that would be the equivalent of running. I'm going to walk right into church with my girls with my back straight and no tears."

"I'm going with you." Haley decided on the spur of the moment. "Maybe God will give me an inkling of an idea about why Mama and my sister didn't tell me about my birth when I was a grown woman."

"You think God will talk to you more in church than right here?" Risa asked.

"I need answers, and I can't find them in this house." Haley shrugged. "Maybe I'll get a sign, or a hymn will spark a memory. One never knows, but even if I don't get a sign at all, I'm going to support you and the girls."

"Thank you." Risa drank the last drop of her whiskey and set the empty glass on the coffee table. "They say that the definition of stupid is doing the same thing over and over again and expecting a different outcome."

Haley nodded and waited for Risa to go on.

"From the time I was a little girl, I wanted my mother to love me like she did all her friends at the church," Risa said with a sigh. "Looking back, though, I can see that I married Paul to get away from Riverbend. We eloped because I knew Mama would fuss about having to spend money on a wedding. She wasn't sad the day that we drove away in his pickup truck. She just stood there on the porch with this big smile of relief on her face and waved as we left."

"Was she happy the times when you came back to Riverbend for homecoming?" Haley remembered how her mother would make all her favorite desserts and food when she was able to come home for the parade and festivities.

"She seemed to be, but then I was only here for a couple of days. It was an eight-hour drive from our place in Kentucky, so we'd drive down on Thursday and back on Sunday. That left Friday, and we were busy with the parade. Then Saturday, we were packing up to leave the next day. That was the only time I got to see her during all those years, and she was more than ready for us to get going early on Sunday," Risa said. "As controlling as he was, Paul was happier to see us return home than Mama was when we could only come for a couple of days a year."

Haley listened, but she couldn't help but reevaluate all the hard feelings she'd had toward her own mother since she found that letter and her original birth certificate. Nadine, her mother/grandmother, had loved her enough to give her a good home and take care of her at a time when her own biological mother, Frannie, was too young to do the job, and never complained one time. When Haley moved to Alabama, Nadine had stood on the porch and shed tears as she had driven away.

I was loved, Haley thought. *That's what was important.*

"Facing reality isn't easy." She pictured the test lying in the bathroom drawer. Her mother would have been disappointed that Haley wasn't married, but she would have been excited about the baby. Haley wondered if her mother hadn't felt like that when she found out her fifteen-year-old daughter was about to have a baby—disappointment and excitement at the same time.

"But we have to face reality if we're ever going to put the past to rest." Risa's voice sounded tired and wistful. "I've got to do that so the girls and I can move on. I can be thankful to have had a mother like

Stella, who taught me *how not to be* when it comes to raising my own girls."

"You have a good attitude, my friend," Haley said.

"I guess we are *all* four—or maybe I should say five, if we include Wade—paddling the same canoe." Risa poured herself another double shot. "So I'm not the only one with problems."

"Yes, we are." Haley finished off her milk and stood up. "Jessica and Wade are trying to find a permanent place to put down roots after twenty years of living out of a duffel bag. They're both worried that in a few months the other one will grow weary of staying in one place. Mary Nell is fighting with her feelings of giving so many years to that sorry sumbitch, Kevin, and then getting dumped."

"And Jessica and Wade are doubling that first problem by fighting the sparks between them," Risa said as she stood and headed toward the kitchen with her empty glass in her hand.

"You saw it, too?" Haley followed her into the kitchen. "I thought maybe I was imagining things."

"I can almost feel the heat between them." Risa rinsed her glass and put it in the dishwasher. "But we have to let them find their own way through this, and not try to help, right?"

"I suppose so," Haley answered, "but it sure is tempting to give them a little push, isn't it?"

"Nope." Risa shook her head. "What if we did, and it was a disaster like what happened with me and Paul? Or like Mary Nell and Kevin? We better just let them figure things out on their own."

"Now who's the counselor?" Haley giggled.

Risa threw up her palms in a defensive gesture. "Not me. I'm having trouble controlling my own life. I'm not smart enough to help anyone else. But I'm really glad I've got this roommate who is able to help all of us through these difficult times."

Haley gave her a quick hug. "Don't underestimate yourself. You've helped me a lot tonight by just talking to me. So, thank you."

"You're welcome, but I really think that you are just saying that to make me feel better. Good night, and thank you for"—Risa headed for the door and then turned around—"for everything."

"Welcome," Haley muttered and went straight to the bathroom just off her bedroom and took the pregnancy test.

She laid the stick on the counter, pulled up her underpants, and went back to the bedroom. The directions said two lines would appear within one minute if she was pregnant. One line meant that all the stress had simply caused her to be late.

The clock beside her bed had never moved so slowly in her life. Seconds took hours, a full minute was just short of eternity, but when it had passed, she couldn't force herself to go into the bathroom. A dozen steps from the end of her bed to the vanity would tell the tale of her future and present her with the most difficult decision she'd ever made. If there were two lines, she would resign from her job and become a bartender-slash-waitress. No way could she go back there and tell the baby daddy that she was pregnant. He was happily married now and should have been shot for not telling her he was engaged when they were having their fling.

"Men should have to mark their foreheads with a red *X* when they become engaged, or at least wear some kind of a ring like women do to let the world know they are taken," she mumbled as she forced herself to go to the bathroom.

She closed her eyes when she reached the door and leaned against the vanity for several seconds before she opened them. Everything was slightly blurry at first, but then the stick and the two lines came into focus.

She put the lid down on the toilet and sat down with a thud. Staring hard at the test, she tried to will one of the lines to disappear. A family was always something years away for her, and now right there in two lines no more than an eighth of an inch long, her future unveiled itself. She was going to follow in her mother's footsteps. Only she was thirty-eight, not a teenager, and she didn't have a mother to step up and adopt her baby.

"I'm going to be a single mother," she whispered as the tears began to flow down her cheeks.

But you have a support system in your friends, the voice in her head reminded her. *Maybe a new little life is exactly what this team needs to take its mind off all the other problems they have.*

Chapter Nine

Jessica had just put on a pot of coffee on Sunday morning when her phone rang. She sat down at the kitchen table and answered it. "Mornin', Haley. What are you doing up this early? Last night you said you were sleeping until noon."

"Risa is going to church this morning, and she needs our support. After last night, there's no telling what Stella is liable to do or say to her or the twins," Haley said. "I'm going with them, but I thought we should all be there. Will you come, and will you tell Wade? I understand he hasn't been in church since Danny died, but we need him and Oscar both. They're part of our team."

"What time do I need to be there, and what church?" Jessica yawned. "And yes, I will tell Wade. Have you talked to Mary Nell?"

"Services start at eleven. Be there fifteen minutes early and we'll all go in together. It's the little redbrick church out at the end of Main Street. And I've talked to Oscar. He said he'll bring Mary Nell with him," Haley answered.

"And we can sit on the back pew so we can escape right after the last *amen*, right?" Jessica asked.

"Oh, no," Haley said, "we're going to sit up front so Stella can see us. Risa is not going to let anyone control her, remember?"

"Then I guess I'd better not wear camouflage pants and my military boots," Jessica said with a giggle.

"Maybe you should." Haley laughed with her. "It might show Stella that her daughter has the support of the army behind her if you and Wade are both there."

Wade came into the kitchen, waved, and went straight to the coffeepot. He filled up a mug, took a sip, and set it on the counter. Then he opened the refrigerator and pulled out a stick of sausage and a can of biscuits and started making breakfast.

"Is Oscar coming with us for sure?" Jessica asked.

Wade turned around and raised an eyebrow.

"Later," Jessica mouthed.

"Yes," Haley answered, "so between us all, we should fill up a complete pew."

"I'll be there," Jessica said, "but right now I need to have my first cup of coffee so my eyes will open. See you there."

"We'll be waiting for you," Haley said and ended the call.

Wade poured a second mug of coffee and took it to Jessica. "Good morning. I'm surprised to see you up this early."

"Good morning to you, and thanks for this. I'd like to sleep late, but"—she shrugged—"old habits get in the way. You've been out two years. Does it ever get better?"

He went back to the stove and crumbled sausage into a skillet. While that cooked, he popped open the can of biscuits, arranged them in a pan, and slid them in the oven. "You'll have to ask someone that's been out longer than me for that answer. No matter when I go to bed, I still wake up before six every morning. You want eggs with sausage gravy and biscuits? If so, you'll have to fry them."

"Yes, I do, but I like scrambled better." Jessica stood up and carried her coffee across the room. She pulled a carton of eggs from the fridge, cracked two into a bowl, then glanced over at Wade. "How many do you want? And about that phone call. We're all going to church this morning to support Risa, who has decided not to let Stella control her. Do you want to go with us?"

"Yes, I'll go to church to be there for Risa. I will stand with the rest of the team for Risa and the girls, but I'm pretty sure it won't be for my own soul." He stirred flour into the sizzling sausage. "Three or four eggs for me, Jessica. I had a great time last night, and I think the twins did, too. We should plan something every couple of weeks for them. They're hard workers and deserve some fun."

"We're *all* hard workers." Jessica added four more eggs to the bowl, whipped them up, and poured them into a skillet. "But the twins have been pulling more than their share. We should put them on payroll."

"I agree," he said. "If they aren't helping Risa in the kitchen, they're working out in the bar toting and fetching for us. Let's put them on at minimum wage and that will give them money for whatever they need in school or for their cheerleader stuff."

"I'll tell Mary Nell to back pay them for thirty hours a week. She's working on getting insurance for everyone this next week. According to her if someone works forty hours a week, we have to offer them insurance." Jessica would have rather been talking about anything other than boring work details. Like maybe whether Wade was beginning to accept Danny's death a little better. He had to get past blaming himself for his brother going into the military before he could move on with his life.

"I'm glad we've got her in the office." Wade shook another small palmful of flour into the sausage and kept stirring. "I wouldn't have any idea where to start with all that stuff."

"It's a miracle," Jessica said.

"How do you figure that?"

"Well, Mary Nell breaks up with her boyfriend and comes home to get her emotions all straightened out, and she's a bookkeeper. Risa gets tossed out of Kentucky like garbage, and she's a fine cook. Haley is home for the summer, and she's a counselor who is listening to all our problems. She will be wonderful behind the bar when some soldier or rancher comes in whining about his woman not treating him right. And the two of us have finished our last enlistment and need a place to call home. It has to be a miracle that threw us all together at just the right time," Jessica answered.

Wade was silent so long that she wondered if maybe he disagreed with her and didn't want to say anything. "I don't believe in miracles or fate," he finally said, "but you're right. It couldn't be anything else. Maybe it's all of our rewards for the tough times we've been through. But going back to doing something for the twins this summer, Oscar told me that there's a craft fair at Burnet next Saturday if it doesn't rain. If it does, they'll have to reschedule since it's outside. We could knock off work at noon and go, but I thought maybe we should talk about the idea as partners before we say anything to the rest of the team."

"Sounds like a plan to me," Jessica agreed as she whipped the eggs with a fork. "I didn't know that you could cook."

"Enough to keep from starving"—he flashed a brilliant smile her way—"but not enough to put on a chef's hat. The way you were talking on the phone, I thought maybe you were meeting someone for breakfast."

"Nope." Jessica shook her head. "Just talking about church."

"I'm still mad at God for taking Danny away from me," Wade admitted, "so if He wants to say anything to me this morning, He better yell. I'm afraid I kind of closed my ears to Him when Danny died. I'll go for Risa, but even if I didn't want to attend services, you would be welcome to use my truck."

"Thanks." She could hear a little catch in her own voice when he reached for the milk and his arm brushed against hers. "I need to find a small vehicle or truck of my own pretty soon so I don't have to depend on someone else to take me places."

"No need to hurry," he said. "You can always use my truck."

It seemed like a whole new set of hot little sparks every single time she even glanced over at Wade, and the few times they locked eyes, the electricity between them got even steamier. She was thirty-eight years old, for God's sake, not sixteen, and that meant she had to be an adult and get this attraction under control.

"What time do we need to be there?" Wade asked.

"Fifteen minutes until eleven so we can all go in together, and Haley says we're sitting near the front." Jessica scooped the scrambled eggs into a bowl and carried them to the table. She liked sitting down with everyone three times a day for meals, but eating with just the two of them that morning turned things more intimate and personal.

"Then we don't have to eat in a hurry," Wade said as he took the biscuits out of the oven. "And we can even do a little work before we have to get ready and go. We've got enough of the pews torn apart that we need to figure out where to measure for the actual bar. I'm still two ways about where to put it. I keep second-guessing myself on where to place it. Got any ideas?"

Jessica thought about the two places they had talked about and finally said, "I like it against the wall into the fellowship hall. That way if we ever draw in a big enough crowd to have a live band on weekends, we'll have a stage for them to use."

Wade nodded as he toted the rest of the food across the room. "Probably for the best, and when we don't have a band, we can put the jukebox and a couple of tables on the stage, and the mechanical bull off to the end like we talked about."

Jessica raised an eyebrow. "Did we agree to buy a bull?"

"Lily and Daisy will be disappointed if we don't," Wade answered with an extra sparkle in his green eyes. "I'm betting Lily will want to be first."

"I wouldn't take that bet for anything. That girl is fearless." Jessica put a forkful of eggs into her mouth. Family—related or not—that's what made it easy to put down roots.

Risa awoke with a sense of dread and almost told Haley and her daughters that they would either skip services that morning or go to a different church. Then she considered the example that she would be setting for her girls, took a deep breath, pasted on a smile, and went downstairs to the kitchen to start a pot of coffee. If she let Stella intimidate her, it would be just like all those years when she was a teenager and trying to make her mother love her, and the years she lived under the shadow of Paul and his mother. The first thing she'd told Lily and Daisy when they crossed the Kentucky state line into Tennessee was that no one was ever going to tell her what to do or make the rules for her life again. She was on her second cup of coffee when Haley arrived with Lily and Daisy right behind her.

"Mornin', y'all. Mama, do we have to go to church this morning?" Lily asked. "Granny Stella is going to be a handful if we do. I know I got to respect my elders, but it's getting awful hard to keep my mouth shut and my language all sweet and ladylike."

"Might as well get it over with," Daisy said as she headed for the refrigerator. "I love Sunday morning, when we get cold cereal for breakfast."

"What do you mean, 'get it over with'?" Lily asked.

"She's full of hissy fits. Hand me that chocolate cereal, please," Daisy said. "She'll have a special one for when we show up in church after we didn't bow down to her demands when she issued the ultimatum she did. The fit will just get worse and worse with time. Way I figure it is that we might as well nip it in the bud this morning."

Lily handed her the cereal and took two bowls from the cabinet. "You're probably right. Maybe we should dress like the women who stand on street corners"—Lily wiggled her eyebrows—"she's accusing us of being."

Risa was about to take a sip of coffee and jerked her head around so fast that she spilled part of it on her faded nightshirt. "When did she accuse you of that?"

"Last night when I went back to the concession stand for a root beer," Lily answered. "She was helping get the wagon cleaned up, and she said she wouldn't be surprised if we didn't use the Sunday school rooms for 'other things.'" She air quoted the last two words. "I don't think she was talking about Bible classes."

Risa stiffened her back and set her jaw. "What did you tell her?"

"That Jessica was living in the evangelist's room, that Mary Nell was using one of the others for an office, and that we had turned another one into a storage room, but"—Lily shrugged—"that when me and Daisy got eighteen, we might think about her suggestion."

"Good Lord!" Haley sputtered.

"If you can't beat 'em, join 'em." Daisy got the milk from the refrigerator and sat down beside her sister. "I'd wear a hooker dress if I had one, but Granny Martha didn't let us go to church without being dressed like ladies. You got anything flashy that I might borrow, Haley? We're about the same size."

"I work in a school, so no, I don't have clothing like that," Haley answered, and Risa could see her bite back a grin. "The flashiest thing I have would be a red sundress that's got big yellow sunflowers on it. You are welcome to borrow it if you want."

"Yes, ma'am, I would love to borrow it," Daisy answered.

"And I've got a pale blue gingham checkered sundress that comes to my ankles." Haley turned to focus on Lily. "It's got a stretchy top, and it would probably hit you at the knees, if you want to wear it."

"You bet, and thank you," Lily said. "Is that all right with you, Mama?"

"Of course it is." Risa managed a smile, but all the while she was regretting that her girls had to have two ultra-strict, overly religious grandmothers. They should be allowed to explore their own personalities.

Don't be so tough on yourself, the voice in her head scolded. *Growing up in the shadow of Stella, then marrying right into another family that was just as bad, you didn't have much of a role model for raising daughters, but you're on the right track now.*

Mary Nell was sound asleep when her cell phone rang that morning. She groaned, rolled over, and grumbled, "Twice in one morning when this is the only day that I get to sleep in."

"This had better be a life-and-death situation," she said as she hit the "Answer" button without even looking to see who was calling.

"It is," her father said. "You've got one hour to crawl out of that bed, get dressed, grab a bite of breakfast, and go with me to church so we can support Risa and those two sweet girls of hers. If you had married Danny right out of high school, I could have granddaughters their age to help."

"Okay, Daddy." Mary Nell brushed her red hair out of her face and sat up in bed. "I can't go back and undo what I did or didn't do, but isn't it nice that Risa is willing to share her girls with us? I would love a cup of hot tea after I'm out of the shower and dressed. I can't believe you are going to church. You haven't been since Mama passed away."

"Me and Wade are both mad at God for taking our loved ones away from us and leaving Stella Sullivan on the earth, but I'm not about to let those precious girls face off with that old witch without some backup today," Oscar said. "I'll put the teakettle on for your tea. Don't waste time primpin'. You're beautiful just the way you are."

"Thanks, Daddy," Mary Nell said and ended the call.

She stood under the hot shower as long as she dared and thought about what her father had said. Even though she hated to admit it, he was right. If she hadn't let Kevin sweet-talk her into leaving college and moving to Nashville with him, she might have had a family by now. Just thinking those thoughts set her biological clock to ticking so loudly that she put her hands over her ears.

"Hush—I know how old I am and that I'm looking menopause in the eye." She stepped out of the shower and wrapped a towel around her body. She padded back to her room, shot the clock beside her bed a dirty look, got dressed in a sleeveless pale-blue dress, and twisted her curly hair up into a messy bun.

"Well, well, look at you all dolled up." Oscar smiled from the kitchen chair where he was reading the Sunday paper and having what was probably his fourth or fifth cup of coffee.

"It's a sacrifice, but I'd do anything for Risa," Mary Nell said.

Oscar laid the paper aside. "Your tea has been steeping for five minutes."

"Then it should be just right." Mary Nell removed the tea towel from the top of the cup and tossed the tea bag into the trash. "I've got a confession, Daddy. I've been mad at God for taking Mama from us, just like you. And mad at myself for being so far away that I couldn't spend more time with her there at the end. This will be the first time I'll have been in church since she died, too."

"I understand." Oscar picked his newspaper back up and folded it neatly. "We needed someone to blame, and God is a good candidate, but maybe it's time for all of us to realize that maybe God needed your mama in heaven."

"He couldn't need her more than we do." Mary Nell sat down across from him at the table and pushed the paper over to one side. "You do know you can read the paper online these days?"

"Yep, but I can't put a computer under a project when I'm painting like I can a newspaper or put my boots on a computer when I polish them," he said with a grin.

"You got a point there." Mary Nell's earliest memory was watching her dad polish his work boots. She closed her eyes and could see the boots sitting on the newspaper and could almost smell the black polish that he used every night. From that her mind went to the last fight she had involving Kevin. He had gotten furious because she didn't have his cowboy boots polished and ready for him to wear when he went to sign the contract for a record deal. He had told her that he damn sure didn't need her in his life anymore, and she could pack up and be gone when he got back.

"I pay the rent and bills on this place," she had told him. "What you bring in doesn't even support all the demos that you are constantly making."

"With my signing bonus, I don't need you anymore. This apartment is in my name, anyway, and I'll be moving to something bigger and better than this dump," he'd yelled as he shoved his feet down into his unpolished boots.

"You can have your apartment," she said through tears that she refused to let fall. "The rent is paid until the first of this month. I'm tired of you and of doing the work so you can chase the glory. I'm going home to Texas. Don't write, don't call, and don't even think about following me when your so-called career winds up in the toilet."

He'd growled something offensive and then left. She had quit all three of her jobs that day and was on her way to Texas by dark.

"It wasn't the boots," Risa had told her when they FaceTimed after she made it home to Riverbend the next day. "That was just the excuse he gave for putting you out of his life."

"What are you thinking about?" Oscar butted into her thoughts.

"I might ask you the same thing." Mary Nell opened her eyes and took a drink of her tea.

"I was thinking of ways to get rid of Stella so she doesn't hurt those girls' feelings ever again," he said, "but they were all illegal, and would land me in jail. Just in case you ever do give me a grandchild or two, I don't want them to see me in an orange jumpsuit. Orange doesn't go with our red hair."

Mary Nell reached up and touched her flaming-red hair, which was so much like her father's. "It really doesn't, does it? But we could ship her off to a remote island somewhere and make sure she could never get back. Maybe the folks there would have church services twice a day and she would love it."

"Or maybe she could start her own church," Oscar said with a serious nod. "But for now, you better finish your tea so we can get to the parking lot about the same time as the other folks."

"I'd rather be going to the old church bar this morning," she grumbled.

"Me too, but even God rests on Sunday"—Oscar got to his feet—"and that don't change even if I'm angry with Him. And, honey, it don't matter if our bar is named Back Home, Danny's Place, or even the Honky-Tonk. Folks are always going to call it the Old Church Bar."

"I imagine they will." Mary Nell didn't really care what they called it as long as it prospered and she had a job. It had been a very long time since she'd been as happy as she had since Jessica and Wade decided to make a bar out of the building.

She slung her purse over her shoulder, crossed the kitchen and living room, and locked the door behind her when she left the house. Oscar had the truck started and the AC going, but in ninety-degree weather, the cab hadn't cooled down much by the time they reached the church parking lot. Haley, Risa, and the girls were standing beside Haley's car. Jessica and Wade were just getting out of his truck.

When Oscar had parked, Mary Nell opened the door and waved at the rest of the folks as she slid out of the seat and put her feet on the ground. Everyone started moving toward the front of the church, but no one entered until they were all there.

The building wasn't as big as the one they were remodeling into a bar, and it had a redbrick exterior instead of peeling white paint, but the steeple was still on the top of it, and the windows were stained glass. Mary Nell wondered if it had an evangelist room and who might sleep there. Churches could hide all sorts of things.

Oscar nudged Wade with a shoulder. "I didn't know you were coming."

"Had to drive Jessica anyway, and I can't let you go in there alone for the first time in years." Wade clamped a hand on his shoulder. "I'm here to support Risa and the girls, and to shove you out of the way if lightning starts flashing."

"Thanks, partner." Oscar laid a hand over Wade's. "I'll do the same for you."

"That's what friends and partners do," Wade said and removed his hand. "Are we ready to go face the devil?"

"If you mean Stella, I believe we might be," Oscar answered. "I'll bring up the front, and you can fall in at the back. We'll put the ladies between us in case there's a battle right here before services start."

"Sounds like a good plan to me," Wade said.

"It does not!" Risa stomped her foot in protest. "I'm leading the way with my girls right behind me. My mother does not need to think that I can't stand up for myself."

"That's my mama!" Lily patted her on the shoulder.

"Then get after it, girl," Oscar said. "Lead the way and we'll follow."

"Shall I call cadence as we march in?" Jessica asked.

"I'm wearing high heels, and I never was real coordinated," Mary Nell said, "so let's just parade in and sit beside Risa. The front two pews are always free, so I imagine that's where she's headed."

"You got that right," Risa said and opened the door.

Haley walked down the center aisle beside Risa. Both girls followed, and Wade and Jessica fell in next, leaving Mary Nell and Oscar to bring up the rear. The choir director had stepped up behind the podium when they paraded down the center aisle. The buzz of whispered conversations stopped abruptly, and a deafening silence filled the whole sanctuary. Usually Jasper, the choir director, had to clear his throat several times and maybe even tap the microphone to get everyone's attention, but not that morning.

Mary Nell could see folks digging in purses and pockets, bringing out cell phones. Folks' thumbs were doing double time as they sent messages to people who hadn't come to church that morning. She could easily imagine what they were typing: *Jessica Callaway has the nerve to come to our church this morning.* Or maybe it was: *Poor Stella will be humiliated that Risa has come to her church, and you should see the way her girls are dressed.*

"Got awful quiet," Oscar whispered. "Think they all might be considerin' leavin' the building in case lightnin' comes shootin' down past the ceiling fans?"

"Maybe so, or just leaving it in protest to us being here since we are all so evil." Mary Nell slid into the second pew on the right beside Jessica.

"I'd like to welcome everyone this morning," Jasper said. "Let's start off with a congregational hymn. We will begin our service with number thirteen this morning, and I'm asking everyone to open up your hearts and sing loud enough that the angels in heaven can hear us."

She settled for the second pew, leaving the first one empty. Jessica grabbed the last hymnal from the back of the pew in front of her and turned to the right page and shared it with Wade, but instead of singing, she leaned over and whispered, "Stella is right across the aisle from us."

"I can feel the heat coming off her glares," Mary Nell said just above a whisper. "Surely she won't say anything to Risa in a church house."

"We'll hope not," Jessica said out the corner of her mouth.

"Shhh," Wade said ever so softly. "We're tempting God as it is. We don't need to talk."

"Might was well get struck dead for a sheep as a lamb," Jessica told him. "And besides, I can't sing anyway."

Wade tried to sing, but his thoughts drifted, and he kept losing his place, so he finally quit. The last time he was in this very church, he had sat alone on the front pew. He hadn't heard a word the preacher said that day. Danny's closed casket was in front of him, and he felt as if he couldn't breathe. Maybe ten or twenty people sat behind him—a few of Danny's classmates, and some members of the church who never missed a funeral or a wedding.

He didn't feel like an elephant was sitting on his chest this morning like he had at the funeral, but sitting so close to Jessica sure put an extra beat in his heart. He liked having her in his life and was grateful to have someone to share the joy of a new venture with, who also understood his past.

After the singing, the preacher took his place behind the lectern. His sermon that morning was all about forgiving and forgetting. Wade wasn't ready for that, so he blocked the preacher out and thought about redesigning the bar. When the preacher asked an elderly gentleman to give the benediction, Wade bowed his head like everyone else and gave thanks that the service was finally over so he and Oscar could grab a burger at the local diner and go play dominoes with a bunch of older guys at Oscar's house.

He stood up with the rest of the folks and turned to walk out into the aisle. Oscar and Mary Nell had already stepped out in front of Stella, who had stopped at the end of her pew and glared at each person as they made their way from between pews. Wade could have sworn that the whole church was suddenly hotter'n a barbed-wire fence in hell just from the expression on Stella's face.

Haley, the last one to face Stella, nodded and whispered out the corner of her mouth like a gangster, "This is not the time or the place to create a scene. Not even God will forgive you for being ugly to your kinfolks in a church house."

Stella crossed her arms over her chest. "Don't you give me advice," she said aloud.

"Mother"—Risa took a step back and looked Stella right in the eye—"Haley is right. Don't test *me* in God's house or you might be embarrassed."

"You are a disgrace to me," Stella spat. "I don't want you in my church. Go find another one, or else just stay in that bar you're helping build on Sunday morning. I'll tell you one thing." Her finger shot up just an inch from Risa's nose. "There are some of us that won't take this layin' down. We are planning a demonstration at your bar on Tuesday evening, and we're asking the whole congregation to come out and sign our petition to the city council to revoke your right to build anything in that church. We would rather see it burned to the ground than have a house of God turned into a honky-tonk."

"Bring it on," Oscar said. "We will be waiting. Do you plan to just sing hymns as you protest, or will there be preaching?"

"We will sing God's hymns until He hears us and sends lightning to strike that place," Stella said. "I've been praying every night that God will set it on fire, and I believe He hears the prayers of his faithful Christians."

"That sounds like 'Lizzie and the Rainman.'" Lily giggled.

"In that song, Lizzie dances around a fire to make it rain. Are you going to dance around the parking lot to bring down fire, Granny Stella?" Daisy asked.

"Are you going to wear clothes or dance naked?" Lily asked. "Either way, I'm going to stand out by the road and turn this into a TikTok. It should be a great show."

"You!" Stella's finger waved over to include the twins. "You both should be put in foster care. Your mother isn't fit to raise you, and I don't even know what a TikTok is."

"Whoa, now!" Daisy took a step forward. "You are not going to talk about Mama like that."

Stella gave her a push, snarled her nose like a skunk had just sprayed her, and marched up the aisle with half a dozen women behind her. Lily caught her sister to keep her from falling, and said in a loud voice, "Did you just push a *child*? That was a mistake, Granny Stella. God doesn't hear the prayers of mean people. And as a fine Christian woman, you should know that Jesus loves little children."

Stella didn't even turn around, just kept marching forward and out of the church.

"I'm going to order pizza to take to my house," Haley said. "We can all meet up there and talk about this away from the public ear."

"You ladies go on and hash it all out," Wade said. "Oscar and I have a regular Sunday afternoon date with a bunch of guys for a domino game. We're going to grab a burger and get on out to his house."

"Besides," Mary Nell said in a low voice, "neither of you want to hear all the griping, do you?"

"You got that right." Oscar nodded. "See you all tomorrow morning at the bar, if it hasn't burned down by then."

"I doubt that very much," Jessica said. "Like you said, if God wanted the building to be a church, He wouldn't have knocked the steeple off the top of it."

Chapter Ten

*H*aley was so glad that the slight morning sickness had passed and she was able to eat pizza and breadsticks for Sunday dinner. During church services she had made up her mind that this afternoon she would tell the others about the pregnancy, but now that the time was there, she wasn't sure she was ready to confide in them.

"We need to practice," Lily said as she divided the last piece of pizza to share half with her sister. "Granny Martha might have been a bossy old girl, but she was right when she told us practice makes perfect."

"Yep," Daisy said as she took a bite of her slice. "Backyard or my bedroom?"

"We're kind of noisy, and these folks probably want to talk about the bar or Granny Stella's little hissy fit. I really thought she'd do something even worse than she did," Lily answered. "We better practice in the backyard. If I drop anything in your spick-and-span room, you'll gripe for a month."

"The whole reason I suggested the backyard was because there wouldn't be a place to even sit in your bedroom without moving clothes or shoes," Daisy shot back.

Haley bit back a giggle. "I sure wish I would've had a sister to banter with like you girls do."

Lily waved a hand around the table to take in everyone. "You do. Sisters don't have to be blood kin. They can be heart kin."

"Amen," Haley said.

Jessica and Mary Nell both nodded.

"Out of the mouths of babes." Risa blew a kiss toward the twins as they left the room, then waited until they were completely gone. Then she sighed and said, "Thank God for y'all. I got a text from Paul late last night. He wanted an address to send the divorce papers."

"Well, he certainly didn't let any grass grow beneath his feet on that, did he?" Mary Nell finished off her sweet tea and pushed her chair back. "Did he say what he was asking for? Is he going to fight you for custody?"

"No, he said it's just pretty simple. If the girls want to see him, they're free to come to Kentucky anytime. Other than that, he owns no property, and the only thing we have together is two vehicles. He gave me the oldest truck when the girls and I left," Risa answered.

"That sounds good to me," Jessica said. "I see we've all got empty glasses, so I'll just bring the pitcher to the table."

"Have you told the girls?" Haley asked.

Risa shook her head. "Not yet, but I will before bedtime. He said that he won't fight me for custody, but he intends to call them and give them the choice of where they want to live. They can either go back to Kentucky to live with him or stay here, but he wants to be a part of their lives."

"How's he going to do that?" Haley was glad to have something to think about other than that positive pregnancy test. "Is he going to drive down here for every school event this year? Or is he going to send them plane tickets to Kentucky for the holidays?"

"Probably neither," Risa answered, "but maybe they can FaceTime with him and the rest of the family."

Jessica couldn't imagine how it would affect Risa if either or both the twins decided to go back to Kentucky. They weren't even her daughters, and yet, just thinking about the hole their leaving would make in her own heart caused Jessica to go all misty eyed. She had served with the same team for years, knew when they had marital problems, when their wives had babies, and yet, she had never felt as close to them as she did Risa and the girls. Maybe Lily was right when she said that sisters could be of the heart.

"You don't think they'd go, do you?" Jessica's voice cracked.

Risa's chin quivered, and Haley laid a hand on her shoulder. "Everything will be all right. Those girls love you, and they'd never leave you."

"I hope not," Risa said. "They've been the only bright spot in my life, but they should be allowed to make their own decision. Martha was strict and overbearing, but the girls loved their cousins, and they had to leave their friends and the school they had attended all their lives."

"They should know that he's going to call," Haley said as she refilled all the tea glasses. "That way, they'll have time to talk about it and make a decision ahead of time."

"And not get blindsided," Mary Nell said and grabbed a paper napkin from the middle of the table to wipe her eyes. "That's tough, and I'm speaking from experience."

"Want to talk about it?" Haley asked.

"No . . . yes . . . ," Mary Nell stammered. "I don't know. It's been almost a month, and I kind of put the whole experience in a box and taped it shut. But here lately it seems like the tape is letting go, and I get so angry. One of the ladies I worked with called me a couple of days ago. She said that Kevin was flying high about getting a record contract, running up credit card debts and doing lots of partying, but something fell through with it, and he's back playing whatever gigs he can get."

"Karma is a bitch," Jessica said. "He'll probably show up on your doorstep, begging you to come back to Nashville with him, so you can be his meal ticket again."

"They won't ever find his body if Daddy gets ahold of him, so he'd do good to stay out of Texas," Mary Nell said with a long sigh. "He would probably be real smart not to even try to get in touch with me."

"Would you go back if he offered?" Jessica's chest tightened. They all four needed each other for mental support.

"No, that ship has sailed," Mary Nell said with a weak smile. "I loved him at one time, though, and I believed that someday he would get a break. He promised me that we would start a family as soon as that happened."

Haley's mouth went dry at the mention of starting a family. This was the perfect time to jump right in and tell them she was pregnant, but her throat had tightened.

The haunting sound of a fiddle floated in from somewhere close by, and then a banjo joined.

"Is that 'The Devil Went Down to Georgia'?" Jessica asked. "It seems like a strange song for the girls to be practicing their cheerleader moves to."

"Times have changed, but not that much." Haley smiled.

"They aren't practicing for cheerleading," Risa said and then laid a hand on Mary Nell's. "I loved Paul when I married him, but after we'd been in Kentucky a few months, I hardly recognized him as the same guy I'd eloped with. You're not too old to have a family if you want one."

Haley opened her mouth to say that she was pregnant, but Jessica got ahead of her.

"Would you have another baby if you remarried?" Jessica asked Risa.

"No, I would not." Risa shook her head. "I've got my girls, and right now I don't think I'll ever want to get married again. Someday in the far distant future, I might date, but I'm never living with a man again."

"Not even if he's not a mama's boy?" Jessica asked.

"I wouldn't trust myself to take that kind of chance," Risa answered.

"Who says I've got to be married and have a husband to have a family?" Mary Nell said. "I'm thirty-eight, for God's sake. If I want a baby, I can talk someone into helping me the natural way or I can go to a sperm bank."

"Thank God that we live in these days and not back fifty years ago," Jessica said.

"Amen to that," Haley said. All the doubts that her friends would think she was stupid for letting herself get pregnant by an engaged man disappeared. "We are independent women who can make our own decisions."

The music out in the yard changed to a snappy Irish song.

"I recognize that tune coming from the backyard," Jessica said. "I heard it, or something like it, when I was on R & R in Ireland a few years ago. A young lady with long black hair was playing that song in an Irish pub when I went with my team several nights in a row."

The fiddling and banjo playing changed to an old hymn, "I'll Fly Away."

"What are the girls practicing out there?" Jessica asked.

"Their fiddle and banjo," Risa said, "not their moves for the try-outs. When they do that, I watch them and give them pointers. Martha insisted that all the granddaughters take music lessons on the instrument of their grandmother's choice so they could play in church. Lily plays the fiddle. Daisy is on the banjo. One of their cousins played the piano."

"No boys?" Jessica asked.

"Sure, but they only played if they wanted to," Risa answered. "Girls played when they were told to get their instruments out. Like I've said before, boys and girls have different sets of rules in Martha's culture. The drummer was one of the male cousins, and another one played steel guitar. On Sunday afternoons, we all had dinner and the kids played for us. I imagine the girls miss those times."

"Men!" Haley huffed, but at the same time, she vowed that no matter what gender her baby was, the rules would be the same.

"Yep," Jessica agreed.

"Hey, you don't have man problems like us," Haley argued.

"But I have down through the years," Jessica argued back.

"Such as?" Risa asked.

"Such as she's got feelings for Wade, but she thinks she can't do anything about them because they are partners in business," Haley said, needing for them to talk about that to give her a while longer before she admitted that she was pregnant.

Jessica gasped. "Why would you say that?"

"Because it's the truth," Risa answered. "We can all see it, but you have to decide what you're going to do about it. We can't make that decision for you."

"Got any suggestions?" Jessica's face turned a faint shade of red. "I thought I'd hidden all those feelings fairly well."

"We're here if you want to talk about it," Haley said, "but don't let something good slip through your fingers."

Mary Nell pointed a finger toward Jessica. "We thought you and Haley were the smart ones who didn't get married or tangled up with a guy that just wanted you for the paycheck you brought home."

Haley held up both palms. "Don't go grouping me in with smart people. I've made my share of mistakes."

"Oh, yeah?" Jessica said. "Name one."

"I had a fling a while back." Haley stopped and took a drink of her tea. "I met him at a church social, and he wasn't wearing a wedding ring, so . . ."

"Did you find out he was married?" Jessica asked. "I flirted with a guy in Ireland at the bar where I heard the fiddle music. He tried to pass himself off as single, but I saw the white line where his wedding band should have been and told him to get lost."

"Nope, but I've decided that guys should have to wear an engagement ring just like a woman does," Haley answered.

"Then he was engaged?" Mary Nell asked.

"Oh, yeah, he was, and he didn't tell me until a few days before his wedding was to take place. He said I was his last fling before he had to settle down to the white picket fence and the van full of kids and soccer equipment that would come later." Haley's tone had a razor-sharp edge even in her own ears. "And to top it all off, he was marrying one of the teachers at my school. I'd even helped her pick out her wedding cake, but she referred to her fiancé as Mark, and the guy I met used his middle name, Andrew."

"Holy crap!" Jessica gasped. "You actually helped her pick out her wedding cake, but you had never met the man she was going to marry? How did that happen?"

"She had all these pictures of wedding cakes in the teachers' lounge and asked my opinion. We talked about how many guests she was going to have, and how much each cake would feed, and her colors, and then together we chose a cake," Haley explained. "We weren't friends—just barely acquaintances. I remember thinking at the time that she must have needed an outside opinion."

"That's one strange coincidence," Jessica said.

"Oh, there's more. Mark Andrew Roberts has been hired as the new principal in the school where I work," she said. "He lived south of Montgomery, and she had never brought him to the school to meet any of the teachers."

"Does he know that you are the counselor there?" Risa asked.

"He does now, but in his opinion, what we did was between two consenting adults and shouldn't affect either of our jobs. It won't affect mine because I will be sending in my letter of resignation tomorrow morning," Haley said and took a deep breath. Admitting the next part was going to be tougher than telling them about her fling with an engaged man.

"No! You can't let him have that power over you," Mary Nell declared. "If you *want* to stay in Riverbend, we'll all have a celebration if you do, but don't let that lousy rascal have power over you."

"Call me selfish, but I'm glad you're staying here," Risa said.

"Me too," Jessica added.

Haley turned to focus on Mary Nell. "Truth is that I'm taking all the power from him. I just found out last night how my biological mother, my sister in real life, must have felt when she found out she was pregnant. Only she was fifteen, and I'm thirty-eight. I'm sure the feeling is the same in both instances. I'm pregnant."

Total silence filled the room. To Haley, it seemed as if the ice in the tea glasses even stopped melting for fear of making a noise. The music in the backyard ceased, and the air in the kitchen was suddenly too heavy to breathe.

The twins came through the back door, laid their instruments on the cabinet, and stopped in their tracks.

"What's going on in here?" Lily asked.

"There's tension like we felt at Granny Stella's house," Daisy whispered.

"I'm sorry," Risa said. "It's not tension. It's confusion. Haley, would you tell them?"

"It's about a baby," Haley said. "I'm going to have a baby, and we were discussing whether I should tell the father. I was about to say that someday I will be honest and tell my baby why there's no father in the picture."

"Congratulations," Daisy said. "Do we get to still live here?"

"Of course," Haley answered. "I might even need a babysitter on the nights when I work at the bar."

"I love babies," Lily said. "I'll take the job anytime you need me."

Jessica rounded the table and bent to hug Haley. "We're here for you. Anything you need, you just remember that we're going to be the best aunts in the whole universe to this baby."

"But, Haley, don't you think you should tell the father?" Mary Nell joined them, making it a three-way hug.

"No, I do not. I've thought about it a lot, and he doesn't deserve to know," Haley answered.

Risa pushed back her chair and got in on the hugging business. "Whatever you decide, we're behind you."

Haley grabbed a napkin from the pizza place and wiped tears from her eyes. "I don't want to be the cause of his new marriage failing. That woman that I helped choose a cake is a nice person, and she doesn't deserve to have her life turned upside down. I wouldn't marry him if he was the last man on earth. Marriage means trust, and after what he did, I wouldn't trust him as far as I could throw him. Mary Nell, I know Oscar has been fussing at you about a grandchild. You can tell him that he can be grandpa to my baby since the little critter won't have any grandparents."

Jessica, Risa, and Mary Nell moved back to their chairs, and the twins rushed over to hug Haley.

"This little baby will be like us now that we've been tossed out, but Oscar is a wonderful grandpa role model, and he'll be so good with this new little girl or guy." Daisy finished hugging Haley and went to the refrigerator, where she took out a couple of Popsicles. She handed one off to her sister and went on to say, "We're proof that kids can get along just fine without a daddy."

"You are so right," Risa agreed.

"Daddy will be elated, and believe me, he will be first in line to babysit for you," Mary Nell said with a smile. "Look at us, solving problems."

"God, I'm glad to get that off my chest." Haley sighed and paused for a moment. "Thank you all for your support. Guess it goes to prove that the one percent chance of getting pregnant on the pill is a reality."

Risa nodded toward her girls. "I hope you are hearing this loud and clear."

"Yes, ma'am," they chorused.

"What if the baby is a boy? None of us have brothers or know anything about boys," Jessica asked.

"We'll learn, and besides, Paul has five brothers and all of them have sons. I've got a pretty good idea about how *not* to raise boys," Risa told them.

"And we've got Wade and Daddy to help us out in that area," Mary Nell said. "Now that the shock is over, I'm excited for you and for us. I'll be your birthing coach."

They all began to offer their services for coaching at the same time, and then Lily stuck her fingers in her mouth and whistled. For the second time everything went quiet in the kitchen.

"We're happy about a new baby, but that's not going to happen for a while. Daisy and I have come up with a plan that we would like to talk about right now concerning the protest Granny Stella is threatening us with," Lily said.

"We're all ears." Haley nodded, glad to have the conversation turned to something else so she could catch her breath. She had expected support, but the extent of what she had just gotten put a lump in her throat as big as a grapefruit.

"You've got the floor," Mary Nell said.

Daisy pulled out a chair at the end of the table and sat down. "We figure that they'll show up in the parking lot with their hymnbooks. So we thought we'd set up a table on the porch with bottles of cold water and some store-bought cookies on a pretty plate."

"That's sweet of you," Jessica said.

"Not really," Lily told her as she dragged a chair across the floor and sat down beside her sister. "Way we figure it, we don't want any one of those old folks having a heat stroke out there in parking lot, so we'll make sure they have water, and the store-bought cookies are kind of a slap in the face."

Risa refilled her tea glass. "How is giving them water and something to eat an ugly gesture?"

"Well," Daisy said with a giggle, "me and Lily are going to put another table out back between the church and the barn. We're going to make cookies all day tomorrow and have the good-tasting ones on our table, right next to a tub full of cold soda pop and beer. Then the two of us are going to play the banjo and fiddle for the folks who come around to the backyard. We'll entertain them until the last one leaves."

"Oh. My. Goodness." Risa gasped. "Mother will have a fit."

"Yep, and no one will even see her have it"—Lily nodded—"because she'll be the only one left in the parking lot when the evening is done."

"I love it. Bravo to you girls for coming up with this amazing idea." Haley clapped her hands.

"The bar will foot the bill for the drinks, and we can take the microphones from the church out to the backyard so that your music will be heard all the way to the river and beyond. Please make peanut butter cookies. They're my favorite," Jessica said.

"I want chocolate chip," Haley said. "That's what I've been craving all week, and now I know why."

"Any other requests?" Daisy asked. "We know that Mama likes sugar cookies. What about you, Mary Nell?"

"Cookies and doughnuts are my absolute weakness, so I'll eat whatever you make, but Daddy loves snickerdoodles," Mary Nell answered.

"Okay, Sister, we've got our orders and permissions," Lily said. "Now let's go upstairs and practice our cheer moves, and let these old ladies talk about babies."

"Old!" Jessica's voice went up an octave.

"You're lookin' forty right smack in the eyeball," Daisy said. "That's old."

They each took a bottle of water from the refrigerator and escaped up the stairs before anyone could say anything else to them.

"Men, menopause, kids, divorces, deaths, friendships," Jessica said. "It's a good thing we've got each other. My confession today is that y'all are right about this horrible crush I've got on Wade. I know it would be crazy for us to get involved."

"Why?" Haley asked. "Neither of you are engaged, married, or dating someone else, are you?"

"No, but we are partners," Jessica answered.

"We can almost see the sparks between y'all when the two of you are in the room together, so your confession doesn't shock us like Haley's did," Mary Nell said.

"Or like my girls' suggestion for the peaceful demonstration did." Risa shook her head. "Who would have thought those two would come up with a plan like that?"

"Like mama, like daughters," Jessica laughed. "And I've been careful, so how did y'all know about the attraction I have for Wade?"

"Sisters know those things," Haley answered.

"Nothing can come of it," Jessica declared with a sigh. "Like I said, we're partners, and it would be very awkward if we started something, then broke up."

"You'll never know unless you give it a try," Risa said.

"I believe the two of you are secure enough in your own selves that if you did break up, you could still be adult enough to make your partnership work," Haley said.

"Me too," Risa agreed.

"Honestly?" Jessica asked.

"I made a mess of my marriage, but that doesn't mean there's not a happy-ever-after out there for you," Risa said.

"And I screwed up my relationship," Mary Nell told her. "I should have walked out of that situation years ago, but somewhere down the road, I hope to find someone who still wants to have kids in our *old* age."

Jessica turned to face Haley. "We are not old. We aren't even really middle-aged yet."

"Don't look at me like that," Haley said. "I'll be staring sixty in the eyes when this child graduates from high school, and that is *old*. But if there is a happy-ever-after floating around out there, I hope you find it. You deserve it for everything you've done for us."

"Motherhood," Risa said with a smile. "My mother sure gives us a role model in what not to be."

"And, Risa, you give us a role model in what to be," Haley said.

"Here we are," Jessica said. "Risa is a mother with teenage girls. Haley is about to be a single mother. Mary Nell and I are jealous of you both because we want a family. We had great mothers, so we've got role models to go by. We've come a long way from those cheerleaders from twenty years ago, haven't we?"

"Speaking of that," Mary Nell said, "I got a letter from the homecoming committee reminding all former cheerleaders to get their forms sent in if they want to ride on the float. It was forwarded to me from my address in Nashville, and they'd like to have our answers by July first."

"Not me," Risa said. "My mother would throw raw eggs at me if I got on that float."

"If Risa isn't going to ride on it, then I'm not," Haley declared.

"Or me," Jessica answered.

"So the vote is unanimous. We will not be riding on the homecoming float for the cheerleaders," Mary Nell said.

"One for all, and all for one." Haley felt better than she had in weeks.

Chapter Eleven

The whole bar had smelled like fresh-baked cookies all day. Jessica, along with Oscar and Wade and the rest of the crew, had made several visits to the kitchen to grab one of their favorites right out of the oven. The twins had made cookies on Monday, but then they'd gotten worried about having enough, so they had decided to make a few more on Tuesday. They were just finishing supper that evening when a crunch of gravel and the noise of several vehicles out in the parking lot signaled the arrival of lots and lots of cars.

"Well, crap!" Risa sighed. "I was hoping Mama couldn't get enough people to come out, and she would give up on this thing."

"Or that maybe she was just blowing a lot of hot air when she made those threats," Jessica said.

"Not me," Lily said with a head wiggle. "I want a big audience for me and Daisy to play for this evening. Come on, Sister, let's get the two packages of plain old sugar cookies put on a tray and taken out to Granny Stella's table."

"You do that," Daisy told her, "and I'll start taking the platters of the good stuff out to the backyard."

Seeing the excitement in the girls pumped Jessica up almost as much as she'd been when she was being dropped into a war zone on an important mission. There was always that adrenaline rush when she and the team went into that mode, and she had thought she would never feel it again. This wasn't a life-or-death situation where she was rescuing a hostage, but it did make her feel alive.

She had always wanted a sister, but that evening, she wished that she'd had a twin. Someone who could finish her sentences, argue with her, and yet have her back when the going got tough.

You've actually got three sisters who are as close as twins would be. Her mother had popped into her head, and Jessica could swear she got a whiff of Chanel No. 5, the perfume her mother had always worn. When Jessica had cleaned out her mother's closet, her clothing still held the scent.

"Want me to take the cookies out to the front?" Jessica finally asked. "You don't have to deal with her and her protesters. I'll be glad to take care of it for you."

"No, that's my job." Risa picked up two packages. "I want Mama to see that I'm not backing down from any of this."

"I'll take the case of bottled water." Oscar tucked a twenty-four-pack under his arm and followed Risa across the kitchen. "This is more than I would have done for those lousy protesters, but it will show the folks that we aren't evil, I suppose."

"That's the idea," Mary Nell told him. "But if they want the good stuff, they'll have to wander around to the backyard."

Wade carried dirty dishes to the sink and looked out the window. "There's more cars out there right now than there ever was when Elijah had services here."

Haley, Mary Nell, and Jessica finished clearing the table and put leftovers in the refrigerator, then crowded around the window to peer out at the people climbing from their vehicles with hymnbooks in their hands. Stella looked downright proud of herself as she marched up to within six feet of the porch. With a straight back, and her head held high, she had plastered a smile on her face that said for everyone to look at her and know that she was wearing robes of righteousness.

More like self-righteousness. This time Oscar's gruff old voice was in Jessica's head.

"Think we should step out there to support Risa and welcome everyone?" Jessica asked.

"Yes, ma'am, I sure do," Wade answered, "but we don't have a microphone set up out front."

"I'm not a tiny thing," Jessica told him. "And I can be heard when I raise my voice. You just be there to push me out of the way if Stella brings a pistol out of her pocket and starts shooting at me."

Wade motioned toward the door with his hand. "Then lead on, and I'll stand beside you."

Jessica straightened her back and muttered one of the basic training cadences as she marched toward the front door: "They say that in the army, the chicken's mighty fine. One jumped off the table and started marking time."

Wade got into step beside her and joined in the cadence. "Oh Lord, I wanna go, but they won't let me go home."

"We make a fine pair, don't we?" Jessica giggled as she spun around on her heels and saluted sharply.

Wade returned the salute and opened the door for her. "Yes, ma'am, we surely do."

The crowd had gathered around Stella as if they didn't have any idea what to do now that they were there. The queen bee had given them orders, but now they waited to see what they were to do next. Several of the folks stared at the long table where cookies had been set on one end and a case of water on the other as if they didn't know whether they might be poisoned. Jessica clapped her hands, but no one paid any attention to her. Then Mary Nell rushed out the front door and handed a microphone to her.

She flipped a switch on the side and said, "Hold it pretty close to your mouth. It will beat trying to yell over the top of the wind and the folks talking. Poor things act like they don't know what to do. Stella didn't do a very good job of organizing it past getting everyone to come out here. They're acting like they're lost."

Haley came out of the building and went over to stand beside Risa and Oscar. Jessica glanced at all the members of her team, held the microphone close to her face. "Hello, everyone, if I could have your attention . . ."

"No, you cannot have our attention," Stella said. "We are here to pray to God that, if this church can't be used for a holy place of worship, He will send a tornado to blow it away or lightning to set it on fire. And we plan to sing hymns until it gets dark to show God that we are serious."

"Well, in that case, we will leave you to your prayers and singing in a few minutes," Jessica said, "but please know that there is water for when your throats get parched, and cookies if you decide you need a little sustenance for the next hymn."

"We don't eat with sinners." Stella raised her voice over the buzz of whispered conversations and the wind making little knee-high gravel tornadoes across the parking lot.

"Are you a Pharisee or a Sadducee?" Risa asked. "They are the self-righteous ones that ridiculed Jesus for eating with sinners."

"I am a Christian, and I do not even take a drink of water from a sinner," Stella yelled.

Risa took the microphone from Jessica. "Then I guess you'd all best go home and never go to a church social again, because if I've read the scripture right, it says that we have all sinned and come short of the glory of God. If you don't even eat a cookie or have a bottle of water because it's offered from the hands of those you judge as sinners . . ."

"I've heard enough of you trying to justify your actions," Stella shouted. "We will start by singing the first hymn in our books and sing one after another until God hears us and brings down his wrath upon this place. I'm asking that everyone sign this petition. It's letting the city council know that we do not want God's house made into a bar."

She marched forward, laid the petition on the porch, and held it down with a wooden cross.

"Would all the city council members raise their hands?" Jessica asked.

Not a single hand went up.

"I guess the council knows that we are outside the Riverbend city limits, and my lawyer assures me that we are within our rights to turn this building into a bar or whatever else we want it to be," Jessica said. "Now, y'all can get on about your singing and praying."

The wind rustled the leaves in the pecan trees at the end of the building and surrounding the parking lot, and carried the whine of a fiddle and the sound of a banjo around to the front yard. The tune was a fast bluegrass song that put Oscar to keeping time on the front porch with the heel of his boot.

"May I?" Wade asked as he reached for the microphone.

Risa put it in his hand.

"Y'all might want to sing really loud because we have a little show going on in the backyard that could drown out your music up here in the front of this building, and folks, that's what it is—just an old building that hasn't been used for a church in many years. It was a church, and now it's going to be a bar and grill. Risa will be cooking for us, so if you ever want to come out for supper, you're welcome. We haven't decided on a menu yet, and it could change from night to night. We'll be open at six and won't close until two in the morning. Now you can get on with your singing and petition signing." Wade handed the microphone back to Jessica.

Two older gentlemen left the group and meandered around the side of the building. Jessica and Wade followed them, leaving the crowd to sing their hymns, to drink lukewarm water and eat store-bought cookies if they didn't think either or both would be committing a mortal sin. By the time they reached the back of the place, several folks were already having cookies, drinking cold soda pop or beer, and finding chairs. The first two old guys waved them over to where they were seated.

"This is pretty nice back here under the shade trees," Amos Dailey said, "and if these cookies are any indication of what will be cooked in this place, then I'll be coming out here to eat."

"Me too," Fred Johnston said, "and I might just buy a beer or a double shot of Jameson and do a little dancin'."

"Why did you come out here tonight?" Wade asked.

Jessica suddenly recognized the two old fellows. They had aged in the past two decades, but she remembered they had owned the small grocery store in Riverbend. When she was a little girl, Amos would always give her a lollipop when she and her mother went in to buy a few items. He was tall and lanky and had lost what little hair he'd had way back when. His angular face had deep wrinkles, but his faded blue eyes twinkled when he smiled. Fred was short, and even rounder than he had been when Jessica left Riverbend. His plump baby face had few wrinkles, but his brown eyes were as full of life as his old business partner's were.

"We wanted to see what all the fuss was about." Fred popped open a can of beer. "Seems like Stella's been awful busy stirring up crap, and we just wanted to see if it was true. I'm glad we did. Those girls are really good on that fiddle and banjo and these cookies are mouth-waterin' good."

"And now we know that it is true, but we don't care what Stella says." Amos pushed up out of his chair and went to the table to get another handful of cookies. "But we wasn't expecting to have cold beer, good food, and entertainment. Hell, Wade, I ain't puttin' my name on that petition. This is fun."

"Me neither," Fred declared, "but it's a silly idea that Stella has cooked up anyway. I say it's a good idea to use this building for something. It's just going to sit here and rot away to nothing if you don't."

"Thank you." Jessica picked up a platter of cookies and began to move among the crowd that continued to grow with every song the twins played.

Wade followed behind her, stopping to talk to folks and inviting them to get something cold to drink, pull up a chair, and enjoy the music.

When Jessica's platter was empty, she went back to the kitchen to refill it and found Wade standing at the sink with a beer in his hand. "I had to come see how things were going out front. I can see everything from here."

Jessica joined him at the window and was amazed to find that there were only about ten people out there in the parking lot, and not a one of them was singing.

Risa had brought a chair out from inside the church and sat down at the end of the refreshment table. She would far rather have been out in the backyard listening to her girls play, but since no one was singing in the parking lot, she could hear the music just fine. She hoped that her mother and the remaining people saw her as being as cool as a cucumber, but on the inside, her stomach was a ball of nerves. They made it through two hymns, and then Stella glared at her and turned to say something to one of the few folks left to support her.

No one had stepped forward to add their name to Stella's on the petition. The wind swept the pen onto the ground, and the paper curled up around the wooden cross. A piece tore off and floated out across the parking lot.

Risa had to remember the bitterness in Stella's voice and the hatefulness in her actions when she had spoken to Lily and Daisy to keep from feeling sorry for her mother. Seeing all the friends she had thought would back her leaving one by one for the backyard, then watching the wind blow away the top of the petition—the very part that had her name on it—had to be tough.

"How are you doing?" Oscar brought out a chair and sat down beside her. "Those girls of yours are very talented. They could be playing for the Grand Ole Opry in Nashville."

"Thank you for that, Oscar, but they just do it for fun. Have they done any singing yet?" Risa asked.

"Not yet," Oscar answered. "How about this crew? Think they'll give up and go home?"

"I'm not sure what they'll do now. Mother has been whispering to the diehards that are still here behind her hand and glaring at me for the most part," Risa said and then smiled up at Lulu Swenson, her mother's neighbor, who had come over to the table. "Evenin', Miz Swenson. Can I get you some cookies and a bottle of water?"

"I thought I got a whiff of chocolate a while ago," Lulu said.

"You did, but you have to go around to the backyard for those," Oscar told her and then lowered his voice. "I know for a fact that you go up to San Saba to the Rusty Spur at least once a month. I've seen you there lots of times, drinking whiskey sours and dancing the leather off your boots. Why are you throwing in with Stella on this?"

"Shhh . . ." Lulu put a finger over her lips. "She's my neighbor, and she could cause a lot of problems for me if she thought for one minute that I wasn't upset about turning a church into a bar. Truth is, I think it's a good idea."

"Then tell her so," Oscar said.

"Not going to happen," Lulu said as she picked up a cookie and a bottle of water. "And don't you go tattling on me for going to the Rusty Spur, either."

"My lips are sealed as long as you keep your name off that petition," Oscar teased.

Lulu gave him a brief nod and went back over to stand with Stella, who now only had three other women with her.

"Can the twins sing as well as play?" Oscar asked.

Before she could answer, the girls' voices seemed to surround the church as they started singing "Hush Hush." Risa giggled at the lyrics, which seemed to fit the whole situation that evening.

"They're really good. They sound a lot like the Pistol Annies." Oscar kept time to the music with his foot and by patting his knees with his palms.

"Yep, and Lily can do a fairly good cover of Alison Krauss, too." Risa was proud of her girls. "Their other grandmother would have a pure old Kentucky hissy fit if she knew they were singing a song like that, though. She insisted that they only sing hymns and gospel music when we had family gatherings. I let them play and sing whatever they wanted at home."

Oscar pointed at the parking lot. "If you'll look at Stella's face, you'll see that their Texas grandmother don't like it any better than their Kentucky granny did. If her blood pressure gets any higher, we might have to tote her off to the hospital."

"How can you tell her blood pressure is on the rise?" Risa asked.

"Her face is red, and she's fairly well humming with anger. That would make a saint's pressure go sky high," Oscar told her. "Here she comes. Get ready for a sermon."

Little puffs of dust boiled up at Stella's feet as she stomped across the gravel parking lot. She picked up the wooden cross. "You haven't won!" She grabbed the paper, wadded it up, and threw it at the building, then stopped a few feet from the porch. "I'll keep praying, and God hears my prayers. The Good Book says to pray believing, and I do."

"Good night, Mama." Risa waved.

The girls had started singing "My Church" as the last of Stella's friends left with her. When Lily sang the lyrics asking if she could get a hallelujah, the whole crowd behind the building answered with a loud "Hallelujah!"

Chapter Twelve

"The name Back Home does kind of sound like an antique store."
Mary Nell yawned as she sipped her coffee and watched the sun
rise. Not long ago she would have been frosting doughnuts at one of
her three jobs, grabbing a sip of coffee when she could, not sitting on
the porch and drinking it at her leisure.

"I keep telling all y'all that folks are going to call the bar the Old
Church." Oscar poured his second cup from the pot he'd brought out
and set on a table in front of the porch swing.

The sun was just coming up, giving definition to the trees around
the property. She'd been born in this house, lived in it until she was
eighteen and went off to college, and now she was back in the same
bedroom that had been hers all those years. She might have felt like a
failure, going back in time, but she didn't. She felt liberated and free
at last. That tune to the old song by the Gaither Vocal Band that her
mother had liked so well came to her mind: the lyrics to "Thank God I
Am Free" talked about being like a bird out of prison, and that's exactly
how she felt.

"Doesn't matter what they call it. The lawyer will be filing the final
documents for the business license by closing time today, and he has to
have the name of the bar on them. I like Danny's Place, but I also like
Preacher's Bar and Grill." She set the porch swing in motion with her
bare foot. One of her first memories was of sitting on her father's lap in

the porch swing after supper. He would read a children's book to her. More often than not it would be a Dr. Seuss book because she liked the singsong of the rhyming words. Later on, when she was a teenager and far too old to listen to her dad read books, she had gotten her first kiss from a boy on that swing. The night before she packed up what she wanted and left with Kevin, she and her dad had sat on the swing. He had begged her to reconsider and stay in college until she finished her degree. Now she was back on the swing, holding on to the chains and listening to them creak with each movement. They seemed to be singing "Thank God I Am Free."

"I need to put some oil on those chains," Oscar said.

"The creaking is talking to me. They're singing one of Mama's favorite hymns this morning," Mary Nell said with a smile.

"Whatever it's singing, it's not on key." Oscar chuckled. "I kind of recognize the tune, though. Can't remember the name of the hymn, but it talked about being free as a bird."

"That's the one," she said.

Oscar tilted his head to one side. "I think they might be singing 'Danny Boy.' Think they're trying to tell us something?"

Mary Nell began to sing the lyrics to the old Irish song in her alto voice.

Oscar pulled a red bandanna from the bib pocket of his faded blue overalls and wiped his eyes. "You sound just like my sweet Nellie when you sing, and she loved that song. You should have been the one to try to get a toe in the door in Nashville. Kevin didn't have what you've got."

"What makes you think that?" Mary Nell took the bandanna from him and wiped the tears from her own cheeks and handed it back to him. "You know I can't ever let anyone cry alone, especially if it brings back memories of Mama."

"Memories of her are all we have left, so we have to cherish them whether they make us sad or happy." He stuffed the bandanna back into his pocket. "And I said that about your singing because Kevin can carry a tune and stay on key, but he doesn't sing from the heart and soul like you do. You feel every word that comes out of your mouth."

"On some songs, maybe." Mary Nell took a sip of her coffee and remembered thinking that every song on the radio was meant for her as she made the twelve-hour drive back to Riverbend from Nashville. She had sung along with some of them, cussed with others, and cried with a lot, but they had helped put distance between her and Kevin.

"I like Danny's Place," Oscar said. "It's got a nice ring to it, and it doesn't sound like a honky-tonk as much as something like the Rusty Spur or Longhorn Bar. That's what I'm going to vote on this morning."

"Me too," Mary Nell agreed, "and I don't think we need to add *bar and grill* under the name. Just plain old Danny's Place."

"Honey, there won't be anything plain about our bar and grill," Oscar said with another chuckle. "It's going to be the best place to eat as well as get a drink or a beer and do some dancing in Burnet County."

"What if things get rowdy?" Mary Nell asked.

Oscar stood up and flexed his muscles. "Then I get to be a bouncer. But we've thwarted a peaceful demonstration with cookies and entertainment, so maybe the twins could be bouncers instead."

"I don't think rowdy soldiers will respond to homemade cookies." Mary Nell started into the house.

"Maybe not." Her father got that twinkle in his eyes. "But one of them rowdy soldiers might be someone that you could . . ."

Mary Nell held up a palm. "Don't go there, Daddy. I'm thirty-eight and most of those guys will be in their teens or twenties. If I ever get involved with a guy again, you can bet your bottom dollar that I will take a lot of time to get to know him, and . . ."

"And," Oscar butted in, "he has to pass my inspection, and be as good a man as Wade."

"Don't go there, either," Mary Nell said. "I'm going to get dressed. Risa said she was making waffles this morning. I can almost smell them cooking. There are no sparks with Wade, Daddy, and I want electricity and chemistry and someone who makes me feel like a queen. And if I can't have the whole enchilada, then I'll just be an old-maid aunt to Risa's twins."

"That's exactly what a father wants for his baby girl—the whole nine yards, but not to be an old-maid aunt. You have such a big heart that you deserve a family," Oscar said with a nod.

Haley ate some crackers, drank some sweet tea, and lay very still until the nausea passed that morning. She wondered whether her sister or mother—or whatever she was supposed to call the woman who birthed her—had morning sickness when she was pregnant. Or whether maybe the birth had been so horrific for a fifteen-year-old that she made a vow to never, ever have another baby. Frannie had eloped with an older man when she was past thirty, and they had never had children, much to Nadine's, Haley's mother-slash-grandmother's, dismay. And then a couple of years ago, Frannie had died with a sudden heart attack, the same thing that had taken Haley's mother from her recently. She wondered if she would go the same way sometime in the future, but the thought disappeared when her stomach rolled again. She might die of nausea and not even live to see forty.

Everything was so confusing, especially at six o'clock in the morning, when her stomach was even rebelling against tea and crackers. But having Risa and the girls in the house helped her not to feel so alone. Lying there and trying not to move even an eyelid, she realized that she would never be alone again. She would have a child to take care of, to love and watch grow up, and she would have friends who were willing to be part of the village that everyone talked about when it came to raising children.

Someone rapped softly on her door, and then the hinges squeaked. Risa poked her head inside and asked, "How's the sickness this morning?"

"Not so good, but give me time to throw on some clothes, and I'll be ready to go. If you aren't going to let your mama scare you, then I'm not letting this baby control me." Haley pushed the covers back and was surprised that the crackers and tea had begun to ease the nausea. "See, it's mind over matter, and from what I read, this can all possibly end when the second trimester begins, so that's only a couple more weeks."

Risa came into the room and sat down on the edge of the bed. "I didn't have sickness with the twins, so I wouldn't know. I had a couple of sisters-in-law who were pregnant at the same time, but they had boys, and I always blamed it on that. Jessica, Mary Nell, and I talked, and we decided that you shouldn't be lifting and helping with the construction work. You'll be helping me out in the kitchen from now on. When I have to be away with the girls' school stuff, you'll need to know where things are."

"Yes, Mama." Haley managed a weak grin.

Risa air-slapped her on the arm. "I'm only telling you what you already know. You're the smart one of us, so use that big, beautiful brain of yours to take care of yourself."

"Look where smart got me." Haley's grin turned into a chuckle. "But now that I've had some time to think about it, I'm warming up to the idea of having a baby in my life. I've always wanted a family, but time kept slipping by, and it seemed like I always wanted more than a guy could give me. This was an accident, but it just could turn out to be a miracle."

"What do you want from a guy if you ever find one that you'd be willing to spend the rest of your life with?" Risa stood up and took a few steps.

"All the bells and whistles that go past just hot and heavy sex. I want to feel all tingly when he brushes my arm, or when he does something really sweet for me, like brushing my hair or giving me a back rub without expecting sex as a reward afterwards." Haley stood and went into the tiny half bath off her bedroom. She left the door open a crack so she and Risa could continue to talk.

"Do you really think men like that exist outside of romance books?" Risa asked.

"If they don't, then let's talk to Mary Nell and Jessica about making a pact not to settle for anything less than . . ." She couldn't think of the right word.

"Tingles," Risa finished for her. "I'm going back for a second cup of coffee. Holler if you need me. The girls and I will be in the kitchen."

When Haley had taken a quick shower and brushed her teeth, she felt much better. She laid a hand on her flat stomach and then turned to look at her reflection in the long mirror hanging on the back of the door. Her body was about to undergo changes, and life was never going to be the same. Her mother used to tell her that God didn't do anything by accident. He had a plan in everything He did.

As she stared at her curvy body, she wondered if her biological mother had done the same thing that she was doing that morning— feeling queasy and staring at a flat stomach that was soon to be bulging. Did her mother tell her the same thing about there being no coincidences in life? If so, then did Nadine give thanks to God that He had given her another child to raise, or had she done it out of duty?

You know better than that. Her mother's voice was so clear that a chill chased down Haley's backbone. *I could not have loved you more if I'd given birth to you myself. I am your mother.*

"Yes, ma'am," Haley said with a nod toward the mirror.

Dark clouds blocked out the sun by the time Risa, Haley, and the girls were headed out of town toward the old church. Risa shivered in spite of the heat that morning. She had hated storms her whole life. It seemed like they always brought more than flashes of lightning, crashing thunder, and hard rain. She could attach a storm to every single bad thing that ever happened to her.

"Looks like rain for sure," Lily said. "Good thing our jobs are inside, isn't it?"

Daisy covered a yawn with the back of her hand. "I love rainy days."

"Why?" Haley asked from the front seat.

"Because Mama would let us make cookies with her since we couldn't go outside and play. My first memory is when you let me and Lily stand in chairs on the other side of the bar that separated the kitchen and dining room in our trailer and cut out sugar cookies," Daisy answered. "I always liked to make angels and snowmen."

"Mine too," Lily agreed. "I liked to cut out Christmas trees and Santa Claus."

"Y'all wanted to cut those out and decorate them even in the summertime." Risa smiled. "I'm glad you have good memories, but I absolutely hate storms."

"Why?" Haley turned to focus on Risa.

"They remind me of hard times. Thunder was so loud when Paul and I eloped that we could hardly even hear each other's vows. The sun came out later that day when we were in a cheap motel, and then it stormed again when we went home to get my things and tell Mama I was going to Kentucky," Risa explained.

"It was storming when Granny Martha told us to pack up our stuff and get out of Kentucky," Lily remembered.

"But it wasn't when Granny Stella told us to leave," Daisy said. "Does that mean she might come around later on down the road?"

Risa made the turn onto the gravel road leading back to the church. "Haley, you are our guru when it comes to psychological things. Does this mean Mama will have a change of heart?"

"That's totally up to her," Haley said, "but given her past, I wouldn't put money on it. How does that make you feel, Daisy?"

"It makes me sad," Risa answered before Daisy could. "Not for me as much as for Mama. Granny Stella is missing so much by not allowing me and the girls into her life, and she doesn't have any joy."

"I don't want to grow up to be like her or Granny Martha—either one," Daisy answered. "That's how it makes me feel."

"That's good," Haley said.

As usual, a cloud of dust followed the truck as Risa drove back to the old church. She could see blue skies ahead of her and dark clouds mixed with a gray fog of dust in the rearview mirror. But she was in the company of her family—twins by blood and a sister of the heart with two more sisters waiting at the bar. If there were such things as omens, she had them all right there in the truck on the way to her new job. The dark times in the past would come to her mind occasionally, but the future held blue skies. Her girls were with her, and their memories were good, and what she had with Haley and the rest of the team went so much deeper than just friendship.

"I'm happy," Risa muttered.

"Me too," the twins echoed from the back seat.

"I will be when this morning sickness is over," Haley added.

"It won't be much longer, and then you can use the excuse that you're eating for two," Risa said with a smile as she parked close to the front porch of the bar but didn't turn off the truck engine. "Okay, ladies, today we have to vote on a name for the bar. Mr. Yandell, the lawyer, says all the final paperwork, now that we've all been approved for everything, is being filed today."

"We've kicked around a lot of names, but I really like the idea of Danny's Place," Haley said.

Risa watched a couple of squirrels play chase on the old church steeple, which still sat at the end of the building like a little child in a time-out chair. Should they put it back on the roof and paint whatever name they chose on it? Risa didn't think so. It had been knocked off for a reason. Maybe so that the building wouldn't look like a church anymore.

"Mama, are you thinking or worrying?" Lily asked.

"Thinking," Risa answered. "Oscar says they'll call it the Old Church no matter what we call it, but I think Danny's Place might stick better than Back Home or anything else that we've come up with."

"Even better than Wade's Place or Jessica's Place?" Haley asked.

Risa nodded. "It's just got a nice ring to it."

"Why are we even thinking about Danny's Place? Isn't that just Wade's brother's name that died a while back?" Daisy asked. "What's he got to do with our bar?"

"There's a story that Jessica shared with us," Haley answered and went on to tell her about Danny's dream of owning a tiki bar when he got out of the service.

"And Danny graduated with all four of us," Risa said. "If any of you have a better idea, then present it at the breakfast table, but I like the sound of Danny's Place, so that's what I'm voting for."

"Me too, but for now better get on inside and put on the coffee," Haley told them. "Now that the queasiness is gone, I'm starving."

"Danny's Place does have a nice ring to it. How did he die?" Lily unfastened her seat belt.

"Wade hasn't shared that with us yet, but I imagine it was in the line of duty," Haley answered.

Daisy slung the back door open and got out of the truck. "If I was going out to have a few beers and dance, I could say I was going to Danny's Place for a burger. It wouldn't be a lie that would cause Granny Stella or Granny Martha to drop down on their knees and start praying for me."

"Yep," Lily agreed, "and you old ladies better get a move on. The first big raindrop just splattered against the windshield."

"Old!" Haley gasped.

Daisy and Lily barely beat Risa and Haley into the foyer, and then the downpour began. Lightning flashed and thunder rolled. Risa couldn't help but wonder if the past was sneaking up on her and bringing trouble with it.

Wade jogged from his trailer to the back door of the church, dashed inside just before the rain started, and headed down the hallway toward the aroma of coffee and something that smelled like cinnamon. When he was only a few feet from Jessica's room, she opened the door and fell into step with him.

"Good morning. This kind of day makes me glad that I moved out of the RV. You should consider fixing up the last Sunday school room and moving inside," she told him.

"Good morning to you, and thanks for the offer, but right now, I'm happy in my little travel trailer," Wade said. "I smell cinnamon. I thought Risa said we were having waffles this morning."

"Yep, but she made some with cinnamon, some plain, some with chocolate chips, and then some with blueberries." Jessica's hand brushed against his as they crossed the bar area.

That giddy feeling that macho Texans and guys weren't supposed to have flooded through his heart. His hands went clammy as he stood to one side to let her go into the kitchen ahead of him. "Too bad we aren't serving breakfast when we open."

"We could put breakfast on the menu for those early morning hours," Risa said. "I'm makin' waffles to order this morning. Lily has had cinnamon with brown sugar sprinkled on the top. Daisy had chocolate chip with powdered sugar. And Haley is having chocolate chip with peanut butter and marshmallow crème smeared over them."

Wade chuckled. "I'm surprised she didn't want dill pickles on top of that."

"That actually sounds pretty good. I just might order that for my second one," Haley told him without cracking a smile.

"With a boiled egg on top?" Wade teased.

"No, with strawberries and crushed potato chips," Haley shot back at him.

Wade threw up a hand in defeat. "You win."

"I was serious," Haley said. "Risa, could you get strawberries next time you go to the store?"

"Of course," Risa answered. "What can I make for you, Jessica?"

Wade crossed the room, poured two mugs full of coffee, and handed one off to Jessica.

"Thank you," she said with a nod. "I'll have a Daisy waffle this morning, and Risa, please know how much we all appreciate you doing this."

"And I appreciate having a job and a place to live that's not filled with stress," Risa said as she poured batter into the waffle iron.

Oscar and Mary Nell came into the kitchen and set their umbrellas in the corner. Mary Nell pulled her shoulder-length hair up into a messy bun and secured it with a pencil. "I love the smell of fresh rain, and Lord knows we need it to settle the dust on the road and the parking lot, but it plays havoc with my hair."

"You're not getting a bit of sympathy from me," Oscar said with a deep chuckle. "I almost hate seeing the day we open the bar. I'm getting spoiled to us all having breakfast together and talking about our day."

Wade glanced around at his newfound family and sent up a little silent prayer of thanks. Then he realized that he had just thanked God for something for the first time since Danny was killed, and a tiny measure of peace filled his heart. He wasn't replacing his brother with all these people, but in their own way, they were each helping him to get past the anger he'd been harboring.

That's a good thing. Danny's voice was clear in his head. *Anger robs you of happiness and joy.*

Risa handed Jessica a plate with her waffles on it and turned to Wade. "What would you like?"

"Cinnamon, please, with powdered sugar on the top," Wade said.

His life had changed so much since that night he'd come out to the old church to get away from town. The parking lot had been his getaway place ever since Danny had died. It was far enough from town to escape the noise of traffic, and he could sit on the tailgate of his truck and look at the stars. Sometimes, a summer night breeze brought the pungent smell of the river up to him, and a few times, he could have sworn he heard a fish flopping in the water. That had to be his imagination, he thought, since the river was so far away. But the very idea of a big catfish stirring things up brought back memories of times when he and Danny had gone fishing at the dock after dark.

"Earth to Wade!" Oscar nudged him.

He left the past with a jerk and returned to the present, wondering what he'd missed. "Sorry, was someone talking to me?"

"Yep," Lily answered. "We were talking about making a decision on the name of the bar so that you or Jessica can call Mr. Yandell this morning."

"We've all cast our vote for Danny's Place," Daisy said. "So no matter what you decide, majority will win anyway. Oscar still maintains that it will be called the Old Church."

"Thank you all for this." Wade's voice cracked. "It means a lot to me. Danny always wanted for us to own a bar. He wanted one on the beach, but he would be honored to know that"—he stammered, then regained a measure of composure—"that he's being remembered this way."

"Then it's all settled. The formal name is going to be on the papers as Danny's Place, but we all know what everyone is going to call it," Oscar said. "Risa, I want one of those blueberry waffles. Can I do anything to help you?"

Risa handed the next waffles out of the grill to Wade and nodded. "Thanks for the offer, and yes, you can put on another pot of coffee."

"I'll do it," Mary Nell said. "You don't want Daddy to make coffee. He makes it so strong it will melt the enamel off your teeth. And soon as you get Dad's waffle done, you are going to sit down and let me make one for you while I decide what I want."

"I won't argue with you." Risa handed Oscar his waffle and took her place at the table. "I'll have a plain one with maple syrup. I say we make tiki drinks after work today to celebrate the formal naming of our bar."

"With umbrellas and fancy glasses?" Lily asked.

"I'll pick them up when I go to the store later," Wade offered. "And the liquor to make them."

"For us, too?" Daisy asked.

"Virgin drinks for you two," Risa answered.

Wade sat down beside Jessica and took time to look around the whole table at each of his friends. Apart from Oscar, they had all come back home with baggage, but with each other's help, they were unpacking it—one piece at a time.

Wade waited until everyone had left that evening to get into his truck and drive to the cemetery. He sat down in front of the tombstones and ran a finger over his brother's name, Danford James Granger. "I'm back, Brother, with some news that will put a tear in your eye if you can hear me. The team decided to name the old bar after you. It's officially Danny's Place, but I want you to know that Oscar still says it will be called the Old Church. I hope not. I want people to remember you and completely forget what that building was in the beginning."

A flock of starlings settled in the tree above the gravesite. They came in with force and noise but soon settled down to roost for the night. Wade shifted his gaze over to the empty plot next to his brother's place.

It didn't have a tombstone yet, but someday he'd have to write up what he wanted done when he passed away. Did he want his full name—Buford Wade Granger—on the headstone? His mother's maiden name had been Ford, so she'd used that in both her son's names. He'd always hated his first name, but that's what he'd had to go by in the army. After he finished basic training, the guys just called him Granger, and he didn't mind that so much.

"I can't believe how much has happened in such a short time, Danny," he whispered.

A couple of the birds in the branches above his head cawed at him for disturbing their sleep, but he just laughed at them. "I can't believe that I'm this happy. It's been a long time since you and I had a good laugh." He lowered his voice even more. "Having friends has helped so much. I wish you could be here and visit with the bunch of them. We've all got different problems, but they don't seem so big when we've got each other."

"Amen," Jessica said.

For a minute he thought he was just hearing her voice in his head, but then a shadow passed over him, and he looked up to see her standing behind him. "Jessica?" he asked, as if unsure it was really her.

"I'm sorry for intruding," she said. "Something made me all antsy, like just before we went out on a mission, and I decided to go for a drive. I don't even know how I ended up here. I parked the RV back there a ways, and just started walking through the cemetery, trying to find a place where I thought my folks would be at peace. I'm talking too much." She took a deep breath and sighed. "I should go now and let you finish your time here."

Wade patted the grass beside him. "Have a seat and meet my folks and say hi to my brother."

"Are you sure?" Jessica asked.

"Absolutely." Wade looked up at her. "Jessica, don't ever feel awkward or nervous around me. We're partners—and friends as well. Have a seat and let's talk about where to put your parents' ashes."

She sat down and sighed. "They won't be happy in the ground. I'm the only reason they settled down here in Riverbend. If they hadn't had a child, they would have probably stayed in the army and traveled the world."

"Why did they move to Riverbend?" he asked.

"Daddy's grandparents lived here, and he loved to come visit them when he was a little boy. Sometimes, his folks would bring him to stay with them when they were trying to get moved from one base to another, then pick him up a couple of weeks later," Jessica explained. "Uncle Elijah had stuck around these parts, so he would take Daddy fishing. Daddy had some great memories of Riverbend, and he worked at home on the computer, so he could live anywhere. As soon as I graduated and enlisted, they moved to Orcas Island. And I'm talking too much again."

Wade could have listened to her read the dictionary—or the back of a cereal box, for that matter—just to hear her voice. "Not at all. Go on and tell me more."

"We just had Uncle Elijah when I was growing up." Jessica reached out and touched the tombstone. "It's so cold, even now in the summertime. I'm going to take my folks back to the Palo Duro and spread their ashes out there, where Mama was raised."

"But your dad liked it here," Wade argued, "and you won't have a place to come talk to them."

"Daddy would want to be in whatever place would make Mama happy," Jessica said. "And I can talk to them anywhere, Wade. I've already proven that. On the beach in Maine. In a forest in Kentucky. In an old church parking lot."

Wade thought about how many times he'd talked to Danny while he was driving down that dusty old dirt road and nodded. "Yep, you're right. Now that you've made the decision, when are you going to do that?"

"When the time is right," Jessica answered. "I'll know when they're ready for me to take that step. Maybe if we have a few days between the finishing of the bar and the grand opening. But I really think I'd better be finding a different vehicle of my own in the next couple of weeks. It's not easy to unplug everything in the RV, and with no AC, it feels like I'm traveling in a tin can."

Wade laid a hand on her shoulder, and the chemistry between them got even hotter. "Jessica, what are we going to do about this thing between us?"

"I don't know," she whispered.

"Well, when you figure it out or want to talk it through, I'm here." He removed his hand and stood up. "Want to get an ice cream? You can ride with me, and then I'll bring you back to the cemetery to get your RV. That way you won't have to maneuver that thing through town."

"Yes, and thank you," she said with a nod.

He reached out a hand, and she put hers in it. The tingle didn't shock him that time.

At first Jessica didn't notice Stella and Lulu in the Dairy Queen ice cream place, but pretty soon she could feel the heat of someone's eyes on her and turned to see Stella glaring at her.

"Ignore them," Wade said out the side of his mouth as he stepped up to the counter and ordered a double dip of chocolate mint.

"I'll have a chocolate brownie sundae with the whipped cream and the cherries on top," Jessica said. Then she whispered, "It's hard to ignore someone who is shooting flames at me."

The lady brought their order and Jessica reached in her purse, but Wade quickly laid a bill on the counter and said, "Keep the change."

"Thank you, but—" Jessica started.

"Friendship has no buts," Wade told her. "Let's go sit in that booth over there." He pointed to the other side of the room from Stella.

"Nope," Jessica said. "Risa doesn't let that woman control her life, so I'm not going to, either." She marched across the room and stopped at Stella and Lulu's booth. "Good evening, ladies. Did y'all decide you needed something cold after this blistering-hot day?"

"We always come here for ice cream after Wednesday night church services." Lulu's face turned scarlet in a deep blush. "I shouldn't even eat ice cream when I'm trying to lose weight, but I always drive Stella to church, and she likes to come here afterwards."

"Are you following me just to make me miserable because of what happened at the old church last night?" Stella asked through gritted teeth. "If you are, you can go home to your honky-tonk and tell my daughter that I'm still working hard to make it impossible for y'all to ever open that place."

"Bless your heart," Jessica said.

"Explain yourself," Stella growled.

"I feel sorry for you. What we're doing has already been researched by my lawyer, and there's nothing you can do about it, Stella. I don't like you. You've been mean to my friend and her girls, and it will take a lot for me to ever forgive you," Jessica said. "Now, my ice cream is melting, and it would be a sin to let even one bite of this beautiful sundae go to waste while I was talking to you. So again, bless your heart, and I hope you take that exactly like I mean it."

"Well!" Stella huffed. "Shame on you for talking to your elders like that."

"Shame on you for treating your only child like she's dirt," Jessica said with a fake smile on her face. "Now, Wade, I'd like to go over to the other side of the place after all. I want to enjoy my ice cream, not watch it melt from the hot, glaring eyes of these women."

"Yes, ma'am," Wade chuckled and led the way to an empty booth across the room.

Jessica slid into the seat and dug deep into her sundae. "Sometimes, my temper gets the best of me. I'm sorry if that offended you, but I'm not sorry that I said it."

"Honey, if I hadn't had an ice cream cone in my hand, I would have clapped for you. I agree that the way Stella is behaving is a shame," Wade said.

"Someday she's going to be sorry." Jessica filled her mouth with ice cream, but not even the cold could take away her hot anger.

"My mama used to say that sometimes it's too late to do what you should have been doing all along," Wade said and then bit into the top scoop of his mint chocolate ice cream cone.

Jessica took another bite and noticed that both Stella and Lulu had their cell phones out. It didn't take a rocket scientist to know that tomorrow, folks all over town would be gossiping about what she had told Stella and would be wondering if she and Wade were dating—or maybe even sleeping together. To paraphrase what Rhett Butler had said in the *Gone With the Wind* movie Jessica had watched with her mother several times, frankly, she didn't really give a damn what any of them thought.

Chapter Thirteen

Three weeks seemed like forever in one way. In another, the time had gone by so fast that, looking back, Haley had trouble believing it wasn't just yesterday that Jessica had come home and they had all met out at the church parking lot. She flipped through a magazine that morning as she and Mary Nell waited in the waiting room for a nurse to stick her head out the door and call her name.

Name?

She laid her hand on her stomach and thought about what she should name the child. Should the whole team vote on it like they had when they named the bar last week? No, the name should be her choice, and hers alone. That decision made, she turned her thoughts toward her own name. Had her sister given it to her, she wondered, or had her mother? Frannie must have filled out the birth certificate, because Vanessa Haley did not sound like a name her mother would have chosen after naming her own child Frances Irene.

"Are you nervous?" Mary Nell asked.

"Very much so," Haley answered, "but at least I wasn't sick this morning, so the first trimester must be coming to an end."

"Do you have a good idea of exactly when you got pregnant?" Mary Nell asked.

"Not really," Haley answered. "I kind of figure it was the last night we were together, but it could have been before that. I thought I'd missed the first period because of stress."

"Haley Macall," the nurse called out.

Haley stood up and said, "Thank you for coming with me. Everything is still surreal, from Mama's death to us making the decision to work with Jessica and Wade, to being pregnant. I'm not sure I could do any of it without all of you."

Mary Nell stood up at the same time. "You are very welcome, but it's only by the luck of the draw that I got to be the one to come along today. Jessica and Risa are both jealous and sitting by their phones."

Thinking about Oscar holding straws in his big, calloused hands and letting Risa, Jessica, and Mary Nell draw to see who got to go with Haley to her first doctor's visit put a big smile on Haley's face. "All right then, let's go see if we can find out when this critter is due."

"'Critter'?" Mary Nell frowned. "Not *little angel* or *sweet baby boy*? And I didn't realize that I could go in with you. I thought I'd have to sit in this waiting room."

"Nope." Haley shook her head. "'Critter' is good for today. I don't imagine we'll know what the sex is until later, and right now I don't care if we have a boy or a girl. And support means you go with me."

"That's a great attitude," the nurse said. "How long have you been partners?"

"We're not partners, as in married partners," Haley said, "but we've been best friends since before we went to kindergarten. I will be a single mother, and my three close friends are going to help me raise this child."

"Well, it's great that you have that kind of support." The nurse led the way back to an examination room.

"Yes, it is," Haley agreed. "This is Mary Nell Wilson, one of those friends I just mentioned."

The lady pointed to her name tag. "Gloria Anderson. I will be your nurse through your pregnancy. We like to form a relationship with our patients from the start to make them feel more comfortable. The first thing we are going to do today is weigh you."

"Here's where we find out how much damage Risa's cooking has done." Haley stepped up on the scale. "We're remodeling an old church into a bar at Riverbend, and Risa will be the chef. She's been practicing on all of us."

"I heard about that." Gloria wrote down a number, but didn't say it out loud. "I can't wait until you've got it up and running. I love to dance on the weekends, and I'll be one of the first people to walk through the doors. Jukebox or band?"

"Jukebox here at first," Mary Nell answered. "Maybe a band later, when we get our bar legs under us. This is all new. None of us have ever done anything like this before."

"Long as it's music and the beer is cold, I'm good with either." Gloria pointed to an open door. "You'll need to undress in here. Put on the gown and leave it open in the front, then go through the other door into the exam room. Mary Nell and I will be waiting on the other side for you."

Haley stepped into the room, which was no bigger than a closet, and sat down on the bench to remove her shoes. Her hands trembled and went all clammy. She had never been claustrophobic, but the walls began to weave, and she couldn't breathe. She bent forward and put her head between her knees to keep from passing out. She had accepted that she was pregnant and the idea that she would be a single mother, but the exam would leave absolutely no doubt in her mind. Sure, she'd been sick and the test had been positive. But she'd told herself that the sickness could be stress, and the test could have been wrong. Hopefully, if her doubts had been right, the team would be relieved and not disappointed.

Finally, the dizziness subsided, and she was able to get undressed. She even opened the adjoining door into the exam room with a smile on her face. "I feel a little exposed in this thing," she said as she wrapped the gown around her a little tighter.

"We all do," Gloria said. "Hop up here on the table, and I'll cover you with a sheet. Dr. Jeannie will be in soon."

Haley lay back on the bed, and Gloria spread a fresh-smelling sheet over her. "You just rest a few minutes, and we'll be back to do the first ultrasound so we can determine a due date." Then she left the room and closed the door behind her.

"Dr. Jeannie?" Mary Nell raised an eyebrow.

"I did my research. She's the best OBGYN in the area. I had a female doctor in Alabama and really liked her," Haley answered.

"Are you nervous?" Mary Nell returned the magazine she had been looking at to the rack.

"Probably more than Frannie was when she found out she was expecting me," Haley admitted. "She was fifteen, and I'm thirty-eight, and yet, I imagine that I'm experiencing some of the same feelings that she did. When I first read Mama's letter telling me that Frannie was my biological mother, I was really mad at her—at them. I'm understanding and appreciating their decisions a lot better now."

Mary Nell stood up from the chair where she'd been sitting and paced around the room. "I can't imagine how nervous you must be, because I'm so jittery that I can't even be still. I can't imagine raising a baby all alone, but then I'm not as strong as you are. If I had been, I would have left Kevin years ago."

Haley drew the sheet up to her chin. "I'll just be glad when this visit is over, and I'm not alone. I've got all of you. Please tell me you aren't leaving and going back to Kevin."

"There's not enough dirt in Texas to make me do that," Mary Nell answered, "but I've got to admit that I might give him another chance if I was still living in Nashville. I've got a weak spot where he's concerned. I think it's the female version of knight-in-shining-armor syndrome. I rode in on my white horse and saved Kevin and his dreams. Down deep, I liked having him need me, but that's not what a relationship should be, is it?"

"Absolutely not," Haley answered. "What can I do to help you get over that syndrome?"

"Shoot the horse if I get on it and say giddyup," Mary Nell answered.

"I've never killed anything, but I will have my gun ready if I see you saddling up," Haley said with a nod.

A tall lady with gray hair pulled back into a ponytail at the nape of her neck knocked on the door and then came into the room with Gloria right behind her. "I'm Dr. Jeannie, and I'll be taking care of you." Her voice was calming and soft, and immediately the tension that Haley was feeling eased up. "I understand this is your friend Mary Nell and you've got a support team with the rest of your friends."

"Nice to meet you," Mary Nell said.

"Always good to meet friends of my patients who are willing to help them." Dr. Jeannie smiled. "Gloria tells me that you will be a single mother."

"That's right," Haley said.

"I am a single mom to a daughter who's now a senior in college," Dr. Jeannie said. "As women, we're tougher than folks think we are, and with a good support system, you'll do just fine."

"Thank you for that," Haley said. "I've been pretty nervous about all this since I took the test and it turned out positive. Motherhood at thirty-eight is scary."

"Motherhood at any age is scary, but you've got the advantage of maturity on your side, Haley," Dr. Jeannie said. "These teenage girls I see think that motherhood is finding a cute name and playing dress-up with babies like they're dolls."

Haley wondered if that's what Frannie had thought about when she was pregnant, and if she was the one who came up with the name Vanessa Haley. Did she ever play dress-up with her, or after she'd given birth to her, did she even help with the baby chores?

"I don't feel so mature," Haley admitted. "Being a single mother wasn't the way I planned to start a family."

Dr. Jeannie chuckled. "Me either, but I wouldn't trade the experience of having my daughter in my life for anything in this world." She extended her hand. "If you'll lay back, we'll get started and see how far along you are."

Haley put her hand in the doctor's and eased back on the narrow bed. Everything was going to be all right. If a medical doctor could raise a child and have a practice of her own, that gave Haley the courage she needed to do the same.

"We do things a little different here," Dr. Jeannie said as she pulled a machine over closer to the bed. "I will be your doctor, and Gloria will be your nurse at every visit, and I do my own ultrasounds rather than outsourcing them. So, let's get started. To me, hearing the heartbeat and seeing the tiny little being is one of the most exciting moments of the pregnancy, and I love being here to share it with you."

She folded back the sheet and gown until only Haley's belly was showing. "This will be cold at first," she said as she applied the gel. "You and Mary Nell can watch the screen and see your baby. Don't expect much more than a peanut right now." She turned a knob and began to run the wand over Haley's stomach. "The sound you hear is the heartbeat. Looks like you've got a healthy baby. Heartbeat is 140, and everything is looking good. You'll begin to feel fluttery movements before long, since you are already about to finish up the first trimester. According to this, you are ten weeks and three days along, with a due date of January fifteenth."

Haley did the math in her head. She had gotten pregnant that last time she had sex with Mark, as she had thought. That was the night he'd finally told her that he was engaged and getting married in another month. He'd been amazed that she was throwing a fit, because they had agreed that this was just a casual fling from the beginning.

All those thoughts disappeared from her mind when she realized that the thump-thump filling the room really was her baby's heartbeat. That little peanut she was seeing on the screen was a human being, and right after the first of the year, she was going to be a mother. The full impact of it all hit her with such force that it brought tears to her eyes.

"The heartbeat won't tell us a thing." Mary Nell handed her a tissue. "I did some research and found out that anything below 140 is a boy and anything above is a girl. If I'm reading that number on the screen right, it's right on the button at 140. Guess you'd better pick out a name for a boy and one for a girl."

"A healthy baby would be enough for me," Haley answered, almost breathless with emotion. That tiny little thing that looked like a lima bean was her child, and it already had a heartbeat. She fell in love in that moment in a way that words could not describe, and wondered if Risa had felt this surge of emotion when she heard the twins' heartbeats for the first time.

"It looks like you've got your wish for a healthy baby at this point for sure." Dr. Jeannie removed the wand and turned off the monitor, which made Haley even more emotional. She wanted to stare at her baby moving around a little longer.

Gloria took a couple of black-and-white images from the printer and handed them to her. "Here you go. The first pictures for the baby book."

Haley hugged them to her chest and wished that January would hurry up and get there so she could hold the baby instead of a picture. "Thank you."

Then she heard a sniffle and turned to see Mary Nell dabbing at her eyes.

"That was the most beautiful thing," Mary Nell said. "I'm so glad I got the long straw."

"It is, isn't it," Dr. Jeannie said. "There's just something about this first time that fills a mother's heart with love. I'll see you in a month, and Gloria will explain our scheduling to you, but if you have any problems, call us. Or if you have a worry about something, we're always ready to listen."

"Thank you," Haley said around the lump in her throat. Nothing had ever affected her like the images she held in her hand.

Dr. Jeannie wiped the gel from Haley's stomach and helped her sit up. "I'll see you in a month. By then you might be feeling a few little flutters."

"Thank you, again." Haley suddenly couldn't wait for every stage of the pregnancy, and planned to record every day in a journal so her baby would always know how much he or she was wanted.

Haley taped the pictures of the baby to the mirror above her dresser that evening. Her friends had looked at the two images so much that she was surprised there was anything left of them. Before she went to bed, she kissed her fingertips and touched the image. "Good night, sweet baby. We're going to have a wonderful life together, I promise. You'll have Wade for a male role model and Oscar will step in for a grandparent, and you've got three wonderful aunts, and two cousins that can't wait for you to arrive."

She was still too wound up from the afternoon to go right to sleep, so she reached for the book she'd been reading on the night-stand. She didn't have a good hold on it, and it fell on the floor and scooted under the dresser. Haley dropped down on her knees and felt under the piece of furniture that had sat in the same place in her folks' bedroom since she was a toddler. Her hands closed around the book, and she eased it out.

But the book in her hand was not the one that she had been read-ing. It was a worn copy of *Dr. Seuss's ABC*. She rolled over to sit with her back against the dresser and stare at the book, a faint memory coming back to her. Just before Frannie had left home to go off to college, she had set Haley on her lap and read the book to her. When she finished reading, she had hugged Haley tightly, and explained that she was going away, but that she would always, always keep her in her heart. She had even laid Haley's little hand on her chest and said, "You will always, always be right here, my precious little girl."

"Not *sister* or *daughter*," Haley muttered, "but *precious little girl*. I think she did love me. When I kissed her good night, her face tasted salty." She opened the book to the yellowed pages. "It seems fitting that I should read this book to you today since my biological mother read it to me," she told the baby growing inside her. She began to read.

When she reached the part about camels on the ceiling, an envelope fell out into her lap. She picked it up and found her full name on the front of it: Vanessa Haley Macall. She didn't recognize the handwriting as her mother's. Her hands shook as she carefully ripped it open and removed a letter written on lined paper with three holes in the side. She just knew it was from Frannie—and she was right.

Her eyes scanned the page, then went back to the beginning to read each word:

> My dear child,
> I'm leaving tomorrow, and I don't know if you'll ever find this letter. I'm your mother, not your sister. It kills me to leave you behind when I leave for college in the morning, but it has to be this way. I want you to know that your father was my first love. We were both only fifteen, and he came to work for my dad in El Paso. To make a long story short, I got pregnant, and Mama said that they would adopt you and raise you as my sister, and your father was more than willing to sign the consent forms before he went back to New

Mexico. His name was Larry Morino, and he died in a car wreck before you were born.

Leaving you is so painful that I don't expect I'll come back very often, but I can't leave without at least telling you how I feel and hoping that someday you will find this note in the last book I read to you. I couldn't take care of you properly at fifteen, and now that you are legally Mama and Daddy's child, I can't bear to watch you grow up and not tell you that you really are my daughter and not my sister.

Your father and I listened to Van Halen that summer, and "Secrets" was our song. I wanted to name you Vanessa Halen, though Mama said she would only concede to Haley. To her, Halen sounded like a boy's name, so we compromised. That's just a little bit of news that you might not know unless Mama finally decides to tell you about your birth.

I wish you all the best life can offer, and hope you grow up to be a well-adjusted woman.

Again, I love you,

Your mother, Frannie

Haley read the letter three more times with tears dripping onto the paper every time. When she finished, she laid it on the floor and sobbed worse than she had even at her mother's funeral. She wasn't aware of anyone knocking on her door or pushing it open and coming into her room until Risa sat down beside her and wrapped her up in her arms.

"It's going to be all right," Risa said. "We're here to help you however we can. Don't cry. There's lots of single mothers out there in the world, and this baby is going to be loved and spoiled and—" She stopped and stared at the letter. "What is that? Is it what your mama wrote to you? Why are you dragging that out tonight?"

"Read it," Haley said. "It's from Frannie. She wrote it when I was three years old, the night before she left for college the next day. Why was it under the dresser? Did Mama leave it there, knowing that I would find it when she was gone?"

Risa picked the letter up, read it, and then hugged Haley again. "She loved you. Now you know that she didn't just forget about you, but that she stayed away out of love. She wanted you to have the best life."

"Do you think if she was still alive"—Haley reached over her shoulder and got a tissue from a box on the dresser—"she would be disappointed in me? Here I am, repeating her mistake."

"No, I don't." Risa folded the letter and put it back into the envelope. "I believe she would be very proud of you, and who knows—maybe neither you nor this baby were mistakes. Until we are old and have time to look back, sometimes what looks like a mistake is really a blessing. You are smart and independent, and just remember that everything happens for a reason. We might not know what the reason is at first, but a few years on down the road we'll understand. Want to go out to the kitchen and get a glass of milk and maybe some cookies?"

"Yes, I do." Haley held on to the book with one hand and pushed herself up off the floor. "And I want to talk about the memory that popped into my head when I picked this book up. Frannie read it to me that last night before she left to go to California to college. I think she might have been crying when I kissed her good night."

"That means she was sad to leave you." Risa draped an arm around Haley's shoulders and led her out to the kitchen. "Sit while I pour us some milk, and we'll dip our peanut butter cookies in it. And tell me how you felt."

"Thank God we all came back home," Haley said with a long sigh. "Right now, I feel like you're the counselor instead of me."

"Good," Risa said with a smile. "That means I get to pay you back just a little for all you've done for me and my girls."

Chapter Fourteen

The air was heavy with anticipation, and the slight wind blew sand in Jessica's face. She stood perfectly still between the two houses and held her breath as she waited for the signal from her commanding officer. A high-ranking enemy had been spotted going into a place across the road with several of his team. Her five-person team's mission was to surveil, report back that the target was really in the house, and then quietly retreat after the house had been marked.

Things seldom went as planned, though, and suddenly, half a dozen men surrounded her, automatic rifles in their hands. Jessica's heart pounded so loudly in her ears that she hardly heard the first shot, but when the second one ricocheted off the stone wall of the house right beside her, her training kicked in, and she defended herself. Bullets zinged past her head, and men fell to the ground. Seconds seemed like hours, and she prayed that those who were dead weren't members of her team.

Her heart pounded in her chest. Her pulse raced. She tried to throw her gun to the ground, but it was glued to her steady hands. Her superior officer grabbed her by the arm and pointed toward three other shadows moving into the darkness. Light began to shine from windows out into the sandy yard, where no grass grew and where children played and chased each other during the daylight hours. Jessica's ears rang so badly that she covered them with her hands, and she began to jog, but when she heard the screams of a child, she stopped and turned around. A little girl had come from one of the houses and was kneeling over a dead body.

"No! No!" Jessica dropped to her knees. Her heart pounded in her chest so hard that she couldn't even hear her teammates yelling at her. Her hands were clammy and the rifle slipped away, landing on the dirt and sending a puff of sand into her teary eyes.

One of her teammates pulled her up, grabbed her rifle, and shoved her into a vehicle. They were all elated that they'd taken out a high-ranking enemy, but Jessica couldn't blink away the sight of that little girl crying for her father or maybe even her older brother.

"That little girl lost a loved one," she said.

"For the greater good." A teammate patted her on the shoulder.

"Get over it, Callaway," another one said. "You were doing your job. We rescued the hostage and took out a major player. This was a success."

"Tell it to that child," she said and turned away from the guys. When she got back to the post, she took a long lukewarm shower, but it did nothing to wash away the pain in her soul.

She awoke with a start, sat straight up in bed, and wiped the sweat from her face with the tail of her nightshirt. "It's just another nightmare," she told herself. She checked the clock and stretched out again.

This time the dream started after the gun battle, and the little girl who was lamenting had blonde hair. Jessica dropped her weapon on the ground and went to comfort the child, but when she got there, the man on the ground was Wade Granger. Jessica couldn't breathe, couldn't think, and her heart felt like a stone in her chest.

Wade awoke with a start and was on his feet before his eyes were fully open. He turned around twice, bumped his shoulder on the edge of the cabinet, and stubbed his toe on the corner of the booth that served as a dining table. Going back to sleep wasn't an option, and besides, it was just an hour before he would normally be awake and ready to go to the bar. He dressed in faded camouflage pants and a brown T-shirt with an army logo on the back and headed outside.

He made his way to the front of the old church, thinking all the while that Oscar was probably right about what people would call the place. He unlocked the door, eased it shut, and quietly made his way to the kitchen in the dark. He switched on the light over the sink rather than the overhead and put on a pot of coffee. It had just begun to drip when he heard Jessica screaming. His first thought was that someone had broken into the building and was hurting her. Without a second thought, he ran from the kitchen to the hallway and didn't even hesitate before rushing into Jessica's bedroom.

The only light in the room came from the two motion-detecting floodlights that had come on when he had walked across the parking lot. He glanced around for a split second, then realized that Jessica was flailing about, weeping, and screaming one word—*no*—over and over again. He crossed the room and sat down on the edge of the bed.

"Jessica, wake up," he said in a normal voice. "You are having a nightmare."

A fine sheen of sweat glistened on her face. A steady stream of tears flowed down her cheeks and dripped on the pillowcase. He reached for a tissue and gently dabbed away the moisture.

"Jessica, you have to wake up," he whispered.

"Don't be dead," she muttered as she reached out to touch his chest. "Please, God, don't let him be dead. I'm sorry. I didn't know it was you. I thought I was firing at an enemy. Wake up, Wade. Stay with me. I will never forgive you if you die. I need you."

Wade took her hands in his and held them tightly. "Jessica!" he said in a loud voice. "Wake up."

Her eyes popped open, but they were unfocused. She stared straight ahead into what Wade could only describe as an abyss. "Jessica, look at me. It's just a nightmare. I'm right here. I'm not dead," he said.

She turned her head slightly, and fresh tears flooded her cheeks. "I'm so sorry, Wade. Forgive me."

"For what?" he asked.

"I took you from your beautiful daughter, and she's weeping for you. If you can hear me, you can . . ." She stopped talking and sat up, wrapped her arms around Wade, and soaked the shoulder of his T-shirt with more tears. "You are alive. It was just a dream."

"No, darlin'." Wade pulled her even closer to his chest and gently massaged her back. "It was a nightmare. Was it about one of your missions?"

She nodded but didn't let go of him. "In my dream, I killed you, and your daughter ran out of the house, and I . . ." She leaned back and raised a hand to touch his face. "You are real, aren't you?"

"Yes, I'm real." He tried to smile, but it didn't work. He'd had the nightmares that were so vivid they brought on sweats and emotions so raw that words couldn't explain them.

"I could smell the blood and taste the sand blowing into my mouth when I cried," she whispered.

"I know," Wade said. "I've been there and felt the same thing. The dreams are so real that it's a wonder we haven't had heart attacks from them."

Jessica leaned into him again and laid her head on his shoulder. "Thank you for rescuing me tonight."

"Anytime, darlin', anytime," he said.

She leaned back again and stared right into his eyes. A kiss would start something that neither of them could finish, and yet he found himself drowning in the depths of her brown eyes. He dipped his head slightly and was about to taste her lips when the headlights of a vehicle shone through the window and right into the room.

Jessica jerked her head around, and his kiss landed on thin air. "It's too early for Risa and Haley," she said. "I'm going to see who it is coming around here at this time of morning." She hopped from the bed and headed out of her bedroom.

Wade followed behind her, wondering how someone could be so fragile one second and so fearless the next. "Hold up, Jessica. I'm going with you. It's probably just a fisherman who's going to walk from here to the river."

"If they start shooting at us, you duck, roll, and run," she said. "I've already mourned for you once tonight, and that's enough."

Wade opened the front door and stepped out on the porch just in time to see the bright red taillights of a vehicle driving out of the parking lot. "Whoever it was must've made a wrong turn?"

"No, they didn't. That was Stella's car," Jessica told him. "I got a glimpse of the bumper sticker that says 'Let Go and Let God.' She was driving it when they came out here to protest."

"She doesn't let *anything* go. Why would she be out here in the middle of the night?" Wade wondered out loud. "Do you think she's praying over us?"

"No, I think she's praying over the church and warning us." Jessica pointed to a piece of paper tacked up to a porch post.

Wade jerked it down and walked over to the end of the porch where the light was better. Jessica peered over his shoulder, and they read it at the same time. There was a hand-drawn cross at the top of the paper, and a quote from Psalm 58 below it: *O God, break their teeth in their mouths; pull the fangs of the young lions, O Lord.*

"Is she talking about knocking Risa's teeth out?" Wade asked.

"Or is she suggesting that the twins have fangs?" Jessica answered with a frown.

"I think she's calling on God to tear us apart as a team, so that we will give up on our idea of the bar. She's at least one of those people who are affected with BCCS," Wade answered. "Let's go inside, tear this up, and keep it between us. Risa doesn't need to know that her mother is pulling stunts like this."

"I agree," Jessica said with a nod. "They already know that she's mean, but this goes way beyond that. This is personal. It's not just against the bar, but against them. What is BCCS?"

"Bat Crap Crazy Syndrome. I'm not sure there's treatment for it, and I'm pretty sure there's no cure," Wade answered.

Jessica got so tickled that she snorted, and Wade thought even that was cute. There she was in a pair of pajama bottoms, an oversize T-shirt with Betty Boop on the front, and laughing hard enough to snort at something he said. The morning had started off just fine in his books.

"Do I smell coffee brewing?"

"Yes, you do." Wade opened the door and stood to the side. "I had just made it when I heard you crying out. At first, I thought someone had broken in and was torturing you."

Jessica crossed the foyer and the sanctuary, then right into the kitchen. "Do you ever wake up in a cold sweat and think that if you can just turn on a light, everything will be all right?"

"Yes, I do. Monsters are afraid of the light." Wade went straight to the counter, poured two mugs of coffee, and carried them to the table. He pulled out a chair for her and then sat down right beside her. "It seems like light dispels the darkness in our souls as well as the natural darkness. Do you want to talk about the nightmare? Is it the same one over and over?"

Jessica nodded and then took a sip of her coffee. "It was our last mission as a team. I was sent home to Maine a week later to get all the paperwork done." She told him the story in a monotone. "Tonight was the first time the little girl had blonde hair in my dream."

"Well, darlin', I'm alive and right here beside you," he said with a smile. "Ghosts don't make or drink coffee."

"Do you think we'll ever get over the dreams?" she asked.

"I hope so." Wade laid a hand on her shoulder. "According to therapists and army shrinks, talking about it with someone helps, but until now, I've not met anyone who understood."

"Well, I understand." Jessica patted his hand. "Thank you, Wade, for being there for me, and for not being dead."

"You are so welcome." He removed his hand and picked up his mug. "We can help each other get through this, but why do you think you dreamed that I was dead?"

"I think it's out of fear that something will happen because I'm so happy," she answered.

"I'm right here, and it'll take more than a nightmare to kill me. Evidently, I've got a little blonde-haired girl in my future," he said.

And I hope that she looks exactly like you, he thought.

Chapter Fifteen

Jessica relived the kiss that she had almost shared with Wade every night when she went to bed. Some of the time she blamed it on her fragile state when she came out of that horrible nightmare. Other times she wished that it had happened so she wouldn't have to wonder how the kiss would have affected her every time she looked at him—and that was often.

There had been no more threatening notes tacked on the porch posts, and when they'd gone to church the past few Sundays, Stella had given them dirty looks but kept her mouth shut. That evening Jessica carried all the condiments for hot dogs out to the table that had been set up behind the church for their big Fourth of July celebration. A big bowl of scooped-out watermelon balls was already there, covered with a towel to keep the flies from helping themselves to it, and Oscar was busy cooking hot dogs in the new firepit he had built for them.

"Independence Day means more to me this year than ever before," Mary Nell said as she and the twins set up chairs. "We are all free this year, kind of like that song that Martina McBride sang years ago."

"Amen," Jessica said, but she thought again of that kiss and wondered if she was really free or if she was yearning for something that could ruin an important friendship.

"Want us to sing that tonight?" Lily asked.

"But not until we have our fireworks." Daisy popped open the last chair and sat down in it.

"Yes!" Lily pumped her fist in the air. "This will be our first holiday in Texas, and we're celebrating with a whole sparkly show."

Jessica sat down beside Mary Nell and asked, "So, did you ever in your wildest dreams think you would be celebrating Independence Day with all of us at this old church? That you'd be leaving Nashville, and Haley would be pregnant and leaving Alabama?"

"Nope," Mary Nell said, "or that you and Wade Granger would be putting in a bar together, either, but it feels right and good. And I'm glad to be where I am. I didn't realize how unhappy I was with Kevin until tonight. A year ago on this holiday, I was in Nashville at the fireworks show. I was miserable. I was trying to shape my whole life around what he needed, what he wanted, and trying to please him."

"Why tonight?" Jessica asked. Then she pointed and squealed. "Look, everyone! There's a shooting star!"

"You saw it first, so you get to make the wish," Wade said as he came outside.

Jessica glanced over at Mary Nell for an answer before she made her wish.

"It's a feeling that's hard to explain, but I'm glad I'm here and not still there," Mary Nell answered. "Now, make your wish."

Jessica closed her eyes and wished for a real, honest-to-goodness kiss from Wade. Maybe then she would stop thinking about it.

Last year, Mary Nell and Kevin, along with some of his friends, had watched the fireworks show in Nashville at Riverfront Park. Like always, it had been spectacular, but Mary Nell hadn't known just how tense and strained their relationship had become by then, not until she came to Texas. As her mother often told her, she had finally put some distance between her and the forest she had been living in. The fireworks package that Oscar had bought for the twins was pretty meager compared to the tens of thousands of dollars that had been spent on the big show in Tennessee. But the laughter and the feeling she had that evening outshone every moment of the big show the previous year.

"And here goes the last one," Lily yelled. "Enjoy it, everyone."

A brilliant blast of red sparkles lit up the dark sky, and everyone applauded.

"Good job, ladies," Mary Nell told them. "Now what do we do?"

"I'm having another hot dog, and a bowl of watermelon," Daisy declared. "Maybe next year we'll have made some friends, and we can invite them to our show."

"Maybe even the cheerleaders, and Mama can talk Jessica, Mary Nell, and Haley into doing cheers for us, too," Lily teased.

"They can do cheers," Mary Nell said with a laugh. "Darlin', if I could find my cheerleading outfit, I couldn't fit into it. You'd think working three jobs would jerk the weight right off me, but it didn't."

"All that I own is out there in that RV or else in my bedroom, and there's not a cute little, short skirt or a tight-fitting top in either place. There will be no cheering from this woman," Jessica declared. "But I'm more than glad to give y'all some pointers if I'm not too *old* to remember how it was done."

"It's like riding a bicycle," Risa said. "Once you get on, you remember how to balance and how to pedal. Haley and I have been helping them with their tryout cheers, but you and Mary Nell are more than welcome to share what you remember."

Mary Nell shook her head slowly. "I'll do what I can, but it's been twenty years. I won't be doing any cheers."

Risa covered a yawn with the back of her hand. "Y'all can stay out here as long as you want, but I'm going to start carrying the leftovers inside. Then I'm going to go home, take a long, hot bath, and read a good book until I fall asleep."

"Awww," Lily whined, "can't we stay a little longer?"

"I'll bring them home after a while," Haley offered. "I'm wide awake, and I'll help with cleanup. I haven't pulled my share today. Go on home, Risa."

"I'm not going to argue." Risa stood up and headed around the end of the church.

Mary Nell heard a vehicle leaving, and in a few minutes, the crunch of gravel told her that another one was arriving. "I wonder what your mama forgot."

"Probably her purse," Lily answered.

A car door slammed, and then a deep voice yelled, "Hello, the camp."

"That don't sound like Mama or Granny Stella," Daisy said.

"Come on around and make yourself known," Wade said, raising his voice.

"I'm Landon Greeley. We were wondering if we could park here and walk down to the river to do some fishing." The light provided by half a dozen citronella candles showed a muscled-up kid who looked like he was either a football player or a weight lifter. He had dark hair and eyes, and his face was clean shaven.

Altogether a good-looking boy, but Mary Nell didn't like the way he was sizing Lily up. She recognized him as the youngest son of Billy Greeley, one of the guys on the football team when she was in high school. "How are you, Landon?"

"Just fine, Miz Wilson. Hello, Oscar. Hey, Wade." He tipped the bill of his cap toward them.

Oscar and Wade waved.

"And you are David Adam's son, right?" Mary Nell asked the shorter kid, who had red hair that touched his collar and a bit of scruff on his face that reminded her of Shaggy on *Scooby Doo*.

"Yes, ma'am." He nodded. "I'm Eli, the youngest of us five boys. Me and Landon will be seniors at Riverbend High this fall, and we're starters on the football team. Landon is quarterback, and I'm his backup."

"Go Gators," Jessica said with a smile. "All of us graduated from Riverbend High School."

"Meet Lily and Daisy. And Jessica and Haley." Mary Nell made introductions all around.

"Pleased to meet all y'all," Eli said. "Is it true that you're turnin' this place into a bar?"

"Yes, it is," Mary Nell answered as she pushed up out of the chair.

"Lily, would you and Daisy like to go fishin' with us?" Landon asked. "We'll have you back before midnight."

"Better not," Lily answered. "Our mama, Risa, isn't here to ask, but maybe next time."

"Sure thing." Landon nodded toward the other folks. "Thanks for letting us use the driveway. You girls want to walk us around to my truck? We could maybe hang out a few minutes. We're always glad to have new girls in our school."

"Sure," Daisy said.

"Are you really twins?" Eli asked. "You don't look a thing alike."

"We're really twins, and we hear that a lot." Lily tugged the legs of her denim shorts down and fell in beside Landon.

Mary Nell remembered those boys' fathers and hoped that they weren't anything like them. When she'd been in high school, the town had treated the football boys like they were royalty, but then that was understandable. Riverbend was a football town and had won the state championship for nine-man football so often they had to put up a new sign south of town to accommodate all the years.

"Let's get this all cleaned up," Haley said. "Like Risa, I'm beginning to feel a nice warm bath calling my name."

"I'm ready to go home when y'all get done, Mary Nell," Oscar said with a yawn. "It's been fun, and it's been real, but this old daddy is tired."

"Go on home," Haley said. "I'll drop Mary Nell off on my way home."

"Thanks." Oscar covered another yawn with his hand. "I'll help get the table and chairs inside first so you don't have to make as many trips, and then I'm going home." He folded and picked up four of the folding chairs, and Wade got the rest of them.

Mary Nell was putting things away in the fridge when Oscar and Wade finished their job. Oscar waved and told them that it had been a wonderful evening and left. Wade did the same thing.

"I need a cold beer. Anyone else?" Jessica asked.

"Not me," Haley said. "I'm driving and pregnant."

"I'll take one since I'm not driving," Mary Nell answered and slumped down into a chair. "This has been so much fun . . . and peaceful."

"That's a strange word for the Fourth of July." Jessica brought out two beers and handed one to Mary Nell.

"Thanks," she said as she rolled the cold bottle around on her forehead before she twisted the top off. "Maybe what I should have said was there was a lot less tension. I didn't realize how much stress I was living with until I got away from it. Reminds me of when Mama made Daddy get hearing aids. He said he didn't know what he had been missing."

"I didn't know Oscar had hearing aids," Jessica said.

"Me either." Haley brought out a pitcher of sweet tea and poured herself a glass.

"I'm sorry," Mary Nell said. "I should have done that for you. Come on over here and sit down with us. And yes, Daddy has had hearing aids for more than twenty years. He can't hear jack squat without them."

"I'm pregnant, but I'm still able to do for myself," Haley said. "I wish I could have a cold beer with y'all, but this will have to do."

Lily and Daisy came in like a whirlwind, both looking like they could chew up church pews and spit out Tinkertoys.

"Those boys already gone?" Jessica asked.

"Yes, and they can both go straight to hell," Lily growled and stomped over to the refrigerator. She pulled out two bottles of root beer and handed one to Daisy.

"What did they do?" Jessica asked.

"They told us that if we wanted to be popular . . ." Daisy blushed as she opened her soda pop and took a long drink.

"That what?" Haley asked.

"That we had to be willing to . . ." Lily's face turned even redder than her sister's.

"Put out?" Mary Nell finished for her.

Both girls nodded.

"Did they mean tonight?" Haley asked.

"Landon tried to kiss me, but I pushed him away. He called me a prude, and that's when he said what he did," Daisy answered.

"Eli said we'd never be popular if we were 'that kind'"—she air quoted the last two words—"of girls. Then they got in their truck and left."

Lily hiked a hip on the side of the table. "They said that . . . ," she stammered. "I feel my face turning red just thinking about it."

Daisy finished the sentence. "That since we were bar bunnies, we should expect guys to treat us like what we were."

"What did you do?" Haley asked.

"I slapped Landon so hard that he almost fell," Lily said.

"That's when they got in their truck and drove away," Daisy said. "I don't think they were really here to go fishing anyway."

"Did y'all sleep with the football players back then?" Daisy asked.

"We did *not*," Haley said. "I didn't have sex until I was in college."

"Me either." Mary Nell wasn't going to admit that the only man she'd ever slept with was Kevin.

"I'd been in the army a year and thought I was in love before I went to bed with a guy." Jessica pounded her left fist right into her right palm.

"I guess we might as well not even try out for the cheerleader squad if that's what it takes." Lily sighed.

"Don't let those rascals tell you what to do or intimidate you," Jessica growled. "If they ever come around here again, I intend to tell them to take their sorry butts back into their pickups and find somewhere else to park."

Mary Nell spoke up. "Don't worry about the tryouts. You will just meet in the gym and do your best two cheers for a panel of judges. Riverbend is a small school, so there's just a teacher who serves as a cheer sponsor. It's not like in the big schools, where there's a flag squad or props for the cheer tryouts. It's just you and the judges. The football team has nothing to do with any of it."

"That's the way it was in Kentucky, too." Lily stood up and carried her empty bottle to the trash. "We always wanted to try out, but Granny Martha said no. Please don't tell Mama about tonight," she said. "It would just worry her. She wants us to be happy."

"I'm telling her soon as I get home," Daisy declared. "We all three promised not to keep secrets."

Lily shot a dirty look toward her sister and then turned toward Mary Nell. "Would you tell your mama about something like this when you were about to be a senior in high school?"

"Senior? I thought you girls were sixteen," Mary Nell said.

"Our birthday is September the first. We'll be seventeen then," Daisy answered. "We'll be young graduates."

"I see." Mary Nell took a long drink of her tea. "To answer your question, yes, I would have told her. Mama and I shared almost everything."

"Jessica?" Lily asked. "How about you?"

"Probably"—Jessica nodded—"but mainly because I would have gone home so mad that she would have known something was wrong."

Haley spoke up before they even asked her. "Nope, not in a million years. I might have done something to get even with them, but

I wouldn't have told my mother, and Risa wouldn't have told Stella, either, would she?"

"Oh, hell no!" Daisy gasped and then clamped a hand over her mouth.

"Don't worry about saying a bad word, Sister. We are not living with Granny Stella or Granny Martha, and hell is a destination according to both of them, anyway." Lily patted Daisy on the shoulder. "So that makes it just a word, like Florida or Cancún, or Paris, France."

Daisy removed her hand. "You are right, and I'm trying out for cheerleader. We'll be the ones who change things if what they said is true. Besides, that was crude and rude of them to tell us that."

"Totally ungentlemanly." Mary Nell held up her beer. "To scumbags who think they can make any of us do something we don't want to do."

"Amen." Haley clinked her glass against the beer bottle.

The other three raised their drinks.

"To us," Lily said.

"To us," the others chorused.

Chapter Sixteen

*M*ary Nell could hear her dad whistling out in his moonshine barn, where he was working on a new batch of elderberry wine. She was sitting on the front porch swing with a glass of sweet tea in one hand and a book that she planned to read in the other, but the sunset was just too pretty to miss that evening. So she laid the book on the swing, which she pushed into motion with her bare foot.

Her phone rang, and thinking it was probably her dad wanting her to bring out a bag of sugar to the barn or maybe to taste the newest blackberry moonshine, she didn't even check the caller ID, answering instead with a cheery "Hello! You should come see the sunset. It's beautiful tonight."

"I would love to be there beside you." Kevin's words were slightly slurred, which meant he'd been drinking. "I miss you, darlin', more than I can ever say in words. I was a fool to let you leave me."

"*Let* me leave you?" Mary Nell's voice went up an octave. "You threw me out, told me you didn't need me anymore now that you were on the rise with that contract."

"Don't be mean to me, darlin'," Kevin said. "I had a lapse in judgment. It's the artist in me. You have to know I love you."

"No, I do not know that." Mary Nell was amazed that she felt nothing for him except anger that he thought he could sweet-talk her into another chance. "A person doesn't treat someone they love like you've treated me, Kevin, and I was a fool to let it go on as long as I did."

The phone screen went dark, and Mary Nell thought he'd hung up on her, but then it rang again, and this time he wanted her to accept a FaceTime call. She hit the right button and held it out from her face. "Kevin, it's over. I'm in Texas. I'm not coming back to Tennessee. Find yourself another sucker to pay the bills while you chase your dream of being a famous country music star."

"Look at me, darlin'." He let one lonely tear roll slowly down his unshaven cheek. "I'm begging. I'll get down on my knees if you want me to. I love you. I always have and always will. I want you to come home."

"I am home," she said. "Where are you living?"

"I was evicted from our apartment, and I'm just staying with one friend after another. I need you to ground me, Mary Nell. Please come home." He was almost whining. "Give me one more chance. I promise this time will be better."

Her knight-in-shining-armor syndrome came out, and it was on the tip of her tongue to tell him that she would consider it when she thought about her friends and how happy she'd been in Riverbend. Then she got mad at herself for even considering giving him a second chance—or talking to him, for that matter.

"No!" she said with such force that it scared a sparrow sitting on the porch railing.

Kevin's bleary eyes narrowed, and his jaw began to work like it did when he'd told her to get out of his apartment and his life. "I won't take no for an answer," he said through clenched teeth. "I'll get in my truck and drive to that miserable little Podunk town and make you see that your place is with me, Mary Nell. We are soul mates."

"I wouldn't do that if I was you. You'd be making the trip for nothing," she told him.

His bloodshot eyes glared at her now. "You are a selfish bitch," he ground out. "I took you away from that lifestyle and gave you something exciting. I gave you almost twenty years of my life, and you can't even give me a second chance?"

"That's right, but if we're honest, I worked and gave you all those years to accomplish your dream. That's long enough, Kevin. Don't come to Texas or—"

"Or what?" He cut her off. "Or your daddy will shoot me?"

"No, Daddy won't shoot you, but I will. I don't need anyone to do my dirty work for me. I'm perfectly capable of doing it myself. I'm hanging up now, and I don't ever want to hear from you again." Mary Nell reached up to end the call.

"This is your last chance for happiness." He was still talking when she made his face disappear.

"Who were you talking to?" Oscar asked as he came around the corner of the house.

"Kevin, but don't worry, Daddy, it's over," she answered as she scrolled down her contact list and called Haley.

"That's a good thing. I'd hate to have to go to prison right here at a time when we're all getting a bar ready to open up for business," he said.

"You wouldn't have to." She smiled up at him as she listened to Haley's voice mail message. "If he shows up here, I'll take care of him, and they'll never find his body."

"That's my girl," Oscar said with a grin.

Haley was on the phone when the call came from Mary Nell. She sent a quick text: On the phone. Will call ASAP.

She got one back that said: Meet me at the bar.

"I'm sorry," Haley said. "That was a friend. What were you saying?"

The woman on the other end had begun to sob. "I shouldn't"—she stopped and blew her nose loudly—"bother you with . . ." Another bout of weeping.

"It's okay, just tell me what is going on," Haley said.

"It's just that you were the counselor, and you helped me pick out my wedding cake, and I need to talk to someone, and"—she stopped long enough to take in a breath—"and my life is in the toilet, and I'm mad, and if I don't talk to someone, I'm going to go to jail for homicide."

"Sweet Jesus!" Haley muttered when she figured out that this was the very woman whose fiancé Haley had had a fling with—the father of the child she was carrying.

"I've been married a month, and I'm filing for divorce tomorrow," the woman said.

"Amanda?" Haley asked just to be sure.

"Yes, I got your number from the faculty list. Can you meet me somewhere for a drink? We need to talk," Amanda said.

"I've moved to Texas and am no longer affiliated with the school. I turned in my resignation a few days ago. I guess they haven't gotten around to taking my name off the faculty list," Haley said, "but I'm so sorry things didn't work out for you." Hopefully that fool hadn't told her about his little premarital affair with Haley.

"I should have listened to my mama." Amanda had gotten a bit of control and was talking in complete sentences. "I'm glad Daddy insisted on a prenup, or Mark would have taken me to the cleaners."

"Did you catch him cheating?" Haley held her breath for a moment for fear that he had told Amanda about the fling he'd had with her.

"No, he just came in an hour ago and admitted that he'd been seeing another woman since the night before our wedding. It's my . . ." Here came the sobs again.

"It's who?" Haley asked.

"She was my maid of honor." Amanda's voice went all high and squeaky. "He said he has found his soul mate, and as soon as the divorce is final, they are getting married."

"Oh. My. Goodness." Haley let all the pent-up air out in a whoosh. "Are you going to work at the school with him?"

"Oh, hell no!" Amanda said clearly. "But neither is he. He's resigned already and he'll be going to work for my friend's daddy in the oil business. He and Missy are moving to Mexico. I hope she's got enough sense to make him sign a prenup."

"That would be good," Haley said.

"Thanks for talking to me. I just needed to vent," Amanda said. "I'm going home to Marion, Virginia, for the rest of the summer. I'll find a teaching job around that area so I can be close to my folks."

"Glad to be of help," Haley said. "I wish you all the best."

"Thanks again. Bye, now," Amanda said.

Haley slumped down in a chair just in time to hear a phone ring again. She rolled her eyes toward the ceiling and gave thanks it wasn't her ringtone this time. She'd had enough of the past coming back to haunt her, and tomorrow she was changing her phone number.

Risa had just finished reading through the divorce papers that had come in the mail that day. Basically, the wording was easy to understand—she could have what she brought into the marriage, plus full custody of the girls, just like Paul had said. She signed her name on the lines where the lawyer had put a yellow sticker and slipped the papers back into the self-addressed, stamped envelope that had been provided, and tucked it into her purse. She would mail it tomorrow on her way to work.

The setting sun threw a yellow glow across the kitchen floor and reminded her of the color of that little sticker designating the place for her to sign the papers. "Yellow is my new favorite color," she said with a smile.

How do you really feel about that? Haley's voice popped into her head.

"Relieved," she muttered, "and yet a little sad that Paul and I won't enjoy being grandparents together some day."

Her phone rang before she could fully analyze her feelings, and she fished it out of the hip pocket of her jeans. When she saw that it was Paul, a dark cloud covered the sun and the pretty rays spreading across the tile floor disappeared.

"Hello, and before you ask, I signed the divorce papers and have them ready to mail tomorrow morning," she said in a curt voice.

"That's good. I want this over with." Paul's tone was icy. "But I want to talk to my girls, not you, and neither of them are answering their phone."

"They're in the backyard practicing their cheers," she said. "I'll call them inside."

"Cheers! You know how we feel about that!" he yelled.

She laid the phone on the table, crossed the room, and motioned for the girls to come inside. "Your dad is on the phone, and he's pretty upset about both of you trying out for cheerleader."

Lily marched over to the table, pulled out a chair, and sat down, then put the phone on speaker. "Hi, Daddy. How are things in Kentucky?"

"I just want you girls to know—" Paul began.

Daisy had gotten two bottles of water from the refrigerator and handed one to her sister before she sat down and interrupted him. "Hey, Daddy. What's going on? We haven't heard from you in weeks."

He started again. "I just want you girls to know that even though your mother has custody of you, I would love to have you come back to Kentucky and live here with your family. Your grandmother and I miss you very much."

"We miss the family, but we are happy here in Texas," Lily said. "Tell all our cousins hello for us next Sunday. We've been texting and keeping up with them on FaceTime. We're trying out for the cheerleading squad, and we've had a job working—"

Daisy poked her on the arm and finished the sentence for her. "We've been helping Mama out getting a restaurant ready to open."

"Paul, where are you?" There was the sound of a door slamming and then Granny Martha's voice. "Do you know what your daughters are doing? I just talked to Risa's mother, Stella, and she says that Risa and the girls have been helping a friend of hers turn a church into a bar. We need to rethink those divorce papers. I will not have my granddaughters doing such a blasphemous thing."

"Huh-oh!" Daisy said.

"I could strangle Granny Stella," Lily whispered.

Risa had to hold on to the cabinet for a few seconds before the room stopped spinning. Lily glanced back at her, and she pasted on a smile.

"I'm fine," she mouthed.

"Put me on speaker," Martha said. "I've got something to say."

"Girls, your grandmother wants to talk to you, so you are now on speaker," Paul said.

"As if we couldn't hear her before." Daisy stood up and crossed over to hug her mother. "It'll be all right."

"Are you both there?" Martha asked.

"Yes, ma'am," Daisy and Lily answered at the same time.

"Is your Granny Stella telling me the truth?"

"She wouldn't tell a lie. She's too afraid of hell for that," Lily answered.

Risa could imagine Martha's expression. Lips pinched. Eyes narrowed. Jaw working like she was chewing gum.

"If I could take you away from your unfit mother and bring you home where you belong, I would," Martha said.

Risa wanted to butt in, but clamped her mouth shut and kept quiet.

"But since Paul has talked to the lawyer and assures me that you have a choice, then I want you to know this. If you girls do not come back here before school starts and that abominable bar opens its doors, then you will never be welcome here again. Do you understand what you are giving up to stay in Texas?" Martha asked.

"Yes, ma'am," they said again.

Lily nudged Daisy on the shoulder and both of them smiled.

"Do you also understand that this family, including your cousins, will be ordered to have no further contact with you?" Martha asked. "I will not have my kinfolks associating with people who are turning a house of worship into a place of iniquity."

Risa bit back tears of pure, unadulterated anger. Neither Martha nor Paul had the right to tell her girls they couldn't even talk to their cousins.

"But, Granny Martha—" Lily started.

"That's the choice you have, and you know what you have to do to be a part of your family," Martha said.

"Daddy?" Daisy asked the question in one word.

"A house divided cannot stand," Paul said, quoting part of a verse of scripture.

"What happened to loving thy neighbor?" Risa asked.

"So, you're in the room, too?" Martha said. "This is not between you and me. I've banned you for your decisions. This is between the family here in Kentucky and the girls. I've spoken, and now we are ending this call. Goodbye."

Haley poked her head in the kitchen door and said, "Mary Nell has a problem, and we're all supposed to go to the bar to talk."

"Thank God!" Risa muttered.

Jessica took a cold beer out to the porch after work to celebrate the framework of the bar being finished that day. They had ordered the mechanical bull and the jukebox, both of which would be delivered the middle of August. The plumber was coming next week to do all the work for the bar's dishwasher and sink, and the electrician would be taking care of what needed to be done for the beer tap and the plug-ins for blenders.

She sat down and braced her back against the porch post where Stella had tacked up her vengeance warning and imagined a parking lot full of trucks and cars. Friday and Saturday nights would be their busiest nights for sure. That was a given. The sun dipped behind the rolling hills and pecan trees, bringing that moment of dusk before real dark set in. The tiny lights of dozens of fireflies flickered out across the parking lot.

"Hey, I thought I might find you out here." Wade came around the back of the church with a glass of sweet tea in his hands.

"I like to watch the lightning bugs and listen to the tree frogs and crickets. We didn't get much of that when we were deployed, did we?" she asked.

Wade sat down close enough to one of the other porch posts so he could use it for a backrest. "I missed the smell of the river when I was over there."

A soft breeze ruffled the leaves on the pecan trees that surrounded the parking lot and brought the scent of the Lampasas River. She closed her eyes and sniffed the air to get the full effect of what the wind was blowing toward her. "I'd forgotten about the way this place smelled when we all came out here, but I didn't forget the sounds."

"You could hear them over all that music and conversation?" Wade asked.

"I was here, but I wasn't here." She turned up her beer and finished off the last lukewarm sip.

"What does that mean?" Wade asked.

"I came with Risa, Mary Nell, and Haley, but I spent most of my time either on the back porch watching lightning bugs or thinking," she said.

Wade chuckled. "That's funny."

"Why?"

"Because I was behind the shed when I came out here," Wade answered.

"Kissing on girls?" Jessica teased. She remembered seeing him a few times, but all too often he would be there and then he was gone.

"Don't you remember me at all?" Wade sat down beside her. "I was the science and math nerd that everyone thought would turn out to be a professor in a junior college. Girls avoided me like the plague, because if they liked me, their friends would think they were crazy."

Jessica nodded. "I understand."

"How could you?" Wade asked. "You ran with the popular girls, and you've always been beautiful."

"Folks say that beauty is in the eye of the beholder. You must be nearsighted, Wade Granger," Jessica teased, but down deep she held on to the compliment like it was a lucky penny. "I was always tall, so most guys wouldn't give me a second look."

"Too bad we didn't know that we were hiding out behind the church and barn back then. Our lives might have turned out different," Wade said.

"Yes." Jessica bit back a sigh.

Her phone rang before either of them could say anything else. Jessica dug it out of the cargo pocket of her camouflage pants and answered it without even looking at the caller ID.

"Hey, Jess! Where have you landed?" She recognized the deep voice as that of Roger, one of her old teammates who had finished his last enlistment a few weeks before she had.

"Roger, it's good to hear from you!" she said. "I'm in Texas. How about you?"

"Still in Maine. Got a job opportunity for you. An independent security firm is working for the base here in Maine, and they need folks to train recruits for the jobs we had. Would you be interested? Pay is great, and we can put the old team back together in a way. We won't live in Maine. The training is done out in New Mexico and Arizona, and we're all used to that kind of hot weather and sand in our boots," Anderson said.

"I have a business going here," Jessica said. "I inherited an old church, and I'm turning it into a bar."

Anderson laughed out loud. "You're joking, right? You are definitely not a bartender. You are a soldier. You don't just turn your training off and on like a water faucet. It's in your blood. Let me tell you about the pay." He quoted her a figure so high that she couldn't wrap her mind around it.

"We're pulling out of—" she started.

Anderson butted in before she could finish. "There will always be wars and people like us who are trained to go in, do the job, and disappear. The recruits that will do what we did need good training."

Jessica glanced over at Wade and thought about Risa, Mary Nell, and Haley, who were all depending on her. "Sorry, but the answer is no. I'm settled in here, and I've found a home."

"Well, if you change your mind, you've got my number, and the offer is open ended for at least a year," Anderson told her. "But I still can't see you as a bartender."

"Tell everyone I said hello, and if you're ever in central Texas, give me a call. First round of drinks will be on me," she said.

"I just might take you up on that. Bye, Jess," he said and ended the call.

"Got a job offer, I take it?" Wade asked.

"Yep, and turned it down." She went on to tell him what Anderson had said.

"That's a lot of money," Wade said.

"You want me to call him back and see if he wants to hire you? You're probably more qualified to do the work than I am," Jessica pointed out.

"No, thank you." Wade shook his head. "I'm happier than I have been in a long time, and I'm not messin' with that."

"Me either." She locked eyes with him and could feel the chemistry flowing.

"I'm glad," he said.

The wind shifted and dust boiled up, signaling that more than one vehicle was coming their way. Jessica set her empty bottle aside and stood up. If that was those two rotten boys coming back, she was ready to give them a healthy dose of her mind. No one would treat the twins like they had and then be brazen enough to expect to have parking rights. No, sir! They could take their sorry little crude asses down the dirt path to the river, and she hoped that they ran over a sharp stick or a nail and got a flat tire. If it was Stella, she would tell her to take her robes of righteousness back to town and stay away from the bar, or church, or whatever folks wanted to call it.

She was surprised when Mary Nell's and Haley's vehicles came to a stop close to the porch. Wade stood up and tipped the bill of his cap toward her. "This looks like a hen party about to happen. I'm going out to my trailer. If you need me, give me a call."

"You can stick around," Jessica said.

"Not tonight. You gals just cuss and discuss." Wade waved over his shoulder.

"We need to talk," Mary Nell said as she marched into the building.

"What's going on?" Jessica asked, following her.

"Everything, and it's bad enough to get out the ice cream," Lily answered as she brought up the end of the parade of women and girls.

Jessica's red-alert senses were crawling—not totally unlike they had when she was out on a dangerous mission. Her thoughts went into overdrive and kept circling around to the idea that one or all of them were going to quit, and there was no way she and Wade could run the bar without their help. Maybe this was an omen that she wasn't cut out to be a bartender, and that she should call Roger Anderson back and talk to him about that job.

She followed all of them into the kitchen. Mary Nell had taken a gallon of sweet tea from the fridge, and Haley was putting ice in six glasses. Risa had brought out a loaf of banana nut bread and set it on the table with half a gallon of butter brickle ice cream and six spoons stuck in it.

"This must be some serious stuff," Jessica said.

"When we get out ice cream, you can bet your sweet ass it's serious," Daisy said.

"Daisy!" Risa scolded.

"That is not a cuss word. It's in the Bible. Jesus rode on an ass. Maybe that little donkey was a sweet ass." Daisy dug deep into the ice cream and put a heaping spoonful in her mouth.

"What is going on?" Jessica asked. "All of you look like you fought with the devil, and he won. Please don't tell me you aren't staying in Riverbend."

"It's my problem," Mary Nell said. "I did battle with the devil, but he damn sure didn't win." She went on to tell them about Kevin's phone call. "I feel like a new person since I stood up for myself with him, but I got to admit, for a split second, I thought about giving him a second chance."

"I'm proud of you," Haley said, "but this must be the night for the past to come back and haunt us. I got a phone call, too." She told them all about Amanda's call.

"How did that make you feel?" Risa asked.

Haley grinned. "That's my line, but it made me feel all kinds of mixed emotions. Anger at Mark for what he did to me and Amanda both. Pity for her, and guilt for me not stepping up and telling her what a son of a bitch he was before she married him."

"That's quite a load for you to carry with the pregnancy and all," Risa said with a sigh.

"Yep, it is," Haley said with a nod, "but y'all are helping me carry it."

"I can agree with that," Mary Nell said. "When I was just about to say I'd give Kevin a second chance, I thought of the happiness I'd found here with y'all. Life is good."

"Agree," Haley said.

"I've got a confession, too," Jessica said. "I got a call from one of my military team with a job offer, but it's not a big thing like Mary Nell. I turned him down. He told me that the job was open for a year if I change my mind. Y'all want to move to Arizona or New Mexico if the bar goes belly up?"

"Oh, hell no!" Haley gasped. "I don't like to sweat, and it gets hotter out there than it does here in Texas. Why would you ask us if we want to go anyway? Did the job offer say you could bring along three friends?"

"And a set of twins?" Daisy asked.

"No, but I sure wouldn't go without you. Risa could get a job at any restaurant on the base, and Mary Nell could keep books, and Haley, you wouldn't need much schooling to be a full-fledged therapist. If they want me, they have to take us all," Jessica answered and winked at Daisy, "including a set of twin girls. But like Mary Nell and Haley, I don't want to leave what we've got here."

Tears ran down Mary Nell's face and dripped onto her shirt. "I couldn't leave what we have and go back to the stress I was living under. We were best friends when we were in high school, but now that we're grown up, we're more like family."

Haley draped an arm around Mary Nell's shoulder and patted her. "I feel the same way. It must be the night for throwing doubts at us, though."

"You too?" Jessica picked up one of the spoons and took her first bite of ice cream.

"This all sounds like a bad soap opera, and we haven't even added our episode to it." Lily licked the spoon she'd been using and carried it and her empty tea glass to the dishwasher. "But mine and Daisy's story is just as bad. Daddy called. Granny Martha came in while he was talking, and . . ."

"She laid down the law," Daisy finished, then went on to tell them what had happened. "Maybe we should all just toss our phones in the trash and get new ones and new numbers."

Jessica glanced across the table at Risa. Her hands trembled so badly that she almost dropped the spoon when she dug into the ice cream. It didn't take a genius to know that all this had shaken her up pretty badly.

"Are you okay?" Jessica asked.

"I had just signed the divorce papers when the phone call came from him." Risa felt totally empty inside just thinking about how cruel Martha had been, yet angry at the same time at Paul for not ever standing up to his mother. "Martha said I was an unfit mother. Do you think she would pressure Paul to get into a custody battle with me?"

"She might," Mary Nell said, "but they can't win. By the time they could even get anything started, the girls would be seventeen. If he makes good on his threat, we'll all pitch in to pay for a good lawyer to fight him."

"Lily and I can make cookies and sell them all over town to raise money for a lawyer," Daisy offered. "I don't want to go back to Kentucky. I might have wanted to if we still had to live with Granny Stella, but now that we've got a home with Haley, I don't want to leave Texas."

"You think Granny Stella is worse than Granny Martha?" Lily asked.

"Yes, I do. Granny Martha is bossy and has to rule the whole family, but Granny Stella is even meaner," Daisy declared.

"We won't take no for an answer if it comes to a custody fight, and you girls won't have to peddle homemade cookies all over town," Haley told them. "Like Mary Nell said, we'll pool our money, and if I have to, I'll sell the house and we'll all move in the extra Sunday school rooms."

"Thank you!" Daisy and Lily said in unison and high-fived each other.

Mary Nell took another bite of ice cream. "What was it that the old pirates used to say?"

"All for one," Lily quoted.

"And one for all," Daisy finished for her.

"Thank God we've all got each other," Jessica told them. "Did you tell Oscar about Kevin's call?"

"Yes, I did," Mary Nell answered, "and when I get home, I'll tell him about Paul's call to the girls, too. He's kind of adopted them as his grandkids. My first thought was to call Haley and get us all together. I felt so sorry for Kevin until I realized that he was just playing me, again, and that he hasn't changed, and all he wants is a person to support him while he follows his dream."

"I understand." Risa had friends—no, she had a family—who would stand behind her. That was more than she'd ever had, and there was no way she would take it for granted. "All Paul wants is a woman who won't fuss about him putting another deer head on the living room wall or another mounted squirrel on the end table. Our house looked like a taxidermy shop."

"Jessica is the only smart one amongst us," Haley added. "She didn't get married or involved with a loser."

Jessica held up her half-empty tea glass. "I made my fair share of mistakes along the way, believe me. I had a couple of fairly long relationships that went in the crapper because I was afraid of commitment."

"Details?" Daisy asked.

"No, ma'am." Jessica shook her head. "They aren't even worth talking about, but rest assured, I've learned my lesson."

"That mean you're not afraid of commitment anymore?" Lily asked.

"It means that I'm trying to put down roots. Before now, I couldn't let myself get serious because of my job, and because of the fact that at any time I could be sent away on deployment for a year or more. And I very likely couldn't even have been allowed to tell the person I was with where I was going, or what I had done while I was gone when I got home. That's no way to enter into a relationship," Jessica said.

"I understand," Haley said. "That would have been rough."

"Yep," Jessica agreed, "but when we get the bar built and everything up and running full speed ahead, I just might be ready to think about a relationship."

"And we get to decide if the guy is good enough to join our team, right?" Lily teased.

Jessica made a motion with her hand. "All of you do. I wouldn't make a decision like that without one of our sessions like this."

She bit back a smile when she thought about Wade saying that they were about to have a hen party. *Thank God for us hens,* she thought as she finished off her tea, then wondered if she should have suggested naming the bar the Hen House.

Chapter Seventeen

When Risa was nervous, she cooked. When she was happy, she cooked. When she was sad, she cooked. The morning the girls took the truck and drove to the school for cheerleader tryouts, she experienced all three emotions, so she made banana bread, orange-date bread, and zucchini bread to put in the freezer. In between times, while the breads were baking, she helped do whatever she could out in the bar. The plumber and the electrician had both taken care of their jobs, and now Wade and Oscar were putting up the long pieces of oakwood they had salvaged from the pews. The big room was beginning to look less and less like a church and more like it had originally been built for a bar.

"Are you going to survive this morning?" Jessica asked as she and Haley held a length of oak for Oscar to put in place with screws.

"I'm not nervous." Risa almost crossed her fingers behind her back. "They've practiced hard, and"—she plopped down in a chair—"I don't want them to be cheerleaders. Not because of anything religious, but because I don't have good memories of our senior year."

"Truth is, I don't, either," Jessica admitted. "I liked spending time with you all. I guess that's why I didn't come back for the homecoming thing."

"Mama made such a fuss about me being out there in a short skirt and showing my 'hind end'"—Risa air quoted the last two words—"that

I wished I'd never even tried out, but like you, I wanted to spend time with y'all. And yes, I'm nervous. I'm happy, and I'm sad. How a person can be all three of those at the same time is a mystery, but it's the truth."

"There's no mystery, my friend, and it's perfectly understandable. You are happy because the girls are getting to do something they've wanted for a while, and their Kentucky grandma wouldn't hear of it. You're nervous because you're worried about how they'll fit in if they do make the squad. And you're sad because you are worried that they will be upset if they don't get chosen, and also because down deep you don't want them to have to deal with all it entails," Jessica told her.

"Hey, what did we miss?" Mary Nell and Haley came into the bar and sat down on the pulpit with Risa and Jessica.

"Risa is cooking," Jessica answered.

"We all know that she cooks when she's on an emotional roller coaster," Mary Nell said. "So, has this cheerleader thing got you worried?"

"Yes," Risa admitted.

"Mama used to say, 'What will be, will be, and what won't be . . . might be anyway,'" Haley said. "I never understood it until recently, and it applies today. Only I think the new way of saying it is, 'It is what it is.' We can't change whether they make it or not, but we can support them in whatever happens."

"Thanks," Risa said.

"What's that wonderful smell coming from the kitchen?" Oscar sniffed the air.

"Risa is making breads," Jessica answered. "Orange-date, banana, and zucchini."

"Nellie used to make orange-date bread for me on holidays, and I haven't had any in years. Now I'm looking forward to the morning break. Y'all heard from the girls yet?"

"Not yet," Risa answered.

"Mama made breads like that at Thanksgiving for me and Danny. Dad didn't like dates, so she made banana nut for him. We had warm breads for breakfast on that day, so it always reminds me of family and good times." Wade picked up a long length of oak and set it in place on the framework of the bar.

Risa heard the door to the building open, and her heart skipped a beat. The moment she saw her girls, she knew the news was not good for them, but she put on a brave face and held back the tears.

"We didn't make it," Lily sighed. "There were four spots, and three of the ones trying out had been cheerleaders for the past two years."

"They aren't all seniors anymore?" Jessica asked.

"Nope," Daisy answered, "but they only choose four since the school is so small. I never heard of nine-man football before today. That's why those boys were so cocky. They're big fish in a little pond."

"But we aren't disappointed," Lily said, "because we made a couple of friends. Two of the other girls who didn't make the team said that they would love to have us in choir since we play the fiddle and the banjo. Ginger plays the piano, and Melissa plays guitar."

"And Ginger's mama is the choir director at the school." Daisy headed for the kitchen. "I'm starving. I need a midmorning snack, and I smell something with cinnamon in it."

"Melissa invited us and Ginger over to her house after supper tonight for a jam session. Who knows, we might even get up a country band and play here at Danny's Place when we're old enough," Lily said.

"You don't have to be twenty-one to play in a bar—you only have to be that age to drink," Wade told her.

"Wow!" Lily's eyes widened. "I've got to go tell Daisy!" She started that way and then paused. "Hey, Mama, can we go over to Melissa's tonight? She only lives about four blocks from Haley's place. We gave her a ride home after the tryouts. We can walk that far if you need the truck."

"Of course you can," Risa answered. "Did you catch Melissa's last name?"

"It's Ginger Davis and Melissa Jones," Daisy answered as she came out of the kitchen with a slice of date bread in her hand. "They're cousins. Did you know anyone by that name when you lived here?"

"Yes, I did." Risa felt like prayers had been answered. The girls weren't cheerleaders, and they had made friends with girls who had similar interests. "Melissa's mom was a Davis, and Ginger's dad is her brother. They were both in the band. I'm not surprised their kids are musical."

"That jumping around took a lot of energy and made me hungry, too." Lily took a few more steps toward the kitchen.

Haley moved over to sit on the floor beside Risa. "They made friends that are probably more like them than the cheer squad. Do you feel better?"

"Oh, yeah," Risa said with a smile.

"Hey, Mama," Lily yelled from the kitchen. "I forgot to tell you that Ginger invited us to go to her church on Sunday. I want to go there so we don't have to deal with Granny Stella."

"Of course you can," Risa answered, "but I'm still going to Granny Stella's."

"You are one tough cookie," Haley said.

"No, just determined to show her that I'm in control of my life," Risa said.

Jessica stepped back from the board the guys were putting on the face of the framework and sat down on the stage. "Now that we've crossed the cheerleading bridge, what do y'all think about going to the all-school reunion on Friday night?"

"How many of our class do you think will be there?" Risa asked.

Wade spoke up. "I'm going. I've never been to one, and I want to see what they're all about."

"We eat some kind of chicken dinner, stand around visiting, and do some dancing to music provided by a DJ, who usually plays country," Mary Nell said. "It's like an older-people prom. The guys slip outside to drink a beer or get a snort of whiskey. No liquor is supposed to be on the school grounds. That rule hasn't changed, but they hide it in their cars or trucks."

"Then when it's over at midnight, someone hosts an after-party, and the real liquor comes out," Risa said.

"Along with the real personalities," Jessica added. "I won't be going to any of those."

"Why not?" Risa asked.

"Seen enough drunks to last me a lifetime." Jessica thought of the parties her teammates had after a mission, and how she'd felt the morning after. "And, for that matter, enough hangovers."

"Me too, but then I doubt anyone invites me to one," Wade said and went back to work.

Risa nudged Jessica on the knee and whispered, "Think you and Wade will dance at the reunion?"

Jessica shrugged. "We danced together at the rodeo. He's pretty smooth on his feet."

"Did I hear my name?" Wade asked.

"Yep, you did," Mary Nell said. "We were wondering how many women you're going to dance with at the reunion."

Wade's eyes went immediately to Jessica. "I don't imagine many will want to be caught dancing with the biggest nerd in my huge class of eighteen graduates."

"Hey, we only had nineteen, and we wouldn't have had that many if there hadn't been a set of triplets in the class," Jessica told him. "And I'll be glad to dance with the biggest nerd."

"Thank you," Wade said with a grin and went back to work.

Risa checked the time on her phone and headed to the kitchen. It was only twenty minutes until noon, and she had soup to heat up and grilled cheese sandwiches to make. The rock in her chest had disappeared. Lily and Daisy weren't too disappointed. Jessica and Wade were in a wonderful place—taking it slow and not rushing into anything. To Risa's way of thinking, that was a good plan. If she hadn't gotten in a hurry all those years ago, she might have had a very different life.

But you might not have had those two precious girls, the voice in her head said.

Chapter Eighteen

*J*essica took a long bath and shaved her legs on Friday night after work. That done, she even used a curling iron to make her blonde hair a little more presentable and applied some makeup. Like Wade, she had never been to one of their class reunions, so she wasn't sure what to wear. She finally chose her simple little black dress—which was sleeveless, stopped at the knee, and fit her curves perfectly—and a pair of strappy sandals. She checked her reflection in the mirror and added a pair of pearl earrings, but she still felt like a giant going to a hobbit party.

She turned around and closed her eyes. It didn't matter what she looked like. Her friends would be there to support her, and Wade had offered to give her a ride, so none of them had to drive all the way out back there to pick her up. Next week, she vowed, she was going to take the RV to Killeen and trade it in on an SUV. She'd thought about a car and then a truck, but an SUV seemed to make more sense since she could haul more people in it. She was all the way across the bar and about to go out the front door when it opened, and Wade just stood there with a grin on his face.

"Can we pretend we're on a date?" he asked.

"You would want to do that?" Her eyes traveled from his freshly shined cowboy boots, up his khaki western-cut slacks, and to the forest-green shirt that matched his eyes. "Any woman there would be glad to be your date. Why would you want to saddle yourself with a giant?"

"I never did go for those petite women." Wade offered her his arm. "For the first time in my life, I'll be the envy of every guy that ever graduated from Riverbend High School."

"With a compliment like that, how could I ever refuse to be your date?" Jessica slipped her arm into his.

"I should've asked you earlier and brought a corsage," he said as he locked the door behind them.

"This is not a prom," she said with a chuckle, "and I'm probably overdressed as it is, but it was this or my camouflage pants."

Wade opened the truck door for her. "You look drop-dead gorgeous to me."

"You clean up pretty good yourself." She got into the passenger seat and fastened the seat belt.

He whistled all the way around the front end of the truck and slid in behind the steering wheel. "I didn't think I'd ever be this happy again after Danny died. I owe you, Jessica."

She smiled across the console at him. "We all owe each other. If you hadn't come to the parking lot that first night I arrived in Riverbend, and if you hadn't suggested turning the old church into a bar, none of this would be happening."

"What would you have done if that hadn't happened?" he asked as he started the engine and drove away from the bar.

"I would have given the church to the city to do whatever they wanted with it and driven my RV on west in search of a home," she answered honestly. "I told myself when I left Maine that I would know where I belonged when I got there because I would feel peace in my heart."

"So, you feel peace?" Wade asked.

"Yes, I do," she said with a nod. "Do you?"

He didn't answer until they turned off the dirt road onto the paved one leading down to Riverbend. "I didn't, but I do now. I feel like I can finally let Danny go, and that . . ." He paused.

She turned to focus on his face. A lot could be read from a person's expression, especially when they were searching for the right words. Wade suddenly smiled, and it reached all the way to his eyes.

"I'm not sure how to say this, Jessica," he said. "We are partners, and getting into a relationship might not be a good idea, but I'd like to see where this chemistry between us would lead, but I've been afraid to even bring it up for fear if it didn't work out, we would . . ." Another hesitation.

Now his face looked less relaxed and more tense. She reached across the console and laid a hand on his arm. The electricity between them seemed even hotter than ever.

"We're adults," she told him. "If a relationship didn't work out, I think we could handle being friends, but if we never see where whatever this is between us might go, then we might be passing up on something wonderful."

"Right!" he said as he turned into the high school parking lot and found an empty space. He turned off the engine and turned to face her. "So, can we call this a real date tonight?"

"Yes, we can." Jessica was tired of fighting the battle between her heart and her mind.

"That means I get the last dance of the evening?" Wade leaned across the console and kissed her on the cheek.

Jessica's heart threw in an extra beat and then raced ahead with a full head of steam. Her face suddenly felt hot enough to melt all her makeup off. Granted, it had been a while since she'd had a boyfriend, but she felt like a teenager out on a first date again.

"Of course, and the first one, too," she answered.

Mary Nell jerked the door open and said, "Y'all are finally here. We've been waiting in my car for you, so that we can all go inside together."

"Strength in numbers?" Jessica asked.

"You got it," Haley said as she stepped up. "Don't you look all fancy. I feel underdressed now."

"All three of you look awesome," Jessica said, "and I feel over-dressed, but this is the only thing I had other than camouflage and a full dress uniform."

Haley wore a strapless blue sundress with cute little wedge heels. Risa was wearing a hot pink sleeveless dress that stopped at the knee, and Mary Nell had chosen a dark green dress with big yellow sunflowers on it.

"Honey, you'd look good in a burlap bag tied up in the middle with a length of rope." Risa looped her arm into Jessica's and led her toward the doors.

"Well, damn it!" Jessica said with half a laugh. "If I'd known that, I would have just borrowed a tow sack from Oscar, and not worried so much about how I look."

Risa leaned over and whispered, "I saw Wade kiss you on the cheek. Does that mean anything?"

"We'll talk about it later." Jessica unhooked her arm and took a step back. She laced her fingers with Wade's, and eyebrows began to raise.

"Jessica is my date tonight, so I won't feel like the nerd I was in high school. From what I hear, folks at a class reunion always revert back to whatever they were when they were seniors, so tonight, I'm a nerd who just happens to be friends with all the cheerleaders from the class a couple of years behind me," Wade explained.

"You are so right," Mary Nell agreed. "I've only been back here for a couple of these things, but the smart alecks are still the same and the shy ones haven't changed much."

"Maybe so, but tonight," Wade said with a grin, "I'm going to be the envy of all the men in the room. I'm walking in with four gorgeous women."

"Next week, the talk around town will be that you have a harem going out there at Danny's Place." Mary Nell pushed a strand of red hair behind her ear.

"Oh, crap!" Risa muttered under her breath. "I forgot that Mama graduated from Riverbend High School. This is our twentieth, so it's probably her fortieth, and she brags that she has never missed a reunion."

"Want to leave?" Jessica asked as she peeled the back off the name tag a young girl handed her and slapped it on her right shoulder.

"Yes, but I'm not going to," Risa answered. "I'm going to stay until the last dance is done and they shove us out the door."

"Good for you," Wade said.

"Wade Granger? Is that really you?" A woman with whiskey breath ignored Jessica and walked right up into his personal space. "Remember me? Good God! Were you this sexy in high school, or did you change?" She tapped her name tag, which read *Brenda Covington*.

"Of course I remember you, and I don't think I've changed all that much," Wade answered. "You graduated with my brother, Danny. Do you remember Jessica, Mary Nell, Haley, and Risa? They were cheerleaders back when y'all were seniors."

"Yep, I remember all of you"—Brenda barely glanced at them before she gazed up into Wade's eyes—"but I remember you the best. Why didn't you ever ask me out?"

"Because you would have said no," Wade told her. "Excuse us while we find a seat. I think they'll be serving the food in a few minutes."

"Who wants food when I can have you?" Brenda laid a palm on his chest. "I hear you are opening up your own bar. When I come home next year for the reunion, I'll be sure to come by and see you. But if you want to give me a little tour later tonight, I'll gladly follow you home."

Wade held up Jessica's hand. "Sorry, but I'm taken."

"Well, darlin', if it don't work, you just call me. I'll fly back here any weekend if you need a little rebound comforting." Brenda winked and headed off to greet another guy who had just arrived.

"And you thought you'd still be the nerd?" Jessica teased.

"I am, but now I'm a nerd with a bar, and that appeals to folks who like to drink." Wade led her over to a table that was still empty.

Jessica glanced around the room and didn't recognize many people, but then twenty years changed most folks. She felt Stella's glares long before she located her sitting at a table with several other older folks. Jessica pitied the woman. She had an amazing daughter and two lovely granddaughters, but because of the tension and hate in her heart, she was a miserable old woman.

Round tables for ten were located along the walls, leaving the center of the cafeteria open for dancing later. Nora Jones and her husband, Quinton, arrived, and came over to their table.

"Y'all mind if we join you?" Nora asked.

"Not a bit," Wade answered.

"I hear that Melissa and Ginger really hit it off with your girls," Nora said as she sat down across the table from Jessica. "The four of them have been texting and talking music all week. I'm so glad y'all moved back to Riverbend. Our girls don't run with the popular crowd, thank goodness, and they need friends that are musical like they are."

"Hey, did you save these seats for us?" Linda Davis asked and sat down without waiting for an answer.

"Sure, we did," Nora said. "I was just telling Risa that our girls have become pretty good friends, and they're going to church with us on Sunday."

"Well, I'm glad to have Ginger running with good girls, and to tell the truth, I'm happy they didn't get into the cheer squad." Linda leaned forward. "No offense meant to you four, but things have changed since we graduated," she said out the corner of her mouth.

"From what I've heard, they sure have," Risa said.

"Hey," Richard, Linda's husband, said, "I hear the bar and grill is coming along pretty good. We'll be among your first customers. Oscar has been telling us about the food, and we do enjoy dancing sometimes on Saturday nights."

"It's looking like we can have our grand opening on the night before the homecoming parade and ball game," Wade said.

"Is it really going to be called the Old Church?" Nora asked.

"No," Jessica answered, "it's going to be Danny's Place in honor of Wade's brother."

"That's sweet," Nora said with a smile. "He was a good guy."

Waiters brought out plates of food, and Jessica took the first bite of the stuffed chicken and poked Risa on the shoulder. "You should have catered this event. Your crumb chicken beats this all to pieces. And that pecan pie looks store bought."

"Are you going to do some catering?" Nora asked.

"If so, I want to book you for Ginger's seventeenth birthday party," Linda said.

Risa shook her head. "I'll be too busy in the bar when it opens to have time for catering."

Nora leaned forward a little and whispered, "If you change your mind, I get first chance for Melissa's birthday party, and we have to get together for lunch someday."

Even though he ate everything on his plate, Wade didn't taste much of it. He heard the president of the alumni association introduce a speaker but couldn't focus on what the man was saying most of the time. Folks around him laughed at the guy's jokes and memories he talked about from fifty years before, when he graduated from Riverbend High School, but Wade kept stealing side glances at Jessica and thinking about the kiss they had almost shared. If the man would just finish talking, Wade could take Jessica out on the dance floor and hold her close like he wanted to do.

"Is this boring you?" Jessica whispered.

"Is it that obvious?" Wade asked.

"It is to me. I've been stifling yawns," she said.

"Want to sneak out?" Wade asked.

"God yes, but how do we? Risa might need us," Jessica answered.

"I don't think Stella will try to wade through Mary Nell and Haley, not to mention Linda and Nora," Wade said. "Let's have a couple of dances and then find our way out of this place. This is twice I've been to one of these things."

"Twice?" Jessica asked. "I thought this was your first time."

"My first and my last," Wade said without even a sign of a grin.

The speaker finally ended his speech and got a standing ovation. Wade wasn't sure if it was because folks really enjoyed hearing his anecdotes or if they were glad that he was done. The president introduced the DJ, who went right into playing a song, "I Hope You Dance," that had been popular twenty years before.

Wade pushed back his chair and held out a hand to Jessica. "May I have this dance, ma'am?"

Jessica put her hand in his. "They played this at mine and Danny's graduation. I wonder if they'll play popular songs from every year."

Wade led her out onto the floor, where she wrapped her arms around his neck, and he began a slow two-step. For a while they were the only two people on the dance floor, but Wade didn't feel uncomfortable. For the first time in his life, he didn't feel like hiding in the shadows.

Surprise, Brother. Danny's voice was clear in his head. *You have lost your nerdiness. Don't ever lose Jessica. She's your lifesaver.*

Wade drew her a little closer and danced her closer to the door. "Stella is leaving. Risa won't need us now, and they all seem to be having a great time."

"I'll need to get my purse and tell them that we're leaving," Jessica said.

"I will wait for you by the door," Wade said, "but if you want to stay longer and visit . . ."

"No, I do not, and I believe I have been to two of these also—my first and last. This just isn't for me, but I am glad we came, so I could have a dance with you. Risa really should reacquaint herself with Nora and Linda since it looks like their daughters are going to be such good friends, and you are right about Haley and Mary Nell being here for her." Jessica raised up just slightly on her toes and kissed him on the cheek. "That's so Brenda won't come try to steal you away."

"Darlin', I can outrun that woman," Wade teased.

"Maybe when she's had too much to drink, but when she's sober, she might be fast on her feet," Jessica joked. "Have you even considered all the women who'll be coming into the bar when we open it? You might have a choice of ladies to dance with at closing time."

"I don't think so." Wade took a few steps toward the door, and this time he stayed in the shadows, where he could watch Jessica walk across the room. He drank in his fill of her, but he was not oblivious to several other men who couldn't take their eyes off her, either.

"Wade Granger?" A guy startled him when he spoke. "Is that really you?"

"It is," Wade said, and tried to put a name with the familiar face.

"Are you really here with Jessica Callaway?" the man asked.

Wade quickly read his name tag, but still didn't remember him. "Yes, Adam, she really is with me. Lucky man, ain't I?"

"I'd say so." Adam clamped a hand on his shoulder. "I hear you are putting in a new business out there in that old church that's been standing empty for years. If you need anything for your new bar, from road signs to business cards, give me a call. I'm in the advertising business, and I'd love to help you out." He whipped out a card that said "Adam Pritchard Signs and More" on it, and stuck it in Wade's shirt pocket.

"Thanks. Jessica and I are about to leave. Y'all have a great evening," Wade said. He and Oscar had already talked about hiring another guy named Zach for the job, but if he was too busy, they just might call on Adam.

"I can think of better places to have a good time," Adam chuckled, "but my wife loves these reunions. I'd rather be home watching a ball game on television, or even mowing the yard."

"I hear you," Wade said with a nod.

Adam walked away and spoke to Jessica when he passed her coming back across the floor. Wade suddenly felt ten feet tall and bulletproof. Danny had been right—Wade had lost his nerd status, and it was all because of Jessica.

"So where do we go now?" Jessica asked once they were outside.

"Wherever you want," Wade answered as he led her across the parking lot and opened the truck door for her. "We came. We saw. We listened. We left."

"I like the last part best of all," Jessica said.

"Me too." Wade closed the door and then hurried around the back of the truck.

Jessica was glad that she had come, because for the first time ever, she didn't feel like a giant sunflower in a flower bed with a bunch of pretty little pansies or even marigolds. She was there with Wade Granger. Back in their high school days, he'd been passed over just like she had been, but tonight, she'd seen the way the women all took a second look at him. Brenda had certainly not been the only one at the reunion who would like to have a chance at him. She was just the one brazen enough to try to get between Jessica and him.

"Name your poison," Wade said when he was behind the steering wheel.

"Let's drive to Killeen and get a hamburger and french fries," Jessica suggested. "I didn't eat much of that supper. I guess I've been spoiled to Risa's cooking, because what we had tonight tasted like sawdust mixed with a little cheese."

Wade started the engine and drove out of the parking lot. "Your golden chariot, a.k.a. my white pickup truck, will take the princess wherever she wants to go. And, honey, I would love a big bacon cheeseburger with extra pickles. I agree with you about being spoiled to Risa's cooking."

"I noticed that you were pretty quiet at dinner. Those people didn't make you feel uncomfortable, did they?" she asked.

Wade braked at a stop sign. "Nope. Did they intimidate you?"

"Not one bit. I was there with the best-lookin' guy to ever graduate from Riverbend High School," she answered.

"They didn't bother me, either," Wade told her, "because I was too focused on you to even see anyone else."

"That may be the most romantic thing a guy has ever said to me," Jessica said.

"Then you must have been dating fools." Wade chuckled.

"Probably so, but not a one of them ever lost their taste for food because they were sitting beside me at an event," she told him.

Wade turned onto the highway leading to Killeen and set the cruise control to the speed limit. "I have a confession to make. I had a crush on you in high school, and I wanted to ask you to go to the prom with me when I was a senior and you were a sophomore."

"Why didn't you?" That was the same year Jessica had had a crush on Wade. She couldn't help but wonder what their lives would have been like if he had asked her out. Would they have hit it off as well as they were doing these days? Would they have wound up together and had a family by now? Or would they have hated each other and ruined what they had this evening?

"Fear of rejection," Wade admitted. "You were way out of my league."

"I'll have to disagree with you on that, but for one second let's say you were right. What about now?" Jessica asked. "Have I come down, or have you come up? I feel like you are way out of my league."

Wade jerked his head around to stare at her. "You've got to be kidding me. Would you have gone with me if I'd asked?"

"Probably so," Jessica said with a slight nod. "I had a crush on you at that same time, and Wade, I never felt like I was better than you or anyone else. I was awkward and so tall that I was ashamed of my height and slumped until I got into the military. The only time I stood up straight was when I was a cheerleader. I imagine I was chosen because I was tall and could be the bottom of the pyramid during cheers."

He reached across the console and took her hand in his. "I can just hear the drill sergeant bellowing at the top of his lungs at you."

Jessica could easily visualize her drill sergeant with her hands on her hips, and fire coming out of her eyes when she looked Jessica in the eye and told her to be proud of her height, and never slump. "Yep, she did. I just realized something. Stella Sullivan missed her calling."

"How's that?" Wade asked.

"She would have made an amazing drill sergeant. Can't you just see her yelling at recruits and kicking a metal trash can down the center aisle of the barracks to wake them up before dawn?" Jessica asked.

"Yes, I can," Wade agreed. "We're almost to Killeen. You want to go into the burger joint, or would you rather get it to go and take it to the park?"

"What would you rather do?" she asked.

"I don't like to share my toys," he answered.

"Me either, so let's go to the park, and when we get finished eating, will you push me on the swings?" Jessica asked.

"Anything you want, darlin'. I'm your knight in shining pickup truck tonight," he answered, "but why would you want to swing?"

"You don't remember, but one time when I was in first grade and you were in third, we had an Easter egg hunt at the Riverbend City Park. I was the tallest kid in class, and—"

He butted in, "Two of the girls were teasing you. I took you by the hand and led you over to the swings and pushed you until it was time to walk back to the school."

"I felt pretty that day, and I didn't even thank you," Jessica told him.

"You were always beautiful," Wade said as he pulled in behind a line of cars moving toward the takeout window. "You had on a yellow dress and white sandals that came off when I swung you too high."

"And you put them back on for me so I wouldn't get my feet dirty," she said. "That might have been the first crush I had on you."

He finally got to the window, ordered their food, and added a banana split. Then he turned toward her while they waited. "I wish we would have had more courage in those days."

"Not me," Jessica said. "I think fate was waiting on us to grow up and be adults before she made it possible for us to get to really know each other. We might not have worked out back then."

"You think we will now?" he asked and then handed the girl who was passing the food out to him a bill. "Keep the change."

He gave the long, narrow plastic dish to Jessica.

"I hope so," she answered. "I've fought the attraction ever since I got home."

"Me too." He drove out onto the street and headed toward the city park.

When he had parked at the edge of the park, he turned to her and asked, "Want to eat in the truck before we go swing?"

"No, let's go over to that picnic bench." She pointed to one under a huge shade tree. "I'm not real graceful, and I'd hate to get grease from the fries on your truck seats. If I drop one or two on the concrete, it won't matter."

"It will just become ant food," he told her as he got out of the truck. "I'll take the food if you'll carry those two root beers."

They sat side by side and Wade used the paper sack their food was in as a placemat. "Ketchup?" he asked.

"Yes, please, but not on my fries. I like to dip them, and this burger smells really good," she said as she unwrapped it.

He squirted ketchup out onto the edge of the sack, dipped a fry into it, and fed it to her.

His fingers brushed against her lips, and the sparks around them reminded her of the Fourth of July fireworks. "You are a romantic," she said. "I think you've been hiding it behind the nerd you wanted everyone to believe you were."

"I'm glad you think so," Wade said and then unwrapped his burger and took a bite.

"I don't think, Wade Granger," she told him. "I know."

When they finished their food, he cleaned up their mess and put it all in the nearby trash can. Then he returned to the table and held out his hand.

She put her hand in his and said, "There's no music, but I'd love to dance if you'll hum a tune."

"May I please have this time to swing you, ma'am?" Wade asked.

"I was so involved with the food that I'd forgotten." She let him pull her up and liked the feeling she had when he kept her hand in his all the way over to the swing set. He gave her time to get seated and then pulled her back a long way and gave her a good push forward.

This time her shoes didn't fly off, but the stars and moon sure seemed brighter than they had even when they were on their way to the reunion. The wind rushed past her face, and when she stretched out her long legs, she touched the bottom limb of the tree in front of them.

"You've got to swing with me," she said. "This is exhilarating."

He sat down beside her, pushed off with his feet, and waited until they were going at the same speed to reach over and grab the chain on her swing. She did the same with his, and soon they were one, even if they were in two separate swings.

The moon, what there was of it, had begun to dip lower and lower in the sky, but Jessica didn't want to go home. Still, tomorrow was a workday, and she was a bear when she didn't get enough sleep.

"We should be going," she said.

"It is almost midnight." Wade brought the swings to a stop. "But my truck doesn't turn into a pumpkin when the clock strikes twelve times."

"But at my age I do require a little beauty sleep," she teased.

"Darlin', you won't need beauty sleep when you are ninety." He took her by the hand and led her across the playground and opened the truck door for her. She thought he might kiss her then, but he didn't, and she was more than a little disappointed.

When he had slid into the driver's seat, she said, "Thank you for that compliment. This has been the best date ever."

"For me, too," he told her as he started the engine.

When they reached the bar, he got out of the truck and, like a gentleman, opened the truck door for her again, and walked her up to the porch of the bar. She moistened her lips and got ready for the kiss, but he simply pulled his key from his pocket, opened the door of the bar, and stood to one side to let her go before him, then followed her across the foyer, what had been the sanctuary, and down the hall.

"This may seem crazy, but I'm walking you to your door," he explained.

She stopped at her bedroom door and turned around. "Maybe what's crazy is that it's not crazy."

Wade took a step forward, tipped up her chin with his fist, and stared into her eyes. She barely had time to moisten her lips before his eyes fluttered shut and his mouth closed on hers. The first kiss was sweet. The second one was so hot that Jessica could have sworn that she heard the fire sirens in Riverbend going off.

Then he stepped back, took her hand in his, and kissed the knuckles. "Thank you for the best night of my life. I'll see you tomorrow morning."

"Thank *you*," she said breathlessly.

He turned, started to walk away, then turned back. For a minute she thought maybe he had changed his mind and would return for another kiss or two or three. If he did, she intended to pull him into her bedroom and lock the door.

"I just wanted one more look at you to take with me for my dreams tonight." He winked.

"You really are a romantic," she said.

"I hope so," he said with a smile.

Chapter Nineteen

The Annual Craft Festival in the Riverbend City Park brought in people from all over the area each year. Folks rented space and brought in everything from baked goods and handmade quilts to crocheted items, picture frames, and a multitude of other things. That Saturday, if Jessica could have seen the place from an airplane, she was sure the view would have looked like a mass of ants scrambling from one booth to the next. She'd wondered if the turnout would be good, since they'd had to reschedule it because of rain. Thank goodness the sun was shining brightly today.

Lily and Daisy left with Melissa and Ginger as soon as they arrived. Wade and Oscar saw a big display of hand-painted mirrors and went in that direction.

"Guess that leaves us four," Jessica said. "Where do y'all want to go first?"

"It looks like the booths are set up along the outside and then two rows back to back right down the middle. I haven't been to one of these since before I graduated from high school, but it looks pretty much the same," Mary Nell said. "Let's begin right here and work our way around the outside and then do the ones that are left. But first, we haven't had time to talk about anything other than the bar all week, and there's never been a moment when we were all four together." She turned toward Jessica. "What's going on between you and Wade? Did y'all go straight home after the reunion? I'm dying to know."

"Me too," Risa said. "I tried to corner you several times, but finally got the idea you didn't want to talk about it. Did he hurt your feelings?"

"Or are you just holding it in because it was really good, and you don't want to share for fear you'll jinx it?" Haley asked.

"No, we didn't go home until about midnight, and yes, Haley, you are right, and so are you." She nodded toward Risa. "But he didn't hurt my feelings. It was the most wonderful night and date of my life," she said and told them about going for burgers and swinging.

"Oh. My. Gosh!" Risa gasped. "That really does sound like the most romantic date ever."

"Did he pay for the food?" Haley asked.

Jessica wondered what that had to do with anything, but she nodded.

"Did he walk you to the door and kiss you good night?" Mary Nell asked.

Another nod.

"Details!" Haley clapped her hands. "We need more details."

"My toes curled. Sparks danced around us. He's definitely not the nerd we thought he was when we were all in high school," Jessica answered. "And when he walked away, he turned back and said he wanted one more look to take with him for his dreams. Is that enough detail?"

"Sweet lord." Mary Nell fanned herself with her hand. "That's the sweetest thing I've ever heard. If Kevin had said things like that to me, I would still be with him."

"And since then?" Risa asked. "What's been going on after we leave in the evenings?"

"Nothing. Not one kiss, or anything but hard work on the bar." Jessica shrugged. "I'm not complaining. We're not hormonal teenagers."

"We might be grown-ups, but our hormones haven't died yet, and the heart wants what the heart wants," Haley said. "You can't tell me all that didn't set your hormones to whining for more."

"Nope, I can't, and we'll have to wait and see what the future holds. Now, back to this craft fair. Where do we start?" Jessica asked.

Mary Nell shook her finger at Jessica. "Don't you ever hold on to good news like that for a whole week again without telling us."

"I promise I won't. There just wasn't a time when we were all together and Wade or Oscar wasn't close by," Jessica told them. "Now, the first place that I'm stopping is at the baked goods booths. I've been craving cookies ever since we had that little demonstration at the bar."

"We can always make more. The girls love to bake, but Haley is supposed to be the one doing the craving, not you." Risa stopped in her tracks and stared at the booth not far from them. "You sure you want to stop at the first booth?"

Stella and Lulu were sitting behind a table covered with baked goods. A sign that said that all proceeds would be donated to the missionary fund at the church was propped up on the table. As usual, Stella had already spotted them and was alternately whispering to Lulu behind her hand and shooting dirty looks across the park right at them.

"Are you okay?" Jessica asked.

"I should've remembered that she would be here," Risa answered. "She was all in a tizzy about it for weeks when we used to talk about it on the phone."

"Remember that old Ray Stevens song about Santa Claus?" Haley said with a giggle. "Stella is like the man in the red suit." She waved her arms around and said in a high-pitched, singsong voice, "She's everywhere, she's everywhere."

"And so are we," Mary Nell laughed with her. "From the look on her face, I'd say she's more agitated than we are. I'm going to go over there and buy a dozen cookies. The money is going for a good cause, and I know we can each eat three. Then we'll go on down the row and get a slushy drink to wash them down. Snickerdoodles good with all y'all?"

"I'll buy half a dozen of Lulu's key lime cupcakes." Risa started that way. "I see an empty picnic table where we can sit. Wade and Oscar will be here soon, so I'm sure they'll help us eat them, and maybe Wade will even offer to push Jessica on the swings if those kids ever get off them."

"Shhhh." Jessica pointed across the fairway. "Wade and Oscar are coming this way."

"Hey," Wade said when they were close. "It's only a few minutes until the twins and their friends are playing in the gazebo. Think maybe we better head that way?"

"We're going to buy some cookies and cupcakes first," Risa answered. "I cook when I'm nervous, but since I can't do that out here, maybe eating will calm me down. They've played in front of a crowd before, but it was all family."

"Hey, now," Oscar argued. "They played for the church demonstration, remember?"

"Yes, but that was different," Risa told him.

Wade laced his fingers with Jessica's. "Are you as nervous about them as Risa?"

"Almost," Jessica answered, liking the way his big, calloused hand felt in hers. "They didn't seem a bit antsy, so I don't know why we all are worried."

"I'm not." Oscar frowned. "There's nothing to be nervous about. I just wish there was a talent scout here at the festival. Wouldn't it be awesome if they got a scholarship to a good university based on their musical ability?"

"Yes, it would." Jessica led the way to Stella's booth.

"What can we do for you?" Lulu looked like she was a bunny rabbit that had wandered into a coyote convention. She pointed to the sign. "All the proceeds go to help the missionaries in Africa."

"If you want something, buy it and get going." Stella's tone was somewhere between disgusted and downright hateful. "I don't want people thinking that I'm having anything to do with any of you."

"Our money ought to be as good as anyone else's cash," Oscar said.

"And like Lulu says, it's going to a good cause." Risa rounded the end of the table, bent down, and gave her mother a hug. "I forgive you for all the mean things you've said and done, but my forgiveness is not for you as much as it is for me. I don't have room in my heart for all that ugliness, and I chose to just let love live there."

Stella went as stiff as a board and shivered like the devil had just kissed her. "Get thee behind me, Satan," she growled.

"I don't see horns and a forked tail on Risa," Jessica said, "but I also don't see wings and a halo on you."

"Just go," Stella said.

"Lulu, I'd like that plate right there with the dozen snickerdoodles, and the one with the key lime cupcakes, and then that one with the cinnamon rolls. How much do I owe you? We can tell when we're not welcome, so we'll take it to go instead of staying around here to visit with y'all," Haley said.

"I'll be your pack mule and help you carry this if you'll share with me." Oscar had already reached for two plates. "Mary Nell, get that last one, and I'll make a mad dash for that picnic bench over by the gazebo. It'll be like we're at a dessert theater."

"Are you going to come over and listen to your granddaughters play?" Risa asked her mother.

"I am not," Stella stated. "If they were playing hymns in church, I might have listened to them. I can't believe you have let them learn that awful country and bluegrass stuff. I wish Martha would get full custody of them. That way I'd know they were being raised right."

"Martha has shunned them and made all their cousins do the same. I wouldn't call that being raised right." Risa shrugged and turned to walk away.

"I'm not through fighting against the disgrace you are bringing to a house of worship," Stella said, raising her voice.

Risa whipped back around. "You need to pray to God to help you with your spirit, Mama. It's as far from being Christian as hell is from heaven. And that old building hasn't been a house of worship in decades."

"I can't believe you would talk to your mother like that," Stella whined.

Risa just shook her head and joined the rest of her friends as they headed toward the concrete picnic bench. The bunch of them had barely gotten seated and the plastic wrap torn off the plates when the Chamber of Commerce president, Richard Davis, stepped up to the middle of the gazebo and tapped the microphone. "We've got a special treat for you today, folks. For the next hour, my daughter and her three friends are going to entertain all y'all with a little music. Let's give them a big round of applause."

Several of the folks clapped and whistled, and some of the people brought their lawn chairs up a little closer when they heard the whine of the fiddle begin, and then Lily stepped up the microphone and said, "This one is called 'The Hunter's Wife.' We're dedicating it to our mama. Y'all might recognize it if you've ever listened to the Pistol Annies."

Risa blew a kiss their way and laughed out loud. "This could be my theme song. I didn't even know they had been practicing this one."

"Good kids you got there, Risa." Oscar fired up the crowd by starting to clap in time with the music. Soon, everyone was doing the same.

Jessica was glad that she and Wade had had a couple more weeks to figure out that the attraction they had for one another was something real. She forgot all about Stella's hateful words, her glares meant to fry Risa as well as the rest of them into nothing more than a pile of bones, and the ugly way she had treated her own daughter. She put it all away and enjoyed the kids' music. What she liked even better than the songs they played and sang was having her hand tucked into Wade's. To her, that subtle sign meant they were a couple, and it felt so right.

Chapter Twenty

According to Jessica's phone calendar, the mechanical bull and the jukebox were both arriving that day—a week before the twins' first day of school so they would be there for the excitement. She stood in the middle of the room and soaked in the diverse atmosphere. Western for Wade and Oscar, beach for Danny, and fancy for the twins. To some folks the mixture of all three might seem downright crazy, but to Jessica, it felt perfect.

Oscar and Wade used the last of the oakwood from the pews to close up the opening for the baptismal. When Jessica thought about the baptismal, she still felt like she had been raised up out of a dark past into a bright future that she wouldn't trade for anything.

When they had been at the craft fair, Oscar had bought a set of mounted steer longhorns that measured six and a half feet across, and just yesterday he and Wade had hung them above a tiki hut that the guys had built around the jukebox. It was hard to believe there had ever been a hole in the wall with a giant bathtub back there. Beneath the horns was a sign that Oscar had commissioned a local guy, Zach, to make: a long piece of rough wood that said "Danny's Place." With the tiki-looking lettering, it blended the look of western horns and the tiki hut perfectly.

She turned around to stare at the bar itself and the wide mirror behind it framed in gold gilt etched with the name of the bar in fancy lettering that the twins had picked out. Western. Beachy. Fancy. All in one place.

Now if only she and Wade could find that perfect place in their relationship. Not that she was complaining about where they were after only two and a half months, but she wanted more. They had settled into a relationship that involved good-night kisses after long talks every evening when everyone had gone home. She was more than ready to take it to the next level, but every evening he had gone off to his trailer, and she had spent the rest of the night alone in her bedroom.

Wade came through the front door, crossed the room, and slipped his arms around her waist from behind. She could feel the steady beat of his heart against her back, and as always, the touch of his body pressed so tightly against hers caused visions of leading him back to her bedroom right there in front of whoever was around, and even God if he still visited the building sometimes.

"I think the sanctuary has lost its halo and wings," he teased.

Jessica covered his hands with hers. "It kind of did that when we started tearing the pews apart to salvage all the oak. I love the mirror, the horns, the tiki hut—all of it. They all go together like an eclectic family."

"Which isn't bad as long as our relationship isn't dysfunctional." He nuzzled the inside of her neck.

"We may be the least dysfunctional couple in the whole world," she whispered.

"That's the way I feel, too." He tipped her chin up and brushed a sweet kiss across her lips.

If she didn't take a step back, the only work that would get done that day would be in her bedroom with the door closed and locked. With a sigh, she moved away from him and said, "The bull and the sign for outside will be here by noon, but I can sure feel Danny smiling down on us. If he was here, he'd be the first one on the bull."

"What was that sigh all about?" Wade asked.

"I wanted more than a kiss," she said honestly.

"Me too, but that's a big step that we shouldn't take lightly," Wade said. "Speaking of Danny riding the bull, he would probably insist on being the first one to plug quarters into the jukebox, too."

"That was a quick change of subject," Jessica said.

"Yep, because, darlin', I've wanted more than a few kisses for a long time now." He nodded.

"I'm ready for that next step anytime you are," she said.

"Oh, honey, just name the time and place," he told her.

"We'll talk about that later tonight," she said with a smile. "Now back to the bull and jukebox. I've promised Daisy she could do that since Lily gets to ride the bull first."

She could still feel his breath on the soft spot below her ear, and just thinking about it sent waves of warmth through her whole body.

"Hey, where is everyone?" Oscar yelled. "I could use a hand."

He rolled in two long pews stacked precariously on top of a wheelbarrow. "I found these hiding behind a bunch of empty boxes at the back of the barn. What do y'all think of putting them against the far wall for folks to sit on between dances?"

The pews didn't look quite as long as the ones that they'd torn apart. "I wonder what those were used for," Jessica said.

"Probably they were deacon's benches," Wade suggested.

"I guess the sanctuary might not have quite lost its halo and wings after all, but I've got a better idea," Jessica said. "Roll them right back outside, and let's put them on the porch. That way the customers will have a place to sit when they go outside for a breath of fresh air."

"Now why didn't I think of that? One on each side of the door, right?" Oscar asked.

Wade stepped over to lend a hand and steady the pews while Oscar eased the wheelbarrow across the foyer and back outside.

Jessica followed, stepped off the porch, and kept walking out into the middle of the parking lot, where she eyeballed the two shorter benches when they took them off the wheelbarrow. "Hey, what if we have Zach paint *Danny's Place* on the back of the pews? Maybe if we remind folks enough, they'll begin to call this place by its rightful name instead of calling it the old church bar."

"I like that a lot," Wade said and then pointed to a truck coming their way, kicking up a cloud of dust behind it. "There's our outside sign now. You can tell him what you want painted on the pews. He'll probably want to take them back to his shop. There's no way the paint could dry out here without getting dirt in it."

"What's going on?" Mary Nell asked, coming out of the building. "Oh, the sign has arrived!" She sat down on one of the pews. "Where did these come from? I thought we'd torn all the pews apart."

"I found them in the barn," Oscar said.

"Well, it's a good place to use them," Mary Nell said. "Folks will have a place to sit if they've come out for a breath of fresh air or to smoke. You might want to put up a couple of those things to throw cigarette butts in, at the end of the pews."

Before anyone else could say a word, Risa's old truck came to a halt in front of the porch, and the twins beat her and Haley out into the parking lot. All four of them grabbed bulging grocery bags from the truck bed and hurried inside.

"Don't let him start putting it up without us," Lily yelled.

"We want to watch it," Daisy said as she brought up the rear. "And where did you find those things?" She nodded toward the pews.

"Hiding in the barn," Oscar repeated with pride.

Zach, the sign guy, as Oscar referred to him, hopped out of his flatbed truck and waved. "Y'all ready for this?"

"You bet we are," Wade said. "Can I help you?"

"I never turn down help," Zach answered. "I plan to use the two supporting poles that are already in place. They're metal and set in concrete, so the first thing I'll do is take this old one down. Then I can sure use an extra set of hands to keep this new one steady on the jack until I can get it bolted down solid."

Wade laid a hand on Jessica's shoulder and gave it a gentle squeeze. "You and the girls decide what kind of lettering you want on the pews while I do this little job. Things are sure working out for us, aren't they?"

"Seems like it." Jessica sat down on the end of one of the pews.

"Decide what?" Lily and the rest of the team joined them on the porch.

"We're thinking of having our logo put across the backs of these pews and leaving them out here on the porch." She waved a hand to take in both benches. "We need to decide what kind of lettering we want, so Zach can get busy on them."

Risa sat down beside Jessica. "They're church pews. My suggestion is that we use the fancy lettering that's on the mirror behind the bar. Kind of blends the church with the bar, doesn't it?"

"Maybe we could add a couple of palm trees on either side," Lily said. "That would really make it look like a tiki bar."

"And on the other bench we could ask Zach to put some longhorns across the top of the lettering," Daisy suggested.

The twins, Haley, and Mary Nell all took a seat. Lily whipped her phone out of her pocket and found some art for everyone to look at. Oscar meandered out to the spot where Zach and Wade were putting up the sign.

Haley pointed to clip art of a palm tree. "Maybe Zach could spread the actual logo out a little more so that it covered most of the back rather than making it the same size as the etching on the mirror and fix the palm tree so that the leaves kind of laid over on the end of the lettering."

"Yes," Lily agreed, and went on to find artwork for the horns.

"Does sitting here make y'all think about singing hymns?" Jessica shivered despite the heat.

"No, it makes me think about how far we've all come this summer," Lily said.

"It doesn't bother you that you can't keep in touch with your cousins?" Risa asked.

"Nope," Daisy answered. "We've been so busy with our new friends and our music that we're okay with that. How about you old girls? Y'all regretting your decisions about living here and making a bar?"

"Old?" Risa raised an eyebrow.

"Older than we are," Lily said with a grin.

"No regrets here," Risa said.

"Or here." Haley laid a hand on her still flat stomach. "Not a single one."

"Not me," Mary Nell added. "Life is good."

"Yep, it is," Jessica added.

Mary Nell pointed toward the sign going up out there at the edge of the parking lot. "We've almost done it this summer, ladies. We wanted to be ready to open in time for homecoming, and it looks like we'll make it."

"I'm glad we named it Danny's Place," Haley said. "It has a nice ring to it."

"Have y'all seen the Pistol Annies video when they're singing 'Hush Hush'?" Jessica asked. "That's what comes to my mind today. That church at the beginning of the video reminds me of this one, only this one doesn't have a steeple, and all the secrets they tell about in whatever town they're singing about is Riverbend all over again."

Mary Nell pushed a strand of red hair back up into her messy bun. "You got that right, but then most small towns are rumor mills."

"And big towns," Haley said. "Our high school had more kids in the system than the population of Riverbend, and the rumors were just as bad as they are in a small town. What are we going to do about that steeple anyway?" She nodded toward the thing still out there beside the church.

"Oscar has a plan for the wood in it," Jessica answered. "He says it's going to be a surprise. Look!" She pointed. "They're setting the new sign in place already. I thought it would take longer than this."

"It's really official now," Haley said. "We are all working for Danny's Place no matter what the people in town call this bar."

"It's kind of anticlimactic." Lily sighed. "I was hoping for a clap of thunder or maybe a bolt of lightning. I wanted a sign from heaven so that I could prove to Granny Stella that she was wrong about God hating us for what we're doing. If lightning didn't strike the building, then it would be pretty good proof."

Risa draped an arm around Lily's shoulders and drew her close for a side hug. "We don't need proof of anything, my child. Everything is working out for all of us pretty well."

"Don't include me in that *all of us* business," Mary Nell whispered. "Kevin called again last night. He promised to go to rehab and therapy if I'll just give him another chance. He even says he would be willing to move to Texas and be content just to play gigs in this area. I don't know how long I'll be fighting this war, but I keep telling him no."

"His name should be Linus," Risa said.

"Why's that?" Mary Nell asked.

"You are his security blanket," Risa answered.

"You got that right," Mary Nell said with a sigh and a nod.

"He has found out too late that he'll have to find another security blanket, though, hasn't he?" Jessica asked.

"Yes," Mary Nell answered with conviction, "but if I didn't have y'all to talk to, and have the fear of disappointing Daddy again, he might be able to talk me into giving him that second chance. He looked so pitiful, and it's hard for me to say no."

"We are here," Haley said, "anytime of the day or night."

"You might want to kick me out of that basket of all of us having things working for us, too," Risa said.

"No! You're not going back to Kentucky, are you?" Jessica gasped.

"Nope, but Martha could file unfit-mother charges against me, so everything isn't going too well for me, either."

"But Daddy hasn't offered to leave all his dead animals behind and move out here with us, has he?" Lily asked.

"The devil will pass out snow cones in hell before that happens," Risa said and turned to focus on Haley. "You haven't mentioned anything about your baby daddy in a couple of weeks. Is everything all right in your corner of the world?"

"Everything is great. Remember that next week, we find out whether we get a girl or a boy."

"And we start to school next week," Daisy said. "This summer went faster than any one we've ever had, and we have to think about what we're really going to do when we finish our senior year."

"The world is our oyster," Lily quipped.

Jessica was surprised to hear someone as young as Lily quote Shakespeare, but she was right about that. The pearl in her own oyster was Wade, and things were going to work out for them—she felt it in the depths of her soul. She probably shouldn't be impatient, but she kept thinking that things were going too well, and that the other shoe would drop any minute.

"Look!" Daisy squealed and pointed toward the sign. "It's up and in place. Isn't it beautiful?"

They were all so engrossed with the new sign that they paid little attention to Zach as he drove across the lot and the three men loaded the old steeple on the back of his truck, then drove it back to the barn. In just a few minutes, all three men came back to the porch.

"I could sure use a bottle of water when we get these pews loaded up," Zach said.

"We got water, tea, and cold beer," Risa told him.

"Tea sounds great," Zach said as he picked up the end of the other pew.

Daisy went inside and brought out a glass of ice and a gallon of sweet tea. She set it on the edge of the porch, and said, "Help yourself. Anyone else want something to drink?"

Oscar pulled a bandanna from his pocket and swiped sweat from his face. "I'd take a cold beer."

"Make that two," Wade said.

"Y'all wouldn't want to rent out that barn, would you?" Zach filled his glass and drank half of it down. "The place where I work now has been put up for sale. I like quiet when I work."

Jessica chuckled. "This is going to be a bar. We'll be open until two in the morning. Do you really think you'll have peace and quiet here?"

"I work in the day and usually knock off no later than six. Right now, I live in the loft above the small warehouse on the outskirts of Copperas Cove, where I work. They tell me in three months I have to be out because my place will be razed to make a golf course," he said. "I'm looking for a place to relocate. I'd gladly rent the barn and buy that RV out there. I see you've got a 'For Sale' sign on it. You don't have to give me a decision today, but I'd appreciate it if you'd think about it." He finished off his tea and poured another glass.

"That's where I keep my tools," Wade told him.

"I take on no more than two projects at a time," Zach said, "so all I need is a corner, but for now, I thank you for this sweet tea. I'm going back up the road to get busy on this steeple. Oscar and I've talked about what to do with it. What do you want on the church pews?"

Wade raised an eyebrow toward Jessica. "Have y'all decided?"

"The same thing you worked on the mirror. Lily picked out some artwork that she could send links to on your phone if that would work. Do you think maybe you could carve it into the wood, rather than just painting it?" Jessica asked. "That way it would be permanent."

"Sure thing." Zach nodded. "Do you want the carved part to be stained darker than the oak or painted?"

"Stained," Wade said without hesitation.

"You got it. I'll have them ready as soon as possible." Zach tipped the bill of his hat toward the ladies. "See y'all then."

Daisy grabbed Oscar by the arm and whispered, "If you'll tell me what he's going to do with that steeple, I'll make you a whole batch of chocolate chip cookies this afternoon."

"Much as I love those, I want it to be a surprise." Oscar shook his head. "I will tell you this, though. Stella Sullivan is not going to like it one bit, and after the way she's treated you and Risa, that brings me great pleasure."

"Daddy!" Mary Nell scolded.

"Hey, don't fuss at me. Vengeance might belong to the Lord, but He's the one who knocked that steeple off the roof of this place, so I don't reckon He will care what I do with it." Oscar twisted the top off his beer and took a long drink. "Now, unless I'm mistaken, I hear a big truck coming and I'm pretty sure that's going to be our bull. Which one of you won out to ride the critter first, and what did you decide to name him?"

Lily raised a hand. "I'm riding first."

"And his name is Bodacious," Daisy answered. "I researched the names of mean rodeo bulls."

"That's a pretty famous bull," Oscar said as the truck backed up to the porch.

"Yep, and our bull will be even more famous because he's going to be the only one in all of Burnet County. Heck, we're going to be as big as Billy Bob's," Daisy told him.

Lily stepped up in front of everyone and spread her hands out wide. "All y'all need to step back. Bodacious is about to be turned loose from this truck. He's going to come out mean and snortin' and pawin' at the ground, but I'm determined to tame the critter."

Jessica giggled and then laughed out loud at Lily's antics. Soon the whole bunch of them were guffawing. The guy, whose name tag read *Billy*, jumped out of the truck and shook his head.

"I've seen people happy to get their electronic bulls, but never this happy," he said.

"Then you never delivered one to a couple of sixteen-year-old girls, did you?" Wade asked.

"That I have not." He opened the back of the truck, and there was Bodacious lying on his side. "Show me where you want this old boy set up and I'll get busy."

Wade slipped his arm around Jessica's shoulders. "It's coming together one step at a time," he said, "but I keep waiting for something to set us back."

"I know exactly what you're talking about," she said with a nod. "I hope when it does, we can work our way through it."

"We will," Wade said. "Together we can conquer most anything. What do you think about selling your RV to Zach?"

"I'd sell it to anyone who has the money to buy it, but what if it's contingent upon us renting him part of your space in the barn?" she asked. "What do you know about him?"

"That he's a damn good sign painter, and that he was about two years ahead of me in school. He was a loner, too, and he's never married, is basically shy and a good man. Sometimes he plays dominoes with Oscar and me on Sunday afternoons. He comes along with his Uncle Gary when he isn't working on a job," Wade answered.

"Do you like him well enough to share your barn and this place with him?" Jessica asked.

"I guess I do," he said. "I don't reckon I'm going to have a lot of time for odd jobs once we open up for business anyway, so I won't be using my woodworking tools very often. They could be pushed all the way to the back of the place."

"You decide that part, and we'll talk among us about letting him park the RV behind the barn if the deal works out," she said. "Right now, we'd better get in there and see if Lily can stay on old Bodacious for the full eight seconds."

"And then let Daisy choose the first song on the jukebox after she has a ride," Wade agreed.

Together, side by side, and in step with one another, they crossed the porch. Leaving the August heat behind and going into the cool foyer made chill bumps pop up on Jessica's arms and neck. "That's kind of a shock to the skin," she muttered.

"Yep, but it sure feels good," Wade agreed.

Billy had Bodacious up and running in less than two hours, showed them how to work the controls, then got back in his truck and left without even a wave.

"A man of few words," Mary Nell said when he was gone.

"Yep, but we weren't paying him to have a conversation with us," Haley said.

"Daisy, you got your five dollars ready?" Lily picked up an old straw cowboy hat from under the bar and jammed it down on her head.

Her sister held up a bill. "I'll add five to it if you let me control the switch."

"Bring it on, Sister," Lily said. "This is my lucky hat, and I'm saving for a pair of cowboy boots. For now, I'll be the first girl to show Bodacious who is boss and do it in my bare feet."

Jessica was so happy that she wanted to hug herself. Then, out of the clear blue summer sky, a feeling of doom settled over her.

A vision of the little girl that she dreamed about so often popped into her head. Was that the other shoe dropping that she had feared and Wade had mentioned? Was the thing that would ruin her and Wade's relationship the fact that neither of them could get over the past, and move on to the future?

What if Lily got hurt on that thing? Sure, there was padding all around it to soften the fall if she didn't stay on the mean-looking critter for eight seconds, but time didn't matter here. She could get thrown off and hurt in two seconds or even six or seven. She could land wrong, break a rib, puncture a lung, and die in seconds. In that moment, Jessica wished that she had never agreed to buy the damned thing.

Risa laid a hand on her arm and whispered, "We can't protect them from everything, but I'm terrified about letting either of them get on that thing."

"Me too," Jessica said in a low voice. "They've become like my nieces, or maybe even my daughters."

Lily climbed on and settled on Bodacious's back, wrapped the rope around her left hand, and threw her right one up in the air. "Let 'er rip, Daisy," she yelled.

Lily gave it all she had, but she took a tumble after six seconds and got up giggling. "That's enough for me. I'd rather play in a band as ride bulls, but it was fun. Your turn, Daisy, and I owe you ten dollars."

"We'll see. If I stay on eight seconds, then you owe me." Daisy jerked the hat off her sister's head and crammed it down on her light brown hair. Then she climbed up on the bull's back and got into position. "I had it at medium speed, so you can't make it go any faster than that."

Lily just giggled again, and when Daisy was set, she pushed the controls all the way up to the fastest speed. Bodacious twisted and turned and bucked. Daisy made it to six seconds and slid off the side flat and landed on her butt.

"You cheated," she yelled at her sister. "You made him go faster for me and harder than I did for you."

"Yep, I did," Lily said. "You told me not to, but I didn't promise that I would. Now we don't either of us owe the other one money. Besides, Granny Stella and Granny Martha would have matching hissy fits if they knew we were betting. Have you got your quarters ready for the jukebox?"

"I do and I've got my song picked out." Daisy got up rubbing her butt. "I'll stick to playing music. I like folks clapping for me better than I like getting thrown off that thing."

"Good choice," Risa told them both, and then whispered to Jessica, "Things are still working out. I'm glad y'all bought old Bodacious. Now Lily will hopefully go to college and forget about riding bulls."

Jessica blew out a lungful of air she hadn't even realized she was holding in. "If either of the girls got hurt bad, I was going to burn that thing."

"I wonder what song Daisy has picked out?" Haley asked.

"*Three* songs," Daisy said. "I get three for my money."

"Is the first one that song y'all played by the Pistol Annies about a hunter's wife?" Wade asked as he sat down and pulled Jessica down to sit beside him. "I thought that was pretty cute, and it's on the jukebox."

"I'm thinking it will be 'My Church,'" Jessica said.

"Nope," Oscar disagreed with a shake of his head. "I bet it's something more modern, like maybe one of Blake Shelton's songs."

Daisy put the quarters into the jukebox and turned around. "Are y'all ready for this?"

"Don't tease us," Lily scolded her. "Just push the buttons."

"This is my part of the show, so don't rush me," Daisy threw back at her sister. "I've given this a lot of thought, and y'all might need tissues on the first one."

She whipped out a box of tissues from the tiki hut and carried them to the edge of the stage, where she set them down between Jessica and Risa. "The second one and third ones just seemed to be fitting," she said as she returned to the jukebox and pushed the buttons. "Here we go!"

Jessica knew that the song was "Danny Boy" within five seconds of the soft violin music lead-in to the lyrics. Tears rolled down her cheeks and dripped onto her shirt. She didn't like for people to see her cry, but there was no controlling it, and then Wade buried his face in his hand and his shoulders shook as he wept. She wrapped him in her arms and raised his chin with her hand. Then, cheek to cheek, their salty tears blended together.

Mary Nell grabbed a fistful of tissues and wiped her eyes. "I hope Danny can hear this and is looking down on his tiki bar."

Risa pulled the tissues over closer to her and Haley. "Dammit, Daisy, you've got us all weeping."

"Me too." Daisy knelt in front of her mother and laid her head on Risa's lap. "I couldn't think of a better song to christen the jukebox with than this one. I didn't know Danny, but I feel like I do. Lily and I have never even seen a picture of him."

"He was a kindhearted guy when we knew him. He was more outgoing at that time of his life than Wade, but he had a big heart just like Wade does." Jessica finally got control of her emotions. "Thank you, Daisy, for giving us this beautiful gift today."

"You are welcome," Daisy said. "Now get ready to raise your hands to heaven and shout *hallelujah*! 'My Church' is the next one on the list."

Oscar put away his bandanna and shouted louder than any of them when the lyrics asked them to give her a hallelujah. He got up, grabbed Mary Nell by the hand, and did some fancy swing dancing around the barroom floor. "We needed this after hearing 'Danny Boy' and remembering the man who gave his life for our freedom," he said over the top of the music.

"Well, it is our church." Jessica dried up the last of her tears and then wiped Wade's face. "Are you all right?"

He hugged her tightly. "I am now, and I will be from now on. How about you? Regrets?"

"Not a single one. I'm home, and I'm happy," she answered. "And you'll think this is an insane time to get a message from the universe about where to bury my folks, but I just did. I'm going to put them between the church and the barn and put up a small stone to mark the place. They wanted me to be happy, and I am, and I do want a place to go talk to my mama every now and then."

"When you are ready, we'll take care of it"—Wade kissed her on the forehead—"and, honey, I don't think it's crazy at all. And after this song, I'm going to show the twins the pictures I have of Danny on my phone. They need to see the man that the bar is named for."

"Last song coming up," Daisy yelled. "It's 'Neon Church' by Tim McGraw. We should have thought to put a neon sign up."

"I love this song." Lily began to dance all alone out on the floor. "I like the part about a jukebox choir and a bunch of honky-tonk angels."

Wade stood up and held out a hand toward Jessica. "I think they're playing our song."

She put her hand in his, and he led her out to the middle of the dance floor. She wrapped her arms around his neck, and he drew her close. "We're going to be all right. I just know it. We deserve what we've got, and with all our friends around us, we're going to kick that other shoe out the door if it drops."

"Yes, we are," she said, and she meant it.

Chapter Twenty-One

When everyone had gone that evening, Jessica went out to the bar and plugged some coins into the jukebox. She pressed the buttons to play "Lead Me Home"—a song that probably would be better suited to a funeral, but every bit of the song seemed to apply to her life. That night she was burying the past and going forward. The lyrics asked God to take the singer's hand and lead him home, and Jessica felt like God had done that for her. That a bar remodeled from an old church could be compared to heaven might not fit into some folks' way of thinking, but to Jessica, it was perfect. She stepped out into the middle of the floor in the semidarkness and closed her eyes. She weaved back and forth until the song ended.

The next song was "If Tomorrow Never Comes" by Garth Brooks. One minute she was dancing around alone, the next Wade had appeared out of nowhere and taken her in his arms. He sang the words to the song right along with Garth.

"This was on the radio when I was getting ready for bed, and I had to come out here and tell you . . ."

She took a step back and led him down the hall to her bedroom. "I don't ever want to face the world without you, Wade Granger, but I damn sure don't intend to waste another moment of what we have today, either."

"This is a big step," Wade whispered. "I've been ready for it for a long time, maybe since we were teenagers."

"Me too." She pulled him into her bedroom and kicked the door shut with her bare foot.

Wade awoke on Tuesday morning and sat straight up in bed. For a few minutes he thought he was still dreaming, and then he realized that Jessica was curled up beside him. His phone lying on the table next to the bed told him it was five o'clock, Tuesday, August 16. He propped up on an elbow and stared his fill of Jessica. Her blonde hair was splayed out over the pillow, with one strand stuck to her forehead. The sheet covered her body, but he didn't need to see her without clothing to know what she looked and felt like. The night before had told him all that and more.

She opened her eyes slowly, reached out to touch his face, and said, "You are real. Last night wasn't a dream."

"I was just thinking the same thing." He moved over and brushed a soft kiss across her lips. "I'm in love with you, Jessica. I want us to live together, but all I have to offer you is a tiny travel trailer."

"I want us to live together, too," she said, "and I do have this bedroom, a nice bed, and a bathroom we can share."

"So?" he questioned.

"But . . . ," she started.

"There are not buts in real love, just ands," he told her.

"What does that mean?" she asked.

"*But* means there's a reason for something not to work. *And* means there'll just be more and more added on to what we have now," he answered.

"I was going to say, but I want to keep this between us for a little while. I don't want to share you or the news," she told him.

"No problem," Wade agreed. "We'll tell the rest of them when the time is right. Right now, though, it's more than an hour until Risa arrives to make breakfast."

She moved over closer to him. "I've got an idea about how to spend that hour."

"I'm reading your mind right now, and I like your idea," Wade said.

A week later, Risa awoke with sadness in her heart. She had never been ready for the first day of school, and that morning she dreaded even more seeing her girls get into the truck and leave. This would be their last first day, and she would only have one more year with them before they went off to college. She made their favorite pancakes that morning, but they were almost too excited to eat. Now it was time for them to walk out of the bar and drive to school—their first time ever to drive and not ride the school bus.

"I can't believe you are letting us take the truck to school." Lily slung her backpack over one shoulder. "Man, Daisy, we are almost adults."

"*Almost* is the key word," Mary Nell told them. "Treasure this year, because being an adult isn't nearly as much fun as it looks like."

"Amen to that," Haley said. "Mary Nell is giving you some good advice."

"Yes, she is, and learn from all our mistakes instead of repeating them," Risa said.

"This is some pretty heavy conversation for the twins' big day." Oscar piled three more pancakes onto his plate. "I remember the morning that Mary Nell left for the first day of her senior year. Her mother cried, and I wanted to go get her and take my family to a remote island somewhere far away."

"Are you going to cry, Mama?" Daisy asked.

"Nope, I'm going to pray that you have the best year ever." Risa crossed her fingers under the table like she had when she was a little girl and told a white lie.

"Aww, that's so sweet." Daisy pushed back her chair, rounded the table, and gave Risa a hug. "Are you going to walk us to the porch and wave as I drive away?"

"I'll be the one driving," Lily said.

"I'm the oldest," Daisy argued.

"Only by two minutes," Lily countered.

"Daisy drives today, and you drive tomorrow." Risa settled the argument. "And if you can't agree or forget whose turn it is, then I'll take you to school and hold both your hands all the way to the door like I did when you started kindergarten."

"Yes, ma'am." Lily didn't waste a second in disagreement.

"And you better thank Jessica and Haley for saying that I could use their vehicles if I need something so that you can have the truck for school," Risa told them.

"Thank you!" the two of them chorused at the same time.

"It's time to go if we're going to pick Melissa and Ginger up on the way," Lily said. "I'm sure glad we've got a back seat in the truck. We'll see y'all as soon as school is over."

The moment Risa heard the truck leave, she covered her eyes with her hands and began to weep. "Don't any of y'all look at me. I'm ugly when I cry."

"I can't let you cry alone." Jessica left her chair beside Wade and hugged Risa. "We've got this whole year with them. We won't waste a minute of it, and we're all grateful to you for sharing them with us."

"I can't even imagine sending this baby"—Haley touched her stomach—"off to preschool, much less think about him or her going to their senior year."

"Time passes so quickly. Just look at this summer," Oscar told them. "Don't take a minute of it for granted. Y'all have got a wonderful friendship among you, and Jessica and Wade, you've got something beyond that. Cherish it."

"You'll get no argument from me, but how did you know about me and Jessica?" Wade asked.

"We all know," Risa said. "Right now, I don't want to think about how empty my life will be when I can't see my girls every day. They've been my lifeline to sanity all these years."

"Just keep the lines of communication open. You've got all this wonderful technology these days." Oscar swiped a tear from his eye. "Now, let's get busy before we get even more maudlin. Zach called last night. He's bringing the two church pews home this morning. Have y'all decided whether you are gonna rent the barn out to him or what? I noticed you took the 'For Sale' sign off the RV."

"I sold it to him," Jessica said. "He's going to take it today and get the AC fixed or replaced."

"I thought it best that we all make a decision about letting him park it on the property." Wade shrugged. "What do you think?"

"No problem here," Oscar answered.

"Like he said, he'll be working in the day when we're all sleeping, and sleeping at night when we're all working," Mary Nell reminded them. "I don't have a problem with him being here. Haley?"

"He seems like a nice guy," Haley replied. "If Oscar and Wade vouch for him, I don't care if he lives on the property."

"Me either." Risa was glad for something to think about other than her girls leaving for their senior year.

"What kind of rent do you think we should charge for letting him work out of the barn?" Wade asked.

"How about we ask him to get his license to sell liquor and beer and fill in behind the bar for us when we're shorthanded?" Oscar suggested. "My wine and moonshine business has suffered this summer with all this remodeling, and I'd like to get back to it. Zach could be a real asset to the team if he's willing."

Risa got up and refilled all their coffee mugs, then sat back down. "I like that idea a lot. That way, maybe one of you can leave the bar and take over for me in the kitchen if I need to be at the school for something the girls are involved in."

"Then I'll ask him if that would work for him," Wade said, "and if no one is going to eat those last two pancakes, I'll have them."

Risa shoved the platter over closer to him. "Do any of you realize how much I love all this? Being asked for my opinion, and us all discussing things? I had decisions made for me my whole life until now, and it's sure a good feeling."

"I sure do." Mary Nell put two spoonfuls of sugar in her coffee. "It makes me feel like I matter."

"We're all good for each other," Haley agreed. "I'm glad that my baby is going to have this particular village to help raise him or her."

Jessica stood in the middle of the foyer with everyone else and stared at the coat and hat rack Oscar had made by cutting the old steeple down. He'd used the wood from the bottom to make fancy little hooks to hang things on.

"That is awesome," she said.

Oscar smiled and nodded. "Thanks, but it's just a hat rack. We needed to use the thing for something other than firewood to roast hot dogs and wieners, and one day I really looked at it. It was too tall to use all of it, and that six-sided shape wouldn't let us put it out on the road to use for a sign of any kind."

"I offered to paint a sign on it, but Oscar said if folks didn't know this was Danny's Place, then they were probably blind or drunk," Zach said.

"Well, Oscar did good with the coatrack, and you did an awesome job on those last two pews," Risa said.

"Zach, you should join us for lunch today for doing all this." Mary Nell sent a smile his way. "We need to celebrate these final jobs."

"Awww." Zach looked down at his well-worn work boots. "I wouldn't want to intrude."

Mary Nell looped her arm in his. "Nonsense, it's just lunch, and you've got to eat. Come on inside and sit with us. Risa is a wonderful cook, and she's been sad all day because her girls started back to school."

"And this is their last year," Wade said.

Oscar clamped a hand on Zach's shoulder. "When Risa is sad or happy or angry, she cooks. Today she's sad, so the whole bar smells like homemade bread."

Zach blushed and raised one shoulder in half a shrug. "I never turn down homemade bread, but I'm sorry you're sad, Risa."

"I've got lots and lots of support here. You'll find out that we're basically a friendly lot when you get moved in."

"I promise to keep things quiet when whoever lives out here is trying to sleep during the mornings," Zach said.

"That's good, because Jessica and Wade might shoot you if you don't," Mary Nell told him.

Jessica hung back with Wade a little longer after the rest of the family—that's what they were now instead of just a team—made their way across the parking lot and into the building.

"I thought I wanted to keep things quiet for a few weeks or months, but evidently everyone already knows," she said.

"Do they know we're living together?" His green eyes glittered.

"I'm not sure about that, but I'm ready to tell them that we are, and that I'm buying a vehicle and that I'm ready to bury my folks' ashes," she answered. "I'm at home, and it's time to put my folks to rest."

"Actually, we can share my truck." Wade drew her into his arms and hugged her tightly. "I can make a wooden cross to mark the spot until you decide on a headstone." He cupped her face in his big hands and kissed her. "Now, about living together. I want more than that, but I'm not in a big hurry. You can tell me when you are ready for the next step."

"Why, Wade Granger, are you proposing to me?" Jessica flirted.

"No, I am not. When I do, you won't have to ask that question. You will know," he answered.

Chapter Twenty-Two

*W*e're on the countdown." Jessica pointed at the clock on the kitchen wall. "One hour until we open. Is everyone as nervous as I am? What if no one comes tonight?"

"Then we'll open again on Tuesday night and hope they come then," Wade said. "We have advertised in newspapers in every county all around us, and we even bought some airtime on the local radio."

"Plus, all the controversy that Granny Stella tried to stir up had to give us a little bit of advertisement." Lily looked up from the last tomato she was slicing. "Food prep is all done. Daisy and I are ready to help build burgers and wash dishes when the rush hits."

"I just hope there is a rush." Jessica smoothed down the front of her T-shirt, which was imprinted with the bar logo.

"Hey," Mary Nell scolded, "there will be no bad vibes an hour before we open. We are going to have a full house, and there's going to be people outside waiting to get in. The inspector said we can have a max of one hundred people, and we'll hit that mark by six thirty."

Zach chuckled. "You dream big, madam."

Mary Nell shook her finger under his nose. "Don't you call me that, and yes, I do dream big."

"Yes, ma'am." Zach nodded, but the twinkle in his eye told Jessica that he was flirting.

"Well, I'm proud of everything you kids have done this summer." Oscar brought out a stack of red plastic cups and a pitcher of sweet tea. "I vote that we toast the new bar before we open tonight. Whether one person comes out to our grand opening or we have a million, we have created a family while we've been working on making a bar out of this old church building the past few months. That's pretty danged awesome in my book. I was afraid a relationship between Jessica and Wade would be a bad thing, but I was wrong, so here's to them, too!"

He poured tea for everyone and held his cup up. "To the old church family."

"Hear! Hear!" The rest of the team picked up their cups and held them high.

Wade took a drink, set his cup down, and slipped an arm around Jessica's waist. "My mama used to tell me that working together makes the best friends. We are proof positive of that tonight. I'm going to plug enough money into the jukebox at exactly six o'clock to play six songs to get the night rolling. Anyone have suggestions?"

"'Danny Boy' should be playing when the first customers come in," Haley answered.

"And then 'My Church,'" Lily suggested.

"I agree with Lily. Looks like we've got our first—" Risa stopped and pointed out the window above the sink. "Oh, no . . . ," she stammered. "Mama is out there. She's parking in the middle of the lot and just sitting in her car."

Daisy rushed over to the window and draped an arm over her mother's shoulders. "We knew this might happen."

"And there's Lulu pulling up right beside her," Oscar noted.

"I wonder if they've enlisted the whole congregation to come out here and just park so that folks will think we're full?" Haley asked.

Jessica kept checking on the lot for the next half hour. No one else showed up, and at ten minutes until opening, she began to get really antsy. At first, she'd thought Stella was just a big bag of hot wind, but maybe the woman had more influence over the town than Jessica had realized.

Then vehicles began to arrive, two and three at a time. Men and women alike who were definitely military got out of trucks and cars and gathered in clusters to talk. Then Stella and Lulu got out of their cars and started putting brochures on windows. A few folks grabbed them, glanced through them in a couple of seconds, and tossed them on the ground.

"Looks like our job tomorrow after church is going to be cleaning up the parking lot," Zach said.

"Kind of looks that way," Wade said with a wide grin. "Okay, folks, it's time, and it looks like the parking lot is full."

"I see folks coming down the road," Haley said. "That means they're parking way out there and walking in. We're going to have a good grand opening."

"In spite of what my mother is doing," Risa growled. "Y'all hold down the fort. I'm going out there."

"Don't give her the satisfaction," Haley said. "She just wants to get a rise out of you."

"Let me take care of this one," Oscar said. "From the way the folks are crowding up to the door, you are needed in here. Man your posts, everyone. Mary Nell, Zach, and Wade need to be behind the bar. Risa and the girls, get ready for a rush. Jessica and Haley will be working the floor, and I'm going to be everywhere after I come in from the parking lot."

"But . . . ," Risa started to argue.

Oscar laid a hand on her shoulder. "What I've got in mind will work better than anything you could say or do."

"We need you too badly around here for you to be thrown in jail," Risa said.

"She's right," Jessica agreed. "Let me go talk to Stella."

"I'll take Jessica with me as a witness if that will make y'all better. Looks like our first rush might be more interested in beer and shots than in food. The porch is full of military folks." Oscar headed for the door leading out of the kitchen and down the hallway. "Jessica and I are going out the back door. Wade, you start the music at exactly six o'clock and wait by the coatrack to kind of welcome the newest folks. Jessica, you get the key so you can unlock the door and let 'em in."

Jessica trusted Oscar, so she followed him, but she sure hoped the argument that was bound to happen wouldn't cause the customers to turn and run. She glanced over at the wooden cross marking the spot where she and Wade had buried the coffee can holding her folks' ashes, and then toward the barn, where she could see her old RV sitting. Zach was fitting in well with their eclectic group.

"What do you want me to do?" Jessica asked when they had rounded the end of the building.

"When you hear the music, open the door and turn 'em loose," Oscar answered. "The rest is my job."

"What are you going to do?" Jessica hoped that Oscar wouldn't land in jail for whatever he had planned.

"I'm going to fix the Stella problem," Oscar said with a nod, "so that it's over and done with. Hey, Tommy!" He waved. "You here to take pictures for the *Riverbend Weekly News*?"

"Yep, I am. Does that get me a drink on the house?" Tommy teased.

"You bet it does, if you'll take a picture of me dancing and put it on the front page," Oscar yelled above the noise.

"You got it." Tommy gave him a thumbs-up.

Jessica had to weave among dozens of people to get to the bar's front door to unlock it. When she heard the first notes of the music, she raised the key and yelled, "Welcome to the grand opening of Danny's Place." Then she unlocked the door and stood to one side.

She didn't count, but it seemed like twenty or thirty people had gone inside when suddenly there was Stella in the middle of the crowd, with Oscar right beside her. She looked absolutely mortified, and he had a huge grin on his face.

"Turn me loose," she growled as she passed Jessica.

"I'm afraid you'll get trampled." Oscar winked at Jessica and nodded toward the foyer. "The Good Book tells me to love my enemies. I don't want to get thrown out of heaven for not protecting you from all these people."

"I will not step foot in this place of iniquity," Stella hissed.

Jessica whipped around in front of the next customer and followed them inside. "Danny Boy" had finished playing and "My Church" had started when Oscar marched Stella out onto the dance floor, grabbed her hand, and swung her out, then brought her back to his chest. Several flashes from phones and a big one from Tommy's camera lit up the dance floor.

"You are the devil's spawn," Stella said in a loud voice.

Oscar wrapped his arms around Stella and held her so tight that she couldn't get away. He whispered something in her ear and more flashes went off. When the lyrics asked for a hallelujah, everyone shouted.

Jessica caught Wade's eye across all the people, and he winked and mouthed, "We did it."

She blew him a kiss and then turned to see Stella storming across the dance floor and out the door.

"That should take care of Miz Sullivan for now and forevermore," Oscar told Jessica.

"What did you say to her?" Jessica asked.

"I told her that a picture of her dancing with me in a bar would be somewhere in every newspaper in all the surrounding counties, even if I had to pay for ads thanking everyone for coming out to our grand opening," Oscar answered.

"Are you really going to do it?" Jessica asked.

"You heard Tommy promise, didn't you?" Oscar waved at a couple of elderly men who were claiming barstools. "When everyone sees her dancing and looking like she's having a good time, her smart-ass plans to destroy us won't hold a bit of water."

"She'll call it fake news," Jessica said.

"Yep, and that will make it seem more real. Haven't you heard that stirring the crap pile just makes it stink even worse?" Oscar disappeared into the crowd.

A few minutes before closing time, Wade plugged in a few more coins and played "Danny Boy" again. When it ended, he picked up the microphone from behind the bar and said, "Thank you all for being here tonight for our grand opening. Our plans are to be open Tuesday through Saturday from six p.m. to two a.m."

Wade herded the last few stragglers to the door and locked it behind them, then went straight to the kitchen, where everyone else was gathered. "We did it, folks. We had an amazing first night, but what was all that business with Stella here?"

"What!" Risa gasped. "My mother was in the bar?"

"Not by choice," Oscar said, "but yes, she was here, and yes, she danced with me, and yes, her picture doing that will be on the front page of the newspaper on Wednesday when it comes out, and no, she was not happy about any of it. But that should stop her from being so nasty in public to all of us."

"Sweet Lord!" Risa's eyes were as big as saucers.

"Yep, He is very sweet at that." Mary Nell giggled.

"Did anyone see what those brochures were all about?" Haley asked.

Oscar laid one on the table. "Looks like it says that folks should turn from iniquity and be saved." His phone rang, and he pulled it from his pocket and raised a finger. "Yes, this is Oscar," he said and listened for a few minutes. "It's negotiable. What have you got to give me?" He rolled his eyes and shook his head. "That won't do."

Wade was standing close enough that he heard a woman yell, "Then you can go to hell. I'll tell everyone the picture was doctored." When Oscar put his phone back in his pocket, Wade raised an eyebrow.

"That was Stella, trying to make a deal," Oscar said. "I guess the folks that had cell phones posted on social media, so the newspaper will just be an afterthought. She's been getting calls all night, and she's plenty mad. She doesn't realize that I might have the power to keep it out of the newspaper by offering Tommy a few more drinks, but there's nothing I can do about the internet."

Lily whipped out her phone. "It's blowing up Snapchat. They're saying that an old couple was the first ones to dance at the grand opening of Danny's Place. You can't see your faces so well, but I can tell it's Granny Stella."

Wade bit back laughter. "It's been a night to remember, but I'm beat. The party is over. Let's turn out the lights and clean up the mess tomorrow afternoon."

"I'm all for that," Jessica said. "Church starts at eleven, so it's going to be a short night."

"Give me a hallelujah," Lily said.

"Give me an amen," Daisy said and then covered a yawn.

Jessica could hardly hold her eyes open, but she managed until Wade finished his shower and crawled between the sheets with her. She cuddled up beside him and laid her head on his chest. "Do you think every night will be this busy?"

"Probably not, but I expect Saturdays just might." Wade rubbed her back.

"I liked that we opened and closed with 'Danny Boy,'" she whispered. "It seemed fitting."

"It did," Wade agreed. "Maybe we should do that every night."

"I think so. Have I told you today that I'm in love with you, Wade?" she asked.

"Couple of times, darlin', but I'll never get tired of hearing it," he answered. "And I love you right back."

Epilogue

NINE MONTHS LATER

*Y*ou do know that if we'd gotten married right after basic training, we could have kids this age," Wade whispered to Jessica as the senior class marched down the sideline of the football field and took their places in front of the stage.

"I was just thinking the same thing, but I'm glad that things worked out for us the way they have. We had a beautiful little private wedding at the bar at Christmas. I loved every bit of it."

"And now we've got our little guy on the way, and he should be here by homecoming in the fall. Do you think they'll want y'all to ride on the float this year?" Wade teased.

"If they ask, we'll probably turn them down like we did last year," she told him. "We'll let the ones who still relive the glory of being cheerleaders in the past have that honor. I don't need that kind of claim to fame."

Haley leaned forward from right behind them. "I agree with Jessica. Do y'all realize it was one year ago today that we all met in the parking lot of the old church? Fate steps in again."

"Ford is chewing his fist." Oscar handed the four-month-old baby over to Haley. "He doesn't care about a graduation. He wants a bottle.

There's Mary Nell and Zach coming up the bleachers. I'm so happy for them. He treats her like a queen—or better yet, like a father wants a man to treat his daughter—and she's so happy since I finished the loft apartment out in my barn so I could move out there and give them the house. I'm hoping that Ford will have a little cousin before long."

"Wouldn't that be wonderful?" Jessica touched her belly, which had just begun to protrude.

"It's about time. Ain't a one of y'all getting any younger," Oscar said.

The superintendent of Riverbend Schools tapped the microphone and said, "We'd like to thank you all for attending the Riverbend High School graduation this afternoon. It's been a year to remember."

"Yes, it has," Risa said with a smile.

"I'm not ready for them to go off to college this fall," Oscar said.

"Me neither," Risa told him, "but I'm going to give them wings to fly."

"Are we going to be that comfortable when it's time for our son to graduate?" Wade whispered to Jessica.

His breath on the soft part of her neck still caused tingles to chase down her whole body. She hoped that when they were married fifty years and sitting in rocking chairs on the front porch of the house they were going to build not far from the bar, she could answer yes to that. But that afternoon, sitting there in the heat, without a cloud in the blue Texas skies, she wanted to hold on to what she had found and never let any of it go.

"I'm just going to enjoy every day I get with you and this baby, and all our friends," Jessica answered. "Family is what makes life worth living."

"You got that right," Wade said.

"It's the gospel truth." She smiled over at him.

Author's Note

Dear Readers,

I've heard that the eyes are the windows of the soul. I don't doubt it, because the eyes portray so much expression—sadness, happiness, anger. I'm not arguing with that at all, but I believe that music is the window to the heart. Sometimes my characters tell me that a song speaks to their heart more than words could ever do. That's the case with the folks in *Riverbend Reunion*. Several songs came into both Wade's and Jessica's minds, as well as the twins', during the course of them telling me their stories. I hope that you enjoy listening to the songs when you read the story. They were all pretty adamant about their selections, and sometimes even woke me up at night to visit with me about them.

As I've said before, it takes a village to help produce a book from a simple proposal to what you hold in your hands today. My thanks to all the folks in that village: to my agent, Erin Niumata, and my agency, Folio Literary Management, for everything you do; to my Montlake editor, Alison Dasho, and my entire team there, from copy editors and proofreaders to cover artists and all those who work so hard at promotion, for continuing to believe in me; to my developmental editor, Krista Stroever, the best of the best, please know that I appreciate your advice and suggestions so much; and to all my readers who continue to support me—you are truly the wind beneath my wings. And last but not least, to my family, who understands that deadlines often have to come first—thank you for everything you do so I can live out my dream.

It's not easy to leave my characters behind when I finish a book. I spend so much time with them that they become real to me. I hope that you feel that way when you reach the last page, and that they have touched your emotions.

Until next time,
Carolyn Brown

About the Author

*C*arolyn Brown is a *New York Times, USA Today, Washington Post, Wall Street Journal,* and *Publishers Weekly* best-selling author and RITA finalist with more than 125 published books. She has written women's fiction, historical and contemporary romance, and cowboys-and-country-music mass-market paperbacks. She and her husband live in the small town of Davis, Oklahoma, where everyone knows everyone else, knows what they are doing and when, and reads the local newspaper on Wednesday to see who got caught. They have three grown children and enough grandchildren and great-grandchildren to keep them young. For more information, visit www.carolynbrownbooks.com.